GODS OF LEGEND

ALSO BY E.M. WILLETT

LORDS OF RUIN, BOOK 2, DEAD BLOOD VOLUME I

HEIRS OF ETERNITY, BOOK 3, DEAD BLOOD VOLUME I

GODS

OF

LEGEND

Book 1
Dead Blood Volume I

E.M. Willett

Title: Gods of Legend
Author: E.M. Willett
Copyright ©2025 by E.M. Willett

ISBN:
eBook ISBN: 978-1-969649-56-1
Paperback ISBN: 978-1-969649-98-1
Hardcover ISBN: 978-1-969649-58-5
Published by Pine Tree Press

www.pinetreepress.com
Printed in USA

DEDICATION

*For those who look into the dark
and find it staring back.*

CONTENTS

ACKNOWLEDGMENTS

To my younger self, for pursuing a dream. To my family, for their unwavering support. To you, dear reader, for entering the Kingdom of Vanguards.

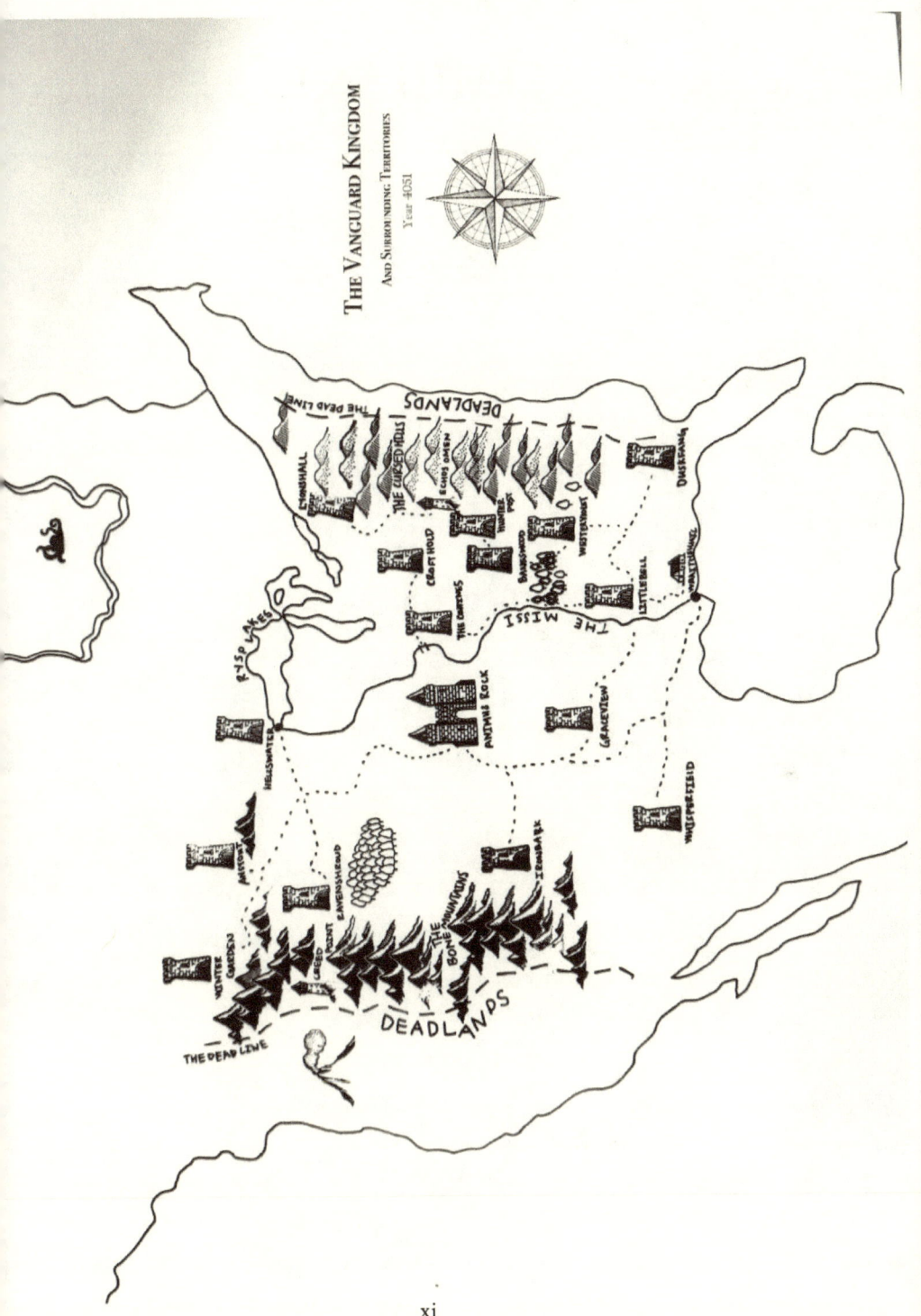

TIMELINE

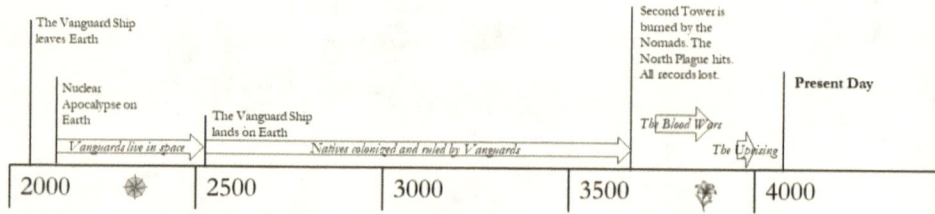

The Vanguard Ship
leaves Earth

Nuclear
Apocalypse on
Earth

The Vanguard Ship
lands on Earth

Second Tower is
burned by the
Nomads. The
North Plague hits.
All records lost.

Present Day

The Blood Wars

Vanguards live in space

Natives colonized and ruled by Vanguards

The Uprising

2000   2500   3000   3500   4000

PROLOGUE

INTRODUCTION

———— ᗺXᏟ ————

A paradigm-shifting breakthrough was made in the 21st century. An American scientist and billionaire, Alabaster Beaumont, discovered that humanity is far more complex than it had previously been thought to be. He was a geneticist. In 2026 he published a paper detailing his findings.

He discovered there are two types of humans. *Homo sapien,* and a second, that Alabaster called *Homo sacrum,* or sacred humans.

Homo sacrum appear to be identical to *Homo sapien,* except lack a certain protein in their blood. But that small difference leads to enormous gaps when it comes to processing and utilizing consciousness. These differences allow *Homo sacrums* to manipulate physical reality, if they are in the correct conditions.

Jesus Christ, the Buddha, the Prophet Muhammad; Alabaster speculated that all these historical figures, and many more, were in fact *Homo sacrums,* not *Homo sapiens.* They did not perform miracles. Instead, they had abilities deeper than what *Homo sapiens* could understand.

Like the old saying goes—magic is a name for what science hadn't explained yet.

Homo sapiens are bridled by their own logical thinking, trapped within the confines of what is presented to them at face value. *Homo sacrums,* however, can reach beyond the veil of reality. The existence of *Homo sacrum* explains the occurrences of prophets, priestesses, shamans and witches throughout history. Even mental disorders and personality disorders and neurodivergence oftentimes, as well. The scientist postulated that these individuals are not necessarily gifted or cursed, instead, they are simply of a different genetic makeup than the rest of humanity.

Homo sacrums can conceptualize and manipulate reality

differently than everyone else.

He hypothesized that approximately 15% of the population alive in the 21st century had the *Homo sacrum* genome. But not all presented abilities.

It is a radical thought, that there are different types of consciousness. Different types of people. That not all humanity is created equal. The scientist was laughed out of every conference he presented his findings in. No one in the scientific community believed him. He had proof, but it was far too controversial for the mainstream to accept.

Regardless, Alabaster built a cult-like team around his findings. He himself was of the *Homo sacrum* bloodline and it became his lifetime obsession to document and detail everything that could be known about it. To do this, he turned to human experimentation.

Alabaster and his lead scientists presented their findings at a conference in 2030, showcasing the otherworldly abilities that *Homo sacrum* possessed if properly nurtured. That meant little EMF exposure, no consumption of meat or dairy and excessive access to nature, sunlight and fresh air. A man with super strength, able to lift a car. A woman able to manipulate emotions, simply through prolonged eye contact. A child that could fly, although it was just a few inches off the stage.

Still, the exhibition took the conference by storm. Alabaster and his team thought they'd done it, brought *Homo sacrum* into the public eye, but they were mistaken.

Instead, the elite feared the monumental shift that this knowledge would cause. Imagine some humans with unknowable powers. What could that mean for the status quo? Instead of accepting the findings as fact, the knowledge was rejected. Every transcript from the conference, every video, every message sent from a cell phone, was confiscated and deleted. Talk of what occurred there, banned.

The elite, fearing the power of *Homo sacrum*, conspired to keep that branch of humanity oppressed. First through contaminating the water then through mandating unnecessary vaccines to ensure the people would never learn of what they had the potential to become. But as Alabaster and his team continued to push, the elite decided that more drastic measures must be taken. A plan was enacted to release a chemical into the atmosphere that would alter the genetics of Homo sacrum and forever mute their abilities. In those living and for all generations to come.

Alabaster and his team were prosecuted for human experimentation, then escaped into hiding.

THE VANGUARD LAUNCH SITE, LOCATION CLASSIFIED

About 2,000 years ago...

Oh, how he wished they had more time. How he wished things had gone differently. The Council might have understood, if only they had made more significant progress. But his team hadn't made the progress he'd hoped for. And the Council didn't understand.

Not at all.

Alabaster couldn't help but replay the hearings over in his mind. The shame he felt from all those eyes judging him and dismissing his vision was more than he could bear. But like a dark cloud, the memory hung over him. All over the news he and his brilliant team were compared to war criminals. Their trial, equated to the trials of Nazis scientists in the wake of WWII.

How did it ever come to this?

These same thoughts looped over and over as he watched hired crew members, paid exorbitant amounts for their secrecy, flittering from checkpoint to checkpoint, ensuring the spaceship outside would be ready to launch. Such a bold move. But where else was there to turn?

Although he stared ahead intently at the action beyond the windowpane in the remote desert they'd chosen for secrecy's sake, he felt he wasn't fully there. A large part of his old mind kept running back on itself. How did this happen? The Vanguard Mission was meant to save humanity, not tear it apart. How did this happen? How did this happen?

Over and over, the thoughts pounded in sync with his beating heart.

"Alabaster." He felt slender fingers with precisely manicured nails creep across the shoulder of his finely tailored suit. He snapped out of his loop of thoughts.

"Isolde," the elderly billionaire replied, placing his own twisted, inflamed hand atop hers. He didn't turn, leaving his black eyes focused ahead, still studying the chaos. Men were shouting in preparation for launch at midday directly outside of the trailer's massive window.

"Tout va bien?" Isolde asked softly. She leaned towards him. Her chestnut hair brushed against his wrinkled neck. "Mon amour." She brought her hand to his weathered cheek and turned his head gently as she dropped down to his eye-level where he sat, practical lab coat gracefully buckling at her knees. "Is everything alright?"

She looked at him with concern followed by a heart-melting smile. The old man gazed woefully into her mischievous hazel eyes.

Alabaster Beaumont was strikingly handsome, once. He had an etched face with cavernous cheeks and a thin sprinkling of once-black hair. Now, in his late eighties, the man's striking features appeared harsh, sometimes terrifying, with papery skin drooping from pronounced bones. "Yes, Doctor Brochet," he said, low and deep. His black eyes, vapid and soulless. He'd given everything to the Vanguard Mission. And it had brought him to his knees. "This is my dream. Things couldn't be finer."

He pulled at his fingers nervously, massaging tired arthritic knuckles.

"We will achieve our aims," Isolde said. She leaned closer to him, rounded breasts pressing together beneath her lab coat. "We will find another way. Something different than the mass," she paused, eyes narrowing, "*genocide* they plan."

Isolde was a brilliant scientist on the forefront of ground-breaking neurological research. Her focus was the neuroscience of personality and how that related to genetics. She set out to prove that there is indeed a connection between the mind, body, and spirit. And, if that connection could be properly understood, one could theoretically manipulate reality.

Alabaster recruited her for the Vanguard cause when she had just finished her PHD at the age of twenty-four.

"They cannot hold us back," she said. "The Mission is everything." She was passionate yet practiced. She cleared her throat lightly, adjusted her coat slightly, and raised her high arched eyebrows until the old man looked up. "We will, Alabaster." She spoke with familiar inflection. "The Vanguard is our final journey," she said. "It is your vision," she added, gaze ablaze with conviction, "as it is mine."

Alabaster Beaumont studied Isolde Brochet's ardent expression in careful silence, stroking his chin with a gnarled hand. She watched him sympathetically. His eyes darted back and forth, searching deep in hers for anything other than what he saw. Unquestioning loyalty, ambition, devotion. What happened to true belief? *Is there such a thing anymore?* Alabaster brought a crunched hand to his forehead and scrunched his eyes. *Where did I go wrong?* He echoed over and over to himself, in his thoughts. The loop started again. It always did. *Where did I go wrong?* He woefully sighed.

The trailer door burst open. Isolde Brochet popped up from where she kneeled, curls glistening in the buttery morning light. She hurriedly adjusted her lipstick with the nail of her thumb, then breathed into a wide smile as she turned.

"Mercury!" Isolde said. "Is everything on schedule?"

A man glided through the door like a fleeing shadow.

Mercury Graves, a respected neurosurgeon before joining the Vanguard cause, had tree-branch shoulders, an angled face, and pointed jaw. His pristine white lab coat, although the longest size, stopped unnaturally short above his knees, nonetheless. His hair was raven's wing black, glistening purple in the right light, and long for a man. He wore it in ample waves patted down in the morning with a rinse of water, then smoothed back to reveal severe widow's peak. He was young, much closer to the thirty-something Isolde's age than the ancient Alabaster's eighty, with steely-brown, sunken eyes, narrowing at what he saw.

Mercury was particularly disliked among the members of the

Vanguard, mainly for his apparent disinterest in forming personal bonds. They'd joke and call him soulless. He only seemed to have a slight affection for Isolde, favouring her in nearly every vote or debate there was.

Mercury tucked his hair behind his ear with his one hand as he held a tablet in the other. He looked down, ignoring both Alabaster and Isolde, poking at the electronic screen carefully. "Nearly there," he finally said, slowly. "A slight mishap," he added, looking up suddenly.

"Mishap?" the old man asked, irritated by the impersonal man just like his other followers were.

Isolde turned with a clacking, high-heeled step of concern, then crossed her arms.

"The participant attempted to renege."

Alabaster felt the last thin thread holding his psyche together snap. He erupted, pale face reddening quickly. "What?!" he bellowed, thoughts racing. "I thought that was dealt with!" If Mercury told the truth, all could be lost. It certainly would be. Alabaster's voice lowered to a faint, thunder-like rumble. "Tell me that is all."

"Not all," Mercury said unapologetically.

"Spit it out!"

"The media."

Alabaster's black eyes widened, watery and full of fear. "The media?"

The media was the Vanguard's downfall from the beginning. Alabaster's team had been painted as insane, power-hungry and downright villainous. Evil, even. Public opinion was fully against them, despite Alabaster's ultimately noble intentions. The people of Earth didn't understand what the G.N. was planning. Even the G.N. didn't fully understand it. When Alabaster tried to spread word of what was to come, how his team was planning to save everyone from the covert mass manipulation by the world's elite, he was accused of sharing fake news to incite terror and uprising. His mind started to loop again. It was so different from his childhood. His youth. The modern media was one beast he didn't fully understand.

"The media?!" Isolde's deeply accented outrage cut the makeshift field office, a practical trailer outfitted with standard, necessary office furniture and stark-white, wallpapered trailer walls. She clacked forward several steps until stopping right in front of Mercury. Although she believed him, Isolde had to see for herself.

"Give me that," she said forcefully, grabbing the tablet.

He sighed but allowed her to have it, then nonchalantly shrugged. "Check for yourself," Mercury said with a glint in his sunken eye. "Word has broken." He held both hands casually behind his back while standing comfortably. "We are found out." He paused, a slight smile on his curled lips. For Mercury, the taboo nature of their practices made them that much more enticing. He almost enjoyed being chased. "Again."

Alabaster's etched forehead buckled. "They will come for the participant," he said. "All is lost." He swung his head towards the trailer's bay window as he pulled at his hair. He sighed loudly as he eyed the buzz outside, dozens of eager workers in navy blue jumpsuits performing final checks and maintenance about a makeshift launch pad.

Isolde shot a communicative glare at Mercury, who mouthed, "*I'm sorry,*" unapologetically, as Alabaster turned his head.

She mouthed back, "*Useless,*" then shook her mane of hair with a scratch of long nails before clacking over to the flustered old man's side.

"Mon amour," she said, breathy and low, dropping to her knees against next to the old man's state-of-the-art electronic wheelchair. She placed a hand on his frail thigh, swimming in his prodigious suit. She squeezed. "Launch is in mere hours," she said. "Let them discover us. We will be untouchable," she added, tone dropping to a murmur. "We will own the stars."

Alabaster was still painfully anxious. "You say David reneged," he spun his head, papery skin of his neck pulling across tightened tendons, rapid heartbeat pulsing through the thick artery in his throat. "Then he is no longer a participant."

David Minney was a globally renowned holistic healer as well as a self-proclaimed shaman. He'd written dozens of books about the therapeutic power of thought and garnered quite a following worldwide before Alabaster recruited him for the Vanguard. He had agreed to join their cause, offering himself to be experimented on. Until now.

Alabaster's wildly passionate eyes darted across the floor in panic, until locking on Isolde's as she squeezed his thigh. "He was the only one of us with the genes to achieve your theoretical aims. Without his blood, we will never get close, according to your own research! But he is sworn in. If he has reneged." The man paused, imagining David's trusting sky-blue stare. "We cannot break the Code," he said, ancient voice faltering, white spittle sticking to the corners of his lips.

There's a reason for the Code, for times like this. If they were to break it, Alabaster thought, it made them no better than the rest of the world. Then the elite he so despised and the governments under their thumb. The G.N.

"It... it... it is as law!" he added emphatically.

The Vanguard belief system was primarily centred around a code, referred to as the Code. The Code was written by Alabaster Beaumont himself. It outlined modes of conduct for any member of the Vanguard, including procedure for dealing with defectors. They are not to be altered or harmed in any way. No matter what.

"Alabaster," she said firmly, patience dwindling. "This is how far you have come, mon amour." Isolde placed a warm hand on his face, shifting his head up and out at the bay window. "Look," she said. "How far we have come," she added, gently gracing his cheek with her sharp knuckles. "You have shown us the way. The way past ourselves, and on, through to another world. Another way. You have focused our genius. The ultimate aims we were all born for, that you tested us for, are right before our eyes." Her gaze widened with childlike excitement.

Alabaster couldn't help but think to himself again, "*What have I done?*" He'd meant to save humanity. To give humanity another path, different from the one it was being forced down now. One of the inner works. Self-sacrifice. Ultimate freedom.

But looking into Isolde's eyes, he realized the dangerous seed he had planted. For her to argue to use the participant unwillingly was, why, it was cruel madness! That wasn't what Alabaster Beaumont stood for. Not at all.

"No longer will the weak continue to rule, misguided and unchecked," Isolde proclaimed. "It is for us, the strong, to rise above. To become what we were meant to be," she said, disdain masquerading as passion. While Alabaster had intended to promote peace and equality for all, the younger ranks of his Vanguard team were poisoned by the promise of power and superiority. Genetic manipulation to create a new, better race. "The others," she lowered her voice, "the *nonbelievers*," she said, pausing for emphasis, mischievous gleam in her eye, "are lost to us. You taught me that, mon amour."

Isolde shifted closer to the old man and gently stroked his wrinkled cheek with her warm hand.

He stared at her timeless, poignant beauty and frowned. *What have I done to you?*

"Humanity is on the cusp of its dream," Isolde said. "That is owed to you."

"The Code," Alabaster interjected, baritone vacillating. "We are nothing without the Code." He'd written it so many years ago for this very purpose, to ensure this thing he'd created never grew bigger than could be controlled. He squinted and his breaths wheezed. "The followers," he said slowly, revelling in the painful gravity, eyes searching across Isolde's gorgeous face. "Our poor followers," he said with a pained cry, thinking of all the threatened souls dependant on his philosophy. "Without the participant..." he trailed off, eyes wild, tasting failure on the back of his tongue. "Without the participant, I have failed them." He wheezed in self-pity. "We cannot take off. We must not," he muttered, mind spinning, heart thumping. "I was so wrong."

"Alabaster," Isolde said cooly with a frustrated bite. She scooted closer to him then leaned up over the padded armrest of his wheelchair. She was nearly in his lap, breasts spilling out of her blouse onto his knees. The old man raised a black eyebrow, and even amidst his internal turmoil, glanced lustfully down. She bit her bottom lip, lipstick smudging over her straight, white tooth. "Alabaster," Isolde repeated, warmly, as if to a child, noticing the smudge in the chrome on the wheelchair, clearing the lipstick with her finger. She pulled his drifting head violently to look at her, again. "Alabaster," she said a third time, "we have come too far to turn back now."

"She's right," Mercury interjected from the corner of the trailer, in monotone, reminding the others he was there. He leaned against the far wall, arms crossed, as if casually observing passers-by on the city street's sidewalk. "Too far."

"What do you infer?" Alabaster called out.

"The G.N. wasn't bluffing," he said. "David leaked our coordinates to save himself, it seems. The internet is in an uproar. By my calculations," he added, "troops will arrive within the hour."

"Impossible!" Alabaster bellowed, eyes darting. "We are lost," he moaned. "Is there nothing we can do to change his mind?" He looked with hope-filled, pleading gaze to Mercury. David Minney was their only chance. There was no time to find another. Perhaps he would change his mind.

"Nothing," Mercury said as Isolde silently glared.

"*Useless*," she mouthed at him.

Mercury shrugged back, smirking, enjoying her frustration greatly.

"Nothing!?" Alabaster jumped forward in his chair, red-cheeked and wheezing. "Everything worked for, sacrificed for," he sighed, "is lost."

Isolde took his arthritic hand into hers and patted it gently. "Mon bien-aimé France," she said. Her magnificent eyes searched off to the side. "Even she is gone," Isolde added bitterly. "As your cherished States will be, shortly." She fake spat. "These nations are bloated, overblown far past potential, propping up the meek and punishing the strong." She paused and allowed the weight of her words to settle. "The G.N. knows nothing. Fools, all of them. The Mission is only lost if we allow it to be."

The ancient man softened watery eyes. "What are we do to?" he asked with palpable vulnerability. "What am I to do?" In all his years, confidently amassing a fortune of billions, this was a first. He dropped his head and ran his crumpled hands through white hair, feeling hopeless. His life's work was lost.

"This isn't the Alabaster Beaumont I know," Isolde offered playfully. "Where is the grand leader who inspired us all? Who brought us together? Discovered the truth of *Homo Sacrum*? Where is the man we follow to salvation? Where is the genius who wrote the Code?"

Alabaster softened slightly. "It was so clear then. I was a younger man." Spittle stuck between dry, cracked lips as he spoke. He placed shaking hands into his wrinkled lap. "The last decade feels like a century," he said sadly. This mighty man, wealth to purchase a nation, had never seemed so human, so small. His head popped up. "How much time do we have, Graves?" He barked at the willowy man hovering by the shadow of the doorframe.

He gestured at Isolde. "She has the tablet."

Isolde huffed. Mercury Graves's chilly ways were so irritating. But he was useful. "Oh, fine," she said under her breath. She lifted the translucent device and poked at it with a clack of her fingernail. Her indignant brow widened in humbled shock. "Oh," she said softly. She glanced quickly at Mercury, who smugly nodded once.

"Isolde?" Alabaster asked.

"I told you," Mercury said.

Isolde's shocked expression fell to panicked wrath. "Unacceptable," she bellowed. She rose quickly from her squat beside the wheelchair, stormed to Mercury with tablet white-knuckle clasped in one hand while flipping her hair over her shoulder with the other. She dramatically held out the tablet to him.

"Fix it."

"You heard him," Mercury offered, gesturing his head slightly to Alabaster. "We are lost." His sunken eyes teasingly danced; especially once Isolde frowned.

Isolde sighed. "Must I do it all myself?"

"Seems so."

Isolde ignored Mercury. She marched back across the modest space to Alabaster's side, pointed heels echoing hollowly against the manufactured trailer floor. She lowered again, this time only crouching instead of kneeling, both hands-on knees, prominent nose only inches from Alabaster's pallid, anxious face.

"What am I to do?" he asked with wide eyes.

"We need the participant."

"But he has refused," Alabaster began. "He's defected. He's..."

Isolde fiercely interrupted.

"All of our experiments require him, mon amour. Of the hundreds, thousands tested, David is the only one with the correct genetic makeup, the correct blood. The correct brain chemistry. The correct neurological development. How could we know it would be one of our own?" Although she had known before they ever reached out to David, of course. She spoke evenly and calmly but her hazel eyes burned. "The specimens we used for the exhibition were just parlour tricks. We need to push further." She used all her willpower to stop herself from slapping Alabaster like she wanted to. She was so close to greatness and this old bastard was all that stood in her way. Alabaster nodded with her as she spoke, eyes wild and darting, unconvinced. "We need David Minney, no matter what," she added resolutely. "It is the only way."

"You don't mean..." Alabaster trailed off in horror. "Isolde, we can't," he said in a hush. "David is Vanguard Elite. He's... he's..." the old man stuttered. "He's one of us." His hands trembled in his lap. "If the man has reneged, we are lost," he said softly, mostly to himself, eyes down.

"What is the difference between him and the other specimens?" Isolde asked coldly. "Alabaster, we have been running tests for the better part of a decade."

It was what the Vanguard team had been condemned for most brutally by the nations of the world. It was their regular practice to experiment on any individuals willing to submit to their testing. True, specimens were typically compensated afterwards, if they survived, that is.

The others have been collateral damage, means to an end, the same as any fallout of war, Alabaster thought wilfully. "Why, because he has been inducted! He is a believer!" he shouted; face red. Irate. How could she question this? "He is one of us. To do what you insinuate would be upmost betrayal," he added sombrely. "Are there not others?"

"None," Mercury interjected from across the room.

Isolde huffed again, dramatically glaring at Mercury quickly to indicate, "*shut up*". She took a breath and scrunched her eyes briefly while exhaling slowly, personifying false calm. She looked back at Alabaster. "We need him," she said. "Or else, yes, all is lost."

Her cold words cut a jagged wound through the old man. His darting eyes glassed in terror. Over and over, in his mind, he repeated, *what have I done?* The loop felt like it was going to swallow him whole, until he was nothing but those resounding thoughts, dragging guilt and painful shame across his heart like a knife drawing blood with each pass.

Isolde glared at him, watching his pathetic, anxious ticks, waiting for him to respond. It was all she could do not to gag when she looked at him. But Isolde was smart. And manipulative. She glanced up to see Mercury tapping on his wrist with his pointer finger.

"*I know,*" Isolde mouthed silently to him. "*Hold on.*" She lowered and placed a gentle palm on Alabaster's panic-stricken face. "It's not too late," she said softly. "Not at all. We are so close. Bellamine assured me last night that the plans are air tight. The ship meets every safety check. We could take off right now if we wanted to! There are five years of provisions already packed away, and the filtration systems and self-sustaining bio garden is functioning and ready. By his calculations, you've built the ultimate spaceship, mon amour," Isolde added affectionately. "To keep your people free. Free from the manipulation and oppression of the G.N. Free to continue our work uncontested."

Alabaster frowned. "Yes, yes," he distantly said.

"By the time we land back down on Earth the world will understand that you are her true savior," Isolde cooed. "Why, imagine... in the wake of what's being planned..." she trailed off with a slight smile. "Once we land, they'll realize they need the knowledge we bring, the salvation we share, and will allow us to resume our practices. Unrestricted by the government, how to not succeed?"

"Bellamine's men checked it?" Alabaster grunted. He glanced to the titanic spacecraft vertically constructed on the massive pad outside. "He confirms it will perform as has been promised?"

"That is what I am telling you now," Isolde said through a clenched-teeth smile, impatience seeping through her mask. "Five years should be no problem at all. He says if we wanted, we could say up there for hundreds. Until the hull started to break down around us. Yet who would be bête enough to do that," she added with a flashing smile.

"Hmmm," Alabaster grunted, shuffling bent knuckles and crumpled fingers in his lap. "My son is here already?" He spoke as if he was in a world all his own. Isolde couldn't imagine the oppressive power of the loop. It was crushing him.

"He is," Mercury interjected, to an eyeroll from Isolde.

"We are humanity's last hope, Alabaster," Isolde said, getting the man's focus by using his given name firmly. He raised black eyes to meet hers like a child looks to his mother. "It's for their own good."

"That's what I've always believed." Alabaster's voice groaned, cracking at the back of his throat like a mighty tree about to fall. "So many lost to the world before they've been given a chance to live in it. So many indoctrinated with hogwash ideologies, fed lies, poisons, so far from what they were meant to become. So many trusting governments that betray them and they thank them for the privilege. Isolde, my love," he said," it was only when I met you did my eyes open. You, and your work... the possibilities that the right kind of science opens to us." He paused, pulsing his jaw and swallowing hard. "I wanted to help the world," he said, sole tear welling in his eye. "I wanted to free them all. I was able to explain all the suffering I've caused away, because it was for the greater good, you see." He trailed off. He sniffled. "Where did I go *so* wrong?"

"Just think," Isolde pressed, "just one more sacrifice, then. If that is your goal, David is the key."

Alabaster felt at the end of his rope. "What will you have me do?" he asked. "Betray our own?"

Isolde stood in a huff. *That's exactly it,* she thought. She waltzed with echoing clacks to the wide window and placed her fingertips delicately on the glass, lowering fingernails against it with impatient crescendo. She mindlessly fiddled the buttons on her blouse with her other finger and thumb, watching the rising sun glint off a roasting sand dune behind the monstrous spacecraft, constructed entirely in secret.

Make-shift trailers circled the launch pad and functioned as laboratories, bunkers, and prisons for the tight-knit, cult-like team.

"If only one of the other specimens showed promise..." Isolde offered, then trailed off. "If we had known David's feelings earlier, perhaps, if we had time, something could be done." Her accented sentiments dripped honey. She kept her eyes on the masterpiece outside. "There simply isn't time," she said. "And, besides," she paused, biting on her lip and narrowing her eyes, mon amour," she added half-over her shoulder, eyes still locked on the impressive Vanguard ship ahead, "you are forgetting that there was an agreement. David knows what he is here to do." She swallowed, lowering her tone for emphasis. "There is no backing out. We must preserve the *Homo Sacrum* genetics. The stakes are too high."

A bone-shattering crack followed by a sad thud echoed in the modest trailer behind Isolde. She spun in a turn, dark waves bouncing about the stark white shoulders of her lab coat.

"I was almost through to him!" She shouted in vain, eyes large. She studied the concave, leaking wound on Alabaster's right temple. "He was about to agree!"

"You were taking too long," Mercury said. He set the heavy stool down, seat edge gory and bloodied. At her indignant glare he said, "You know we don't need him. We've got the child."

Isolde's stunning eyes sparkled playfully. "What if I was fond of him?"

"He's demented," Mercury said. "That wasn't the man we knew." He paused, digesting the languid pooling blood beneath the crisply dressed man, crumpled at the foot of his wheelchair on the floor, snow-white hair stained with gore. "Age overtook him. He'd forgotten who he was." Mercury paused again. As he studied warm corpse, he ran his tongue over his teeth. "It was Alabaster who was lost."

"Is he dead?" Isolde asked. She took trepid steps across the trailer, then knelt at bleeding Alabaster's side. His mouth gaped inhumanely open and his watery, blood-specked eyes were glassed and wide. Mercury glanced down and shrugged. Isolde raised a plucked, black eyebrow at him. "The treatments have made you so cold," she observed, slightly smiling. Proud of her work.

"David is already on board," Mercury offered, turning his willowy shoulders slowly to face her.

She paused. "He did not renege?"

Mercury baited the pause, hanging on Isolde's questioning look. "He did," the sunken-eyed man finally confirmed. "It just doesn't matter."

Isolde smiled wide, blood-red lipstick to match the sticky pool on the floor. "He's dead," she confirmed after feeling no heartbeat. She dropped her hand from Alabaster's cooling, sinewy neck.

"A martyr for the cause, indeed," Mercury offered, unmoving eyes cast down.

"If what you say is true and the G.N is on the way, we must launch urgently," Isolde said, concerned, yet confident. She tucked side-parted hair behind both ears. "Is everyone here?"

"Yes," Mercury Graves blinked at the body. "All sixteen of us."

THE VANGUARD SHIP, SPACE

Five years later…

"Captain," Lugaid Norland croaked as he stumbled onto the Vanguard ship's bridge.

The man's world was on fire, yet he was powerless to put it out. The flames consumed him. He couldn't breathe. Lugaid swallowed hard, pulling at the high collar of his grey uniform, sixteen-pointed compass rose on breast. His jade-green eyes darted wildly as his spiky Adam's apple danced up and down his long neck.

Captain Byron Bellamine slowly turned, snapped out of his daydream of life back on earth. What life could be like with Cesarina and the child. He wore identical attire to Lugaid, although slightly embellished to indicate his rank. His oversized ears overshadowed his typical Anglican features, straight nose, strong jaw, even-set round eyes, all highlighted in blue-hue by the ambient, artificial lighting spanning the creases where the ship's ceilings met the walls. Byron's walnut-colored hair, greying at each temple, was tight-buzzed to his rounded head. He had weary undereye bags of a man twice his age. The years weighed heavy on him. He stood with hands clasped loosely behind his back, gazing out at an endless blackness dotted with dainty stars.

He turned as he heard the uneven footsteps. "What is it, son?" Byron faced the incoming Second-in-Command and was instantly disturbed by what he saw.

Lugaid's pale skin was awash with terror, stark-white like he'd seen a ghost.

"What is it, son?"

"I've just come from Communications," Lugaid said, panting, trying his best to remain calm, although it was impossible given what he'd just learned.

Byron stood statue firm. "A hitch in preparations?" The five years aboard this damned ship were nearly up. They were due to land back on Earth shortly. He hoped it was just that.

Lugaid shook his head. His blond hair shuffled on his long forehead. His eyes were unblinking, locked on Bryon.

Byron took a heavy-booted step. "The treaty was signed." He frowned. "If it's the G.N.," his tone warned.

"It's not the G.N."

Seeing the typically stoic young man so rattled was unsettling, but the ship's Captain resolved himself to be calm.

"It's... It's..." Lugaid muttered, emotion stabbing the back of his throat.

"Son?"

He swallowed painfully as he met Byron's eyes. "It's gone," Lugaid croaked again.

"Gone?" The Captain was puzzled. "What do you mean *gone*?" He smirked at the strange thing to say.

"I can't go home," the young man said hollowly. "You don't understand, though, I have to get home." His eyes were wet and teary now. His voice trembled.

Byron reached Lugaid, putting both hands on his shoulders. "Son!" he shouted, shaking him once, fully unnerved at seeing his prodigy so traumatized. "Out with it!"

"I fucking told you!" Lugaid shouted now too, tears leaking from the corners of his narrow-set eyes freely. "It's all fucking gone! New York City. Chicago. L.A." He sniffled hard, choking, coughing when he tried to swallow. "Paris, London." He bit down, flexing his jaw to try and calm himself. The action was futile.

"Gone..." Byron hesitated, dropping his hands from Lugaid's shoulders. They all knew this was a possibility, nuclear war, yet a very remote one, all had thought. "What do you mean, *gone*?" The words echoed in his mind after he said them like a pebble kicked down a ravine. It couldn't possibly be true.

Lugaid was in a frenzy now, eyes wild with horror, darting about, not focusing on anything. "Oh, and don't forget about home," he said, chuckling in a blood-curdling laugh, high-pitched and forced. "Pssssshhhhhhaaa," he whistled through pursed lips to sound like a bomb, then gestured his hands to indicate a mushroom-clouded boom.

Byron's voice faltered. "What do you mean *gone*, Lugaid?"

The crazed young man made the gesture with his hands again, palms facing each other, flicking fingers upwards and out. "Boom," he whispered, then manically laughed, eyes wild, insane with grief and pain.

"Son," Byron stepped forward. He pulled the unstable young man to a seat on the floor. "You said home. Did you mean?" He asked, already anticipating the truth, not wanting it to be so. Despite Lugaid's mechanical, insane nodding, Byron shook his head in disbelief. He asked anyway. "Washington, D.C.?"

"I. Fucking. TOLD YOU!" Lugaid bellowed. He lunged at the older man and shoved him away before collapsing onto himself in a whimpering sob. Byron's brow pinched and he re-approached. He put a sympathetic arm around the distraught young man.

"Maeve was pregnant when I left," Lugaid confessed, followed by a heart-piercing groan. He buried his head into the older man's shoulder, clinging to the gold band on his left hand's ring finger like a life raft while lost at sea. "I have a daughter, Captain," the young man said, bittersweet tug at the back of his throat. "Or, I had…" He trailed off into a pitiful a sniffling wail.

"Why did I never know, son?" Byron asked, nearly tearing up himself. None of them were meant to have children. The Vanguard Code didn't permit it.

"It was only five years," Lugaid replied woefully, words hollow in the back of his throat. "I'd come out a king. We had nothing before, you see?" He looked at Byron as a sinner to absolution. "I had to leave them. We found out right before I left. It was never in the plans." His tenor cracked. "I had to."

Byron patted Lugaid's shoulder. "Sure, sure," he said glancing away. "Tell me though," he asked, voice heavy with concern, "what proof is there?"

Lugaid barely heard. "I never even met her," he whispered. "My own Cecelia. My little flower." He started to sob. "I would have been home in time for her fifth birthday."

"Son!" Bryon shouted firmly. "Pull yourself together," his tone was cold. "You are on a mission. I am sorry," he added sympathetically, "for your family, but if it's true what you say, you are not the only one who has lost."

Alas, Lugaid spoke true.

Every major city in every leading nation of the world fell to nuclear war. Massive mushrooms of destructive, fiery grandeur dotted the blue and green planet beneath the Vanguard ship adrift in space. Wide-eyed and awash with fear, the crew was forced to helplessly witness their own planet's descent into ruin. Communications with every station on Earth went silent. Not one signal could be picked up.

There was nothing they could do but watch.

"We have all lost a great deal," Byron's baritone shook the crew members. Lugaid stood by his side with a steeled jaw and bloodshot eyes, biting his lip when the Captain spoke. A wisp of murmured confusion swept across the team. "It is true. I can confirm the reports." Gasps, and an anonymous "no!" rang out. Byron held up his hand and the tempestuous crew fell silent. "Our worst fears, realized."

A supernaturally pale young man shot from his seat. "You corrupt my father's vision!" Albert Beaumont's grey, compass-rose uniform hung from his frame like a sheet from a rail. He shook his finger accusingly. "He would be so ashamed," the young man, barely a proper teen, scathed, "of all of you!" His thick black hair was accented at each temple with two premature snow-white streaks, and stuck up several inches from his head, shaking with his gesticulations.

"Albert," Isolde Brochet said carefully with practiced cadence. "Mon chéri," she added warmly as she stood from her seat then sauntered to his side; flawless, voluptuous frame evident even through boxy uniform and lab coat. All eyes were on her as she crossed the cramped quarters, just like she preferred it. "You mistake the gift we have been given," she said, placing herself gracefully in a chair near to him. Nearly five years had passed and her hair was now cropped to her chin and middle parted, but she still wore her signature red lipstick.

"What gift?" the snobbish boy scoffed.

Isolde turned her head to Mercury Graves, unchanged from years ago, apart from a few fine lines beside his eyes. "After what the Earth has," she paused, searching for the English word, "sustained," she finally said with heavy accent, sweeping her head to address everyone, then resting her eyes back on Mercury's bulbed, beady ones. "When will it be safe to land?"

"It is not so simple."

"Oh, Mercury," Isolde teased, and the room flittered in a muffled laugh. "Don't be so literal, for once."

Mercury's eyebrows fell. "Naturally," he said cooly. "It will be centuries, if ever."

The crew collectively gasped, protesting amongst themselves in shock.

"We'll die up here!" the squirrelly, underbite-ridden Paden Busk protested. Paden, an abnormal psychologist, had a strong interest in studying mental illness, as he came from a family rife with schizophrenia. His life's work was about fixing psychotic brains.

A woman with a bumped nose and jet-black hair, heavily rounded with pregnancy, leaned far back in a chair with hand rubbing her stomach. Her expression was lost. "What about the baby?! I can't have her up here!" Cesarina Calvanese, a leading paranormal researcher and psychic medium, shook her head in shock. "I can't." She paused, expression contorted. "Even she will die here," she whispered under her breath, patting her burgeoning belly.

Byron glanced to his lover with heart crashing emotion, feeling horrible guilt for their tryst. To have a child born into the world like this…

"There must be another way," the charismatic scientist

Kipling Demos reasoned, sly eyes pleading for a way out. Kipling saw the world differently than his contemporaries, part of why he was recruited to be a member of the Vanguard elite. His work was focused on the biology of mind control. He sat forward, placing elbows on both knees. He spoke with his hands, fingers open, clasping them together and back. "Let's be reasonable, Mercury."

"It is you who knows no reason," Mercury retorted.

"Ooooo," Kipling held his fingers up, wiggling them mockingly, taunting the odd man for the umpteenth time. It elicited a murmur of chuckles, like it always did.

Mercury eyed him evenly, never moving or saying a word. Only his sunken eyes appeared to smile.

"Cut it out, both of you" Byron Bellamine said, taking back control of the room.

"Don't you all see?" Isolde said, standing from her close seat next to scrunch-faced Albert. "This is our chance."

The group murmured again, shocked by her words, until Byron shouted, "QUIET."

Isolde nodded to him, then continued. "Let us take this as a sign, from our founder and father Alabaster himself that his work is not complete. Let us vow to dedicate our lives to this cause, the same as the lives of the children that come after us," she added, gesturing towards Cesarina. "Have we forgotten who we are? What lies in our blood? Have we forgotten our Code? Have we forgotten why we're here?"

A few positive murmurs.

Edmund Regnard, a neurobiologist with sickly skin and a pig-like nose, grumbled loudly, "No!"

"That's right!" she said enthusiastically. "I thought not!" Her wide, brash smile flashed. "Do not mourn your loss. Celebrate what you have won!" She studied her colleagues' serious faces. "Complete freedom over your experiments. Dictation over law. The governments hunting us are gone. The G.N. is gone. Nothing stands in our way now!"

"But, Isolde," Jasmine Duran, a psychologist focused on the study of I.Q., interjected, small face tilted up in fear, tinny voice cutting the room. "If what Mercury says is true…"

"It is true," Mercury said flatly.

"He's right," Alexander Thorne, botanist, confirmed from where he sat to the side of the control room, part of Byron's crew, white-blonde eyebrows raised high, poking at a flashing flat screen.

Jasmine ignored him and repeated herself. "If what Mercury says is true, what life is there here? What mission is left? We have failed them," she said sadly, gesturing limply out a side porthole over the passing Earth as horrifying black clouds billowed in tiny pocks across the surface. She was one of the few who believed in the true cause as Alabaster did. Not one who saw the cause their own way, for their own gains.

"You must think bigger," Mercury said, eyeing the room playfully.

"He's correct," Isolde cheered, pleased for once with Mercury. "We have been given the gift of time!"

"How?" Daemon Dale, mercenary turned crew member, recruited for his unusual strength and *Homo Sacrum* blood, asked in a grunt. "How is anything about this," he paused in a frown, "tragedy a gift?" The large man leaned forward sceptically, glancing around at his comrade's questioning faces, voicing the group's general concern. He scratched at his fire-red beard once.

Braden Warn and Geralt Horne sat on either side of Daemon, in full agreement with his comment, nodding fiercely. Everything they did was in line with their beloved friend turned leader. Both Braden and Geralt had followed Daemon since they left military service decades ago. After Dameon was accepted into the ranks of the Vanguard for his *Homo Sacrum* genetics, he made sure Braden and Geralt were tested and when they too were *Homo Sacrum*, were recruited as well.

"Why, we've been gifted centuries of time for our own selves and our descendants," Isolde said, "free to experiment here on the Vanguard, exactly as we choose!"

Her eyes glinted with terrible fervour. How could the others not understand what she saw? Isolde was nothing without her vision.

"What then?" Kipling pressed. "After the Vanguard, what's next?"

"Once we have conquered the stars," Isolde said, flashing her brightest smile, "our blood will remould the land." She paused, letting the sentiment settle over all who listened like dust.

She glanced out a rounded glass porthole at the green and blue earth dotted with black clouds below.

"It will be ours."

THE VANGUARD SHIP, SPACE

About 200 years later…

Indeed, the Vanguard team stayed on their spaceship and continued their experiments. They intermarried and interbred for generations and generations, creating an entire society of Vanguards that all adhered to Alabaster's original Code.

Each of the original Vanguard cult member's bloodlines evolved differently, based on what their aims were. The entirety of the ship was filled with every type of laboratory and library and the children chose their fields of interest young and were expertly schooled to continue experimentation and evolution of humanity by the time they were in their teens. Everything they did revolved around the Mission. After over 200 years in space, they achieved impressive results.

The Beaumont bloodline was the first to obviously evolve. A young child named Vlad Beaumont threw his plate across the mess hall with nothing other than his mind. He was only three years old, but was afterwards condemned to a life sedated, so his brainwaves could be mapped and his neurology studied. His DNA was utilized to further the Beaumont bloodline, resulting in a class of people who could move things with their minds.

The Bellamine bloodline gained super intelligence. They were known for building technology that the other bloodlines relied on. The ship's captain was also typically of that bloodline.

Several members of the Brochet bloodline developed physical regeneration. They were able to endure wounds only to have them rapidly heal, although they still felt the pain. The tests for this were exceedingly brutal and reserved for babies, although the specimens typically didn't present their abilities until puberty.

Typically, all Vanguards didn't present abilities until trauma was incurred, or puberty. Beaumont was a notable exception.

Busk, alternatively, was notably powerless. Some members of the bloodline could manipulate water droplets slightly, but only under the correct EMF conditions. After generations of experiments on them, hopes were low that they would produce any abilities of note. They were known as not powerful at all. Their bloodline primarily kept the ship running, working in mess, or as hullhands.

The Calvaneses, however, were exceedingly powerful. Every single female in the Calvanese bloodline developed empathetic dominion. They were able to control feelings simply by being near someone. In the beginning of the emergence of this power, chaos ensued. It caused extremely unpredictable actions. Many of which resulted in death. For this reason, the Calvanese were sequestered to their own wing of the ship, with their own dedicated laboratory. Only Graves dared venture to their wing, for they were immune their powers.

Durans developed the ability to turn invisible, or phase-shift from one location to another. They were discouraged from using their ability because miscalculations resulted in quick deaths.

The Demos bloodline developed oath binding, where any pacts or vows made with them were nearly impossible to break, and if broken, the results were dire.

Dale developed super strength.

Graves developed soul harvesting. Only Brochets could withstand them. Everyone else avoided them fearfully.

Horne was the only bloodline that extended their research to animals of all kinds. Mammals, lizards, fowl and insects. Specifically, they developed deep empathetic connections with dogs. These specially bred animals followed the Hornes around if they were appendages. But they also experimented with different types of animals, creating entirely new species.

Minneys were known for their healing abilities.

Norlands were known for their berserker-like tempers and

often relegated to their own wing of the ship, like Calvanese.

Morfit with its bloodline focus on altered states of consciousness, mastered lucid dreaming and astral projection. The younger members of the bloodline often used their ability to play tricks on their schoolmates. As did Duran with their invisibility and shifting abilities.

Regnard developed the ability to manipulate frequencies. It was a particularly dangerous ability living in a spaceship therefore all Regnards were given a serum to dampen their abilities temporarily, until further research could be completed and their powers could be controlled. They often worked as assistants for the other bloodline scientists.

Thorne, primarily botanists, experimented with all types of unusual plants producing many unique, even magical types. More notably though, though mere happenstance, some Thornes developed temporal sight as well. That meant they could glimpse possible futures.

Finally, some in the Warn bloodline, not all, could manipulate the perception of time.

It was right after supper, when the lights were flashing. It was time to return to quarters. Dymphna Thorne was awash with sadness. She was failing at her lessons. She did not take to botany the way that the other Thornes did. The plants hated her and she hated them. She was careless with sterilizing tools and couldn't stand the way dirt felt under her fingernails. She hadn't even evolved a single dandelion. Her classmates, brothers and sisters and cousins, teased her mercilessly.

"Dymphna will be a hullhand!" her cousin Alfia squealed in the mess hall. "The plants shrivel when she nears them," she lowered her voice, scandalously whispering loudly to all the other girls at their table. "She's a powerless Thorne."

"We'd love to have you," Linton Norland yelled from down the mess hall. "Wouldn't we boys?"

The other young Norlands, Hornes, Demos and Busks that

sat at the same table whooped and hollered gleefully. Hullhands were known for their lack of power. They were also typically male. The few women relegated to their ranks were less than lucky.

"Stop it," Dymphna whined, putting her head into her hands, hiding behind her long blonde hair.

She hung back from the others, waiting until the mess hall cleared. She wanted to be alone. As she made her way through the winding corridors of the Vanguard ship, she did her best not to cry.

Then, the corridor lights flickered slightly. The temperature didn't change, but she felt significantly colder. As if frost settled upon her soul.

Graves.

Dymphna turned, listening for footsteps, but heard nothing. She silently crept to the next corridor and peeked around it.

"Got you!" Cormac Duran cried, materializing out of nowhere. Dymphna gasped, startled. Shortly after, his brother Clement appeared as well.

"No fair," Clement shouted. "You cheated!"

Dymphna exhaled, leaning against the cool wall behind her. She watched the pale boys with black hair disappear again and heard their running footfalls down the long hall.

"Dymphna," a cold voice breathed in her ear.

She nearly screamed. Reynold Graves slipped a hand quickly over her mouth. She tried to look away, but he held her head firmly. His dim, unfeeling eyes settled on hers.

"Do not scream," he said.

It hurt to look at Reynold. Dymphna's eyes teared, from her earlier sadness and now fear. The Code expressly forbid Vanguard attacks against Vanguards, however, there was a grey area when it came to Vanguards without power. Their society had stratified at that point into the higher class of powerful Vanguards and the lower class of Vanguards without. Dymphna was nearly fourteen years old and had not displayed any of the characteristic Thorne powers. If she did not present power soon, she would be relegated to hullhand or test subject.

As a girl, she would likely become a test subject. There was a chance she would end up pinned against a wall by Reynold anyway.

Dymphna blinked her eyes slowly and Reynold lowered his hand.

"Good," he said.

"What do you want, Graves?" Dymphna asked warily.

"I want to look at you."

Dymphna's heart seized in her chest.

"You… you can't," she said, cowering against the cool wall behind her. Reynold's frame towered over her. He was barely a teen, yet already as tall as a man. "The Code," she said, glancing both ways down the hall. It was empty. They were alone.

"Fuck the Code," he said, smiling. "Besides, you are not powerful. I heard your kin squawking about it at supper." He lowered to whisper in her ear. "That means you will be mine soon anyway."

Each bloodline utilized their test subjects differently. Graves, for all intents and purposes, swallowed their souls, absorbing their knowledge and gifts, to further evolve their own bloodline. While each Vanguard bloodline was mostly tight-lipped about the experiments there were overseeing, rumors spread. Everyone knew about Graves. And even if they didn't, they could feel it. It hurt to be near them in the soul. Like their eyes siphoned all hope.

"I won't," Dymphna said proudly. "I am powerful," she added meekly. "I know it." And she did, deep down. But she had no proof. The plants did not grow for her. She had no mind for botany. Still, she had hope in her heart that she was meant for more than a life imprisoned.

Reynold was enlivened by Dymphna's protesting. The hope she felt fuelled him.

"Show me," he said tauntingly.

She looked at him, hard, as if she wanted to smack him across the face.

"You can't do this," she said. She felt pressure on her chest, as if there were hands pressing down on it. She tried to look away from Reynold, but her gaze was fixed, like his beady eyes were hooks. Her voice caught in her throat from terror.

A smile crept across Reynold's handsome, skeletal face and his dull eyes began to sparkle.

Dymphna felt her hope fading. The warmth that it brought her even at her lowest began to recede and was replaced by frost. She shivered. She was theoretically afraid but could barely feel it. Her terror faded, too. Everything that made her feel like herself began to escape her. The world around her seemed to dim, until everything was lifeless.

Reynold couldn't stop smiling. He nearly laughed. He had never tasted a soul so good, and hopeful, and pure. But there was something else too.

As Dymphna was nearly sucked dry of life, her body seized. Her eyes shut and Reynold's concentration fell. She dropped to the floor of the corridor, white-bright lightning shooting from her fingers and toes.

Reynold gasped and backed away slowly, until taking off in a sprint down the hall.

"Help!" Reynold ran down the spaceship's corridors towards the Bridge. He skidded as he stopped. "Help! Something happened to a Thorne girl!"

Several heads turned. Cormac Bellamine, the Captain, was the first to speak.

"Where is she?" he asked loudly, but calmly.

"Not far from mess," Reynold said. "Follow me."

Cormac Bellamine, his Second in Command Roman Brochet, and the oldest member of Reynold's own bloodline Angelina Graves walked hurriedly behind Reynold. They reached Dymphna quickly.

Dymphna was lying on the floor where Reynold left her, motionless, with pale green eyes impossibly wide.

"Is she dead?" Angelina asked in her elegant, wavering baritone.

Roman Brochet knelt. He felt her pulse.

"She lives," he replied.

Right as his hand touched her skin, Dymphna sat up. Her eyes darted back and forth.

"I see castles," she said hollowly. "Sixteen of them."

"Go get her bloodline," Roman commanded Reynold. He dutifully bowed and darted off towards the Thorne wing of the ship. "Girl," Roman addressed Dymphna. "What is your name? What do you see?"

"The castles are soaked in blood," she said distantly. "Built with the bodies of the lost. Their eyes cry the blood. They show what has been lost. We are all that remain. We must save them."

"Girl?" Roman shook her shoulders, but Dymphna remained frozen, apart from her darting eyes. He looked up at Cormac and Angelina watching closely.

"Her power has revealed itself," Cormac said stoically. "She's a Thorne with foresight."

"Another like Artur, then?" Angelina said, not taking her eyes off Dymphna. She remembered the first Thorne with foresight named Artur Thorne, from when she was a girl, nearly a century before. The young man was exceedingly useful for the Vanguard cause and helped them further many of their experiments successfully. The extent of the powers they had gained many attributed to him alone. Although he never spoke of castles.

Alon Thorne followed by his closest advisors, alongside Reynold Graves, arrived quickly from around a corner.

"Dymphna, no!" cried her mother, Celia. She dropped and threw her arms around the girl. She shook her, but Dymphna didn't move. "What happened to her?" She looked scathingly at Reynold, then Angelina, "Did you do this, Graves?"

Angelina's thin eyebrows rose high, approaching her grey widow's peak. "Unlike your bloodline, Graves follows the Code."

Alon stepped forward. "Angelina," he bowed, "I apologize for Celia's brashness."

"Alon, you know they did something to her! Look at her! I'm telling you; she's gone. I... I can't feel her anymore," Celia looked at the elder of their bloodline pleadingly.

But Alon knew that nothing was worse than offending Graves. Not even losing a daughter.

"Did she say anything?" Celia asked more softly, stroking Dymphna's hair.

"No," Roman said resolutely.

Angelina looked at him pointedly. Her lip twitched, but she did not smile. Cormac frowned. Neither said a word. Reynold shifted from foot to foot, studying the tops of his boots carefully.

"How could this happen?" she said, looking from the other Thornes to the Captain, then Roman and Angelina. "Have you ever seen anything like this?"

"Her body is unfit for power," Angelina said. "If she once held the promise of it, she does no longer."

"No…" Celia whispered. "I know she is late. I know she nears her fourteenth birthday and yet no power has been witnessed. But please. Please! Do not declare her powerless. Please do not. She is so bright, so good. So beautiful," Celia said, stroking Dymphna's comatose face. "Please don't condemn her to that life."

"What life will she live as a vegetable?" Roman said. "Drawing resources without contribution."

"Brochet speaks true," Cormac said gently. "It is illogical to declare otherwise."

Celia had always known that it was a possibility. Especially as Dymphna aged and the other Thornes discovered their gifts of accelerating plant growth or communing with the plants to give, or receive, special abilities, and she did not. But Celia's five other children were powerful. Dymphna was her youngest. She was sure that the girl held power too. She knew it from the moment she was born and she looked into the little girl's pale eyes.

"Fuck logic," Celia said angrily.

"That's enough," Alon said. He looked wearily at Angelina. The years had worn hard on Alon. He was tired. "We surrender Dymphna Thorne as powerless."

"No!" Celia wailed, clutching her daughter. Several hullhands grabbed her and pulled her from Celia. The other Thornes held Celia back.

"Thank you good Alon," Angelina said cooly, gaze shifting slightly to watch the commotion, then back to the Thorne elder.

"Certainly," Alon replied, with Celia's screams echoing all around him.

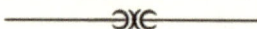

Reynold retreated to his quarters awash with emotion. Confusion. Dread. But also, pride. He truly did not believe Dymphna had power or he would not have fed on her soul so. Like all Vanguards, he lived and died by the Code. And to do what he did was the highest offense. He attacked another powerful Vanguard. He was all but dead.

Why did Roman Brochet lie for him? And the Captain? And his terrifying elder Angelina? What did they stand to gain from hiding the knowledge of Dymphna's power? Reynold didn't know, but he thanked his Ancestors, regardless.

Then, he was hit with a wave of information. Images, sounds and smells washed over him until he was immersed in their depths. He found himself in another place. Another time. He watched a man that looked like him but with nearly translucent grey eyes riding a horse, a hawk perched on his shoulder, with two other men following behind.

The other men had red eyes.

BOOK 1

LITTLEBELL CASTLE

Almost 2000 years later...

"Praise the Horned! Praise the Horned!" a shrill voice called out down the Littlebell castle corridors. "The babe is charmed! Hail the Horned One, Minney has another charmed one! Finally! Oh, praise the Horned!"

The frantic woman scurried down the castle's yellow stone hallways alerting all who were near. She shouted with a wide smile at all who would listen to her cries.

She had waited beside Sia, the Lady of Littlebell, for moons, hoping her prophesy would come to pass. Gertrude felt it was her duty, after all, since the Horned Woman chose her to bestow the vision upon. She'd known since she'd had the dream that a great blessing was to befall the Minney bloodline as a reward for their overwhelming good-natured kindness, despite ill-treatment from other bloodlines, during the Blood Wars. That was what the Horned Woman told her in her dream. Gertrude always had visions that came to pass and she assumed this one was no different.

She'd run just as frantically then, one year ago, to address Littlebell's Lady Sia, to tell her what she'd seen.

Unlike the Vanguards in other realms, Littlebell's Vanguards were willing to listen to her. Gertrude was proud to hail from such a progressive place. She'd heard whispers about Ravenshroud and Anstout, how their natives were little better than slaves. She'd seen bits and pieces of Westerviolet, what lay along Littlebell's border anyway, and it wasn't much better, with sickly thin natives, skittish like deer. She'd passed through Baneswood and it was far too tough for her Littlebell sensibilities, with their rough customs and brutal ways. Open meat markets, public beatings, the ferocity of the Games. She thanked her stars and silently offered a prayer for those less fortunate than herself as she cut around the yellow stone corners, hollering everyone's ears off.

"The babe is charmed?!" an excited shout echoed down the hall, mirroring Gertrude's jubilee. Attendants and costermongers flitting around this end of the castle began to catch wind of Gertrude's shouts. Wide smiles plastered all the faces who heard. Arms robed in the colorful patterns of Littlebell danced and cheered. Soon, everyone was shouting to spread the joyous word.

It had been centuries since Littlebell had a charmed babe living in the flesh, and not a moment too soon, for in the wake of the Blood Wars, Kingdom politics were tumultuous. Sia's elderclaim was continually challenged by the traditional realms. Littlebell needed someone more powerful than she or her son Amos at her helm.

He just wasn't enough.

Gertrude felt a bit sorry for the lad. It was well known that he was to lose his elderclaim in light of the recent babe's birth. There was no contest against a charmed one.

If the prophesy was true to its meaning, this next charmed babe was to alter the face of the Kingdom forever. Gertrude knew how important this child was going to be for the land.

She couldn't stop smiling.

WESTERVIOLET STABLE

About 100 years later…Present Day

It wasn't that Rose was frightened of her mother. She knew Mother would never harm her, but she was petrified of disappointing her. Everyone in Westerviolet was. The Vice Lords stumbled over each other for the slightest chance at catching her eye. The merchant caravans whistled at her from the Commons as she passed through, throwing their wares at her feet, for if the Lady of Westerviolet was seen to be wearing them, they would inevitably be in fashion and all the high natives across the realm, and likely natives throughout Baneswood and Animus Rock as well, would seek them. Even Grandfather was under Sybil's spell. This spoke to her undeniable power. Sybil was a force of nature, terrifying as she was beautiful.

Rose wanted to be just like her.

She clenched the damning piece of parchment tight in her fist and her mind raced with excuses.

"I don't want to go back to the castle today," Rose said.

The little Lady of Westerviolet stood ankle deep in mud and manure across the stable from Col, son of the late Stablemaster, watching him gently groom a mare. Dust swirled in the light between them with each bristled stroke. She studied Col's serious glare. He was intently focused, beads of sweat glinting against his ebony skin, dripping from his short curls. She glanced down at her own pale hands and sighed, feeling an ache deep in her chest that she couldn't explain, like there was something profoundly wrong her. Like she painfully didn't belong.

"I wish I could stay here with you."

The lanky boy turned. "Why?"

She looked up to meet his eyes. "Mother will be cross." His irises were red, like all natives' were. Col's were brilliant shades of red, like polished molten glass. To Rose, they almost seemed to glow when he really looked at her. She loved when he really looked at her.

"You know you have to little girl. This is no place for a Lady."

"I know." Rose glanced up at him. "Is it okay if I stay here just a little while, though?"

The air was heavy and stagnant, like you could bite it if you wanted to. Time itself stood still.

"You can stay if you want."

Rose smiled. "I won't be in the way. I can help!" she cried, then mimicked a bow. "How can I serve you?"

Col winced.

"What's wrong?"

"I don't like that we have to say it," Col said flatly.

"Oh." She opened her eyes wide. "I didn't mean it. I..." She stuttered, face burning hot, throat stabbing in threat of tears. "I didn't know."

"You didn't know?"

"I thought it was just something you said."

"You did?"

If he didn't respond with the appropriate phrase, he would be beaten. Some children never got up. It had always been that way in Westerviolet, but such realities were kept far from Rose, who rarely left the castle grounds. She was never allowed in the city. Her interactions with natives were limited to the foppish children of the Vice Lords and Col, when she was able to steal away from Mathilda's watch unnoticed.

"I..." she lowered her head. "I didn't know."

He exhaled hard against the back of his throat. "It's okay."

"Are you sure?"

Col nodded, brow still furrowed, then went back to brushing the steed. Rose watched him in silence.

"My father taught me who our people really are," Col said over his shoulder. "We aren't supposed to serve you."

"Yes, huh."

He shook his head 'no' with his jaw set.

"That's what Mother says," she countered hotly. "You owe us."

Mother told her all about their heathen ways. All about the old gods and the Landing, and how her people, the Vanguards, came and saved Col's people from themselves a long, long, long time ago. Longer than she could imagine, Mother said. How they knew nothing of farming, or order, or glory before the Ancestors came and built the castles and taught them how to properly behave. She knew everything about it, she thought.

Col laughed to reveal his endearingly crooked teeth. "My people were here long before yours and they were great!"

Rose balked. "Grandfather would not like you saying that."

It was forbidden to speak against Vanguards in Westerviolet. Everyone knew that.

"I know, but I trust you," he said. "You'd never tell him."

Rose smiled and walked to where Col stood to place her hand on the flank of the mare aside his. "Mother says our blood is special."

"It's all a made-up story."

She play-shoved him. "Shut up!" Then, curiosity got the better of her. "How do you know?"

"Know what?" Col frowned. "My father told me."

"Mother doesn't lie," Rose said, and a chill ran down her spine. "I know it is true. Vanguard blood is special."

Col shoved her back. "If you say it is."

Rose's face clouded. How could he tease about something so serious? Something so real? Something so true?

"I'm leaving," she said.

Before Col could respond, already more like her mother than she realized, Rose proudly stormed out, small feet slogging through the muddy ground with comical difficulty.

When she finally reached the creaky stable door, she slammed it behind her.

"Aye!" he shouted. "I told you a creed of times not to do that!" but she was already gone.

———— ƆꞮƆ ————

"How many today, Rose?" Sybil asked over her shoulder as she heard the girl's small booties echoing lightly in the massive space. "You thought I forgot, didn't you? How many?"

Sybil turned in the engulfing hall, ceilings lined with dark-stained timber, arched into the reaches of the Westerviolet North Wing. She narrowed her eyes at the girl's muddy footprints. She could smell guilt on Rose like a river fang smells blood, yet she decided to deal with one punishment at a time.

Rose sulked towards Sybil with a crumpled strip of parchment hidden behind her back.

Towering tapestries lined each wall on either side of the rectangular hall, patterned with stylized serpents biting each other's tails in glinting black and green. The serpent designs spun about one another with sharpened fangs, brought to life by lustrous threads of real silver. In streaming sunlight, the snakes appeared to writhe and breathe, as if by magic. Some claimed they were indeed enchanted by old power and to stare too long at them enacted a curse upon the onlooker, as those that lined the halls of Duskfang were rumoured to function, although sensible people knew such talk was only legend. Still, no one let their eyes linger on them for long.

Horizontal windows lined the eastern and western walls in front and behind Rose as she walked the long distance to her mother. In the deep afternoon, hot rays poured from the west and cast dark shadows across Rose's cheeks.

"Rose?" Sybil turned ominously towards the girl, emerald-laden gown sparkling. "Show me."

Rose's cheeks burned. She held the parchment tight. "I got one."

"Why not the other?" Sybil tapped her boot, wondering what trouble the girl caused now. "What did you do, Rose?"

"I didn't do anything!"

"You had to do something. She doesn't take one away for nothing. You did well the first half of the day it seems." Sybil glanced at the sad paper in Rose's tightly clung fingers. "What happened the second?" she asked with an intense glare. "What did my sweet girl do?"

Rose was unable to meet her mother's eyes. Instead, she looked far up to study the ceiling.

"You won't find what you did up there," Sybil taunted, inwardly amused yet outwardly stern. Rose reminded Sybil of herself at that age. Too beautiful for her own good. And endlessly headstrong. "Why did she take a check from you?"

Rose sighed and lowered her eyes dutifully but still did not respond. "You're trying my patience." Sybil's annoyance brewed. "You must tell me or I will find out from Mathilda herself."

Rose sighed more loudly this time and met her mother's glare angrily. "Mother," her tone warned.

Sybil smirked, stifling delight at the girl's frustration and pride for her strong personality. Alas, Tomas wouldn't stand for such a wilful granddaughter. She was to be dealt with, especially before she was to be sent to Academy. Sybil had to ensure the girl did not sully the proud Brochet name, she had to know how to behave, hence the arrangement with Mathilda. For each part of the lesson day that Rose behaved as a proper Vanguard should, she received a check on a piece of parchment that she delivered to her mother each afternoon, as a report on the day. The girl was to be educated in the ways of Brochet, alongside the worthiest children, High Native born, of course. It was of paramount importance that she knew how to behave.

"What do you pout for?"

"Mathilda is just jealous of me," Rose said. "I'm smarter than her."

"Oh?" Sybil pursed her lips to hide her amusement. "What did you do, Rose?"

Rose mumbled and looked down again.

"Unacceptable. Look up at me like a Lady. Like a Brochet," Sybil commanded. Instantly Rose's head popped up, wide curls bouncing. "Speak clearly and never mumble like that. Even if you speak a mistruth, say it with all the pride that anything you speak should be said with. You speak with dignity or not at all. Do I make myself clear Rose?"

For being such a petite woman, Sybil was unbelievably imposing.

"Yes, Mother."

"Good," Sybil cooed.

The girl was so young and so beautiful, it was impossible to be angry at her doll face. Sybil never had the heart to punish her with anything other than words, although that was punishment enough, as Sybil had a venom tongue. Tomas was different though and had no issue smacking a child, beautiful or not. Sybil thus far had protected Rose from her grandfather but was constantly on edge over it. Rose so far had been obedient enough, albeit curious and wise beyond her years. Tomas often compared her to a difficult mare, fierce and tough but once broken, the best kind of steed. He reassured Sybil that Rose was still young and could be moulded. He was sure her intense thoughts and strange ways would fade with time and she'd fall more in line with the other Vanguard children, especially once she was sent off to Academy. That time was coming shortly.

"Back to the heart of the matter," Sybil said as she shifted her weight, verdant gown shifting in her wake. "The true mystery today. Whatever did my most sweet girl do?"

"I didn't do anything."

"Rose..."

"I only did what Grandfather taught me."

"Nonsense."

"It's true!"

Sybil rested her hand on the wall and felt cool, flat rock beneath her palm. The stone steadied her as it had countless Ancestors before her. Her thoughts briefly shifted to the Ancestors, wondering if even Lord Robert the Great, savior of Brochet, champion of the Blood Wars, had stood in that very same spot, then quickly back to the present. "I doubt good Mathilda would withhold for that," she said, lowering her hand, glaring at her daughter. Her black eyes pierced. "At least she thought you did something," Sybil added as she strolled across the massive hall, Baneswood boots clacking louder than before. "What did she accuse you of then? What didn't you do?"

As Sybil strode, a maiden with the threadlike braids typical of Westerviolet low born natives hurried out of the shadows. The girl's narrow eyes were cast down as if she'd lose them if she looked up. Her bare feet slapped against chilled, speckled marble as she hurriedly polished the smudge Sybil left on the stone wall, ever so slight it was, then scurried back to her hidden position.

Sybil ignored the maiden and outstretched her hand to Rose and led her to an enormous wooden table spanning the length of the cavernous chamber. In the center sat a series of simple vases packed with dark stems that appeared to be crawling out, dotted with white bindweed. The same flowers surrounded the Lunar Tower, just outside the gate, off limits for all but Vanguards. White bindweed was said to have been used by the old gods to bind two people's fates and was thought to be sacred. The bindweed gave off a strong, romantic, nearly offensive scent. Rose studied the creamy petals as she sat.

"Mathilda told me I disrupted the others," Rose said.

She eyed the waxy side of a leaf. It matched Sybil's gown and most of the tapestries in the castle, as it was their bloodline's signature color. All the bloodlines had a color, not only Brochet, that legend said spoke to their inherent powers. Brochet was said to have the gift of immortality in their blood, however in the modern day, this was just a tale told to children. No one of note believed in such things anymore.

Sybil adjusted her fine gown as she sat too. "Did you?"

"No."

Sybil crossed her thin arms. "So, what did you do?" Rose could be such a mystery at times. "Why did she say you disrupted?"

"It was me, but I didn't say anything to them. I didn't *make* them do anything."

Sybil raised her eyebrows. "Rose...What did you do?"

"Am I going to get in trouble?"

"It depends on what you did."

"I don't want to get in trouble."

"Tell me."

Rose sighed loudly from the back of her throat. "I trained them."

"You did *what?*"

"I trained them."

"Oh, I heard you," Sybil replied with a melodious laugh. "How in the Kingdom did you do that?"

Rose proceeded to tell Sybil all about the old tale, where the man rang a bell when he was going to feed his dog, until the dog would salivate each time he heard the bell whether food was served or not.

"Grandfather told me that humans are like animals," she went on excitedly. "If you ring a bell enough times when you feed them, they will learn to bark when they hear it."

Sybil chuckled lightly. Rose frowned with embarrassment. Noting the girl's scrunched expression, Sybil explained, "I assume he spoke in metaphor."

"What's that?"

"He didn't mean it."

"Why would anyone say something they don't mean?"

"He meant that people expect things from you if you let them," Sybil explained. "If you do something for them, they will demand it always. He didn't mean to tell you to ring an actual bell, my sweet girl!"

Rose's glare burned. "You don't know what happened."

"If you make that face long enough it'll stick that way, you know." Rose continued to scowl. "Oh, alright," Sybil relented, curiosity getting the better of her. "Tell me what happened."

Rose puffed out her chest and sat up a bit taller as she turned to Sybil.

"Every day, right before midday meal, I kicked the desk."

Rose wanted her mother to be proud of her for her cleverness. She wanted to be the same as Sybil. She thought the snooty high-born natives she was forced to spend long days with, children of Vice Lords and merchant leaders who cared more about the latest fashions or hangings than the way flowers smell or how fun it is to climb trees, were the perfect way to practice.

"I did it for moons," Rose said. "Today, I kicked when it wasn't time for meal. Everyone got hungry and cried."

"That was very naughty," Sybil scolded, frowning, veiling her pride the best she could. At this rate the girl would be a more skilled manipulator than Ancestor Lucien himself by the time she was of age. Sybil's great-grandfather. A true Brochet. Known for his charm, power and role in securing the Old's prevalence during the Uprising. Inwardly, Sybil beamed. "You must not treat others that way," she said. "Even the earthblood."

"Why not?"

"You just shouldn't."

"Why not?"

"Because I said so."

Rose, hurt, lifted her legs and crossed them under herself. "You don't understand. You're just like Mathilda."

"I hope not," Sybil said slowly. Rose felt the hairs on her neck rise. "I am more than an *earthblood*. I am your mother. No more of this feeling sorry for yourself or being spoiled and ungrateful. No more. Tomorrow you will go to Mathilda and apologize for disrupting. And never again Rose, do you hear me? You are better."

"But Mother, it is so boring!

Sybil rolled her eyes. "Oh, it is not boring." She held her hand out to inspect her unpainted nails. A sign of her old blood and breeding—one of many Sybil bore. She herself remembered her Westerviolet lessons and Rose was absolutely right, they were boring. When Sybil was young, she was much more interested in finding ways to escape the castle or convince Digory to cause mischief on her behalf. Which in retrospect was good practice for her behavior in adulthood, particularly after Rosen died. How she'd pit the Guardsmen against each other when she needed to create a distraction. Or she'd always get the best price on ruby furs from the Baneswood traders. And she could always quell the storm that was her father, Lord Tomas Brochet, elderclaim, as easily as the old gods of legend could quell lightning and thunder.

"You must not pay attention." She shot Rose a teasing glance. "You must be boring yourself."

"It is boring!" Rose squeaked, uncrossing and re-crossing her legs, fiddling with a loose seam on her mud-caked bootie.

Sybil studied her daughter down her own prominent nose. She sympathized with Rose to a point. Learning about the long-dead Brochet Ancestors and their accomplishments and conquests tended to be dull. There were so many of them. But it was necessary tradition. It was the way of Brochet. They honoured their Ancestors above all else. Everything was for the glory of Brochet. The glory of Westerviolet. Ultimately, the glory of their people, the Vanguards.

"At least let me stay in the stables with Col or I can chase firebugs by the moat with Ellie, or I could even play in Pinewood. Father brought me there once when I was small and I still remember how lovely it smelled. Anything other than listening to Mathilda blather on all day. I don't care about what happened to daft old men! I don't care what they saw! What they did! I want to see and do things for myself."

"Rose, enough," Sybil said firmly. "It is vital for you to learn about your history. It's your birth right. It's the first knowledge that all Vanguard children are given, before puberty sets in and other instruction is required. You are to inherit elderclaim someday, as I will from your grandfather, whenever he gets around to deigning it so," she added under her breath. "It is your duty to learn everything there is to know about Brochet so you may lead Westerviolet properly someday." At Rose's morose expression Sybil added, "Don't be ungrateful. You are young. I don't blame you for not understanding that many have died for you. Don't act like you know everything. You don't know how the Kingdom works. You have much to learn of duty and honor. Much to learn about the glory of

Westerviolet."

"Then tell me!" Rose nearly shouted, full to the brim of duty, honor and glory. "It is so boring inside the castle. You know the Lessonroom does not have windows. Not one! I am trapped like a pine hare all day. I just want to play outside. I'm all alone in there." She sighed. "I want friends," she added with a knowingly manipulative sniffle.

"No more," Sybil said curtly, icy words piercing the hall's warm air. "You are tremendously fortunate to be educated in the castle at all. If you'd been born with different blood you could be working in a Morfit field or begging in the Littlebell streets! Or worse, the Anstout or Lyonshall mines. So many children just like you don't have it nearly as good as you do."

"I wish I was working in a field!"

"Oh, my sweet, you don't know what you want," Sybil shook her head, laughing at the girl's naiveite. "You've never worked a day in your life. You just want what seems exciting and different and the opposite of what I'm telling you to do. You're more like me than you realize. It's a blessing and a curse that all women turn into their mothers eventually."

"I'll never be like you."

"If I spoke that way to your grandfather, he'd have my tongue for sup," Sybil warned. "You're fortunate I don't tell him."

Instantly, Rose's mood flipped. "Please don't tell him!" Dark eyes widening in fear, she cried, "I didn't mean it!"

Sybil warmed considerably and, with a loud scrape, scooted towards her daughter in the heavy chair. She looked down lovingly and placed a slight arm around the girl's shoulders. Sybil lowered her dusky, melodious voice.

"You cannot act like this at the Academy."

Rose's eyes instantly lit up and she turned to Sybil with glee. "When?! When can I go?!" Before she gave Sybil a chance to respond, Rose continued chattering eagerly. "Grandfather says there isn't really a rock, not really, but it's called that because it can't be broken into. And all eight towers reach all the way to the clouds! I heard one merchant boy say you can see the Deadlands from the very top! That it has all the treasure of the old gods in it. Oh Mother, can I go?"

All Vanguard children regardless of bloodline were customarily sent to Animus Rock, the Kingdom's capital city, to be educated in the disciplines of history, linguistics, trade and diplomacy. Unofficially, the children were monitored for any residual power that remained in their blood, trickled down from the legends of old and not yet identified by the Guild.

"I don't know if you're ready," Sybil said. Rose was excited and persuasive as well as persistent, and Sybil could not deny that she wanted to go back to Animus Rock herself. She had plans brewing. And Westerviolet had bad memories. It was easy to be lost to mourning and sorrow there; years later, still in the wake of Rosen's death, she had not recovered. Maybe Animus would be good for her. She would have room to weave webs properly, to get closer to her ultimate goal.

"I am! I am! Oh please. I promise!" Rose squealed.

Sybil, grinning, feigned a sigh. "So be it," she said, blinking slowly, "I'll speak to your grandfather."

Rose shrieked and leapt into Sybil's arms. "Oh, thank you Mother! Thank you! I will be so nice and good you will not recognize me."

"I have no doubt, my sweet," Sybil cooed distantly, thoughts drifting from Rosen, to the Rock, to formulating her future plans. "I know how good you are," she said, rubbing her daughter's silky hair as she held her close. She felt Rose's flutter of a heartbeat within her small body. "I know."

WESTERVIOLET LORD'S STUDY

"Father."

Sybil's shrill command interrupted Lord Tomas Brochet as she stormed into his study. She'd internally steeled herself towards her purpose on the long walk down the hall, preparing to face her father, portraits of old Brochets glaring at her from every angle.

He wasn't going to like what she had to say, but she didn't care. She always got her way.

At first glance, Sybil Brochet was a ghost haunting Westerviolet's enormous, ancient castle. Her plunging green gown starkly contrasted her ethereally pale skin. Around her neck was an impressive and unique green-gem pendant on silver, given to her by her mother, passed down through the Brochet women and wives for as long as history had been recorded, and long prior, with encircled serpents in the form of Brochet's emblem. The ouroboros lay between her plump creased breasts.

She stood adjacent the Lord, tapping her boot impatiently. "The girl is trapped," she said. "Rose needs to see the Kingdom. She doesn't know anything."

"You don't know anything," Tomas barked from where he sat. "None of us do." He took a long sip of aubergine Animus wine while leaning far back in his high-back chair, feet and armrests carved serpents. Then he set his drink down on the elderdesk with a thud.

"Don't interrupt me," Sybil said. "This is important."

Tomas raised his bushy eyebrows. "Do you forget I am your father?" His ancient voice groaned like a cart under heavy weight. "I shall do as I wish."

"Are you busy?"

"Yes."

"Doing what?"

Tomas took another long sip as he met Sybil's glare. "I'm drinking," he said. Then, he deep-belly laughed so hard that he jostled his healthy mop of brown hair, greying in his advanced years, salt and peppered all over. His cavernous cheeks and razor-sharp jaw were cleanshaven, revealing his inexplicably youthful vigour. Tomas Brochet aged notoriously well without age spots, heavy jowls, or varicose veins. No one in the Kingdom was quite sure how old he was, including his own daughter. His deep-set hazel eyes, now taunting Sybil, were laden in smile lines from expression and hidden behind spectacles.

It was apparent that he enjoyed toying with his headstrong daughter very much.

"That's not helpful," Sybil retorted.

He snorted as he pushed the glasses to the bridge of his nose with a finger.

"Let's send her early," Sybil pressed on, always focused. Eyes locked on her father. "It would be good for her."

"You believe she is ready?" Tomas said, unimpressed. "Why? Because she is more clever than you? Tradition dictates we wait at least six more moons. The girl is not yet thirteen years."

Sybil scowled as she shifted her weight from foot to foot, then uncrossed her arms. She began mindlessly twirling a piece of nearly black hair with her pointer and middle finger, fallen out of her high-head bun stuck with precious gem pins. Her hair was uncannily long, reaching far past her breasts to her navel. It wasn't in fashion, quite the opposite, especially in the New realms, and that was why she adored it. Sybil's hair spoke to her old blood. It made her feel powerful.

"The girl is too smart for her own good," she said. "And she is just a child! She only sharpens with time." Tomas audibly scoffed and Sybil clarified, "I would not believe it if I did not witness it myself."

Vaulted ceilings loomed over the pair in Tomas's study. The green stone castle walls nearly sparkled in the light from inlayed metallic materials in the rock. The furniture here was fine, yet practical, with intricately carved wood and linens in either black or green. Serpents were everywhere. Quite outdated from a modern perspective, if you asked Kingdom-wide, but it reflected Brochet values as the decor was timeless, yet beautiful. Brochets were known for their affinity for beautiful things. For example, within Westerviolet, the most beautiful natives were held in highest esteem and typically given the most enviable positions. Beauty indicated goodness. Trustworthiness. Agency. To be beautiful in Westerviolet was to be powerful. It was in part why Sybil was so unstoppable. She was as powerful as she was beautiful. And oh, was she beautiful.

Facing Sybil from behind the elderdesk, Tomas removed his spectacles. She continued to twirl her hair, pacing in front of the adjacent man-height fireplace with its gaping mouth unlit and unused in these warm moons. Her bootsteps clacked impatiently.

Tomas glared back. "I cannot fault you for thinking her abilities higher than they are."

Although insulted, Sybil reminded herself to use this negative energy as fuel. "Why do you presume my assessment to be at fault?"

Tomas exhaled slowly. His forehead wrinkled deep.

"Father, are you alright?"

"Must you make me say it?"

"Out with it, old man."

Tomas rubbed the bridge of his nose as he shut his eyes. "I hate to do this, but it is to prove a point," he said, "for your own good."

Sybil's smile dropped from her face with a crash. "I don't know what you're talking about," she said, nose wrinkled, displeased with his reaction and the wafting stink permeating the study. "Must you leave it open?" She gestured to the far window overlooking the stable. It loomed over them, reaching nearly to the ceiling with wide, long rectangular panes. The lowest was ajar and the rancid stench of horse shit and hay drifted up and inside. With every breeze, the smell bit at the back of her tongue.

"Yes," Tomas grunted. "I enjoy the scent. It reminds me of my childhood when a stable still meant prominence. When old blood still mattered. Leave it," he barked.

Sybil huffed and tugged at the loose plait of hair. She had faint light freckles across her nose like her daughter did, and a heart-shaped face that scrunched in the same way each time she was displeased. Her impossibly high cheekbones left hollow shadows across the angles of her cheeks and jaw, especially when she frowned. As default, her face rested in a perpetual pout, with black eyes glaring in baited intensity.

"Do you remember when they tested you?" he asked in a lighter tone.

"Vaguely," Sybil said, distracted, scrunching her nose still from the stench of shit in the hot afternoon. The odd men and women from the Guild so many years ago had bored her with their riddles. She'd barely listened to them, only hoping they went away quickly. She'd not wanted to be chosen. Father had never expressed interest in the mysteries of Hidden Den, rather the opposite, or else maybe she would have tried. She'd never told him that, though. They didn't speak about things like that.

"I was certain you were..." He paused, cleaning his spectacles with a small cloth. "Gifted."

Sybil burst into laughter and glided in a few steps before sitting in a chair identical to the one Tomas sat in. "Father!" she exclaimed, tickled by his presumption. "We believe in our blood's superiority, the sanctity of it, not the cursed the power of it." She crossed her legs, smooth thigh flashing. "Magic is a myth from the old days."

"Don't laugh, girl. Whatever you call it, power, magic. It is no myth. Not by far."

She scoffed, "Oh, please," yet internally felt unstable. She saw something in her father's eyes but did not press.

Tomas raised his bushy brows high. "Oldblood Beaumonts had powers that you could not believe," he said, tone low and gravely. "It would curdle your blood to learn the half of it. Insane bunch," he added with a knowing smile. "Gorgeous too, with that snowy skin and raven hair, but I suppose with any real beauty comes a measure of insanity. It is painful to be beautiful. You and the dolts at Animus don't know the half of it," he said with a twinkle in his eye. Sybil wondered if there were bloodlines more powerful than even Beaumont, particularly Brochet, but she knew even if she asked, he would not reveal what he knew. Tomas loved to be the one holding all the shells. "The truth was kept far from the Academy lessons," he said as Sybil sighed impatiently. "You mock me but that is how precious you are to me, daughter."

Sybil hid a smile and shook her head. "Father, stop."

Tomas stood slowly and paced to stand at the far side of the chamber overlooking the stable. A warm breeze lifted the edges of his white cloak, customary garb for the Brochet elder. His thick, grey-peppered hair shifted with the wind. "I mean it," he said, staring outside at the stable. "I thought you were to be one of them. Brochet hasn't had our own Guildsman in over a century and I thought you were the one." He turned to her, eyes searching. Wistful. He spoke sincerely. "Girl, I thought they'd send you to Wraithswail. To Hidden Den."

"I barely remember being tested," Sybil said. "It was a long time ago."

"I was distraught when you failed." Pain casted Tomas's brow. "It changed my view of you completely. I was sure you were Guild."

"Father!" Sybil's outburst was shrill, but Tomas ignored her.

"I'm thankful for it," he boomed.

What Sybil didn't know was that most of Tomas wished she'd failed the Guild's assessment yet possessed abilities regardless. The possibility had always been considered particularly due to Sybil's unique blood. It was a shame the Guild actively worked to suppress Vanguard powers. That they took Vanguards with any promise at all into their ranks, to indoctrinate them and hide them from their own blood. To prevent them from mating, so the future generations were without power. The true treasure in Tomas's eyes would have been if Sybil was as his grandfather Lucien was. Powerful yet undetected. But alas, she'd failed the assessment, and had not shown any abilities since, so she wasn't.

"I went from inflating your worth to seeing what you are and that is a valuable lesson to learn. You cannot let your own sentiment cloud your judgment of the child," Tomas wisely warned. "It is a fool's mistake."

"This isn't a battle," Sybil argued. "This isn't the forsaken Vanguard Council. Father, you don't have to be so cold."

"Sybil, it is," Tomas assured. "It is exactly the world that we live in and the world that controls all the other smaller, less meaningful worlds. It is our place to show them the way. To set the future for generations of our bloodline to prosper. You mustn't ignore the rules, lest you'll lose the game." Sybil scoffed. "Why do you not absorb my wise counsel?"

"Who are you to follow rules?"

He smirked. "I said you mustn't ignore the rules, not that you must follow them."

She groaned, "Father..." but he simply chuckled at her. Sybil persisted her point, crossing her arms dramatically. "So, what about Rose?" she asked with a bite. "What does me failing have to do with her?"

The warmth melted from his tone like ice in spring. "Don't bear an attitude," he growled. "I didn't say you failed. I tell you this as to caution you not to expect more out of your daughter than she is capable, for it will only breed discontent when she inevitably falls short." Tomas's voice rumbled. "Be better than I. Look how you turned out, thinking you know more than you do."

"That's a lot coming from a pompous, overinflated old man."

Tomas turned from the window to glare at Sybil, the intensity of his hazel eyes cutting right through her. "Don't pretend that Rose is ready for something she isn't, just because you want her to be."

"She *is* ready," Sybil said, surprised by her own tone's whine. "You overestimated me, but she's better than I am. Smarter than I am." She swallowed hard. "More beautiful, even, than I am."

"That is true."

"Maybe she got more of your blood than I did, then."

"Yes, likely true as well," Tomas replied. Sybil realized her sarcasm was lost on Tomas, or he ignored it. "She got better blood than you did." He paused and sighed. "Why didn't I find a nice Green Winger like my mother to wed?" he said to himself. "Never should have listened to your grandfather. His ridiculous experiment. You may have turned out better. At least, not so insane."

Sybil's mother had been a woman with many defixes. In Sybil's entire memory she never left the North Wing, much less Westerviolet's castle. Tomas once explained it to Sybil that it wasn't her fault. It was an inevitable result of the madness that flowed in her blood.

"Don't tease. You adored Mother," Sybil gushed. Assessing the mounting protest on his face, she pressed on. "You did!" She pointed at him. "I was small but saw how you held her, even at the end."

Sybil had walked in on her father removing the noose from her mother's neck, too late. Her mother's lips were already blue, but the Lord of Westerviolet kissed them anyway.

Tomas relented, softening, sharp memories flooding in a rush. "I won't deny it," he said, voice catching, eyes crinkling in a half-smile. "But I grew to, over time," he added, smile dropping, lost in a thought. "I had no choice in the matter to start. It was my duty to wed her. She was a hard woman to love, your mother. Deep with secrets that came with her blood. I figure that is why you are so difficult to tame. And why your daughter is as well."

That was one secret Tomas hadn't kept from Sybil. His late wife's ancestry. She was the last Beaumont.

Sybil nodded. "It's hard to deny the resemblance."

"Yes, yes. Like you. Devious blood."

Sybil laughed. "The old crow calls the young one black."

Tomas turned. "Oh?" He walked across the study with cloak billowing behind him, returning to his seat behind the elderdesk.

"Father," Sybil said with an intimate chuckle. "You are a hypocrite. You weave more webs than Thorne. They may not know it, they may not see it... oh, I say it as compliment," she added when she noted his expression. "It is spectacular!" she cooed. "Where do you think I get it from? I may have Mother's eyes, her blood, but where do you think I learned to see?"

Tomas smiled, sated with the warm praise. "I raised you to be smart, that is all. You must always be one step ahead and you must protect your own. Do what makes sense. For the glory of Westerviolet. That's what is right and true. It's the Brochet fate that we love so dearly."

"It's your granddaughter's fate to go to Animus early."

"You are very bold," Tomas said slowly, rubbing his temple, putting his spectacles back on. "Has it been too long since you've been to Animus Rock? I can tell you the place is a traitorous mess. She is far too young."

The state of the Kingdom was tumultuous at best, and it was understandable that Tomas was unnerved to consider sending the youngest of their bloodline so far from home, amongst so many different bloodlines with such poor values. And Sybil agreed. *Rose is better than that filth*, Sybil thought. It wasn't the other Old realms that she and her father were concerned with, per se. Sure, any Thorne children would be manipulative and Busk children would be unpolished. Norland children would likely be brutish, but at least they were pure. Specifically, it was the idea of her mingling with Newblood children that turned Sybil's stomach. Yet she saw it as necessary. Both for Rose and ultimately, herself.

"She has to learn sooner or later," Sybil argued. "She'll be elderclaim after I am."

Tomas grunted dismissively and glanced back down at the daunting stack of parchments under the oblong paperweight.

Sybil's eyes narrowed. "What was that for?" She stood, pacing to hover over his desk. "Rose is to be elderclaim."

"Basil wants her," Tomas retorted, glancing up briefly, then back down at the parchments.

There was an accord, long-ago struck, that indebted Brochet

to Graves. The accord required Brochet deliver Graves a Brochet-blood daughter. Generations of Brochets now had delayed fulfilling the accord. Graves was growing impatient.

Sybil shot an incredulous look. "I'm sure you can handle that wicked old man, father."

"That was never in question," Tomas frowned.

Realizing she'd pushed him a bit too far Sybil smiled in out of context warmth and sauntered to Tomas's side, verdant gown writhing like the tapestry serpents in the horseshit-filled air. She sat on the lip of the massive desk with her hip and leaned towards him. "The Kingdom won't change because we shield it from her," she said. "If anything, it'll cripple the girl. She needs every advantage because I can assure you, the other children have them."

"What can that girl understand of the Old or New?" Tomas scoffed. "Politics are far too complicated for a child. Tell her too much too young and it'll go to her head. She'll cause problems." He adjusted his spectacles. "She's a liability."

"Father," Sybil said tersely, "nothing is going to happen."

"How can you ensure it? How can you guarantee it? Are you going to be at her side?" Tomas challenged, removing his spectacles to look at her.

"Surely," Sybil shot back.

"Not simply to travel, but to stay, you say?" Tomas asked rhetorically as he placed his spectacles aside. He glanced at the windows, mulling it over. "You could be my proxy on Council instead of Hector," he finally said. "And it wouldn't hurt for them to have a chance to see you again. We have not received an offer in moons."

"Father," Sybil's tone cautioned, realizing instantly where Tomas's mind went. He wanted her to marry again. Likely to a Norland. There were dozens of them, all of breeding age, all handsome in a brutish way, and of late Tomas had mentioned his interest in securing Brochet's alliance with Norland amidst the tumultuous state of the Kingdom. Or possibly a Thorne, always powerful, always alluring with white-blond hair and sharp noses. Yet Sybil didn't want to be used as a playing piece.

When first widowed, many offers came from every Old bloodline and she adamantly refused them all. "That wasn't my intent."

"Interest in you has died," he countered. "Let's spark it back."

"I'm not discussing that." Sybil strode with stark, defiant steps, heart quickening as she lost control of the conversation. She had her own plans for marriage that her father was no part of. Not this time. She took a seat in the adjacent chair to Tomas with her back to the gaping, empty fireplace. The old chair squeaked loudly as she sat in a huff, stones on her gown clinking faintly like the late summer leaves rustling outside.

"You are," he commanded like a resounding gong. "It's been longer than acceptable. Too long. Now more than ever we need alliances. We need more Brochets as well. While it made sense to follow tradition years ago, now it makes sense to unite. You mustn't be selfish. It is foolhardy to put all hope for Brochet on Rose. This is a harsh world," he added, clearing his throat. "Extinction is not an option. We require insurance."

"I do not."

He scoffed. "You are a dolt not to do your part."

"My part?"

"You don't know?"

"Father, I do not claim to know all."

"You act as if you do," Tomas said and he took a deep breath. "Your mother lost four babes before you," he said bluntly. He paused, eyes glassed, then added, "and four after."

"Really?" Sybil recoiled, surprised, picking at the skin on her elbow mindlessly. Her veil slipped slightly. "The curse?" she asked in a small voice.

Tomas nodded once, putting his spectacles back on, pushing them to the bridge of his nose. "She was ashamed, so it was hidden from record," he said, glancing down at the parchments again. Silence hung between them. "I am astounded she never told you," he added awkwardly, glancing up. "Judging by your face, she didn't," he said and cleared his throat. He picked up the paperweight rock and rolled it around in his hand, studying her face, waiting for a reaction.

"I was a little girl when…" Sybil trailed off, running through her memories of her mother. Often, she was crying in her chambers. There were days on end that Sybil never saw her. It was certainly possibly she was mourning lost children. "It never came up," Sybil finally said, frowning, a sole wrinkle cut deep between her crunched brows. The only crease on her otherwise pristine face. Strained silence permeated the chamber like fog.

Tomas finally broke the lull, softened by his daughter's stung reaction. "You may escort Rose to Animus Rock early."

Sybil brightened immediately. "Oh, thank you Father!"

Tomas held his palm up and Sybil instantly fell quiet. "If," he went on, "you are wed by Spring Equinox."

"Father …"

"Those are my terms," his deep voice overpowered hers. "If you want your daughter to start so badly, prove it. I believe that is fair price—more than six moons is plenty of time," he added. Sybil began to speak but held her tongue. Watching her considering her options, knowing his daughter, Tomas warned, "If you disobey, I'll give her to the Omen."

"Father!" Sybil gasped loudly as her heart dropped into her stomach and her hands jumped to her mouth. Certainly, she knew of the long ago made pact with Graves, that Brochet was to deliver an oldblood daughter to the Omen for reasons she believed were lost to antiquity, which was why, she believed, her forefathers, and now Tomas himself, refused. Although, there were many truths Sybil was not privy to and Tomas's intention regarding the pact with Graves was one of them.

"Mark my words," he threatened slowly. "Choose a husband or lose your daughter." Sybil's angelic visage seethed wrath. "This is the only time I will offer you," Tomas added impatiently. "I'm allowing you a choice. You understand the rarity, don't you girl? For a true oldblood to choose her own mate?" *He's right*, Sybil thought. It was unheard of. Even Rosen, her lost love, although of the Green Wing and therefore neither Old blood nor New, was chosen in the typical ceremony. Sybil could not think of a time in which an Oldblood woman was permitted to choose her mate, apart from the Calvanese myths of course. "If you refuse," Tomas said, "you will be my pawn."

Sybil slowly nodded, eyes locked on her father's sparkling gaze.

"So, it's settled. You agree?" he pressed again. "You will go with Rose to Animus Rock to find your next mate?" Sybil glanced outside at cotton-white clouds against an egg-blue sky through the wall-height window. She had long ago sworn she'd never love another. All she had in her heart, she gave to Rosen, and it died when he did. But that did not mean that marriage could not be useful.

"Daughter!?" Tomas prompted impatiently.

Sybil spun her head, blinking as if awoken from a daze. Her dark, gem-laden bun bobbed as she nodded.

"Of course, sweet Father," Sybil said warmly, white teeth flashing, black eyes glaring, "of course."

WESTERVIOLET LUNAR TOWER

Sybil went to the Lunar Tower to watch the stars on some nights when she couldn't sleep. She would slip from her chamber, silken Ironbark sleep gown flowing behind her as she dashed through the castle halls, down long flights of stairs, around corridors lit by ancient sconces inlayed in the glittering green stone. Ever since she was a girl, she wanted to run. To get away. To escape. Sybil was a rare bird, the last of her kind, born into a gilded cage, treated to every finery and luxury the realm had access to, and yet it was never enough. She wanted the sky. She wanted to be free.

As she glided through the castle she felt a whisper of that freedom. The warm air filtering through her impossibly long hair as she ran, cold stones on her feet. She knew she was indecently adorned and if her father were to see her, she would be berated at best and imprisoned at worst for lunacy. No respectable Vanguard Lady in their right mind would run barefoot through the castle in the depths of night unattended and unburdened. No Lady, except Sybil Brochet.

When she was a girl at Academy, she would run too. She would run through the defunct parts of the Third Tower, up and down stairs, around vacant corridors adorned with paintings and tapestries from Ancestors long dead and forgotten, wondering who they were. She would imagine how many Vanguards there must have been at one time to justify building such a large tower to educate them all. She would run through Eden and the mysterious maze seemed to answer her, churning out paths more quickly than she could pace. She would go from false realm to false realm, wondering where it all came from. It was her game, of sorts. But as she grew, there was no longer time to run. It was no longer proper. Once she began to bleed, then was betrothed to Rosen, things changed. She learned etiquette. Diplomacy. She learned the pricing structures of the merchants and the reporting patterns of the Westerviolet Vice Lords. She studied the trade routes and educated herself on the turning of crops. She prepared herself to hold elderclaim. She no longer had time for frivolity.

Although, occasionally on thick, warm Westerviolet nights in the late upswing of the year, nearing the equinox, she could not resist. The castle felt particularly laden with secrets, as if it was a breathing entity all it's own, waiting to whisper to her as the evening breeze blew through the open passages from tower to tower. The stone walls, shimmering like the stars above, had their own language too. A cold, dead one that couldn't be heard, only felt, except by Sybil. And she loved to listen.

She'd sneak past any natives milling about on various posts for no reason other than sport. She'd tip toe down the main staircase into the moat's garden, listening to the splashing river fangs writhing and hunting frogs. Apart from Guardsmen and the occasional maidens in the castle, most Westerviolet natives were bred for day. Sybil did not have to do much to avoid them. She did her best to keep to the shadows, sneaking over the bridge, across the moat, down a snaking path leading away from the city, then into the white bindweed that blanketed the meadow surrounding the Lunar Tower.

No one was permitted to enter the meadow, apart from Vanguards. It was almost always empty. The perfect place to find peace.

She didn't bother going all the way to the old ruins and instead lay down in the flowers, looking up at the stars. The exquisiteness of the glinting display calmed her anxiety over plans for her daughter and existential dread over her place in Westerviolet, and the Kingdom. It quelled her longing for her lost love. Sybil did not want to find a husband. She did not want to find a mate. She did not want to obey her father, but, she thought to herself as the bindweed brushed against her face in the warm breeze, that she had little choice. The gold cage around her was tightening. All she wanted to do was break free.

She thought, and thought, until a plan began to formulate slowly.

After what felt like hours, she finally stood, feeling a resounding calmness that laying in her own chamber could not bring, and turned back to Westerviolet. She looked at the massive castle towering over all in its wake, the sad grey city, and even the cursed Pinewood to the side of the meadow, scraggly pines jutting up from the ground like felled deadbloods come back to life. *It will be mine someday*, she thought, the idea of power appeasing her hungry mind for the time being. Sybil, if nothing else, was ambitious. But she wanted more than just Westerviolet. She always had. Although, she told herself, those were just dreams. They had to be. Or did they?

Sybil walked through the white bindweed carelessly and reached the path, firebugs whirling around as if in exhibition just for her. She revelled in the dirt against her bare feet. Such a feeling was a rarity for a sophisticated Lady like her. She shut her eyes.

A twang of an arrow shocked her from her reverie. She spun as a rogue native, a raider wondering close to the castle's walls, crumpled dead not an arm's reach from her. He was carrying a dagger. He was trying to kill her. Sybil studied the man's dirty rags and sunken cheeks with apathy.

An elite Guardsman appeared from the shadows, emerald cloak's hood up. His face was in shadow, apart from his tightly trimmed beard and a flash of red eyes.

"You shouldn't walk alone," Digory said.

Sybil turned. "I'm not alone," she said. She walked back to the castle, knowing Digory was following close behind.

WESTERVIOLET STABLE

"You'll never guess!" Rose cried, running with hands over feet past the four ancient oaks. Ellie followed closely behind, wagging her fluffy tail dutifully. It was the next day, and Rose could not contain her excitement.

Wild violet grass bobbed atop wiry stems on either side of the path to the stable. In this realm alone, the tiny violets bloomed in every season, even winter, and it was from these flowers that Westerviolet got its name. Legends said that the ones that grew within the castle wall protected against nightmares, and most Westerviolet high natives had one stitched into the hems of their sleep clothing. Rose had spent long hours in the violet grass with Ellie, playing fetch, chasing butterflies, or watching the clouds roll by. But this day both Rose and Ellie panted loudly as they sprinted by the violets, into the stable.

"Col! Col! Where are you?" she squeaked, bubbling over with excitement. Her cheeks were red and blotchy and splotched. "I have to tell you the greatest news!" She skidded inside the stable with a creak and slam of the old door, erupting a cloud of hay and dust. Ellie barked happily once, as if to mimic Rose's gleeful cries.

She'd never been so happy in all her life.

The lanky boy popped his head out from a stall. Rose's heart nearly burst when she saw him. Everything was now perfect.

"What is it you yell about?" he shouted, lowering to pat Ellie on her tawny head. "Little girl quiet or you'll scare the beasts!" He grinned, showcasing his endearingly crooked teeth. The dust settled slowly between them amidst neighing horses and occasional clucks of wandering chickens outside.

"Col, Mother said I can go to Animus Rock!" Rose squealed. "Can you believe it?" She slogged through the dirt and manure and hay, unbothered that her expensive small booties were again engulfed entirely with muck and she would surely be scolded by Mother for it, until she stood by his side. "I wonder if the streets glitter like the lessons say," she cooed, giddy with excitement. "I wonder if you really can smell the Confines from across the Missi."

Meanwhile, Ellie noticed a stable cat and took off after him in a chase. The animals spun dust all about the stable until bursting outside through the creaky stable door.

Col joined in Rose's speculation. "I've heard there's a thief on every corner," he said as he cleaned the shoe of a brown mare, "and deadbloods jump out from the alleyways and grab little girls just like you!" Col teasingly poked her with a dirty hand.

Rose's face clouded. She recoiled. "Stop it, no it isn't like that. Not where I will be! Why do you have to be so mean? Maybe that's what it's like where they keep the earth…" Her hand leapt to her mouth, but it was too late.

Visibly stung, Col hung his head. "I know you call me that," he said glumly. "It's okay."

"I'm sorry. I didn't mean to." Rose paused. "Mother calls you that."

His mood shifted. "I told you it was okay."

"Col…"

"What do you want?"

Rose was crestfallen at the change in his tone. "I told you," she said, pleading for his warmth, taking a step towards him as the dirty floor engulfed her shoes. When she went to move, the booties stuck in the muck. She looked down and sighed, then looked up angrily at Col. "Mother will speak with Grandfather about sending me to Academy early." Her eyes darted back and forth, searching his. "Isn't it wonderful?" Rose took forceful steps towards him, pulling out of the booties, feet now bare and dirty like his, feeling mud between her toes. "Aren't you happy for me?" she asked quietly, eyes glassed with the threat of tears.

"It's great," he said flatly. Col glanced at Rose quickly and shook his head, then turned back to tend the horse in the stable. He picked up a short bristle brush to comb the brown mare's mane with slow, even strokes. "Good girl Mable," he cooed in a whisper to his favorite horse.

"It doesn't sound like you think it's great," Rose said. "It sounds like you don't like it one bit."

"You don't know me at all, Lady Brochet," Col replied distantly. "I like it fine."

Rose frowned. "Don't call me that. You know I hate it. I came here excited to tell you because we are friends." She was angry now. "Why are you being so mean?" Rose's once-excited eyes now filled with hot tears. "Why aren't you happy?"

"Rose, I'm busy. I have work to do." His shoulders slumped as he turned his back to her. "Come later. Or don't."

"Collen, please. I didn't mean to call you that," she said to the back of his blond head. "You're my only friend, other than Ellie," she added desperately. "Please talk to me."

Col sighed loudly and slowly turned to face her. He frowned. His red eyes were dim. "How may I serve you?"

Tears were streaming down her cheeks now. "Col, stop it. Stop it!" she cried. "Don't talk to me like that. I love you. You're my friend." She placed her hand gently on his shoulder, but he quickly recoiled.

"Stop that. Don't touch me," he spat. "Go back to your castle. Leave me where the *earthblood* belong."

Rose sniffled, waiting an extra moment, hoping Col would say something to her, but he didn't.

Barefoot and crying, she hurried out.

Rose let Ellie's soft fur engulf her as she wept on the floor of her bed chamber.

She didn't know what she'd done wrong. Collen understood how much she loved him, didn't he? She squeezed Ellie harder.

Dutifully, Ellie nuzzled in closer to Rose and licked her face, as if to say it would be alright. Rose didn't know what she'd do without Ellie. She was given her as a companion when both were very small.

The dog's temperament was no good for hunting or scouting, therefore neither the Hunters nor the Guardsmen had any use for her. This was around the time that Rosen died and Sybil, overwhelmed by grief and unable to entertain her daughter, saved the dog from slaughter and gave her to Rose as a plaything. Ellie grew up right alongside her. In many ways, raised her.

Rose's mother would tease her that Ellie was truly her sister, for the pair looked so much alike. Both Ellie and Rose had huge, dark, expressive eyes. Both were excessively stubborn, as well as too smart for their own good. And Ellie's long fur was dark, and a bit curled around her ears, mirroring Rose's wavy locks. She was small too, the runt of her litter. It's part of why she was taken from the rest of the kennel and gifted to the little Lady. Typically, runts were thought to be of no use and were put down accordingly. Fortune just smiled on Ellie.

Often, to Rose, it felt like Ellie was far more than just an obedient companion. It was like she knew her. Rose would speak to her like she did anyone else, and she knew Ellie could understand.

WESTERVIOLET BED CHAMBER

*T*ap. Tap. Tap.

Rose rolled around beneath her warm, embroidered covers and Ellie stirred from her spot at the foot of her bed. Rose glanced about, groggy until her eyes focused, reluctantly waking from a deep, dreamless sleep. Then she noticed Col standing on the windowsill, backlit by the partial moon. She leapt from her bed and swiftly opened the pane to let the boy into her bedchamber.

"How did you get up here?!" she asked in a loud whisper, glancing quickly outside at dim-lit gardens, stable and mirrored black moat cloaked in night's shadow, illuminated by dozens of dancing firebugs. She looked down to the ground far, far below lined with unforgiving pebbles and wiry flowered grass. "You shouldn't be here," she said gravely.

She had heard the story of her late Aunt Farrah many, many times. How she, in her teen years, became too close with the Vice Lord of Eveningstar's son. How she snuck him inside of the castle. How the misdeed was discovered by the elder at the time and Farrah's grandfather, Lucien Brochet. How Lucien killed not only the boy, but his relatives as well. All forty-two members of his family, and servants, children and all. One child was less than a year, still a babe on his mother's breast. He was the first to go.

"He took them to the lair," Tomas had explained to Rose. "To be dealt with accordingly."

Especially late at night, Rose could hear the wails. She knew what went in the Lair was not good. Not good at all.

"Grandfather will kill you," Rose added with absolute seriousness. "I mean it."

"Don't worry little girl." Col crouched through the

rectangular pane. He was as coy and confident as ever. Rose always admired that about him, how Col always seemed to know what he was doing. Nothing seemed to frighten him. In many ways, he was her hero. "It's okay," he said warmly. "No one knows I'm here." His long, lanky legs came first into the dim chamber. Ellie sniffed him, wagging happily. "As long as we're quiet."

Rose crossed her arms, craning her neck to look up. "Why *are* you here?" She yawned.

Col paused briefly to pet Ellie. "Hey there Elouise," he whispered gently, then looked at Rose. Her hair was unkept and she had faint creases on her neck and cheeks from imprint of heavy sleep. "I'm sorry."

Rose's eyebrows rose high. "You are?"

"I shouldn't have been cross with you."

"You shouldn't have been," Rose agreed. "Why were you so mean to me? I thought we are friends."

Col looked sad. "We are friends," he whispered and took a step towards her. "That's why I'm upset." He sighed loudly, as if dropping a heavy bale of hay. "I don't want you to leave."

"Oh Collen." Emotion stabbed her in the throat. "Come here." She gestured to him with open arms. He happily approached her, and they locked in a warm hug.

When she pulled away, Rose spoke out loud as she thought. "What if I convince Mother to bring you? We'll take horses and you can tend to them! Maybe we could find a place for you in the royal stables, or you can work in the castle we live in there. Somewhere. But you would be with me!"

Stranger things had occurred, Rose thought. Collen could be Stablemaster someday, if something happened to his older brother, and the Stablemaster was known to travel with Vanguards on particularly important journeys.

"Shhh," he hushed. "You know she would hate the idea." He glanced at his feet and sighed. "She hates me."

"She doesn't hate you."

"She doesn't like me."

Rose looked outside at the stars. "Mother doesn't like

anyone." The pair stood in silence in the moonlit bedchamber, warm late-summer breeze drifting sluggishly in through the open window as crickets screeched loudly in the background.

Rose's curiosity broke the lull. "How did you get up here?"

"Maybe I have powers," Col teased.

"Mother says there's no such thing."

"My father told me yes huh," Col argued. "There used to be. Especially the Vanguards with black eyes could do things," he said smartly, remembering his father's tales. "Powerful things." At her sceptical look, Col added, "he said he heard about it from Baneswood traders. They love to tell stories, he said."

"I have black eyes and I can't."

He smiled wide. "Maybe you're broken."

"Hey!" she shoved him, then giggled until, once again, curiosity got the better of her. Rose, if nothing else, was endlessly curious. "What kind of things could they do?"

"Things they shouldn't be able to," he said as he took a seat on her bed, "like move things just by thinking of it. Heavy things much larger than themselves. Father said that's how the castles were built."

Ellie leapt onto the bed and curled up next to Col.

"Mother said that didn't happen," Rose replied as she sat too. "That there were never any powers." She ran her fingers through Ellie's long brown fur. "It's just a story."

"Why make up a story like that?"

"Mother says people are nothing but their stories." She shrugged. "But truly, how did you get up here?"

Col pointed outside to the stone wall overgrown with thick ivy. "Little girl, I climbed."

"That was dangerous." Rose knew how high up her chamber was. Col was certainly brave indeed. "Why?"

"I felt bad that I was mean. You're right that you are my friend. I want to say I am sorry. Truly. I do love you, Rose. You know that."

Rose leapt into his arms for another tight hug, then pulled back abruptly, Aunt Farrah's story in her mind, face pallid in terror. Ellie instantly nestled into her side, as if she felt Rose's fear for herself, with eyes wide with concern. "You must go. If Mother or Grandfather found you here…"

"I know, I know. I will go," he sighed, "but will you visit me?"

"I will!" Rose said happily. Relieved, Ellie wagged her tail. "When?"

"You can help me feed the horses tomorrow at midday."

"I will," Rose whispered. "I'll visit."

"I'm glad you get to go to the Rock, Rose." Col told her softly on his way back to the window. "I really am happy for you."

"Thanks Col," Rose breathed, smiling, following him.

He nodded and ducked out of Rose's bedroom window then quickly scurried down the thick ivy as Rose retreated to her warm covers. She left the windowpane ajar and felt cooler night air rush in atop the sounds of crickets all around.

Rose drifted into dreamless sleep, cuddling with Ellie, wearing a smile on her face. Her heart was full.

Sybil lay awake in the early morn's hours and bolted upright at the sound of scuffling. She peered outside to see the lanky stable boy scaling the ivy on the far castle wall, into Rose's bedchamber. Instead of alert the Guardsmen, Sybil glided to Rose's chamber door and listened to the whispering voices.

Once it was over, she let the boy escape the way he came.

Then, Sybil quietly retreated to her own chamber as if she hadn't witnessed anything at all.

It was morning the next day and Sybil stood behind Rose in her sunbloom-colored quarters as sunlight flickered off the bright walls. Rose sat at a vanity with a polished glass, staring at her own reflection as her mother stroked her curls with a wide horsehair brush. Each swipe separated the thick waves, pouring smoothly over Rose's shoulders.

"When I was a little girl," Sybil said, "my mother would brush each of my hairs one hundred times."

"That would take forever."

"She used this same brush I use on your hair." Sybil stroked with admiration. "You have such gorgeous hair. All who meet you will be jealous. You will never need to use mane, not like those mongrel newbloods."

When Sybil was a child, it was fashionable Kingdom-wide to have long, thick, luscious hair, worn typically up in a bun held together by gem pins. Sybil's mother had hair even longer than hers, thicker too, down to her rear. The hair of natives however, and therefore Newbloods, was typically thinner, so those women would use the mane of a horse to supplement their styles. Although, in the modern day, Newblood women cropped their hair short so use of horse mane was a thing of the past.

Sybil sighed, watching dark strands glide through the brush's bristles. "Beautiful."

Ellie watched with sleepy, loving eyes from where she lay, sunning beneath one of the wide windowpanes.

"Can we be done now?" Rose wined sweetly.

Sybil ran her boney fingers through Rose's curls again, assessing her work. "Fine, that's enough." She set down the old copper brush, embossed with their blood emblem, on the vanity with a clink. She took both of Rose's hands. "I need to speak to you. Come, here sit with me," she said as she led her daughter over to the frilly bedspread with emerald embroidery. "I spoke with your grandfather."

Rose's eyes opened wide. "You did?" she asked with poorly veiled excitement.

"Yes, I did," Sybil said, stifling a smile.

"What did he say?!"

"He told us to pack our trunks and load the carriage for we are to leave for Animus Rock next moon!"

Rose leapt from her seat, squealing in pure delight. The unexpected outburst threw Ellie into throngs of excitement. The fluffy dog mirrored Rose and jumped up, wagging furiously, with a grin on her face. "Oh Mother, thank you thank you!" Rose cried. "Oh, I'll miss you so much. The first thing I will do is write you and I will use the missive every single day!" She paced, muttering to herself in glee. Ellie followed her closely, wagging, smiling, not realizing she wouldn't be permitted to go with her. "Maybe I won't write every single day, because I'll be busy with lessons and with all of the new friends I will make that will be better and smarter and more like me, because they are other Vanguards," she said matter-of-factly. "And I will explore the city and learn how to fish on the Missi and somehow I will find someone to take me to the very top of the Eighth Tower because it's the most beautiful view in the whole Kingdom, says the ballads, and I would like to see that."

Sybil, smiling, grabbed Rose's small hand to pull her back to the bed. "No, my sweet." Rose sat with a confused frown. Ellie, feeling her companion's shift in tone, hovered cautiously at her side. "You can write your grandfather, and Mathilda," Sybil explained, "but you won't need to write me. I'll be with you."

"With me!?" The small girl's eyes clouded. If a gaze could kill, Sybil would be dead. "You can't come with me! No one's mother goes with them to Academy!"

Ellie barked loudly as if in agreement.

Sybil frowned at the beast while exhaling slowly. She had little patience for dogs. To her, like to the rest in Westerviolet's realm, they were little better than vermin. Fit for hunting, possibly guarding, nothing more. It wouldn't be long before that nuisance was removed from her concern, so she pushed the irritating pest from her mind. "Oh, my sweet, I won't go to lessons with you, just escort you to Animus Rock," she explained. "I promise you won't be the only one."

"Mother, no. You'll embarrass me!"

Sybil's frustration showed as her patience dwindled. "I'll do no such thing. I'm not that old, you know. I was your age once. Not that long ago. You're just a girl. Not yet begun to bleed. I don't even know why I speak to you like you're grown. Trust me, you'll be glad I'm nearby."

She adjusted her expertly draped bodice tucked into fitted skirts that flounced out at her knees, all in black silk. At first glance this outfit was more fashionable from a modern perspective with the draping, all the rage at Animus Rock and Croft Hold, but her fitted flounced skirt was something of another time. That was just like Sybil, to stand out. To make something her own. She was known Kingdom-wide for her beauty, charm, and the way that she adorned herself. Wherever she went, everyone looked at her. She wouldn't have it any other way. Although she hadn't gone anywhere out of Westerviolet in a very long time.

"These people aren't like the ones you're used to."

"What do you mean?" Rose asked unsurely, tucking her hair behind both ears.

Sybil laughed and Rose's cheeks blushed. She clung to Ellie's head, scratching behind her ears. "You're the little Lady of a whole Realm," Sybil said as she placed a hand on her hip. "You know that's four Vice-Provinces." She paused. "Have they taught you how big Westerviolet is?"

"Mathilda told us it takes four days to go from one end to the other."

"On horseback," Sybil corrected quickly, moving her own huge mane of hair from one shoulder to the other, nearly blending with the dark fabric of her bodice. "Think about that. As far as you can see and as far as you can run for days and for all creeds around, it's ours. The city is ours. All the villages are ours. The fields are ours. The orchards are ours. The kennels are ours. It's the same as it is here at the castle, with people who respect your grandfather and what it means for you to be Brochet. But there, at Animus Rock, you're just another one in the crowd. Everywhere you go there's a Vanguard girl or boy. You must be tough there. And always on alert."

Rose's eyes narrowed. "What do you mean?"

"I mean there it's not safe like here," Sybil explained knowingly. Rose clung to each word. "Here you're free to run about the castle, then down to the stables, then out to the kennels. Why, even through the commons and in and out of the bazaar! It's because you are important and special here, since there are so few of us and everyone here owes us their lives. Not like at Animus Rock, where they may barely know the Brochet name, some of the earthblood." She spit.

Brochet had the least number of Vanguards left of all the bloodlines in the Vanguard Kingdom. They were nearly extinct. It was only Tomas, Sybil and Rose.

"The people owe us their lives?" Rose asked with wide eyes. "How?" She paused. Her tone hushed. She whispered nearly to herself, "They have to toil."

"Naturally, they do."

"But why?"

"Because we protect them," Sybil said simply. "Westerviolet has the Guardsmen and a good relationship with the crown. That means Warmen backup too. That's very powerful."

"Why?"

"Because it means the earthblood are safe," Sybil replied. "Safety is priceless."

"But they can't do what they want," Rose said. "Col told me his father told him that their people had great tribes a very long time ago, long before the Ancestors even. Before the old gods even. And then we came and killed them. You say they owe us, but we killed them."

"We did no such thing," Sybil said with palpable authority, doing her best not to roll her eyes. "Your little friend is lying to you. That's what the earthblood do. And besides, what the Ancestors did is done, and now in the current state of things the Westerviolet earthblood are lucky to live here and not in a forsaken realm like Lyonshall, or Anasout."

"They don't like being called that."

"Like being called what?"

"Earthblood." Rose put her own small hand on her hip to mirror her mother. "Col says it's bad to call them earthblood."

Sybil's jaw clenched at the stable boy's name, irritated by his influence over her precious, sweet, innocent child. "I don't want you hanging out with this *Col* anymore."

"Why?! He's my friend!"

Sybil shook her head. "You're above him," she said resolutely. "He works in the stables as his father before him and his children, if we allow them to him, will after him. It's the way of Westerviolet. It's the way of the Kingdom."

"I want him to come with us to Animus Rock," Rose said, glancing at Sybil with eyes like Ellie's, but her high hopes were dashed instantly by Sybil's cascading laugh. Rose's cheeks burned and she glanced away. Ellie nestled harder into Rose's side and let out a remarkably faint growl.

"You thought I would agree?" Sybil asked in pleased jest. "Absolutely not." She shook her raven head. "We're not bringing that earthblood animal to the most sophisticated city in the land. I've tolerated the friendship because, frankly, I felt sorry for you and allowed it. But this… this… It's gone too far." She gestured at Ellie. "I'd rather you bring your pest."

Rose crossed her arms tightly at her chest. "I want him to come."

"I know what you want," Sybil retorted. "I told you absolutely not under any circumstances. I will not say it again. You want to go to the Academy. Do not make me rethink my decision."

Stubborn and naïvely unrelenting, Rose pressed on. "He could lead the horses! Col is one of the best," she said, small voice rising. And Col really was. He rode fearlessly, with compassion for his steed, the way that he lived the rest of his life. Oh, how Rose adored him. "His father and brother taught him so well and the ride would be so smooth and…"

"Rose!" Sybil interrupted. "We're going to have to do something about this talking back. My word is final. This isn't a negotiation. You are fortunate I don't tell your grandfather about your friendship with the earthblood."

"His name his Col."

"I don't care if his name is Humphry Bellamine!" Sybil shouted, elevating to a screech, black eyes blazing as her patience dropped entirely. Rose gripped Ellie's fur as if she was a shield. "I am your mother! What I say is what you do, do you understand me?!" Her words scorched. "You are the child. I am the adult. There will be no more questions. No more talking back. I will stop with threats and start with your grandfather next time. Do not test me," she said slowly, words dripping like poison from her hissing tongue.

Rose blinked back silently, challenging with an insolent glare.

"Do you hear me!?" Sybil grabbed Rose's wrist tight. Her thin, cold fingers dug into Rose's flesh like icy knives. "I'll tell him that I can't handle you, and trust me, you'll wish you'd listened to me and left this alone." Sybil's tone was harsh. Images of the Lair's entrance flashed in Rose's mind. "Do you understand?"

Ellie's growl picked up in volume, but she knew better than to strike at Sybil.

"But Mother."

"Don't you dare cry. Stop it, this instant," Sybil commanded. "Rose! What did I say to you?"

Alas, Rose quickly devolved into yowls and sobs, gasping through bubbles of snot and tears, latching onto her mother's thin body and clinging to her; wailing with the kind of misery only a young girl could feel. "I'm sorry!" she cried, "I'm sorry that I'm so bad," though snot and sobs, not really meaning it. She was mostly upset that she hadn't gotten her way. And she knew how her tears could sway her mother.

She was already more like Sybil than she realized.

The outburst sent Ellie into a frenzy. She barked, then growled again at Sybil as she snuggled into Rose's leg.

"Oh hush, you are so dramatic," Sybil said as she rolled her eyes in a huff. "Stop that," she commanded, disconcerted by Rose's tantrum. She couldn't stand to see the girl cry. Sybil sighed once, then absorbed her pitiful child in a close embrace, to Ellie's obvious disapproval. She patted her Rose's head and rocked her back and forth. "You aren't bad. Not at all," she said gently. "There, hush now it's alright," Sybil said, rocking Rose until the sniffling diminished and her ashen face was rubbed red from tears.

"Rose," Sybil finally whispered gently. The girl looked up

sheepishly in the haze of her tantrum and met loving gaze with her mother. "This makes me question whether you are ready for Academy." At that Rose wailed and fell into a fit all over again. Ellie barked, highly concerned for her companion. "Oh hush, don't start," Sybil said dismissively. "This is not punishment. You can't have outbursts, not at our capitol," she explained. "You must be on your best behavior. If they see you like this, they'll think you're no better than a Regnard. Or a Busk! We can't have that. Goodness. Your Ancestors would flip in her grave!"

"I didn't mean it Mother. I didn't mean it!" Rose cried. She rubbed her nose and sniffled. "I... I want to go to Academy. I promise, I'll stop crying!" she wailed through big, dripping tears.

Sybil laughed while rocking Rose. Ellie reluctantly settled at Sybil's feet, staring intensely at Sybil as if to threaten her. Rose's young arms wrapped around her frail mother's back, smooth and pale except for a round mole in the center. "I know how badly you want to go," she cooed," but look at you, you can't stop crying now. What does it mean when you're in front of other children who hate you, just for your name?" Sybil leaned in closer, rubbing her hand over Rose's emerald jumper, feeling the embroidered seams. "You think I make you mad, or sad, or nervous? You won't last a moon there! Not like this. Perhaps your grandfather is right. I hate to tell him, but better than set you up to fail. He's a wise man," she said, nearly to herself now. "He may be right."

Rose tried holding her breath to feign all was well, but gasped and hiccupped air, spitting snot, then wailed in misery at her failure. "He isn't right! He isn't right!" she cried into her mother's shoulder.

"Is that so?" Sybil asked, rocking Rose, biting her lip not to smile. "Tell me then. Convince me." She regained her solemn composure, pulling her daughter out in front of her so she could look her in the eye. Rose was so beautiful, so doll-like, even despite the outburst. She would be a gorgeous woman shortly. "Why are you ready to go to Academy? Real,

Vanguard-blood Academy at Animus Rock with other Vanguard children?" she asked. "What makes you ready?"

"I will never ask for another thing as long as I live!" Rose said quickly, gaze darting about as her chest rose and fell rapidly. "I promise on all of my honor that I will be good! I will bring glory to Westerviolet! To the Ancestors! I swear it," she said with conviction, nodding with wide-peeled eyes. "Please Mother, this is all I will ever wish for."

"I'm unconvinced," Sybil said cruelly. "Stay here, skip your midday meal, think about what you've done."

Rose glanced at Ellie who responded instantly by running to her side. In a small voice she replied, "Yes, Mother" as she scratched behind Ellie's ears. "You're a good girl," she whispered to the dog, fighting back tears.

Sybil stood and turned, pleased at the exchange. She smiled as her boots rapped loudly on the way out.

WESTERVIOLET NORTH TOWER

Digory stood watch while the castle slept. He was an elite Guardsman, one of the few able to survive the rigorous training and torture associated with the lofty title, granting him additional privileges. He was able to choose his post. Most guardsmen preferred the inner corridors at night, free from the legendary Ancestor spirits that were said to haunt the castle walks in the light of the moon, but not Digory. He chose the outer walk of the North Tower, the entrance and exit of Westerviolet's castle, where the wind cut through his chainmail and the dark pressed close.

Below him, the city breathed. Somewhere in the distance, a hunting hound barked, then yelped silent.

He rested his hands on the parapet, gloves scarred and dulled by use. He could have them repaired. He never did. New things drew attention. Digory preferred to be a shadow.

A pale cluster of tiny violets grew between the stones near his boot. They were stubborn things, he thought, fed by nothing but runoff and neglect. He noticed them absently, then frowned. They weren't there the day before.

Digory crouched, careful not to touch them, despite his rejection of the typical superstitions that the Guardsmen clung dearly to. In the wrong places, the tiny violets were said to be a curse, bringing nightmares to any who touched them. Castle gardeners uprooted them and then burned them, scattering them in Pinewood, but the plants always came back. Like longing. Like guilt. Like memories that wouldn't rest.

Digory scanned the wall again, but there was no movement. No sound. Still, his shoulders remained tense. Digory had learned long ago that silence was never empty.

A shadow shifted at the far stairwell and his hand moved to

his dagger before his mind caught up.

"State yourself," he said, low and deep. The shadow resolved into a native carrying a basket of linens, narrow eyes downcast. The nervous maiden was too thin, as most Westerviolet natives were. Digory watched her shaking hands. "Go," he said." The maiden went hurriedly down the steps, small braids jumping as she fled.

Digory exhaled once. He returned his attention to the city, but his thoughts drifted to Sybil. They always did.

Ever since Digory was a boy, he could not get Sybil out of his mind. He had sworn to protect her, not because she was good or kind or even right, but because someone had to. She was unlike anyone he had ever known and within her burned a fire that was consuming and illuminating and damning, all at once. He yearned to be in her presence, then cursed her for scorching him. She was a paradox, infuriating as she was satisfying, and Digory could not resist her. She was worse than ale. Worse than tonic. Worse than blood, even. Sybil was an addiction and Digory could not quit her.

He looked out across the sad, grey city of Westerviolet and sighed.

WESTERVIOLET STABLE

S ybil turned up her nose at the smells of shit and piss and hay mixing with heavy yellow pollen from late summer weeds nearby. Why were the bothersome duties always her concern? When would her daughter develop gratitude for everything that she had been given? Sybil missed the days before Rose was old enough to cause trouble. When she was just a babe, swaddled in Sybil's arms. They'd spent long moons together sequestered in the North Wing. As a new mother, with Rosen out hunting, Sybil had been terrified of harm befalling Rose. Although she wouldn't admit it outright to herself, deep down, she worried that the girl's strange ways were her own fault. She hadn't socialized Rose enough when she was young. And thus, it was her responsibility to make things right.

She hovered in the stable's doorframe watching the boy's lanky outline shovelling hay into a trough. Her flounced skirt fluttered like storm clouds in the breeze.

"Do you want to do this forever?" Sybil asked, melodious voice piercing the calm with time-honed disdain.

Col turned. Seeing who it was, he threw his pitchfork down next to his feet in a mist of dust. He bowed low. His voice shook when he spoke, eyes cast down.

"How may I serve you, Lady?"

"Good." Sybil looked him down, then up. "At least you have manners."

"Yes, Lady. My father taught me," Col said proudly, standing, eyes glued to the dirty tops of his feet, like he'd been trained. He shifted his weight nervously.

Sybil picked her dark skirts up to her ankles and slogged into the stable, dirt and manure sticking to her Baneswood leather boots. One of her many pairs. Another sign of her wealth. To sully such beautifully crafted footwear was unthinkable, since such finery was typically reserved for special occasions. For most, anyway. Yet Sybil wore hers as if they were work boots.

"Your father's name was Burkhart. Yours is Collen?"

The lanky child kept his hands behind his back and his head down. "Yes Lady," he replied softly. "Most call me Col."

"Collen, do you want to do this forever?"

Col didn't understand. "This is my place, Lady."

"That wasn't my question," Sybil replied, mindlessly twiddling the ends of her hair with pale fingers. "I asked if this what you *want* to do this forever. When you think of yourself grown, do you wish to shovel hay? Do you wish to brush the horses of better men for eternity?" She glared like a predator watching prey.

"It's what Father taught me," he said hollowly, almond-shaped eyes squinting in confusion. "It's what my brother does." He had trouble looking directly at Sybil and glanced off to her left at Mable's flank in a stall. "It's all I know."

"Oh, child." She shook her head, thick, long hair glinting even in the dim light. "If you were to go anywhere you wanted, where would it be?"

He looked up to briefly meet Sybil's black stare, then glanced away immediately, as if burned.

"I'm not Vanguard blood, Lady."

"I know you're not. Certainly, you're not. Look at your eyes. All that red," she said casually. "But even so, I imagine despite the odds, a wretched creature like you has dreams. I ask you what they are." The boy stood still; frozen. "You must have dreams, child."

Col was quiet. He had never thought about it before. He had a good life. A charmed one for any native of Westerviolet. He did not want for food, shelter or companionship. Until recently, once able to toil, he was under the stewardship of his own father—a rarity in any of the Vice Provinces—and developed a relationship with the man. His brother too. The three were very close.

When Col spoke, his voice was barely audible, just a breath above a whisper. "No one has ever asked." Then he fell silent once more. Horses neighed and snorted during the interlude as chickens clucked loudly outside. Other than that, it was so painfully still, Sybil could hear the heartbeat in his small chest.

Having to consider what he wanted to do illuminated to Col that he had never been allowed to choose anything in his entire life. This realization hit him like a kick from a horse. But there was one thing, he realized. A desire that burned deeply in his chest.

"I want to see Littlebell," he said.

"There! You see," Sybil cooed warmly, "a wonderful answer. That was not difficult."

Col half-smiled at the praise. Instantly though, Sybil flipped again to ice, and it was as if a winter wind blew through the stable.

"You are friends with my daughter, Rose?" Col took one step backwards, shaking his head side to side furiously. "She isn't your friend?" Sybil was enjoying this. He shook his head "no" again. "Are you sure?"

"She's my friend," Col said in a small voice.

"Good. Why is that?"

"Lady," he shifted, "I must feed the horses."

"Don't change the subject, earthblood. Why is my daughter your friend?"

"She's kind to me, Lady. She likes the horses." Col was still trembling, words catching on his lips and tongue from fear. "She... She helps me take care of them sometimes."

"Is that so?" Sybil's eyes twinkled in amusement. "What do you talk about with her, Collen? What is it that you teach my daughter?"

He could hardly breathe. "Nothing Lady."

"So, you don't speak at all? Curious friendship it must be."

"We speak but I don't teach her anything."

"Oh, so the story has changed. First you were not friends, and now you are. Then you didn't speak, and now you do. What is the truth?"

Col hung his head. "She's my friend." Sybil watched sweat drip from his brow into the dirt and hay. "I speak to her."

"Isn't that sweet?" Sybil said warmly. Her smile reeked contempt. "It is a pity that you would give up your dreams for her."

"Lady?" the boy hesitated. "I do not understand."

"It's a shame to throw your future away, that's all."

"I'm not."

"You are," she said. "For I must concern myself with you."

"She's just my friend," Col frowned. "You don't have to."

"Oh, but I think I do," Sybil said, moving closer. "I cannot lose my only daughter and the fate of Brochet to an earthblood stable boy. I will not. So, we have come to a crossroads. How will we resolve it? How will you convince me that I mustn't need vex? And rest assured, you must convince me."

"She's...she's just my friend," he stuttered again, full, youthful cheeks glazed with tears, flat nose running with snot, hands clenching into tight fists at his sides.

Sybil unceremoniously dropped her hemline into the muck and sauntered with great effort across the stable, then took a place behind the boy. Her glossy skirts instantly caked in mud that crept up the garment like water lapping up a bank and brushed the backs of Col's legs as she lay chilled, bony fingers on his warm shoulders. As his entire body tensed, Sybil deeply sighed. "I will tell you a story," she whispered, lemon-scented breath brushing the back of his neck. "When I was a girl, only a few moons older than you, I had a friend. Against all my breeding and my father's advice, mind you, but I was young and so naive. He was a smart boy, very much like you."

She squeezed Col's shoulders intentionally, thinking of young Digory. The wilful, mischievous look in Digory's eyes as a child was one of Sybil's favorite things about him.

All the hair on the back of Col's neck stood up when Sybil touched him as if he was in water when lightning struck it. Jolts of electricity shot into his body where Sybil's skin met his. It was decidedly painful. Although Sybil felt nothing but calm.

"I thought that earthblood was my friend," she paused, "but

also, I pitied him, just as my daughter does you." A hot tear ran down Col's cheek. "My father warned me of your cunning, your deceit. He warned me how you keep to your own. How you loathe us, despite all we do for you. He told me that the boy wasn't what he pretended to be," she said, squeezing harder. "Alas," she added, sighing, "I didn't listen."

Although Sybil was partial to lying, so far, she was telling the truth.

She violently turned Col to face her, dropping to her knee, there in the stable amongst the horse shit and mud. Col shook in paramount terror as he leaned away, but she held both of his small shoulders tight. Sybil tugged him down to his knees to where even her tiny frame loomed over his lanky one.

"If you are my daughter's friend," she hissed venom, "you will stay away from her."

"Lady..."

"She deserves better than you. You know that is true," Sybil interrupted. "If you care about her, you'll allow her to rise higher than you ever could. Don't drag her down into this shit here with you. Here, where we are right now Collen, this is where you belong," she said as he studied the dirt at his knees. She commanded, "Look at me!" and his head popped up.

He locked Sybil's eyes.

"You have no dreams. You will never see Littlebell. You will never be more than a stable boy," Sybil said smiling through half-clenched teeth. "And you will never see my daughter again. Do I make myself clear?" Sybil spoke calmly. Pleasantly. Devastatingly. "You will stay here in the shit, where you belong."

Col nodded as he struggled to breathe, leaking tears over his dirty beige tunic as Sybil held his shoulders so tight, he would surely bruise. He stared into the Lady of Westerviolet's black eyes, sparkling like onyx, unflinching and unfeeling. "Do I make myself clear?" Sybil asked slowly.

Col managed to croak, "Y... y... yes." He looked down. Sybil smiled knowing Rose would never see him again.

"Do you want to know what happened to my earthblood?"

she asked to twist the knife. Col nodded as he glanced up with teary eyes. "Father caught the boy with mother's necklace, so, he went to the boy's hovel the next day." She briefly studied young Col's terrified face, bringing one hand to his head to stroke his sweaty hair. He could be very handsome someday with his heavy brow and intelligently intense gaze. Not unlike his father. *Such a pity*, she thought. "Do you know what my father, your Lord Tomas Brochet, Westerviolet elderclaim, did when he reached the boy's hovel?" she asked, lovely voice flitting through the pungent air. Col shook his head slowly, sniffling again with eyes peeled open. "He made the boy find rope," Sybil chirped, nearly sneering, enjoying this. "Made him measure the length, then taught him exactly how to tie it." She paused. "Then, he hung the boy's father there in front of him, and his three young earthblood brothers too."

Col trembled while Sybil smiled at him warmly. Her grin was shockingly disarming. It made Col sick.

"I know you no longer have a father," she said cruelly, "but do not push me. I can be creative." She paused again. "Do you not have a brother?"

Col nodded furiously in horrified understanding.

"If she approaches you, turn her away. I don't care how you do it, but you must stay away from her. For your brother's safety, if not your own."

Col nodded again, eyes wide with fear.

"I'm glad you agree," Sybil cooed, mood boosted by how intimately powerful it felt to be cruel. "It would be a pity if you didn't." She dropped her hands, never breaking eye-contact, inwardly pleased with the impact she had on the boy. It wasn't often that she was able to exercise her command on unsuspecting earthblood. Typically, it was reserved for Mathilda, Petra, or the other maidens on castle post. And of course, there was Digory. "Back to work," she barked, pointing as she gracefully stood. "The steeds seem hungry."

Then, she patted Col on the cheek gently before shaking off the bottom of her dress. Shit and dirt flew all over him, still frozen in shock.

At his lack of action, Sybil frowned.

"What are you doing? I told you, back to toil."

Then, Sybil smoothed her skirts, and somehow, despite the mud and shit, elegantly sauntered out of the stable, shirts half stained. "Oh, and never mention this to Rose. I'm sure that is clear," Sybil said over her bare, pale shoulder as she exited the stable, disappearing through the creaky, nearly broken door.

Once she was gone, the little boy collapsed into a ball. He beat at his own forehead, crying into the shit-filled dirt.

After changing into a tight emerald skirt, a white camisole and pointed, frilled brown leather boots with side bone toggles, Baneswood crafted of course, Sybil barged back into Rose's bed chamber.

"You aren't going," she nearly shouted.

"Mother, why!" Rose cried instantly. Ellie stirred from her spot sleeping at Rose's feet. The girl sat at her child's desk clutching a piece of coal. In front of her were morbid sketches of long faces without eyes. Drawing was one of Rose's refuges. She loved to lose herself to that other world she drifted into when creating. And it helped her make sense of her dreams. All those faces. All that screaming.

Sybil crossed the chamber, and she stood at Rose's side. She placed her hand on her hip. "You're not ready," Sybil said at Rose. "You're brilliant, my sweet, and gifted," she glanced to the drawings, "but nothing can make up for maturity of time."

Angry, Rose threw her piece of sketching coal and began to sob all over again.

"I have to stay here and listen to Mathilda in the *First Tower* every day?"

Ellie whined too from Rose's feet, although sleepy, having just woken up from a nap, as if to mirror Rose's sentiment.

"Don't call it that," Sybil chided with an eye roll. "It's hardly the First. Don't be so dramatic, it's crass."

"Mother, please," Rose begged gently, realizing her best

chance to get to Academy like she dreamed was to be in mother's favor. "Don't trap me inside."

"My sweet, someday you will look back on your sheltered mindset with shame." Sybil furrowed her brow. "Nothing else to say?" Rose solemnly shook her head 'no'. "Maybe you do learn. I'll have Petra send up something for you to eat as a reward for this already improving behavior. Wait until I tell your grandfather."

"How long do I have to wait?"

"Until what?"

"Until I get to go to the Academy."

"Hm." Sybil pursed her lips. "I have to think about it."

"Mother!" Rose shouted. Ellie leapt up, fully awake now. She yawned, then stretched her back lazily, all the while looking at Sybil with marked distrust.

Sybil shot a piercing gaze. "Enough!" she cried at her daughter. "And I thought you were doing better. What did I say? What did I just tell you? You can forget about a meal." She paused then muttered to herself, "When will she learn?"

"Mother..." Rose pled, yet Sybil shrilly interrupted.

"That's it, you've pushed me too far. You're staying in here until tomorrow," Sybil put her palm out to silence Rose. "I have gone far too long without disciplining you. That ends now. You have a lot to think about."

Rose glared hate at her mother beneath dark, overgrown eyebrows from her place on the frilly, embroidered white and green bed. She didn't say a word.

"Don't give me that look, it's for your own good," Sybil barked as she backed out of the doorframe. "I love you Rose."

"I love you too, Mother," Rose muttered through a frown. She continued to glare straight ahead.

Sybil closed the heavy wooden door to Rose's bedchamber with a clunk, then a chink as the key's tumblers fell into place. She locked the door like a First Tower gate behind her.

Ellie hurried to Rose's side and put her head in her lap.

WESTERVIOLET BED CHAMBER

I t was early morning, sun not fully yet up, just barely brightening the tops of scraggly Pinewood just beyond the moat and castle curtain wall. Sybil's heart ached. She lay sprawled on her bed, sleep gown pooling around her like blood in water, watching a small flower bug crawl across her ceiling. She would never admit it to anyone, even herself, but she was lonely.

She shut her eyes, pretending it was years before. Pretending she was watching Rosen ready himself for hunting, Rose just a baby in the next chamber, just as she did every day in that late summer season, when the boars were particularly active. Every morning at dawn he would put on his hunting garb, then tie his large boots, silently and methodically, as she watched adoringly.

"Can I come with you?" she'd ask each time he readied to leave, never wanting to be apart from him.

"No," he would say.

"Why not?" she would ask.

He would stand and approach her. He would usually sit down on the bed near her.

"I will miss you too much," Sybil would say, crawling towards him. He'd put his arm around her. She'd nuzzle into him. That was the only place she'd ever felt home.

"And I, you."

Then, as if it was a game, each morning, once he was already dressed, Sybil would begin kissing his neck. Rosen would resist, at first.

"I must hunt," he would tell her with a flash in his brown eyes, hands gripping her thighs hungrily. She would already be unfastening his garb. He would already be kicking off his boots.

"My Queen," he would breathe in her ear as her hand went down his trousers. "I must worship you first." He'd stop her, pushing her back on the bed, diving under her skirts. As the sun rose through the chamber's massive horizontal panes, it illuminated Sybil's face as she succumbed to waves of pleasure.

Afterwards, they would lay together, then later, still intertwined as the birds outside began to wake up, Sybil would nuzzle into the crook of Rosen's arm once more.

"Why do you mock me?" she asked him once.

Rosen didn't move, but Sybil could feel him internally steel. "I would never."

"You call me Queen. But I am not. And I will never be," she added wistfully. She'd let go of her childhood fantasy the moment Rosen first kissed her. His was better than power, and control, and any of the secrets the Eighth Tower held, that prior to meeting him, she dreamed about.

The top of the Eighth tower was said to have the most beautiful views in the Kingdom and hold the most valuable secrets from the most ancient of Ancestors. But Rosen was better.

"You are to me," he said, kissing the top of her head. "My Queen."

Rosen truly loved her, Sybil could feel it deeply, but he never said it. He embodied it. That was why she could trust it. And compared to everyone around her, always flitting about, in her ear, attempting to impress her, fawning over her beauty, Rosen was like stone. He was the foundation she built herself on. That was why when he died, she crumbled.

Sybil opened her eyes, struck by the emptiness in her chamber, remembering the solid feeling that Rosen gave her. Like the wind couldn't blow her away. But now she was like smoke.

Sybil sighed, laying back in her bed, attempting to remember what it felt like to be worshiped. She shut her eyes. She tried to pretend Rosen's large hands touched her, not her own small cold ones, but it was futile. Her throat stabbed with the threat of tears. She frowned. She refused to cry.

If I can't be Rosen's Queen, she thought angrily, *I will be Queen for this whole cursed Kingdom.*

It was the only sentiment that brought her broken heart any relief.

WESTERVIOLET LORD'S STUDY

"I'm not sure it's a good idea," Sybil said.

Tomas was nose-deep in parchment, eyes down. "Your idea," he retorted dryly without looking up, smacking his lips without taking his eyes off it. There was word from Animus Rock, detailing the plans for the impending Council Session. The Kingdom-wide weapons policy was to be revisited and voted on. No small matter. He took a lustful, lingering sip from his Animus wine, then sighed.

It was deep into the evening. Emerald green candles with black wicks burned low in the hearth of the soulless, gaping fireplace instead of a fire. Tomas sat behind the enormous elderdesk carved from a jasper tree and in the bloodline for centuries, dark-stained with countless wood-grain rings of age. He ran his finger over the notch from an angry ancestor's sword long ago as he watched Sybil on the opposite side of the chamber staring at the stable yard below.

"You've already told the girl she isn't going, haven't you?"

"Yes, in not so many words, but I could easily..."

"Easily, what?" Tomas interrupted. "Take it back? Do you want her to learn to stand for nothing?"

"Father, she was crestfallen," Sybil said. "Heartbroken. You should have seen her face. She hates me for this."

"Oh, cursed First," Tomas grumbled. "The girl is a child. Children are fickle. More evidence that she's not ready."

"But she is and I fear she is stubborn. You remember me at that age?" Tomas thought of his daughter's own behavior as a girl. How, when punished for killing a hen, she ran. Hid in a merchant's cart and made it halfway to Littlebell before she was discovered and brought home. It hadn't really been her who killed the hen, it was Digory, but she'd confessed to the crime as she feared Digory would have been hung for it. Tomas knew the truth, although he allowed Sybil to keep her secrets. "She's her mother's daughter."

"Let her run," Tomas grunted, ignoring Sybil's indignant glare. "We'll have a true measure of her nature," he added, adjusting the dark metal toggles on the lapel of his cloak.

"Father…"

"I'll hear nothing else. The die is cast."

"Father, I can just tell her…"

Tomas interrupted again. "You claim she's ready. Let the girl prove it. You have eyes on?"

"She's being watched closely."

"Good," he said. "What do you suppose she'll do?"

Sybil rubbed her temple and pushed dark hair out of her eyes. "If she's like me, she'll try to get free. She'll run."

"What of the boy? The earthblood. He won't cause trouble?"

"Taken care of."

"What if she does slip away?"

"She won't."

Tomas raised an eyebrow.

"Digory," Sybil said simply.

Tomas huffed, fully unimpressed with his daughter's pet. The young man had a lot to prove.

"He is capable," Sybil retorted. "I assure you."

Tomas raised his bushy eyebrows dismissively as he looked back to his paperwork. "We will see."

WESTERVIOLET BED CHAMBER

Westerviolet was known for its evening storms, particularly in late summer when the ripe lemons fell and the river fangs writhed, however it generally tended to experience more lightning strikes, high winds and deep snowfalls than the rest of the land. All sixteen of the Vanguard castles were this way. No one knew why, but legend told that it was due to power remaining in the stone from when they were initially laid by the first Vanguards. That the Vanguards residing in the castle walls in the present day, however far removed from their powerful ancestors, still retained power and the storms could feel it. There was an old Vanguard saying that the older generations still muttered occasionally—*Power recognizes power.*

Rose indignantly paced around her chamber, walking back and forth from her child's desk on the West side of her room to windows on the North as a flash of lightning lit up the sky. Ellie kept her pace, anxiously concerned with her tail up and alert. The finality of Mother's decision reverberated louder and louder in Rose's mind until she felt she was being driven mad. She could not live like this any longer. Wind whipped, howled, and swirled loudly outside as the sky unnaturally dimmed. Birds all about the castle squawked and chirped in confusion and protest. The child listened as she cried, then sobbed, then hardened in contemplative anger.

"You stay here Ellie," she told her beloved companion. "I'll come back for you. I won't be gone forever. I promise."

Ellie whimpered and leaned into Rose's leg sadly. She looked up at Rose as if to say, "Please stay," but Rose simply kissed her head. Even Ellie was not enough to keep Rose in her mother's clutches, if something could be done about it. And

Rose intended something to be done.

She furrowed her small brow in resolve and, clenching her fists, walked to her window to look out at the black mote in the near distance, rippling with heavy raindrops. How many times had she gazed out this same window imagining what lay beyond the castle walls? Today she intended to find out. Rose took a deep breath and sighed as she opened her window. She steadied herself, glancing back at Ellie's forlorn expression briefly, before climbing through its horizontal pane into the balmy, menacing night.

The air was moist and warm, thick enough to bite. Gravid rain clouds hid the night sky and blocked light from the moon. The air churned with pain mirroring Rose's own soul. Her skin was sticky and hot with sweat as she gripped the thick ivy with white knuckles. Her heart pounded in her chest. A mosquito buzzed and bit her neck, yet she barely felt it. She was fully engulfed with her escape. There was no other way.

She inched down the wall as weighty drops began to fall upon her in this late summer downpour. She didn't look down.

Then thunder cracked and Rose gasped. She clung to the ivy tightly and bit her lip not to cry, reminding herself to be brave like her father was said to be. He had carried the title of 'Hunter of Westerviolet' which was no small feat. It meant he was the bravest boar hunter, able to take down the largest and fiercest of beasts. She'd always wished to have met known him and spent long hours gazing at the one portrait of him that hadn't been hidden away, a small painting in a gilded frame, right outside of her bedroom door. Rose loved to compare herself to him, and although she most closely resembled her mother, she knew she had his smile. She wondered, briefly, how different her life would be if he'd lived, imaging riding with him while he hunted, listening to his stories from life in the Green Wing, or walking hand in hand with him through the gardens. Every time she saw a child alongside a father, her heart pinched, but she learned long ago never to speak of such feelings. That was the only time her mother hit her, in a cold slap across the face, when she whined, saying she wished Sybil had been the one to die instead of him. She was five years old.

Rose took a breath and continued to descend slowly. Lightning flashed bright overhead; black clouds clapped again. She jumped and slipped, trembling in determination and poignant fear, fumbling to hang on. She regretted her choice, but she was significantly down the wall now. She had gone too far now to turn back. She glanced at the distant ground, illuminated by lightning flashing and then thunder cracking loudly. The storm was directly above her now. Rose could barely see her hands or feet. Everything was wet and dark. Her heart pounding in her chest was her only companion, apart from Ellie's faint barking from the window above.

The hair on Rose's arms stood on end from the charged air.

Then, in a blinding crack, a heavy bolt of white lightning struck the fourth knotted oak not far below her. The flash instantly broke her concentration.

Rose lost grip.

She fell, reaching towards the wet ivy and dark clouds in futility as she plummeted back.

Then everything went black.

WESTERVIOLET STABLE

C ol was in the stable trying to calm the horses when lightning hit one of the ancient oak trees, splitting the storied trunk in two with its force.

The four oak trees were said to have been there long before even the castle was built. They were gnarled and reaching, with branches wider than the trunks of the trees in Pinewood, interweaving between the branches of their companions to the point the four nearly appeared to be one tree. Their leaves grew chartreuse in Spring and turned to emerald throughout summer, so vast in number that when the wind blew hard through them, it was all that could be heard throughout the commons. When light shone through the leaves, it was like viewing the sun through a precious stone. In the late summer months, the leaves turned leathery, and some began to tinge blood red. In autumn, so many leaves fell that a special team of natives, the Leaf Toilers, was tasked with collecting them and disposing of them ceremonially, by burning outside of Westerviolet castle's walls. Each year after their task was complete the Leaf Toilers themselves, too, were burned. The four oaks stood in two rows, like the corners of a square. The massive trunks were so huge that they nearly touched, leaving a space barely large enough for a person within them, although no one dared enter. Legend said that the trees were cursed.

Col ran outside to investigate and was just in time to see a small figure falling from the castle, long dark hair flapping behind her as she descended. She just missed crashing into the large branches of one of the oaks still standing.

His heart dropped into his stomach.

"NO!" Col cried as he sprinted, but he was too far to reach her in time. Rose dropped like a rock towards the hard ground.

There was nothing he could do.

Just as she was about to land, he stopped and clenched his eyes. Col couldn't bear to see his only friend die this way. He listened for a thud but there was none, only howling wind, the resounding rustle of leaves and cracks of thunder. Ellie's faint barking from the window high above. He peeled opened his eyes then stood, shocked and frozen, soaking in the warm downpour.

He couldn't believe it. He rubbed his face, but no, what he saw was true.

Rose's body should be crumpled and broken and bloody, but she was untouched as if she was sleeping. Had Col not seen her fall moments before, he wouldn't believe it at all.

Rose should be dead.

He dashed to her side where she lay soaking in the rain. Her cloak, smock, hair–everything was drenched and covered in mud. Her white cheeks blushed red. Wet hair clung to her neck and face like tiny blades against her pale skin. Col kneeled next to her, shaking her shoulder, "Rose, Rose," but she lay as still as porcelain.

"Rose," he pleaded, "wake up."

This reminded him of a few moons prior. He'd awoken early, before the cock crowed, to do as he always did. To watch the sunrise with his father before the day began. But that morning was different. Instead of sitting outside, putting his boots on as he ate a barley loaf, Col's father was slumped over in his chair. Col had begged and pleaded, but his father's eyes stayed shut. He never did wake up.

Col lowered to check for Rose's breath. Her face and cheeks were warm. She was alive. Col shook her for a third time. "Rose, please. Please," he begged; heart shattered. Other than his brother, and the horses, Rose was all he cared for in the world. *She must be okay*, he thought. *She must.* Then, Sybil's cruel gaze flashed in his mind.

He looked over his shoulder and added in a whisper, "I'm not supposed to see you."

Still, Rose didn't respond. Col whipped his head around again to make sure no one watched, then looked down at Rose in the rain. He furrowed his brow for a long, painful moment, trying to decide what to do, fighting with himself whether he should obey the Lady or not. Then he sighed as he made his decision. He chose Rose.

Col collected Rose carefully in his arms and walked back to the stable through the whistling wind, rumbling thunder, and the stinging assault of warm rain.

Digory watched the children from his perch at the top of the North Gate through a bulbed glass with fascination.

When the girl was about to crash into the hard ground, all her fingers and all her toes emitted a piercing bright light tantamount to lightning. Time stilled. She seemed to float down the rest of the distance like a feather.

Sybil would want to know what had transpired immediately, but Digory had other plans. He'd follow his Lady's commands and ensure the girl not escape Westerviolet proper. He'd get rid of the stable boy. He'd keep it all clean for Tomas. Sybil was adamant about that. "There will be no talk of this at the Rock," she had commanded, and it was Digory's job to keep it that way. But, Digory thought to himself from his nest in the tower, he would not tell Sybil about how her daughter survived that fall.

At least, not yet.

Sybil had commanded him not to act; just wait and watch. And that's all he did.

Col carried Rose's body in his arms like a doll and burst through the creaky stable door. He let it slam behind himself carelessly, then gently placed her in an empty stable, clean with fresh straw.

Col frantically hurried to fetch her water and a blanket as

flashes of lightning ruptured through wooden slats. Each burst illuminated the children in vertical lines while every horse bucked and whinnied in terror around them. The storm outside was epic and unrelenting. The door to the stable didn't close all the way and was caught by the wind. It flapped loudly against the side of the stable with each gust.

Lighting lit up the sky in a flash again as Col tore onto a storage closet and pulled items out of his way, throwing them on the floor in pursuit of a pair of thick woollen blankets used to lay beneath riding saddles.

With the blankets and a canteen, he darted back. Col tossed the canteen down then hurriedly wrapped Rose's unconscious body, gently drying her hair and limbs. He softly rubbed dirt from her cheeks as he spoke to her.

"Rose, what were you doing?" He burned with guilt masked in anger. "Why did you climb that? Why did you copy me?!" he cried as he patted her wet hair with the edge of the blanket. "Please be okay, please be okay," he whispered. "I'm so sorry Rose. I shouldn't have showed you how to do it. You are too small to climb on your own, and in a storm! Please be okay," Col said, mostly to himself. "I'm so sorry I didn't mean to ruin your life your mother is right that I'm no good. Look at you. This is all my fault. I'm so sorry. Please be okay and I promise I'll never hurt you again."

Weeping, Col lowered his head and clenched onto the thick blanket wrapped around Rose's small body. He burned in misery as he felt the faint rise and fall of her chest, until Rose gasped awake. Col jumped away in shock. Rose's eyes shot open, startled, long eyelashes dewy with rainwater still. She looked like she was searching for something not there, black pupils dancing without focus.

"Rose!" He studied her delicate face. "Are you okay?"

She was silent, blinking as if just awoken from a long dream. "I'm not sure," Rose said. "I feel funny."

And surely, she did, for the fall awakened Rose's innate power, hidden deep in her blood.

In the days of old, there was a ritual that all Vanguards were required to participate in. Adolescents at the cusp of adulthood were put in perilous positions to reveal if they were powerful or not. Vanguard power usually revealed itself when the Vanguard had reached puberty and was about to die. Not all Vanguards had power, and it was impossible to tell if a Vanguard child would be powerful based off blood alone, although oldblood Vanguards, apart from the newblood Minneys, were typically more potent.

Many youths in the past lost their lives this way. The ritual was called the Awakening and had been lost to time. It was forgotten long before the Plague that occurred 200 years prior to our story. The only remaining knowledge of the Awakening and the true history of Vanguard power itself was kept by the Guild, initially created to stifle and thwart powerful Vanguards. And Tomas Brochet too had some knowledge, received from Lord Guy Brochet, the elder before him, son of Lord Lucien Brochet, grandson of the Lord Robert Brochet the Great, the most famous and revered Brochet Ancestor there ever was.

Col collapsed to his knees, smiling wide.

Rose looked at him. "What happened?"

"You fell. From your bed chamber!" He threw his arms around her. "I'm so happy you're alive!" She hugged him back, until Col pushed her away suddenly. "You need to go back to your chamber."

"Col? What's wrong? Why?"

"I…" He hung his head. "I'm not supposed to see you."

Rose scooted herself to sit upright. "What do you mean?"

"Your mother said that…"

Rose screamed, "Mother talked to you!?" and lightning flashed outside.

Col hung his head sadly, remembering the interaction. How could he forget? It was branded into his mind.

"Come on," she said, struggling to stand.

He helped her up. "What are you doing? Rose, wait. You should rest."

"Mother will never let me leave." She paused. "We have to go."

"Go?" Col raised his eyebrows. "Go where?"

"Where do *you* want to go?"

Her determination unnerved him. In that moment, Rose reminded Col of her mother. It shook him to the core.

"Littlebell," he said quickly.

"Then let's go to Littlebell."

"What do you say, little girl?" He smiled, confused. "Rose... We can't just *go* to Littlebell."

Her black eyes burned like coal aflame. "Why not?"

"Little girl, it is so far."

Rose paused then illuminated with delight. "We can take horses!"

"But..." Col groped for excuses before remembering the most important one of all. His own blood. "My brother will be back soon."

Rose lowered her voice. "If mother finds out..." she said, then trailed off. "Col, we have to go."

He nodded grimly, knowing her meaning, believing deep down she was right.

"We will come back for your brother, when mother isn't cross. When I come back for Ellie."

Col was silent, fully overwhelmed. Finally, he nodded as lighting flashed again outside.

"Okay," he offered his hand to Rose. "Let's go."

PINEWOOD

The woods surrounding Westerviolet comprised of pine trees primarily, interspersed with red-berried honeysuckle and thorny brambles lining the forest's paths. Occasionally there was a scrawny maple or wide leafed sassafras. Often large rock formations jutted up from the forest floor like stone deadbloods come alive and cast shadows in a horrifying fashion.

Most natives from Westerviolet avoided Pinewood for it was where the ashes of the four oaks were scattered. Those of the Leaf Toilers as well. Most assumed that meant it was cursed. Pinewood then acted as a barrier between Westerviolet and parts of the Kingdom that lay to the west, keeping the natives bound by their own minds. And they did not dare venture far east either, for on that border was the Cursed Hills and no one wanted the Dread.

The storm had subsided slightly, and dark clouds churned angrily above the scraggly pines. A hawk swooped from tree to tree. Col glanced up briefly, then around himself anxiously. Beyond the path there were many felled pines across the forest floor. To Col, in the twilight mist, the fallen trunks looked like a boneyard.

He stood frozen in a dim clearing, scantly lit by the partial moon, with his hands up. A crossbow stared him down.

Col chided himself for not heeding his brother's warnings, swallowing feelings of shame and guilt for betraying his own blood to help Lady Rose Brochet, a Vanguard. The ultimate betrayal. Or so his father would have thought. His heart thumped so hard he figured it could be heard for creeds all around. He clenched his fists in fear.

A man with tight-trimmed beard, fiery eyes, and a roguish,

threatening glare held the crossbow. This man was surely an elite Guardsman, Col thought, as he wore a hooded, emerald green cloak with dark hammered helmet, black metal chainmail, and most notably, a green glass dagger at his hip, in a hidden sheath to where only the hilt was visible, like a glinting emerald embedded in his belt. As the Guardsman moved, it caught the light every so often.

The Guardsman held his small crossbow with practiced calm, pointed directly at Col's head.

"Either convince the girl to go on her own accord or bring her to me and I'll take her myself," Digory said, matter of fact. "Those are your options. Do either and I'll report you dead. You'll be free to go anywhere in the realms you choose and that will be your reward. But," he paused, taking one ominous step towards the trembling boy with a clank of his chainmail, "if you think you are clever and think you can keep your little adventure up, we will hunt you, and find you, and bring her home, and bring Brochet your head. Or if you think you can let her leave, and go home as if this didn't happen, we'll find you and bring Brochet your head. No matter what you do we take your head." Digory paused. An owl hooted somewhere over his shoulder. "Unless you deliver the girl."

Col took one cautious step backwards, bare feet crunching over damp twigs. "P...please," he said under his breath, tasting the fear bubbling in the back of his throat. He lowered his hands. He felt like he was going to be sick.

Digory took a step forward. His sharp eyebrows lowered over his unfeeling red eyes, smouldering like forgotten coals as his boot sloshed against wet mud and grey-green needles. "I'm doing you a kindness, allowing you a chance to be clear of this mess. I can tell you're a smart boy," he cautioned, flexing his jaw. "Don't do something doltish."

"What about my brother?" Col asked timidly. His heart was full of the guilt of abandoning his post, and more gravely, his kin.

"You'll be dead. He'll find out when he's back."

"But..."

Digory interrupted. "Do you not understand I could have killed you at any point since we've been speaking or over the last day I followed you, but I waited, only to give you a chance to save your own small life." He sighed loudly and shook his head and scratched his beard casually.

Col shivered at the idea that the Guardsman had followed he and Rose for an entire day without either of them noticing. They'd snuck out when the storm was still at its peak, when all the houses and stalls were shut, and he thought they hadn't been seen. He'd even checked all around them as they passed the Lunar Tower and entered Pinewood. If the Guardsman was able to follow them to this point, surely he or his comrades would have no trouble catching them before they made it to Littlebell.

"Okay," Col whispered.

Digory looked at the boy curiously. "Okay?"

"Only if she's safe," Col said. "And you won't come after me," he added with impressive poise.

"On the King," Digory agreed, raising his eyebrows, laying his hand over his heart.

Col nodded, satisfied, sniffling, trying not to cry. Trying to be brave like his brother made him promise he would be. He looked up slowly though pale eyelashes and asked meekly, "Can you tell me the way to Littlebell, Guardsman?"

"Littlebell?" Digory smirked and scratched his beard again. He chuckled once.

"Yes, Littlebell," Col replied with determination and mounting anger, young, proud eyes threatening tears.

"If you follow the Narrow you will be there in three days' time." Digory gestured west and slightly south to the wide pebble path in the distant foreground through a heavy thicket of brambles and late evening fog. "Do we have an accord?" Col hunched with the weight of his circumstances, small flame of hope catching the kindling in his chest. "Boy?"

"Okay." Col spoke softly. "Wait here," he added, glancing up briefly, then down at his dirty feet. He sighed. Before Digory could respond, Col ran to where Rose and he had made camp nearby.

"Good boy," Digory said under his breath.

He smiled as the lanky boy disappeared into the shadows. -

Rose looked up to the sound of Col's crunching footsteps. "You took a while," she said, holding a bundle of kindling where she stood next to their tethered steeds.

"I found something."

"You did?" Rose asked happily. "What'd you find?" She excitedly dropped the sticks with a crash.

"Come with me this way and I'll show you."

She stopped, studying his forlorn expression. "Is everything okay, Col?"

He blinked once. "Trust me," he said, internally wincing. He reassured himself that this was what was best for her. She would be safe. That's what really mattered. And he would be alive. "Come with me." Col took Rose's delicate hand. She smiled up at him, trusting him fully. He kept his eyes locked forward, unblinking, leading her into the dark woods. He couldn't bear to look at her.

"Where are we going?"

Col swallowed hard and set his brow as he tugged Rose through Pinewood. "Just over here," he said.

Rose stumbled over fallen limbs. She scraped her leg against a stick. "Ow!" she cried, razor line of blood across her calf. "Col, it's so dark. I can't see."

"It's okay, little girl," he reassured sadly, eyes already focused on Digory in the distance. "I can. Almost there."

They reached the clearing and Rose's eyes widened in understanding and horror when she realized it was her mother's man standing there with smug grin. She instantly pulled to get free like a ruby fox caught in a snare, but Col tightened his grip on her wrist.

"Col?" She looked to him in confusion, then panic. "What... what are you doing?"

"I'm so sorry Rose," Col said. "This Guardsman found us. He'll kill me. This is my only chance."

Rose's world crashed down around her. Up became down.

She screamed, "We had a chance! We could have gotten far. We could have lost him!"

Digory interjected, "No you couldn't have," with playful timbre as he watched the unfolding scene, crossbow aim softened slightly.

Rose's face was red from shouting. She bucked to tear away. Her hair fell about her cheeks like a manwoman. "Col, why would you do this?" She thrashed and hit and bit. "I thought you were my friend!" Rose wailed in between child's-size blows.

Col sobbed pitifully, barely able to breathe much less speak. "I am!" He choked out the words though sniffles, then tears. "Rose, your mother hates me and is making me stay away from you. This way I don't have to see you every day knowing I can't talk to you. Please Rose I don't want to hurt you. You'll be safe. Look at how you fell. You needed help before you were on your own for one moment!" he cried, clinging to her wrist to keep her in place. His feet dug into wet pine needles. "You are too small to leave. Too delicate. I love you Rose. I'm so sorry Rose. Are... are you still my friend?"

"No!" she screamed, tugging backwards against his grip. "You're lying! Never! Let me go!" Rose scratched viciously at the boy, drawing jagged lines of blood along the dark skin of his wrist and forearm.

"I tire of this, tiny ones," Digory said dryly. He took a few hulking steps towards them, separating the pair without difficulty, then shoved scrawny Col aside and the boy fell clumsily into the dirt. Then, Digory grabbed the petite girl and tied her with a length of rope around her hands and feet like a boar while she screamed and wailed and bucked. Amused by the child-size affair, thinking he must tell Sybil of the extent of their attachment, Digory tossed Rose over the back of his horse and latched her to it like cargo.

The little boy slowly rose to one knee, head pounding with guilt and regret. What had he done? He pulled himself upright, covered in dirt and pine needles, then stood with head hung in supreme shame. "I'm so sorry Rose," he repeated over and over as Digory tied her. "He would kill me," Col reasoned with her, and to himself. "Now I can go to Littlebell." Col pointed at Digory. "He told me how to get there. Like we've talked about! You will understand soon. Someday, will you visit me?"

Rose shot an odious glare. "I hate you Collen and I will hate you forever."

Col recoiled physically, as if he'd been struck.

Meanwhile, Digory pulled a dirty, snot encrusted rag from his trouser pocket and shoved it in Rose's mouth to silence her, then picked his crossbow up, all the while Col watched, paralyzed in horror.

"Boy," Digory said.

Col looked to him with a flash of hope in his glassy red eyes. "Forget Littlebell."

Digory fired. The arrowhead struck the boy in the sternum with a loud crack. Burgundy blood bubbled from the wound like a levy sprung a leak. Col's eyes widened in confusion, then terror and pain as he pawed at his small chest, coughing blood.

"I wouldn't do that if I were you," Digory said. "If you pull it out now, you die. Leave it. It's a nice evening. Beautiful. Enjoy it. It's the last thing you will ever see." He gestured at the black, starless sky with a sick grin, then spurred his horse to a gallop.

Rose watched in silent horror as her only friend in the whole Kingdom writhed and crumpled, spitting blood.

With his dying breath, Collen screamed her name at the hidden stars.

WESTERVIOLET BED CHAMBER

"Digory told me how your little friend betrayed you."

Rose turned away with a groan and buried her face in an overstuffed pillow. She had not left her chamber for half a moon.

"I hate to point out how I warned you."

It was early morning. Birds competitively chirped outside, yet the pleasant cacophony was muffled by heavy, black and grey curtains embroidered with the Brochet ouroboros. Ellie was at Rose's side.

The poor dog had been inconsolable while Rose was away. She wouldn't eat and wouldn't sleep. She growled and bit at anyone who tried to remove her from Rose's chamber. Now that Rose had returned, she stayed tethered to the girl, never once letting her out of her sight.

"Maybe now you will learn that you should listen to your mother," Sybil said. "Only when I became a mother myself, did I realize how right my own was, about everything." She walked the length of the chamber, pulling open dark curtains. "You're too young to worry about boys," she said as painfully bright sunlight spilled into the dreary chamber. Rose wanted to protest but was too dejected to care. "There! That's better. Come now you mustn't pout." Sybil sauntered back to Rose, black gown shimmering in the morning sun like oil, showing off her curves. Most of what Sybil owned was emerald or black and looked as if it was painted on, it fit so expertly.

She sat beside her daughter on the bed. Rose was bundled into her comforters with a stone expression.

"You will see someday that this is what was best for you. There was no future for you with him." Sybil studied her daughter's serious visage for hint of a response, but Rose was silent. She placed her hand on her shoulder.

"At least talk to me. I will always understand. I'm your mother. I understand when no one else will."

She thought back to when Rose was very small, still suckling at her breast. She had so many hopes for her. She'd study Rose's tiny face and wonder what type of great woman she would become someday. Would she marry a Norland, or maybe a Thorne? Possibly even a Dale and secure Westerviolet's alliance with Baneswood further. Back in those days, watching Rose suckle, it was easy to think about the future. Although untraditional for a Brochet mother to nurse a child, Sybil wouldn't have it any other way. Oh, how she missed those days, when she always knew the girl was safe, because she never left her side.

Rose sniffed, face puffy and eyes bloodshot as she turned to look at Sybil.

"I thought he was my friend, Mother. I really did."

Sybil shook her head. "Oh, my sweet, you have much to learn." She scooted closer, smooth black fabric bunching underneath her thighs. "A boy with nothing except his life to lose cannot be trusted. He's like those horses," she gestured towards the window, "nothing more than beasts. All earthblood are the same. If you stand behind them and startle them, they will kick you. It's in their nature to protect themselves, Rose. They know nothing of Vanguard honor." She paused, feeling genuinely sorry for her daughter, then added, "I hate that you had to learn the lesson this way, but it's for your own good."

"But, mother, he cared for me," Rose said in a small voice. "He loved me."

"All the same, he turned you in," Sybil replied. "One evil deed poisons a river of kind ones."

Rose was unable to get Col's screams out of her mind. She frowned. "Digory killed him," she said softly.

"Digory did as commanded. The boy kidnaped a Vanguard. It was the noose for him anyway."

"He didn't kidnap me. It was my idea!"

Sybil pursed her lips and lowered her pointed eyebrows sternly. "Digory did him a kindness."

"He told him he would let him leave!"

"He did, did he? Clever," she said under her breath.

Sybil would have done the same thing.

"Mother, it was awful."

"I'm sure it was, because that is what the world outside these walls is like." Sybil put her arm around Rose's shoulders for a half-hug. Ellie protectively nuzzled into Rose's leg, staring Sybil down. "Even the most handsome men break their word, and the kindest men lie and the supremely pious steal and the most faithful cheat," she cooed in the girl's ear.

"The world is full of monsters, then."

Sybil smiled. "It is full of monsters, you are right. Your little friend was a monster, and he was right outside your door."

Rose's thoughts spun. "If Col was one, how do I know? How do I know when someone will hurt me? How do I know who is bad?"

"I can teach you a trick. Here, come in close to me," Sybil said. "The secret is that everyone will hurt you, everyone is bad, barring your mother, surely, because I love you more than anything. A mother's bond is sacred, and they never want their child to come to harm, for it's the order of nature. A mother must protect her child, but everyone else, in one way or another, will sooner or later do something of harm."

"Everyone?"

"Yes, my dear," Sybil nodded solemnly, believing it fully. "Everyone. It's true."

"Even the Vanguards in the other realms?"

"Oh, my sweet, especially in the other realms. Westerviolet is the safest one!"

"What about the Minneys? Col told me stories. I bet if I were a Minney girl, it would be different!"

Sybil smiled coyly as she re-crossed her legs at the opposite angle. "Is that so?" she asked slowly, leaning closer to Rose, dark eyes sparkling, not bothering to question how this *Col* knew anything about other realms, despite it being illegal. She figured rumors had leaked from Burkhart, given his ancestry, which was no longer a problem, for the man was dead. "I have a story then for you. Have you heard of the blue-eyed charm?"

"I've heard of the Green Charm," Rose said, recounting the familiar Westerviolet legend. It spoke to the fact that all Brochets had power, long before the Plague, stemming from the times of the old gods. It was a major reason why Westerviolet natives worshiped the Vanguard Ancestors with such ferocity. The Brochets were thought to be descendants of those gods.

"No, no," Sybil flitted her wrist. "Not that one."

"Then no," Rose said. "I don't think so."

"It's probably best you have not heard..."

"Please tell me, Mother. Please!"

"You're so young and innocent," Sybil baited, chewing on her lip as she looked down at Rose. "I suppose it is about time you learn." Rose listened to intently as Sybil began. "The Minney's realm is to the west along the Missi. What do you know of them?"

"I've heard about their market."

"The Occident? Yes, that's a good start. What about it?"

"Col told me that they have the biggest market in the Kingdom," Rose said. "The whole city is a market really and they sell everything. Even beautiful things that have no other purpose at all. He said there are painters and singers and furniture makers and shops for clothes and shoes and even toys!" There were not toys in Westerviolet. Rose was often gifted toys from other bloodlines or high natives, but they were discarded. "Can you believe that Mother? Toys sold at market! For anyone with coin to purchase! Even earthblood! I mean natives," she said, to an eyeroll from Sybil. "They make most of it there in their realm and the rest of it is merchants and wandering traders. He said Baneswood traders sell meats and furs there. Hellswater sends fishermen and boats that transport things up and down the Missi. Graceview traders sell spices. He told me the Minneys are the best at singing and dancing and painting, and they have a stage where you can give them coin and get to watch! Not like the traveling bards. There's a whole building for it!"

"What else?" Sybil said curtly, put off by mention of the stable boy. "Enough of what the earthblood told you."

Rose wilted. "I don't know."

"Yes, I know you do." Sybil was unrelenting. She always expected more from Rose. "Littlebell's color?"

"Yellow?"

"And their emblem?"

"I don't know."

"Yes, you do."

"I'm not sure," Rose whined, eyebrows pinching to mimic her mother's characteristic expression.

"Oh," Sybil said. "It's an easy one. You'll laugh when I tell you how easy." Sybil paused and Rose waited. Sybil finally said, "A bell!"

Rose smiled. "I should have gotten that one."

"You should have," Sybil light-heartedly agreed. "But you are right, there are a lot of names and it's difficult to remember them all. I'll tell you some from one hundred years ago."

"That's a long time."

Sybil nodded. "The best lessons come from the past, Rose. History always comes back around."

"Tell me about the blue-eye charm, mother."

"Lilli Minney was the most beautiful girl in the entire Kingdom," Sybil said. "She was kind, and lovely, and caring, the tales claim. Everyone adored her. She was said to be a friend to all. She was also brilliant."

Sybil exaggerated, of course, to make the story more poignant for her daughter, all the while bearing a tangible distaste for this Vanguard of legend, due to her bloodline. Sybil turned her nose up at any newblood Vanguards. And while these events far predated any of the Vanguards she had ever met, save for her great grandfather Lucien, so she had never met Lilli or her immediate kin, she hated her all the same.

Rose was instantly entranced. "She sounds like a princess."

"In a way, she was," Sybil said. "The princess of Littlebell anyway. Remember I asked you if you'd heard of the blue-eyed charm? It lives in the Minney blood. The first Minney was said to be charmed, and he had blue eyes."

"Blue? Really?"

"Oh yes. Like Thorne has pale green, Norland has bright green, Dale has brown, or Brochet has hazel."

"Why don't I have hazel?" Rose asked.

"You have eyes like your grandmother's and mine," Sybil said. Rose nodded once more, soft hair bouncing across her round cheeks. "Now, Minney believes their blue-eyed children have special gifts and are tokens of fortune. Blue-eyes don't come around often, every few generations one is born, so their rarity makes them popular. And, they are notoriously stunning, of course, with those sky-blue eyes against that coal-black skin."

She paused and sighed. Despite disagreeing politically and feeling no sympathy for their strife, and although she'd never outwardly admit it, Sybil was jealous of the historical blue-eye beauty. She couldn't stand anything that took attention away from her own legendary allure.

Sybil was exceedingly vain.

"What did Lilli look like?"

"It is said that Lilli Minney had the most perfect complexion, ebony dark and smooth like spider's silk, with honey blonde curls."

"She sounds pretty."

"She was," Sybil said quickly with a pang of envy, having seen a rendering at Animus Rock before. "Not only that but she was unbelievably talented. A bard, known for her ballads. The girl was a bit of a recluse and would steal away to the outskirts of Baneswood Forest to be alone with her thoughts and to write and sing. In some ways, you're a lot like her." Rose smiled. Sybil, smiling back, went on. "Every bloodline in the Kingdom put in a bid for her hand, but Lilli's mother Sia was staunchly New. She believed her daughter should follow the New tradition and marry earthblood, regardless of her talent or her eyes and what that may mean to the other Vanguards. She sent out a notice that they were not accepting offers for Vanguard proposals and would instead search for an earthblood husband for the beauty."

Rose stared at her mother, spellbound. "I want to be just like Lilli."

Sybil nearly chuckled, shaking her head knowingly. "I don't think that you do. Listen to the whole tale. The Norlands had other plans. Do you know anything about them?"

"They are the Warmen?"

"Founded and rule the Warmen, and train them at a camp near their castle, yes," Sybil nodded. "Do you know its name?"

"I forget."

"Try," Sybil said. "Think really hard."

"I don't remember. Something with a bird?"

"It has a bird's name in it. Keep trying."

"I don't know," Rose frowned. "Just tell me!"

"Ravenshroud," Sybil finally said. "Northwest, close to the Bone Mountains and Creed Point. Ravenshroud's western border is the Dead Line. Several days travel from Animus. It's very, very far from here, on the other side of the Kingdom. Rocky and cold."

"I remember that now."

"Good, do you remember the color?"

Rose furrowed her brow. "Purple?"

"It's a deep, dark purple like a cousin of black," Sybil said. "It reminds me of the deepest part of a sunset. My favorite part. Right before everything goes dark."

Rose nodded.

Meanwhile, Sybil furiously twirled her long plait of hair, thinking briefly about the Norland bloodline. How historically ruthless and opportunistic they were. She admired those traits greatly.

"They believe in intermingling Vanguard blood," Sybil went on. Rose listened, nodding with an uncomprehending, puzzled frown. "Over centuries, generations of Norland descendants became powerful members of society through founding and furthering the Warman and intermarrying with other Vanguards. Recruits are trained at Ravenshroud. It is the nearest outpost for Creed Point, making it vital for weapons creation and trade. Ravenshroud also has farmland to support the Norland forces. The point is, they became integral to the fiber of our Kingdom's society, although never fully accepted by the elite bloodlines."

"Why not?"

"Norland is undeserving. They take whatever they can. They have no class," Sybil said resolutely with a shake of her head. "No honor! They are beneath us."

Rose nodded unsurely while clasping the covers tighter around herself. Ellie was beside her.

"But, unfortunately, like I told you, they're fully integrated into the Kingdom and are necessary to interact with from time to time," Sybil said. She sighed. "Now that you know all of that about his bloodline, you'll understand how it was possible that, one hundred years ago, Lord Bin Norland stole Lilli Minney away. He kidnapped her when she was singing alone in her woods."

Rose gasped. "No!"

"He did," Sybil nodded with a harsh gleam in her eye. Something about misfortune pleased Sybil, the more tragic the better, and she wasn't sure why. "He and his men along with Busk forces marched on Littlebell and set the infamous Bell Tower on fire. They ransacked homes and stole everything they came across. They even made Lili's mother Sia watch."

"Oh no!" Rose gasped again, tiny cry stifled by birds chirping in pleasant cacophony right outside the window. Sun flickered off her sunbloom walls.

"Oh yes." Sybil's retort was nearly cruel. "Littlebell was in tatters. Lilli, the gem of the Minneys, missing, and Bin Norland at large."

Rose asked with a small voice, "Did they get him?"

"Of course not," Sybil chuckled. "Not at all."

"But why!?" Rose shouted. "That isn't fair!" Ellie stirred from her slumber in a start. Upon realizing all was well, she yawned then stretched and fell back asleep quickly, into Rose's side.

"Daughter," Sybil's frustration flared, "fair isn't the same for everyone. To the Minneys it was not fair at all. But to the Norlands, who saw it as a chance to experiment with blue-eye blood for the good of the future, it was unfair of Sia Minney to deny that chance. They saw what they did was right, you see?"

"Why didn't anyone stop them? Why didn't anyone help her?"

"My sweet, they tried," Sybil said, "but the Norlands train the Warmen and have the best fighters. The New forces, even with Morfit backup, were no match. They did try to send troops to rescue Lilli, to no avail. Each was cut down swifter than the last. Bin sent the heads back to Sia as a warning to stop, so they did."

"Why didn't they tell the King?" Rose asked, horrified. "Why didn't he tell them to stop and give her back?"

"Bin Norland was friends with the King at the time," Sybil said simply, not wanting to bother her daughter with the complicated specifics.

Although even if the King had wanted to, he did not have the support Kingdom wide to help. Newblood realms had very little influence over the Kingdom 100 years prior, and although Morfit troops endlessly barraged Ravenshroud attempting to rescue Lilli, it was to no avail.

At the look on Rose's face, Sybil clarified. "So, no one stopped them, no. He got back to Ravenshroud with Lilli, uninterrupted."

Rose asked softly, "What did he do with her there?"

"He hurt her."

Rose turned her head and met her mother's eyes. "How bad?" she asked in a whisper.

"Very badly, my sweet," Sybil replied, trying not to smile, dark plait of hair she twirled bunching in a knot at her fingertips. She sighed as she held the hairs in front of her eyes to untangle them, brooding, remembering the details of the story. How Lilli's decapitated body showed up at Sia Minney's doorstep, although, no one ever found her head. Then Sybil baited Rose. "When you're older maybe I'll tell you more."

"Tell me now."

"I'll tell you when you're older."

Rose frowned. "I can handle it," she said. "I want to know."

Sybil ignored her. "My message is, that beautiful young girl barely older than you, the lovely Lilli Minney, deigned Littlebell elderclaim no less, was snatched right from one of the kindest places in her realm because the world is full of bad people. You must be prepared; vigilant. Never be a victim. Don't be like Lilli."

"What happened to her?" Rose pleaded. "Now you have to finish."

Sybil sighed, tucking the tangled plait of hair behind her ear. She clasped her bony hands in her lap and gave Rose her full attention. "She gave birth to one daughter, but when she would not give Bin Norland a son, he killed her."

Rose was incensed. "He killed her!"

Sybil bit her lip to hide her amusement. "He did, then he gave her body back to her mother."

"Why?" Rose asked with wide eyes.

"Because, sweet, Bin wasn't done causing pain."

"But..." Rose paused, black eyes darting. "That doesn't make sense," she said as she met Sybil's gaze again. "He got what he wanted." She waited for an explanation.

"Some men don't cause pain because it makes sense," Sybil said. "They do it because they like how it feels."

As she thought on this in silence, Sybil noted the resemblance of Rose's pensive face to her own. Her own vanity fluttered. Suddenly, Rose replied with boiling rage. "Why didn't you tell me before?" Her small brow furrowed. "Why, if the Kingdom is this bad, did you hide it from me? You should have told me."

Sybil turned her head to watch passing white clouds against the striking azure sky. "You were not ready to hear."

Rose's anger quickly gave way to fear. "Why is everyone going to hurt me?"

"They are rotten, and evil, and they want to."

Rose's eyes were unblinking like two chunks of coal in ice. "But... why?"

"Because you are like Lilli, but in a different way," she went on. "They want what you possess. Bin Norland wanted the blue-eye and your earthblood wanted to be a bit closer to the top than he could ever hope to be. That was the only reason he wanted to be near you at all." At the look on Rose's face, as if she'd been slapped, Sybil paused. "What? Did you think he cared for you? Did you think he was your friend? You didn't think he loved you, did you? Doltish child, there is no such thing."

"Didn't you love Father?"

Sybil paused. She'd compartmentalized her mind years ago and very rarely thought directly of Rosen, except in the early morning or late at night, when she was alone. More often, his memory would sneak up on her when she was not expecting it, prompted by the little things that reminded her of him. Like neetle flowers. Rosen had been fond of them and would always bring Sybil back a crown fashioned from the yellow blooms when he'd return from hunting. His mention felt like an arrow to her heart. "I told you never to speak of him," she said quickly, eyes instantly glassing over. For the briefest moment, the unconquerable woman looked like she may fall.

Rose instantly knew she'd gone too far. "Mother..." she began, trying to apologize, but it was too late.

"No," Sybil spat, face steeling. "Unacceptable."

"Mother," Rose whined, "why?"

"Not another word," Sybil said through gritted teeth. Her glare sliced Rose. It was as if she transformed. "I came here to ease your sorrow, child, and you wound me cruelly. Whatever did I do to deserve such an ungrateful daughter? It if weren't for your blood I'd have half a mind to give you to Digory and be done with you." With the look of terror on Rose's face, Sybil callously laughed. "Kidding! I was kidding. My goodness, you are such a serious girl. I love you, my sweet daughter, you know that" Sybil said with manipulative warmth. "I wouldn't give you to him," she paused, "unless you were very bad."

Rose stared at her mother with an unamused frown.

"Have a sense of humor," Sybil said in a huff as she shoved a frilly emerald pillow towards the girl. Rose didn't respond. "I love you Rose," Sybil added, noting her pinched expression. "I tell you this to prepare you for what it will be like at Animus Rock. There will be Norland children there, I am sure. Likely Minney, Regnard... You'll need to be prepared to deal with all. It's unpleasant but it is real. I wouldn't be a good mother if I wasn't honest with you." Rose silently blinked at Sybil. "Come here, give me a hug, I demand it. You can't stay cross at me. I am your mother and I love you."

Sybil grabbed her daughter in an uncomfortable hug through the cocoon of blankets, yet Rose was stiff.

Irritated by Rose's chilly reaction, Sybil pulled away quickly and huffed before storming off.

"Ungrateful," she muttered on her way out, thinking her daughter spoiled and soft as she slammed the heavy door behind her.

THE VANGUARD SHIP, SPACE

About 2000 years ago...

A team of scientists from bloodlines Graves, Brochet, and Beaumont stood around Dymphna. She lay on an examining table in the depths of the Graves laboratory. Typically, once a Vanguard was surrendered as powerless, usually around their fifteenth birthday, Graves read their soul and determined where their traits would be the most useful to be utilized in experimentation. Which bloodline's goals and aims the specimen would align with. However, this was not a typical case.

Angelina stood at the head of the team. She lowered slightly to look at Dymphna's tracking eyes.

"She is there," Angelina said, "and powerful," she added to a slight gasp from everyone around, "but barely. As if she's a light, flickering."

Reynold stood back with the other junior Graves scientists, observing as a lesson. Angelina didn't look at him, but he felt her think of him all the same. This made his cheeks flush. He narrowed his eyes.

Drusana Brochet listened carefully, taking notes, alongside Killian Beaumont. She scratched her nose, accidently dropping her pencil. Before she could reach down, Killian twitched his finger and the pencil rose back into her hand.

"Thank you", she said, glancing at him.

"Any time," Killian replied.

"My team," Angelica continued, "has processed her vision."

"What did she say in its entirety?" Drusana asked, "For my own edification." Angelica looked at her questioningly. "My husband informed me of the jist," she said, "but I want to know her words, if you don't mind." She bowed her head slightly. Drusana, like most Brochets, apart from their longevity and regenerative healing abilities, was exceedingly beautiful and charming.

Angelica obliged with a hint of distain. She withdrew delicate spectacles and put them on. She held out her translucent tablet and read.

"I see castles. Sixteen of them. The castles are soaked in blood. Built with the bodies of the lost. Their eyes cry the blood. They show what has been lost. We are all that remain. We must save them."

"Heavy," Killian said, to a resounding chuckle, particularly from the junior Graves scientists at the back of the laboratory.

"Indeed," Angelica said, removing her spectacles.

"You believe you understand the meaning?" Drusana asked.

Angelica looked at Drusana cooly. She could not believe the woman's boldness but held her tongue. It perpetually unnerved her that she could not feed on Brochet souls. They were too powerful. Too regenerative. And the Brochet bloodline acted accordingly. They were not afraid of Graves and it showed.

"When our forefathers first began the Mission, left Earth in the home we know today, an atrocity was committed against humankind." As Angelica spoke, she paced, around the laboratory. The artificial lights lit up her haunting features. "A chemical was released to eliminate *Homo Sacrum* blood," she said.

"Yes," said Drusana. "That is our history."

Angelica looked at her cooly. "This chemical," she went on, "altered the genetics of all human beings exposed, *homo sapien* and *sacrum* alike. It removed any potential for power, spiritual or physical. It also, our research shows, had one additional unexpected effect."

"Which was?" Drusana interrupted.

This time Angelica did not look at her, for she knew she could not hide her scorn. "It impacted occipital lobe. This activated scotopic vision."

"Fascinating," Killian said. "They can see in the dark."

"How does this have anything to do with the Thorne girl?"

Drusana said. She studied the girl's pale eyes, still open wide, tracking back and forth.

"With this genetic alteration that humanity experienced," Angelica went on, "there is one key physical marker."

All in the laboratory hung on Angelica's words.

"The people of Earth now have red eyes."

WESTERVIOLET BED CHAMBER

Present Day

"Stay here, good girl," she whispered at Ellie. "This time I'll be right back. This time I promise!"

Ellie gave Rose a wary look, but obedient as ever, sulked to the bed and curled into a sad ball.

Rose left her dark chamber in the wake of sunset, body pulsing with adrenaline and anger, grief and guilt. She'd lost her only friend, and now, Mother was cross with her too. She didn't like the story about Lilli Minney at all, but she was captivated by it. She felt a strong kinship with Lilli, particularly since her mother told her that they shared similar interests. It made sense to her now why Sybil and Tomas alike wouldn't permit Rose to travel outside of the castle walls, to the Lunar Tower or Pinewood, cursed or not.

Rose walked carefully, out of her room and down the long, dimly lit halls of Westerviolet's castle. When she reached her destination, Rose didn't knock. Instead, she pushed open her mother's weighty chamber door with a protesting groan.

She gasped at what she saw. Sybil was nude atop a wide towel with a large pot of wax bubbling in the fire to her side. There were countless strips of cloth aligned next to her, in neatly organized rows.

"What are you doing?!"

Sybil jumped. "Don't sneak up on me. And shut that door. You'll cool the wax."

Rose scrunched her face. "Mother, what are..."

"Waxing," Sybil said with contempt, as if that fact should already be obvious. "Women have many tricks to be beautiful." She paused, turning her head to Rose. She smiled coyly. "This is mine."

"How does it work?"

"You are too young," Sybil replied, "but, you can stay and watch if you wish." She gestured to the bed. "Here, come over here sit over there."

Rose scurried to the bed then scooted herself back across Sybil's black bedcovers, still wrapped in her emerald sheet. She watched her mother backlit by firelight.

"I learned once that an ancient queen had her slaves pluck and tear hair from her body with hot wax pulled away in strips," Sybil told her, sharp-angled face shadowed from the dancing fire. "I perused the idea. It's better than a thornesblade. Or a ghastly newblood mane! But unlike that ancient queen, I prefer to do it myself. The ritual is soothing for me."

Kingdom-wide, fashion trends tended to align to political belief. When it came to body hair, oldblood Vanguards removed it from their legs, under their arms, and their undergarment region, typically with a thornesblade. Sybil was unique in her use of wax and prided herself on her impeccably smooth skin, compared to her peers, with ingrown hair bumps or stubble. Conversely, newblood women did not remove their hair. Instead, the more hair they had, the more attractive the newblood men considered them to be.

"Now, here, I'll show you how it works." Sybil pointed to her leg. "See all of this hair?" Rose nodded. "I'll take this stick here and drip it in the wax." Sybil grasped a hand-length, flat wooden implement. She stuck it in the viscous liquid. "Then, I'll lay a thin layer on my leg in the same direction that the hair is growing." The fire crackled and popped with fury in the dim-lit chamber. Light flickered across Sybil's nude, pale frame. Her form was tight, only lightly muscled at shoulders and abdomen while soft and amble at chest and hips. "Like this," she said, running a long strip of hot wax down her stubbled thigh in a smooth stroke. Then she picked up one of the neatly organized cloths and placed it on her waxy skin. "Take a cloth, then smooth it over the wax in the same direction you applied it," she said as she did so carefully. "Make sure there's enough at the bottom to grab hold of. That's important," she added as she placed her fingers on the lower end of the cloth below where it touched wax. "Then, pull it free."

With a horrible tearing sound, Sybil ripped the cloth from her leg in the opposite direction of the hair. After, her patch of leg looked like how chickens looked after Petra plucked them. It turned bright red with tiny dots of blood pooling at the surface.

"Didn't that hurt!?" Rose cried.

"Yes, it did," Sybil said calmly while blotting violet oil on the area with a small cloth. The oil, made from the tiny violets from which the castle and realm got its name, was reserved for Brochetbloods only and legends spoke to its power, when applied as an oil, to enchant others, enhancing beauty and allure. Pinpricks of blood mixed with the oil, giving her pallid skin a reddish tint.

"Then why do you do it?"

"Because, true beauty is pain," Sybil said. "It is a burden to bear. A curse."

Rose thought back to the stories she'd heard from her mother of the lengths that her generation and the ones before went to be beautiful. Bone corsets so tight, one could barely breathe. Face paints so thick, they marred the skin to remove. There was even a time, before the Plague, when Vanguards were as common as flies, when it's said many women would break their noses in hope of replicating the famous Calvanese bump, as it was thought to be the peak of beauty.

She grasped the stick once more and laid another strip of wax down her leg. Rose winced just watching her mother, but Sybil did not flinch.

"It doesn't look like it hurts you much."

Sybil chuckled. "I assure you it does," she said. "I've grown accustomed to it, is all." She paused to smooth a strip on her leg, moving carefully as she did. "Just because someone doesn't react to something doesn't mean they don't feel it," she said. "It might just mean they're used to the pain."

Sybil tore another strip loudly from her leg as Rose furrowed her brow. After dabbing more of the oil and discarding the used strips in a small bin, Sybil examined her progress. "Why are you here?" she asked without glancing at Rose. "Why did you interrupt me?"

"I'm sorry, Mother."

"What's that?" Sybil looked up, thick hair bouncing in a sloppy knot on her head, looping waves falling to frame her face, pointed angled cheekbones lit up with haunting shadows from the flames.

"I came here to tell you I'm sorry," Rose said quietly.

"You did? Why?"

"Because you were right and I didn't listen."

"That's true. So, what will you do from now on?"

"I'll listen to you Mother," Rose said, then added glumly, looking down at the worn carpets beneath her feet, "I know you are right."

"That's a good girl," Sybil cooed. "I love you very much. You were right to come to me."

"I know, Mother."

"Are you feeling any better?" Sybil glanced and saw Rose slowly nodding her head with eyes glassy and fists clenched. "Good. I knew you would. You're such a smart little girl, learning how to protect yourself."

She ripped another wide strip of wax from her calf, gasped at the permeating sting of hundreds of thick hairs ripped from their roots, then shivered from a jolt of adrenaline.

"You know, Rose, a lot of women would fear this. They'd prefer the nicks and the bumps, or a mane of hair instead of a few moments of pain," she said. "Don't be like them. Pain is often worth it. But to each his own. I do it as I am able to. It's helpful exercise for me, to conquer my own... self. It's useful to have the capacity for pain, Rose. If you can withstand your own pain, no one else can hurt you." Rose tried to absorb this, nodding unconvincingly. "I'll allow you to do it, wax I mean, when you're a bit older, if you wish. Once you bleed. But only if you wish. Not all are fit for it."

"I will, Mother!" Rose cried quickly. "I'm not afraid." She

leaned forward from her seat on the bed. "I'm like you are."

Laughing, Sybil said, "Very well. You will someday. For now, you are too young and you need settle for witness alone." She ripped another wide strip loudly from the other side of her thigh.

Rose jumped again in empathic pain.

WESTERVIOLET SOUTH WING

"Is it true what they say," Sybil raised a coy brow, "that those beast eyes can see in the dark?"

It was far into the depths of evening. Sybil was smooth and clothed in a tight bodice and draped skirt, billowing down to her pointed Baneswood leather-worked boots. Around her shoulders, a shawl. She was almost always cold.

Here, in the belly of the castle's South Wing, the air was cool and moist. The light, dim. The air, heavy with secrets.

"Yes, it's true." Digory smiled affectionately, gaze set on Sybil. "I've told you that."

"I know but it is so hard to believe you," Sybil said flightily, studying her winsome companion's familiar face. He stood across the cellar from her in his typical Guardsman attire, well fitted to his honed frame, emerald cloak hung around his shoulders, back to the massive casks of Animus wine in huge musky wooden barrels. Digory was a few years older than Sybil and solidly built in intensive athleticism. He wore a stern, yet mischievous expression that melted whenever she spoke.

"You are so loyal," Sybil cooed as she walked towards him, boots clacking against stone, dark skirt bunching about her thighs like a churning storm.

Digory looked at his feet. "It's the least I can do, Lady."

Sybil traced his strong jaw with her eyes. "It was good of me to convince father to spare you, wasn't it?"

His head shot up.

"I was young," he said quickly. "It was so, so many years ago now. I didn't appreciate…"

Sybil interrupted. "I lied to the girl because I had to, you know?" Although she'd never admit it to herself, Sybil felt deep discomfort over misleading her daughter. But it had to be done. "It was for her own good."

"Yes," Digory said blankly. He wasn't sure what Sybil was talking about, but he could surmise. He knew Sybil never spoke of their arrangement outside of the castle walls yet had assumed she'd told her own daughter. The idea that he was totally Sybil's shameful secret sat poorly with him.

"You don't agree? You don't think I should have?"

Digory bit at his cheek. "I didn't say that" he said, thinking she shouldn't have. The girl seemed smart. He would have been truthful with her, if it were his decision. Which it wasn't. Nothing was ever his decision when it came to Sybil. She held all the shells. She always had.

"You might have well. I saw that face you made."

"I didn't make a face." He scratched at his beard, looking away. He knew better than to tell Sybil the truth.

"That boy was not to be trusted," Sybil said. "He was not loyal. Not like you, my dear sweet Dig."

Digory half smiled, knowing the boy he'd killed in Pinewood was as loyal as they came. "You convinced me, Lady."

Sybil glared back in a scathing beam. "What's that mean?"

"Nothing at all."

"The boy had to go." Sybil spoke mostly to herself. "It would not have turned out like you and me. My daughter, while much like me, has too much of her father in her to be able to handle a wild beast. And to interact with any earthblood is tantamount to excursion with the level of animalistic behavior I've witnessed. They are meek creatures with weak constitutions. And their silly beliefs cripple them." She paused. "I mean you."

"Yes, Lady," Digory responded automatically, hands clenched behind his back with his strong chest puffed out.

"It doesn't sound like you agree with me."

"I didn't say that."

"You didn't have to."

"You're paranoid," he said, relaxing slightly, enchanted by Sybil's intensity, with a slight grin and twinkle in his eye. He loved her, no matter how evil she could be. At times, because of how evil she could be.

"I didn't tell her who you are," Sybil continued, taking a few delicate steps towards him. "I changed the outcome of the events. But your treachery was real. And it was perfect example for her not to trust that stable boy. It had to be done."

"I'm convinced," Digory bowed his head, hiding his amused grin. Sybil was in a world all her own. Digory knew he was just living in it.

"You know, you never did tell me why you did it."

His head popped back up. "Did what?"

"Focus. Pay attention," she said angrily. "Stole mother's things." Sybil spanned the length of the room until she was standing a pace or two in front of Digory. He gazed upon her elegant, timeless beauty with wide eyes.

He recalled that night so many years ago, when Tomas discovered Digory had in fact committed the deed. He'd stolen Sybil's late mother's glass bead necklace. He was just a child then, large for his age, with the same mischievous glare. He could see it in his mind's eye as if it was yesterday. Standing in the Lord's Study with Tomas's wrath raining down on him, and Sybil hiding behind his knees.

"Does it matter?" he asked with a sigh. "After all these years? Can't we let it rest? I am in your service now. That is what's important."

"Not at all," Sybil said curtly, gaze unrelenting. "Tell me why."

Digory slowly met her eyes. "I didn't know I'd be caught."

"Awful!"

"Let me finish," Digory stepped forward. He grabbed Sybil's shoulder firmly with a calloused hand, remembering how the weighty Winter Garden necklace felt in his small grip. He'd never before touched such finery. "I meant to bring it back."

Sybil stared indignantly at the man in shock, then grinned wide. "Why in the Kingdom would you do that? Steal my dead mother's necklace just to return it? Absurd. I will never understand your earthblood minds," she added flippantly, gesturing with her hand, yet not pulling away from his grasp.

She would never admit it, but a tingle ran up and down her spine whenever he touched her. As when she touched him.

Digory sighed. He dropped his grip on her then scratched his beard in frustration.

"Dig, look at me," Sybil said warmly. He immediately obeyed. "I am serious, you know? I want to know. Tell me why you'd do such a thing. For years I've wondered. I will command you as your Lady, if I must." She paused. "Don't make me do it, Dig."

She put both her hands on his. His body buzzed.

"It is doltish," he said gruffly, avoiding her eyes. "Leave it."

"I won't."

"Don't make me tell you, Lady."

Sybil frowned; patience gone. "You heard me. I want to know. I command you, tell me why you stole Mother's things."

Digory's flaming eyes met hers. "I wanted you," he said in a deep, breathy growl of a whisper.

"You wanted me?"

He sighed loudly from the back of his throat. "I hoped for a reward. I wanted to ask your father for a position, and…"

"What!?" Sybil squealed, visibly amused. "Why would you ever think he would…" She paused. "What is it, Dig?"

"To marry you, spiteful woman." Digory shoved her away and walked to pace, rubbing his beard in thought.

"Oh, come back here," Sybil said teasingly. "Don't be gruff with me." Sulking, Digory ignored her, studying the casks on the far wall. "Must I command you?" she asked his back.

"Must you remind me of my place?!" Digory shouted as he spun, baritone reverberating about the cellar. A squeak of startled rats nestled between dark casks followed. "Must you so abuse me?! After all I have done for you?!"

There were all the times he'd spied on Tomas's dealings, on her command, risking his own life if he were to be found out. The times he'd threatened the Vice Lords to vote the way Sybil thought best. Times he'd stolen from the missive to bring Sybil news before anyone else. And certainly, all the times he had killed for her, for protection, or politics or simply for sport. It wasn't Tomas, or the Lair, or the Guardsmen who created Digory. Sybil was who had made him the man he was today.

"Now the truth comes out!" Sybil's shrill cadence dripped venom. "All *you* have done for *me*!?" Her tone rose, growing more and more indignant. "I saved your life! What more is there? Tell me, please! Enlighten me," Sybil snarled. "Father wanted to slit your throat. You owe me everything!" She took a three furious paces, skirts swishing, then shoved him angrily.

"What is wrong with you?" Digory cried. Face after face, bloody scene after bloody scene flashed before his eyes. "I have murdered for you!" he shouted at her, recalling all he had done in Brochet's honor. In her honor.

"You have, and will again," she said coolly, crossing her arms at her chest. "You will do anything I say and more."

"I will, and happily!" Digory shouted. Emotion shattered in his voice like glass. "I live to serve you!"

"Then, what is the issue?"

"After all I have done, I expect a bit more, I don't know…" Digory said, flustered, pausing. At the head of an unwinnable fight Digory was unflappable, yet in front of Sybil, he trembled. "…respect. You kick me like a dog. You shouldn't treat me like that."

"You are a dog. No better than the hunting hounds," she said icily. "You disappoint me, Dig. Your lowly blood is showing. There is no way to treat anyone. I'll treat you with the respect you command. Right now, that is none, my red-eyed friend."

"You are heartless."

"You are brainless. The irony is glorious for a piece of earthblood scum like you to accuse a pure oldblood like me of having no heart."

"I love you, vile woman! It is why despite everything in me, I do whatever you command. At the end of the day, you are my world. You are everything, Sybil."

"Enough," she said through clenched teeth. "I've commanded you not to speak that way."

He took a pleading step towards her. "How are you so beautiful and so cruel?"

"Digory," Sybil's tone warned. "My patience grows thin."

"Sybil," Digory rushed towards her, pushing her up against the casks. Her body tensed. "As does mine."

"Digory," Sybil breathed.

He put his nose to the crease of her neck, smelling her soft skin. His hands fought with the flounce of her skirts, searching for her smooth thighs.

She burned with desire. Her mind screamed angrily but her body ached. She was so lonely. But he was so handsome. And his passion was so strong.

Digory reached her leg and gripped it tightly in one large hand. His other found her face. His callouses caught on her delicate skin. She shut her eyes.

Digory kissed her neck, timidly. She relaxed slightly.

"Digory," she said pleadingly.

"Sybil," he growled in her ear.

This couldn't happen. "Digory get off of me," she said in a whisper, but he continued to grope her. "Digory," she breathed again. He didn't stop. His lips found her collar bone. His hand gripped her so tightly he nearly bruised her.

Sybil held her dagger up to his neck. It was small, made from Eversands glass that her father gave her when she was first betrothed. Told her to never let a man get the upper hand.

Digory sighed, releasing her. "You *have* gone mad."

Sybil's eyes narrowed. She was the type to strike out whenever she felt attacked, no matter how slightly.

Her voice echoed shrilly about the cellar. "If you say another word, I'll tell your Lord," she hissed. "I'll undo everything I have done for you as a punishment for your ingratitude! How can you do this to me? Accusing me of these awful things when you are the monster with the cursed earth blood. Woe is me to befriend such a gruesome soul. And yet I care for you. This is my curse that I am too kind and care too much, despite how much it may wound me. I try too hard to be kind and everyone is ungrateful. I have done all I can for you. Dig, you are a lost soul if you continue to fight me for one more moment! You know I will do it. Do not push me." Digory glared silently at

Sybil in paramount hatred mixed with supreme longing as she went on. "Nothing? Are you sure?" Sybil prodded brutally. His eyes spoke volumes, but Digory adjusted his trousers then crossed his muscled arms wordlessly with a rustle of chainmail. "There. Good," Sybil retorted. "Now, on to business."

"You're really going to talk affairs right now?" Sybil always surprised Digory. It's part of why she intoxicated him.

She lowered her arms, placing one on her popped hip. "What better a time? Just because you are a soulless leach does not stop the realm from running," she said, grinning.

"Ouch," Digory replied with half a smile.

All was well between them once more.

Sybil removed a folded letter sealed with emerald wax pressed with the Brochet ouroboros from a hidden sleeve behind her draped skirts. "Take this to Anstout," she said, thrusting it at Digory forcefully.

"What is it?" he asked, taking the document from her, turning it over, wax emblem grazing his palm.

"A letter."

"I see that," Digory answered dryly. "What's it read?"

"If I wanted you to know I would have told you."

"Who am I delivering it to?"

"Anstout," Sybil said.

Digory sighed. *Gravesblood*, he thought, chill running down his spine. The rumors alone were enough to terrify him.

Graves was the most sinister of bloodlines, still openly experimenting on the natives in their realm despite the Blood Council ruling forbidding such action so many years ago. Seemingly due to their realm's inhospitable location, unpredictability of the Gravesblood Vanguards and the ferocity of their army, the King permitted their misdeeds. Gravesblood, while historically menacing, were even more terrifying of late.

"Which one of them?"

"Hector," Sybil replied. "Don't give it to the old man. Hector Graves must be the one to receive this. It goes to him alone."

"Why not use the Missive?" he asked, but Sybil only glared.

"What's it read?" Digory tried again.

"That's none of your concern."

"Does the Lord know?"

"What do you think?"

"Well then, *why?*"

"Don't question me," Sybil said slowly, each syllable a threat. "Do as you're told."

"This isn't Dale or Minney, Morfit even," Digory argued back, speaking with his hands, thinking of what he knew of the Kingdom and her bloodlines. "I need to know what I'm walking into. I fear even the Brochet emblem may not protect me there. Not at Anstout."

"I assure you it will," Sybil dismissed. "We have an alliance."

Digory frowned. He'd heard the stories. Natives who crossed the Anstout border never returned. Ever. No one knew what went on in the Gravesblood Black Hills. The Gravesblood realm was said to be far, far worse than Lyonshall with its mines, Ravenshroud with its fields, or even the Confines with its squalor.

Sybil studied him, shifting her weight to rest a hand on her other hip. "Do you not hear? I say you are protected."

"They are savages."

"How so?" Sybil asked with an amused purse of her lips. "How do you know? Have you ever met a Graves? Spoken to one directly? They are actually quite refined."

Digory laughed. "Come on," he said.

Everyone knew Graves had dead blood.

"You shouldn't listen to rumors," Sybil replied blithely, batting her unlined eyes. "And even if the rumors are true," which she knew that they were, "who am I to judge their bloodline? After it is said and done, Graves and Brochet aims are similar. They aim to overtake the Deadlands. Brochet aims to overtake death itself."

Digory was sceptical. "You can't deny the stories."

"Oh..." Sybil dismissed him with a sweep of her hand. "Father has told me stories of the great Lord Robert, the first true Graves ally. The only Brochet survivor of the Plague. The great hero of the Blood Wars. He was the first to begin the Green Wing tradition, you know. Before that, Brochets wed like Beaumonts. Can you imagine?"

"How long ago?"

"Two hundred years," Sybil said. "Maybe more, I can't remember now. I'm sure it's recorded on a dusty Animus parchment somewhere if you are truly curious of the exact date."

"I don't care," Digory said blankly. He truly didn't. His focus was on the future, not the past.

"I figured you didn't."

"It's different having done it in the past," Digory argued. "I hear Basil Graves is a monster, today. Hector has condemned him in front of Council, but it's rumoured he's still an avid supporter of his uncle's pursuits privately. Herman is probably in on it too. You should hear what the men from the Omen border say."

Hector's uncle Basil Graves was Elder of Echo's Omen, the only realm not specific to a Vanguard bloodline and directly North of Westerviolet. Hector's brother Herman, however, was scandalously moderate for being Gravesblood. He lived at Animus Rock instead of at Anstout or Echo's Omen with other family members.

"Nonsense," Sybil said, shaking her head. "Herman Graves wouldn't harm a beetle. You mustn't listen to rumors. I admire their ingenuity," she added wistfully.

"It's dangerous to be involved with those people." Digory remembered the only time he'd been in the presence of Gravesblood, when Basil Graves visited Lord Tomas, yet once was enough to leave a branded impression. How all the air felt like it had been sucked out of the room when he entered. Like the man himself emitted frost. "I shouldn't even call deadbloods people," he added, glancing upwards briefly, "They're inhuman. I've heard stories that..."

"Don't be silly," Sybil interrupted light-heartedly. "You'll deliver this letter. I'll have no complaints."

"No complaints but at least tell me if I should get out of there quickly. Shooting the messenger is a true phenomenon. I've witnessed it, Sybil," Digory said intimately. *Cursed First*, he thought, *I've shot the messenger myself before.* "And in this case, the messenger is me."

"It's hard to say how he'll take it," she replied carelessly. "Best be cautious."

"I figured as much."

"Is that a problem?"

"No, just…" He searched for the right words, sensing her frustration. "I caution you not to trust them. From what I've heard…"

"Dig, enough," Sybil said with pointed familiarity. She placed a hand on his shoulder. A buzz ran down her spine. "You've heard whispers from half-brained earthblood. My bloodline and Gravesblood remain old allies. I won't have you interjecting your lowly opinion this way. You do not know. You must do as you're told." Her eyes darted back and forth, boring deep into his. "Trust me," Sybil finally said with intimate inflection. "Is that understood?"

"Yes, Lady," Digory replied, half smiling in irony. Sybil was the only one he had any trust in at all.

She pulled her hand back abruptly. "Don't look at me like that."

"Like what?" he asked, studying her like once would a beautiful specimen behind glass.

"Like that."

"Like what?" His red eyes danced like flames.

"You're infuriating," she sighed.

"I'll deliver your letter."

"Thank you," Sybil said hotly, turning prominent nose up at him. "You don't have a choice, you know."

He smiled. "I know."

"There is one more thing you can do," Sybil said, "to ensure your safe passage."

"There is?"

She nodded, leaning towards him, then whispered for a long moment in his ear. Digory pulled back from her with a questioning expression.

She told him to wear a green-plumed hat to present himself to Gravesblood, like what they wear in Wraithswail.

"Really?" Digory asked her after Sybil told him to purchase one before he entered Anstout's realm. "You're sure?" Littlebell or Animus Rock should have the wares available for purchase, she'd said. He'd seen the Guildsman's attendants adorned in that silly fashion during Hidden Den's last visit to Westerviolet. "I'll look..." he paused, imagining himself following her orders, "ridiculous!"

"Absolutely," Sybil confirmed with a wide smile. "I am sure that you will."

ANIMUS ROCK THIRD TOWER

About 100 years ago…

The dimpled boy had other plans for his life. He was not prepared to submit to his fate, not yet, not like this. He waited for nine moons, hoping and praying the babe was not charmed like the old woman predicted, but alas, she was. The cursed little snot was born with blue eyes.

It was all he could do not to press a pillow to its stupid face as it slept.

Amos Minney had spent a lifetime preparing to be elderclaim. He'd rejected unsavoury love affairs and refused to go hunting for illegal mad honey with his friends, all to retain his reputation. He'd diligently executed his duties and studied what he'd been told to study, all because he owed it as his duty to his blood realm. Amos took his birth right more seriously than anyone else in the Kingdom. He deserved Littlebell's helm.

Certainly, more than a stupid babe.

He was tired of watching his mother slowly lose bits and pieces of Littlebell's border lands to Brochet ambition. He was tired of sitting in advisement meetings, only to watch Morfit take advantage of his mother's trusting ways. He knew he was young, but elderclaim gave him power. Clout. He planned to leverage his title into a seat on Council so he could truly make changes to the Kingdom.

He would reinforce the Morfit alliance. He'd clean up Littlebell's drug-infested streets. He'd be more welcoming towards the Faith. He'd attack the sordid bare houses, sullying Littlebell's good name. He'd better police her economy. To do all of this, he'd impose proper taxes. All Amos wanted was some power over his beloved realm, to make Littlebell more respectable in the eyes of other Vanguards.

And he was tired of being teased. Especially by Lucien and Bin.

This was Amos's last solstice at Academy before he graduated into the true Vanguard world. Up until a few moons ago, he was Littlebell's rightful blood heir and held elderclaim. Now, everything he had so recently lost felt like a hot ember in his heart. It was burning a hole through him.

Sitting in the Third Tower Lessonroom for one of the last times ever, hearing the oldblood boys' taunts, Amos felt his charred heart turn to ash in his chest.

"My father says Minney blood is no better than earth blood," Bin Norland meanly teased, black eyes flashing. The boy's strong features and stature spoke to his Norland heritage, yet his coloring hinted at distant Beaumont ancestry. Which was no surprise to anyone. Norlands were mutts of every type of blood apart from native.

"Your father is the son of a kidnapping rapist," Amos retorted, referring to Bin's grandfather, the infamous Gauthier Norland, tired of the younger boy's taunts.

At that, Bin Norland and Lucien Brochet together laughed.

"If that's what you call it," Bin replied with a mean smile. "My father survived the Plague *and* the Blood Wars. My father is a true Vanguard man. A living god. What has your father done?" he paused, eyes taunting Amos like two crows squawking at him. "That's right, he's done nothing! Not a thing! Because he is nothing!" Bin added, then snickered. "I almost forgot, because your father is *earthblood*."

Amos felt his blood boiling but remained calm. If he'd learned anything from all the years he'd spent at Academy with Bin and Lucien, it was that fighting their taunts only fuelled them. He did his best to steel himself to the pale boy's jeering. His only weapon was patience.

"He can't help his lowly blood Bin," Lucien interjected with a smile. No matter what Lucien Brochet said, regardless of how mean-spirited it was, he made it sound warm and charming. "Take pity on your lessers, remember what they teach us?"

"I am not a lesser," Amos grumbled under his breath.

"What was that?" Bin asked, followed by a mean laugh. "It almost sounded as if you were talking back to better men."

Amos rolled his eyes and sighed. He was not in the mood for this. "Come on, Lessonmaster Deila will be back soon. Stop it Bin."

"Hiding behind the Lessonmaster's legs like the Minney you are," Bin observed with dark raised eyebrows. "Can't even converse like a man. How you are going to graduate this year, I know not," he chuckled. "And I have no idea how you will find the stones to be Lord of your realm. I bet if I kicked between your legs right now, I'd hit a soft cunt."

Lucien threw back his head in a loud belly shaking laugh, hazel eyes twinkling, thick auburn hair jostling while he smiled. "But Bin," he finally said to the side while holding Amos's eye," haven't you heard the news?"

"Nay," Bin grunted.

Outside, warm sunbeams cast through the time-warped windowpanes to their far right. The Lessonmaster had not arrived yet and the boys sat atop the desks themselves instead of at seats. Both Bin and Lucien had legs widespread and elbows resting on their knees, billowing their matching grey robes wide. Amos cowered against a cool stone wall.

Whatever Lucien was laughing about was so funny that he could barely control himself. The fifteen years boy snickered and his eyes watered until finally he slowed his breathing enough to speak. "Bin, I can't believe you don't know. It's a joke from the Ancestors themselves!"

Bin was smiling but started to frown at Lucien's goading, unhappy he wasn't the first to hear the news. He was always trying to prove something, true to his Norland name. He waited for praise like a dog at Lucien's feet.

"Out with it, Brochet," he grunted.

Amos tried to brace himself, assuming Lucien Brochet knew about the charmed babe, but nothing could prepare him for the feeling of dismal defeat that washed over him when he heard the words.

"The Minney boy lost elderclaim!" Lucien shouted with a

wide smile, pointing at Amos like it wasn't obvious who he was talking about.

Bin's sixteen-year-old face brightened. "Aye?" he looked towards Lucien to confirm. Lucien happily nodded.

"How did that happen?" Bin asked with wonderment, obviously pleased yet still visibly frustrated he wasn't in the know. "You are eldest son," he said not as a question but more like he was wanting Amos to prove him wrong. What had he missed?

Amos loudly sighed. "It is not official," he said through clenched teeth, lowering his sad brown eyes to the ground.

"That's not what my father said," Lucien countered smartly.

Amos shot up his head with an ever-proud gleam in his eye. "What did your father say?"

"My father said that your mother birthed a blue-eye." Amos's eyes widened. A smile crept across Bin's face. "That's why she sent a Morfit proxy to Council for the last two solstices," Lucien added, matter of fact.

How does Brochet always know everything? Amos thought to himself.

"She was with child," Lucien said, if it wasn't already obvious, "and that child is another blue-eye."

Bin had a dumbstruck look on his face. "I thought they were just legends," he said in awe. "Blue-eyes, I mean."

Amos internally cringed, not sure who he hated more in that moment, the oldblood boys or his own kin.

Lucien shook his head 'no'. "Not legends," he said with knowing authority, yet didn't explain further.

"Well?" Bin looked at Amos, shifting his broad muscled shoulders to face the slight Minney boy. "Is it truth?" he asked, mentally rejoicing at the news, already believing it truth, since Lucien said it was so.

His mother Sia had sworn Amos to keep the babe's birth quiet, but Amos didn't care. He knew that child would lead not only to his own ruin but to Littlebell's as well. He knew whoever she grew into would be no match for the type of men Bin and Lucien would grow to be. Without putting much more thought into it than that, Amos did what he felt he had to do.

Amos slightly nodded. "Truth," he said with a half-smile, pleased he was taking his own life into his own command. "A charmed babe was born."

"Why does he smile?" Bin looked at Lucien, gesturing over his shoulder with his left thumb. "It's as if he's glad he no longer has Littlebell's throne."

Amos's smile fell. "Much can happen in eighteen years," he mumbled cryptically without thinking, irritated. He glanced out the window.

Lucien caught what Amos said. His wheels began turning. "What is it you're planning, Minney?"

"I... I..." Amos stuttered. He hadn't begun to give the feeling he had bubbling in his chest credence, not until now. Whatever love or affection he felt for the charmed babe was taken away with his right to elderclaim. This betrayal was enough to set him in motion. "I.." he faltered. "I don't know what I'm planning," he finally said honestly, deep brown eyes meeting Lucien's playful hazel.

Lucien was instantly proud of the Minney boy, realizing he'd underestimated him fully. Maybe he would be useful after all. "It would be unfortunate if something were to happen to the babe," Lucien said, nearly hissing like a snake, eyes sparkling with malice.

"What are you saying Brochet?" Bin grunted. Lucien met Bin's eye and the young man instantly realized what he meant. "Oh, right," he added. "A shame," he said, trying to act like he'd been able to think as quickly as Lucien.

Noticing his duller accomplice's slow reaction, Lucien slightly smiled. Bin might be thick, but oh, was he useful.

"I do not want harm to befall her," Amos said instantly, stomach knotting at the thought of causing his kin pain. He paused. He reminded himself of everything the babe stole from him. "I... I just want my elderclaim back," he added, then chewed on his lip, deep dimple in his left cheek while he waited for the oldblood boys' reaction.

"Certainly not," Lucien said, smiling still. He knew how

valuable the blue-eye was. If he was able to obtain blue-eye blood for the Lair's experiments, well, he'd ensure his place on the Ancestor Walk forever. His infamy would be undeniable. "No harm to befall her, just that she's…" he paused, "removed from your concern," Lucien finally said.

Amos pressed his brows deeply in thought for long moments. He heard his mother's cautious voice wavering in his ear from not a moon before, warning him of the oldblood realms and their wiles. Then he heard his father's gentle cadence breaking the news that he was no longer to be elderclaim, that there was another child. The gut-wrenching agony of losing his birth right was made worse by how little anyone in his family cared. How did they not see that he would be better for Littlebell than any stupid charmed babe?

Amos brought his eyes up to meet Lucien's and he slowly nodded. "How will it be done?" he asked in a hush.

Lucien hadn't gotten that far but was adept at thinking on the fly. He'd already been taught the Brochet ways well. "It cannot be yet," he said knowingly. "We must wait until the babe is grown. Once she's older we can make it appear she's run away on her own or murdered by raiders. Regardless, once she's grown no one will search for her. Not like they would if she disappeared as a new babe."

The boys all mulled over this plan for what felt like a long time, bright sunlight flickering off their intense faces.

Amos solemnly blinked. "It must be before the babe is eighteen years," he said slowly, lowering his voice to a rasp above a whisper. "She must not receive elderclaim in ceremony," he added emphatically.

"Yes, yes," Lucien said offhandedly, half-smiling, distracted, imagining how honored he would be in Westerviolet when he brought back a blue-eye.

"Brochet," Amos said solemnly. He took a step towards the mischievous oldblood boy. "I am serious. Your blood can have her, I'll even help you take her, but only if it's before she's deigned elderclaim. If not, then it's…"

"Quiet *earthblood*," Bin growled at Amos, taking a step

forward, stopping him before he reached Lucien with a wide palmed hand on his chest. "You heard him," he added, gesturing with his head to Lucien. "We'll see it done. You'll have your elderclaim."

"Thank you," Amos replied, smiling wide, relief cascading over his shoulders like a heavy Wraithswail rain, quelling the deep kernel of guilt he had buried deep in the back of his mind.

I am to be elderclaim, he thought happily. *All is right.*

WESTERVIOLET GARDENS

Present Day

Digory strolled casually through the Moat Gardens, boots crunching against small pebbles. Sticky, overripe lemons piled beneath precisely manicured trees either side of him. These trees were more decorative than productive. Westerviolet was widely known for lemons, it was the realm's main export, and all four Vice Provinces were laden with orchards along with barley fields. And although the Moat Gardens' lemons could technically be eaten, tradition held that the fruits were allowed to ripen and then fall of their own accord, as an offering to the Ancestors.

Beyond the lemon trees were rows of neatly maintained bushes, squat with waxy leaves. Scattered amongst the bushes were delicate primpetals, each with four petals in faint pink, with magenta veins and a pale center, like bloodshot eyes watching Digory pass by. Beyond the bushes and the primpetals, the black mirrored moat teemed with yellow-eyed river fangs, known for their paralyzing venom. They too watched Digory, or so it felt. This time of year, they were particularly active and the dark waters teemed with them.

Digory appreciated the tranquillity the Moat Gardens brought, particularly on late evening walks after secret interludes with Sybil. It gave him time to think away from the ranks of his fellow Guardsman. It's not that the other Guardsmen were not good comrades. They were. The best, in fact. The Guardsman were tight knit, however, although expert soldiers, many were not the brightest. And Digory, with his high intelligence, often preferred silence to arm wrestling contests and crass jokes about maidens.

As he walked pebbles crunched underfoot and birds chirped

shrilly in warn of daybreak, but the sky was still dark. Bleak. It was not yet first light. Digory was distracted and deep in thought after his interaction with Sybil. He yawned and breathed in stagnant warm air. He bit at his lip and pinched his brow as he mulled over his options. Journey to Anstout was no small matter.

A high-pitched voice squeaked from over his shoulder. "Hey! You!" Digory instantly froze with a hand hovering over his dagger. "Who is that? What are you doing after dark? You are not on patrol!"

Digory whispered, "Curses," underneath his heavy cloak hood.

"Who goes there!?" the voice squeaked again.

"Couldn't sleep," Digory said as he turned, lowering his hood slowly to reveal his strong bearded jaw and intense flaming eyes. He dropped his hands peacefully.

"What are you doing here, Guard Digory?" the unbearded, pimple-faced teen grilled in the chirp-filled moonlight. The guard's dark metal helmet, hammered and rounded to his skull, with a triangular nose guard and leather strap, was a too big and flopped about atop hair braided in plaits down to his jaw. The popular Westerviolet style jutted out from the ill-fitting helmet.

Digory looked the gangly guard up and down with a smirk. "How old are you?" Digory asked. He had little respect for any man on dawn post, besides, the boy's countenance didn't help his cause.

"Hey," the young guard whined, tan cheeks burning red. "I am a Guardsman of Westerviolet! Do not mock me!"

"Give it a rest," Digory dismissed. "I'm just on a walk."

"It isn't your patrol! You are not permitted to be..."

"I said, shut up. I don't care where I'm permitted to be. Whether or not something is 'permitted' has no bearing on whether I do it."

The boy shook his head, skin of his weak chin pulling back and forth. "No, no. You're in violation." He stepped forward, puffing out his chest. "You must come with me."

Digory laughed. "I have about ten years and half a man's weight on you. What are you going to do? Make me?"

"I repeat, you are in viola…"

"I heard," Digory interrupted wearily. "I've had a rough moon. I'm out here clearing my head. Let it slide."

Displeasure plastered the young Guardsman's face. "No! I will not. I am a sworn member of the Westerviolet Guardsmen, as my father before me!"

Digory shut his eyes briefly and rubbed his temple, then took a step. "Okay," he sighed, opening his eyes, realizing this gnat wasn't going to stop buzzing easily. "What is your name?"

"Aslf," the teen said proudly, weak chin up. His voice cracked and he coughed twice afterwards to recover.

"Pleasure to meet you Aslf," Digory gestured to him with left fist up, in standard Guardsman form. Aslf returned the gesture proudly. "Goodbye," Digory finished the salute.

"Do not turn on me!" Aslf commanded, pride dropping to scorn.

Yet Digory ignored him. He didn't have time for this. Aslf was a lower Guardsman, barely elevated enough to wash Digory's boots much less question him, in Digory's mind anyway. He turned towards the North Gate where he was initially headed but Aslf lunged forward with his left hand, grabbing Digory by his cloaked shoulder. On instinct, Digory withdrew his dagger and swung to confront the attack, dark emerald cloak rising up and back behind him like a fearsome mossy defix. He smacked the young man with the backside of the dagger's hilt in his ridiculously loose helmet with an echoing clang.

The young Guardsman crumpled to the pebbly path in a heap, unconscious.

"You should have left it alone, kid," Digory said as he looked cautiously over each shoulder.

Violence against a uniformed Guardsman was absolutely forbidden and punishable by death. He wasn't sure even Sybil could save him, if his deed were to be discovered. Trying to formulate a plan, Digory crouched carefully and grabbed the victim's sweaty hands, then dragged him through the wiry violet grass. The boy was thin and Digory was strong, so it was easy work.

He laid the body in a shadow behind the fourth knotted oak tree with its massive trunk charred in a fork.

Then Digory ran his hand over his short hair, took a deep breath and assessed the scene. He lowered his eyes. As he studied the acorns at his feet, he audibly sighed. Digory's neck hair prickled and his gaze shot up at a loud splash from the moat. Just snakes hunting frogs, he assured himself. He exhaled slowly.

He scratched his beard then took a knee beside the irritating boy's unconscious body. He didn't feel anything apart from inconvenienced. In an instant, an idea came to him, and Digory removed boy's dagger from his own hip. It was carved fully of green Eversands desert glass, as all the Guardsman daggers were, with ornate etchings in the hilt and an impossibly precise, perpetually sharp blade.

Digory wrapped the boy's hand around the weapon as if he was holding it on his own accord. Then, he used his own hand to steady the unconscious boy's hand, dragging the dagger's precise blade clean across his throat, legendary sharpness of the glass gliding through his tan skin with ease. After the deed was done, Digory let the boy's hand fall naturally with a dead thud, then stood to assess his work.

Sticky blood poured in a river down the front of Aslf's dark armor and emerald cloak, pooling in a lake beneath the charred forked oak. Once it was clear the boy was dead, Digory methodically wiped his hands on the wiry violets until no trace of blood remained, then sauntered calmly through the cobalt dawn.

-

It didn't take long to reach the stable. Digory expected to find it empty and planned to take a steed that night. He had decided to speed up his plans. Better to be gone before the body he left under the fourth oak was discovered.

Digory shoved open the creaking stable door and took

forceful steps inside. Much to his annoyance, he was rudely confronted by a young man bellowing angrily.

"WHERE IS HE?!"

Just my fortune, Digory thought. "What the curse is it now?"

"My brother!?"

"My fortune tonight," Digory said out loud, shaking his head in self-pity. "I cannot believe my cursed fortune. What the curses?!" he shouted upwards, at no one in particular. He didn't believe in the Ancestors. If they existed, they betrayed him long ago.

"What are you doing here!?" the indignant young man with almond-shaped eyes cried as he stepped of the fourth stable. "I return home and my horses are un-watered, fed, or cared for! My brother is nowhere to be found. Now, a trespasser. I see you wear Guard's cloak. Did the Lord send you?" The young man shakily held a rusty sword out in front of him. The fear in his voice was palpable. Digory glanced to the weapon. "This may not look like much but I... I am skilled in its use."

"I have no doubt." Digory seethed sarcasm. He pointed at the weapon, nearly impressed. "Where did you get that?"

"I am Stablemaster!" The man's voice faltered, yet his explanation held. Stablemasters were permitted one weapon, although it was intended to be reserved for travel, for the horses' protection from black wolves or alike. "Why are you here?" he demanded Digory shakily. "What happened to my brother?"

Digory took a step. "Brother?"

"Collen," the young man clarified hopefully, anger lifting, lowering his rusted sword slightly. "A small version of me. Skinny with long legs. Crooked teeth. Left him here not six moons ago."

"Ah," Digory replied knowingly. *The pup I put down in Pinewood*, Digory thought. He nodded.

The young man took an eager step. "You know what's become of him?"

"Alas, I know the lad. It is a pity."

"Out with it!"

"I hate to tell you."

"You must."

"He kidnapped the little Lady." That much at least was true. Mostly true.

"No," the young man said under his breath, glancing down, then up, stepping closer. "Col would never."

"We went after him," Digory lied, shrugging, "but the boy escaped."

"No…"

Digory took another more confident step. "Heard he was headed for Littlebell," he said. "That's what the girl told us when she came back, in tatters from walking nearly a half a creed in Pinewood alone. It's a blessing she survived."

"I can't," the young man paused, squinting his eyes, white knuckle gripping his sword as if waiting for it to give him a final reprieve. "I can't believe it."

"I'm afraid it's true," Digory said coolly. He patted the young Stablemaster on his shoulder as the man slowly lowered his sword fully to rest. The tip sank into manured dirt and hay. "My condolences."

"I can't stay here," he said under his breath, wriggling his shoulders to shake off Digory's hand. The young man walked a few paces away to hover aside a light beige stallion in the closest stall.

"Where do you intend to go?"

"I can't stay in a place with so many memories," he replied. He turned back to Digory. "Everyone I have ever loved has died or left here," he added distantly, thinking of the morning Collen found their father, knives of emotion heavy in his tone. "It's time I leave too."

"What of the law?" Everyone knew that earthborn like him couldn't just leave Westerviolet, not without permission anyway. This young man wasn't under Sybil's protection like Digory was.

"Curse the law," he boiled.

"If that's the case," Digory spoke like a Demos, eyes darting with his mounting plot, trying to sell his idea. "Come with me."

Distraught, the young man glanced up. "Come with you where?"

"I've been tasked with a delivery," Digory explained. "I'm headed to Anstout."

"Anstout?" The young man scoffed loudly, nearly smiling, raising his blond eyebrows in disbelief. "No one just *goes* to Anstout."

Digory ignored him. "Assist me on the road. I could use one knowledgeable of the beasts. I haven't had as much experience with them, although I assure you that you'll be protected," he said as he partly unsheathed his Eversands dagger so it flashed a bit. "I intend to pass through Littlebell, so you could look for your fiend of a brother." With that, the young man's head shot up. "What is your name?" Digory asked him.

"Ryd," the young man said, hands clenched tight on the lowered rusted sword. His grip was ridiculous, speaking to his inexperience.

"Ryd, you will join me, then? Help me with these horses?" Despite his clear overwhelmed pain, Ryd nodded slowly. "Good," Digory said. Help with the horses will be useful, Digory thought. And, he wouldn't have to kill two men this night. "Let's go."

"Now?" Ryd dropped his sword to the ground. "You just told me my brother is a fiend and missing and expect me to leave in a hurry?" He took a few steps through the stable, horses neighing as he passed by, in anticipation of first light's sup. "I must search for him here first. Can we leave in a few days' time, or a moon even?"

"No," Digory said. "Tonight."

"But why…"

"Saddle one for me. Now," Digory interrupted the dazed young man with his demand, gesturing at the row of, chestnut, amber, beige and calico steeds. Westerviolet's stable was the most impressive in the Kingdom. "I'll be back before daybreak." He turned, emerald cape flapping in his wake. "Be ready," he said over his shoulder as he paced to the door.

"Guardsman!" Ryd took two steps. "Wait. Where are you

going?"

Digory stopped briefly, turning his head to side-eye Ryd. "To gather provisions."

"You're really not going to tell me anything?"

Digory ignored him and turned again.

Ryd furrowed his brow and muttered nearly inaudibly, "Our world is dark..."

Digory stopped, turning to face Ryd from the doorframe, backlit by dusty blue brightening sky. Outside, chirping and whistling fowl serenaded louder and louder.

"What is that? A doltish prayer?"

"No, it's nothing," Ryd said quickly, then sighed. He locked eyes with Digory. "It's nothing," he exhaled loudly again. "I'll go with you."

Digory nodded once, hiding a smile until he turned. Grinning at his own cleverness, he rushed out of the stable with time pulsing at his back.

In the early hours of the morning, Rose sat at the edge of her bed still wrapped in her sheet, staring out far window in reverie. Ellie slept by her side. She rubbed her thumbs over ribbed embroidered pillows and revelled in the stagnant, oppressive air. Though the moonlight was dim, Rose saw the man who killed Col slam the creaky wooden door behind him on his way into the stable. She quickly squinted her eyes and winced as it reminded her of Col, then she bit her lip so hard that it bled. Eyes beginning to tear, she forced herself to lie back into her feather bed. She rolled to face away from the windows.

Rose watched shadows cast on the wall from the white light of the setting moon while imagining what would have happened if she and Col had escaped to Littlebell.

She sobbed herself back to sleep.

NARROW ROAD

Digory and Ryd headed west along Narrow Road as the sun inched higher and higher in the cloudless sky.

Narrow Road had a long history for it connected the castles in Westerviolet and Littlebell realms for as long as history had been recorded. Initially it was called Birch Path and was only dirt. As the years, decades and centuries passed, it evolved into the widened, pebbled road it was in the present day.

The late-summer heat was punishing and unrelenting, especially since today there was no wind. The air hung still and moist. Digory wiped sweat from his brow with his sleeve. Ryd unfastened a canteen from his waist and took a long drink.

Ryd was in shock, unable to process how quickly his life had flipped on its head. Everything he knew and loved was gone. His father, dead. His brother, disappeared. And in his hasty decision to follow Digory, his position and safety sacrificed. His anxiety was palpable. He hoped that proximity to a Guardsman out and about on Brochet orders would be his sanctuary. That he'd be welcomed home with open arms once they returned to Westerviolet, if the journey was successful. Although he couldn't stand the Guardsman, Ryd knew sticking by his side throughout their trip would be the key to his survival. Or he could never return home.

Digory gestured at his canteen. "Tell me that's ale."

"Nay, water. What kind of man are you?"

"The kind who doesn't reserve pleasures for one part of the day. Still, water will do. I am parched."

Ryd's horse paced Digory's and he turned his torso to face him. "Didn't you bring your own?"

"Aye, but it's packed away," Digory said. "Give me yours."

He reached out with one hand, holding the reigns in a messy clump with the other.

Ryd sighed and placed the canteen in the Guardsman's outstretched, beckoning hand. He was so accustomed to being commanded that he didn't give his action a second thought. Digory grabbed it and took a thirsty swig, throwing back his head dramatically, then sighed before recapping the canteen and handing it back. "Appreciate it."

With a grunt, Ryd took it and re-fastened it to his steed's side.

They trotted along until Digory broke the silence. "Do you know why they call this Narrow Road?"

"No," Ryd said dryly. "And I don't care to."

"Why not?"

"I want to find my brother," Ryd said. That, besides, wonderment didn't suit him. He took things at face value; believed what he was told. Even his father's fanciful stories never fully took root in his mind. He was cautious not to be blasphemous in the presence of a Guardsman, wary of offending the Vanguard Ancestors he'd prayed to his whole life.

"You aren't curious?"

"I know what it's called and that's enough for me."

"This road is long and it'll feel even longer in silence," Digory said. "Let's pass time."

Ryd conceded with a defeated sigh. "Fine, tell me then. Why?"

"Why do you think?"

"Well, it isn't narrow," Ryd said as he looked across the pebbled path lined on each side with creeping greenery. "Six men could ride abreast if they wanted to. The more I think, it makes very little sense to call it that at all. I'd say the Keeper's Pass is far narrower, as is Eagle's Walk. Was it in jest, then? Calling a wide road narrow in humor?"

"No." Digory shook his head once. "Wrong."

"Why then?" Ryd craned to look at Digory. "Was there a man named 'Narrow' it was named after?"

"Clever," Digory said, "but no. Anything else?"

"No, not really." Ryd said, gaze caught by a pair of black birds chasing three yellow ones, flitting angrily amidst the lustrous leaves of a passing maple tree. "I tire of this."

"During the Blood Wars, over a century ago now, the New marched on Westerviolet, down this road," Digory pontificated, jostling lazily atop his steed, swatting insects buzzing by his face. "They clashed not far from here. We just passed it, had we veered off, back by that split rock. It was a turning point in the war, they say, devastating for the New's cause. After the bloodshed ended, all the fallen bodies were stacked along the road. There were so many that the walkway became so narrow that barely a man could pass through. Lord Robert Brochet gave this road that name to remind all that the last to attack did not escape. The same fate is threatened to enemies, as warning."

For the first time since they'd departed, Ryd questioned if this man he travelled with could be trusted. "How do you know all of that?"

Digory shrugged.

Ryd turned and looked at him. "No, truly. How?"

"I've spent a lot of time around the castle. I've picked up things."

Ryd grunted.

Digory raised an eyebrow. "Really?" He was surprised Ryd didn't have more questions. Digory was accustomed to everyone hanging on his every word whenever he revealed the inner workings of Vanguard culture. The Vanguards were a notoriously powerful, yet mysterious ruling class. Particularly within Westerviolet's realm. Knowledge of their history was typically hard to come by and made for entertaining stories around the fire. Digory was quite popular amongst his men because of it. Although he only shared the most innocuous stories. He usually kept the good ones to himself.

"Really, what? What is your meaning?"

"You really have no interest in the ones who run our lives?"

"My father taught me that Vanguard affairs are no business of ours, as ours is no business of theirs. We each have our duty."

"What's that supposed to mean? You don't worship the Ancestors?"

"I do," Ryd said quickly as he'd been beaten to do, "but my father taught my brother and I that our people and Vanguards shouldn't mix," he explained with a hint of pride. "We worship them customarily," he said carefully, "but father always advised me to not fall into the trap that so many of Westerviolet do, chasing after the Vanguard stories. It is that way that we forget our own." Digory smirked and shook his head and Ryd's confidence faded quickly. "Why do you laugh?"

"I disagree," Digory wiped sweat away from his hairline with his free hand. "I disagree entirely." Ryd glanced sideways at him. The Guardsman spoke every word with resolve, as if it was an infallible law. He was undeniable. Ryd hated him. "Vanguards have a lot to offer," Digory answered the glance. Grumbling, Ryd looked forwards again. "Why do you pout?" Digory prodded, mimicking Ryd's earlier tone.

"Nothing. Forget it."

"No, what is it?"

"I don't want to talk politics."

"Don't act like a maiden," Digory goaded. "It'll be a long journey if you keep that up."

Ryd glared. "Fine," he said with palpable spite. The intensity of his own emotion surprised him, but he didn't pause. "You want to know what I think? You're the dolt. The Vanguards ruined us, murdered and raped, and," he paused, not knowing exactly where his sentiments were coming from. It was like the words had been within him for a very long time and only now, out of the shadow of Westerviolet, could they be revealed. He lowered his voice to a blasphemous whisper, "*enslaved* us for centuries and you're saying they have... a lot to offer? If you weren't in an honorable profession guarding the stable and helping me find my brother..."

"You know you speak treason, don't you?"

"We are far from the Lord's lair now."

"Ah, so you do not fear me and my loyalty to Brochet? Is that it? My friend, that is a mistake."

Ryd's heart flipped in his chest. The Guardsman was right, he did fear him, but he blindly clung to loyalty for his kin. He was defensive. After all, Digory insulted him. "My father taught me to…"

Digory interrupted again more loudly, "And you talk quite a bit about your father."

"My father was a great man," Ryd nearly shouted. "He taught me everything I know."

"Not everything, clearly."

"What's that supposed to mean?"

"You know what I mean," Digory gestured casually towards the canteen. Ryd frowned. Sweat dripped from the coarse curls at his hairline. Digory exhaled slowly against the back of his throat. "Don't make me say it."

"Say it."

"Your father was a drunkard." His words pierced the warm air between them like a spear. Ryd visibly winced. "A good man," Digory added, for Burkhart had been jovial and well-liked, "but a drunkard. Everyone knew that." He paused and scratched his beard. "I figured you'd taken after him."

"My father was a great man he…"

Digory interrupted again. "Is it the drink that killed him?"

Ryd stopped instantly. He felt like he'd been slapped. It had been. Hudde had told him for moons to cut back on ale, but he hadn't listened. Ryd nodded silently, deeply stung.

"Pity," Digory replied blithely.

After that, the conversation died and the young men continued along in the searing heat in silence. They rode over rolling grassy hillsides dotted with clusters of trees interwoven with ivy and reaching plants with light green tendrils. Every so often, they passed a field of sunblooms or a lemon orchard. The sun was nearly at the highest point in the sky and the wind picked up slightly. The greenery around them looked as if it breathed with each gust.

"Thank the Ancestors, the breeze has found us," Digory exclaimed, wiping his brow again. "I'm sweating more than a

Busk Pawn in the heat."

Then, it was Ryd's turn to roll his eyes.

A wide-wingspan bird glided overhead, shadow trailing them across the hilly ground. Ryd watched it cross the rolling meadows that stretched ahead lined by forests of leafy maples and oaks mixed with skeleton like pines humming with life. Ryd patted Mable. He rubbed her hot and dusty mane, feeling the strong, tinsel muscle in her flank beneath him.

"How are we going to find my brother?"

"I don't give two curses about your brother." Digory turned to see the angry hopelessness on Ryd's face. He yielded. "We'll go through Littlebell. Rumor was he went that way. You can look for him there, if you wish. We'll need to water and rest the horses anyway."

"I've taken the journey up through Baneswood to Croft, but never West," Ryd offered. "It makes sense though."

"Sense?"

"Why he chose Littlebell."

"Why?"

"My father used to talk about..."

Digory interrupted with a smirk, "On and on about your father still."

Ryd frowned. "Forget it."

"I was joking." Digory turned. "Tell me about your..."

"I said, forget it."

The men went silent again. The rising sun beat hot on their shoulders as disembodied birds chirped in pleasant competing songs all around them. Gnats buzzed in their ears.

Ryd eventually broke the lull, curiosity and monotony of travel besting him. "How do you know so much about the Vanguards?"

"I told you, I'm a Guardsman," Digory replied. "I'm near them. I hear things."

"Where are you posted?"

"North Gate."

"How would you hear there?"

"I have great hearing."

"Why would they send a North Gate Guardsman as a messenger? Why not the missive?" Ryd asked rhetorically, knowing Digory wasn't keen to offer details, thinking aloud. "And, you never said. Why the hurry? What is so urgent in this message that we had to sneak out when it was barely dawn?"

"Isn't it incredible the mysteries of our realm?"

Ryd frowned. "Is this all a joke to you?" he spat, cheeks burning hot. He wished he'd never met the man. "I joined you as a partner in your journey with a promise of explanation later and now I demand it," he said forcefully, pulling Mable's reigns until she neighed, stopping in the middle of the path.

Digory's mount Chester halted as well when his companion paused on the trail. More gnats and mosquitos quickly found them, buzzing about their necks and ears in the sweltering, windless heat.

Digory's mood soured. "I didn't promise you shit."

"You aren't posted at North Gate. Who are you? Who did I agree to journey with?"

"You are just now asking me this?" Digory said with mounting frustration, tugging uselessly on his stalwart horse's reigns. "Can't we keep moving?"

"No," Ryd said dryly. "In fact," he expertly dismounted, "I'm not going one more step until you tell me."

Digory flexed his dark bearded jaw, eyes swooping in a glance across the partially wooded, hilly horizon. "We don't have time for this," he growled.

"Why are you in such a rush?" Ryd asked, but Digory ignored him, shaking the reigns of his mount in a futile attempt to spur it to move forward and leave Ryd behind. But Chester was loyal to his companion and Stablemaster, refusing to follow Digory's violent whims.

"Be gentle with him," Ryd said.

Digory kicked Chester again. "Doltish beast won't move."

"Hey!" Ryd shouted. Chester shifted his weight and whinnied, obviously displeased with Digory's treatment, taking steps backwards. "I said, be gentle."

Digory kicked and pulled at the mighty horse again, this time harder. Chester neighed loudly and bucked high on his hind legs, toppling Digory hard to the ground. He landed with a weighty thud on his back that knocked the wind out of him.

"Curses!" Digory shouted. He gasped for air, rolling in the dirty pebbles beside Ryd.

Ryd superficially stifled a chuckle. "I tried to tell you."

Chester waved his tail and trotted to Ryd's side, as if equally amused.

"Shut up," Digory grumbled, rolling to a seat.

"You can't just kick them they are..."

"I said, Shut. Up." Digory grunted. He stood to adjust his armor. He picked rocks out of his chainmail, then dusted himself off.

"Why do you know so much about the Vanguards?" Ryd asked again. Digory ignored the question while he brushed dirt off his trousers. "Tell me," Ryd commanded.

"Alright, alright," Digory sighed, just wanting to continue, "Fine."

"Well?"

"I'm... close to them." he said, righting his cloak, patting his pockets.

"What's that mean?"

"I'm the Lady's..." he glanced to Ryd briefly, "personal Guardsman."

"The Lady?" Ryd rubbed Mable's dusty braided mane. "You mean *the* Lady?" He spun his head, astonished. Digory nodded smugly. "Why say you're a North Gate guard?"

"It's what she commands me to say," he said, then shrugged. "I live in the barracks there. I sit on post. Sybil's very secretive." He did his best not to smile.

"You call her Sybil?" Ryd asked, wide-eyed in unabashed awe. "You really serve her?"

"Don't you serve as well?"

"It's different," Ryd shot back. "I care for the horses, as my father did. It is our way." He felt a stab of pride.

"It's not different at all," Digory argued, checking his weapons after the fall. "You watch the Vanguard's property.

They aren't your beasts," he gestured to Mable and Chester waiting patiently to be mounted on the sweltering pebbly path, "they're theirs. Instead of horses, I watch over the Lady herself. You and I are no different."

"We are different," he argued. "I am loyal to our kind. You are a traitor," Ryd added definitively. He'd seen what duties Guardsman were tasked with, like rounding up and eliminating unapproved spawn. Burning the Leaf Toilers. Or recruiting for the Lair. The darker side of Westerviolet. Westerviolet natives were deathly afraid of the guardsmen throughout every Vice Province. Not just within the castle walls.

"Knowledge isn't betrayal," Digory countered. "Knowledge is power, and the more we know about them the better. They surely know enough about us. More than we know ourselves. That's their game."

"What do you mean?"

"How do you think there are only a handful of them and thousands and thousands of us, and yet they live in castles and we live in dirt? Why is the written word banned for all but Vanguard? Why are we not permitted to marry or leave Westerviolet unless on command? Why are weapons not permitted? I'll tell you why. It's so our people can't get our stories straight for long enough to overtake them. We must believe what they tell us unless we listen in on what they tell each other."

"But you do their bidding."

"I'm to deliver this to Anstout. That's all I know."

"You don't know what it says?"

Digory shook his head 'no' as he removed a folded parchment from his pocket. Ryd took it and felt the wax. The raised emblem shifted with his touch in the oppressive heat.

"As you see, the integrity of the wax holds. Proof that I have no idea what it says, which is proof that even if I could read, which I cannot," Digory lied, "I am not doing anyone's bidding any more than the messenger is the man to declare war. Are you satisfied? Can we be on our way?" he asked rhetorically, snatching the letter back.

"If you serve the Lady, what's she like?"

Digory smiled. "Sybil is a force of nature."

Ryd nodded. "I've heard stories from my father. Fearless on a horse. Said she always got her way."

"Yes, that's Sybil."

"And she's smart?"

"Aye."

"I've always imagined she would be," Ryd replied wistfully. "She stands on her balcony and I can see her from the stable yard. After Lord Rosen died, she went out there most nights. I was youngthen. Everything she wears shines like dewy grass. I've watched her dark dresses sparkle in moonlight like she's a moon bird with charred wings and her hair is thick and glows like dark amber from a pine in the sun. I've heard her laugh and it rivals the song birds." He sighed longingly, after which Digory burst into laughter. "What? What is it?"

"You are something," Digory noted with a broad, handsome smile. "You sure you're the stablemaster, not a bard?"

Ryd frowned. "Why do you say that?"

"Nothing. It's nothing. Can we go?" Digory adjusted Chester's saddle, readying himself to mount. "I'm telling you that we need to be moving." His eyes swept the distant treeline.

This stretch of road was notoriously dangerous. It bordered Hill's Shadow territory.

Ryd contemplated his next words carefully. Digory turned his head, noticing the lull. "Have you ever been," he paused, considering his word choice, "with her?"

"I offer fair warning," Digory deflected, "she's beautiful and dangerous."

"You speak of her as if you really know her. You even call her," he paused, "Sybil," Ryd said with reverence. "Have you lay with her?"

Digory broke into an amused smirk. He hadn't, but Ryd didn't need to know that. "Are you jealous, horse boy?"

Ryd's eyes widened further, looking close to popping out of his skull. "You have?"

"You embarrass yourself," Digory spat. "If you knew

anything of Sybil, you'd know you'd lose your head for thinking of her like that. You best hope I don't tell her. She'd have you hung."

"I didn't think of her like anything. I never said that at all. You did." Although, he had thought of her that way. What man in Westerviolet hadn't?

"You didn't have to," Digory laughed. "You need to lighten your mind. I won't say anything to her as long as we're moving towards Littlebell. Let's get on the road. Then we'll be even." Ryd glared at Digory. "If I were you, I would want to hurry."

"Why's that?"

Digory easily lied again, "With the bounty on your brother's head…"

"What! What did you say?! Why are you just now telling me of this?!" Ryd paced quickly over to Digory until he was close enough to reach out and touch his sweaty beard. Digory was nearly a head taller. Exceptionally tall for a native. His tan skin contrasted Ryd's coal black.

He looked down to meet Ryd's indignant glare. "You heard me. Better than coin," Digory said. "Tomas to give a high title to the first to deliver his head."

"Why didn't you tell me until now?"

"I didn't think it was important."

Ryd scowled. He rubbed his neck. "Alright," he conceded in a deep sigh. "I don't trust you but it's too late now." He paused again. "Alright, alright. I just want to find Col. Mable, Chester, let's go."

"Finally," Digory said loudly.

The pair mounted their red-eyed steeds and continued down the road silently, each deep in thought.

Ryd frowned as Digory smiled.

WESTERVIOLET STRATEGY

G awen was honored by his newly elevated position. The other Guardsmen were certainly jealous, but given his good nature, he took their side-glances and angry whispers behind his back in stride.

"How's it feel to be Second, lad?" the gruff, rust-eyed man asked him in a grunt.

Petrok, the Westerviolet Guardsman elder, an ancient, disagreeable bastard, had a wiry beard and ragged horizontal forehead scar above his right eye, honourably earned during the Uprising half a century prior when a Gold Cape struck him in the head. It bisected his ashen eyebrow, impressing into the papery skin like a cavern whenever he spoke.

"It is a great honor," Gawen answered, eyes on the cavern. He wasn't sure how he felt about his speedy elevation into the elite Guardsman ranks. He certainly didn't expect to be deemed Second, yet after the entire process completed in the wake of Clemmo's death, Gawen was chosen. Who was he to question tradition, Gawen thought, so he accepted his new post with dutiful gumption. "I'm humbled by the appointment," he said. "I will do my best to fill large shoes. Peaceful may he rest."

He removed his hammered helmet and bowed slightly, closing his eyes.

Petrok nodded. "Clemmo was a good man, but old in his ways. It's a curse of old brains. Old thoughts." He hacked in a phlegmy cough. "It's about time for some young blood."

"Thank you, Elder Petrok," Gawen replied, stifling a grin. Petrock was as old and backwards as they came. He was losing his hearing and his breath smelled terrible. He could hardly walk upright and each time he moved he released noxious gas.

Most barely tolerated him. "I will give it my all."

"Good to hear," Petrok grumbled, "good to hear." The Guardsman elder hacked and coughed up phlegm again. This time, he hawked it right onto the stone floor with a faint splat. Gawen flexed his jaw. "Do you have your Topics of Concern prepared?" Petrok asked after he'd righted himself.

"Absolutely, Elder," Gawen replied, blinking cherry-red eyes. "As is customary each week."

"Good, good. Just checking. Just checking. As you are young and unprepared," he added, coughing again. "Could you perhaps," he paused and cleared his throat low, "tell me some?"

"Elder, if you didn't prepare…"

"Quiet!" Petrok leaned forward to rest against the mighty strategy table in the center of the storied chamber. "How dare you accuse me of such? Nonsense," he huffed.

"Certainly elder," Gawen said. He lowered his gaze. It was all he could do not to laugh out loud at the ridiculous old dolt. Petrok's senility was widely known, however, the position he held was an honored one. It put him beyond reproach.

"It is highest honor to sit here. You now have a seat at this mighty table. Do you know how many men of great blood have fallen because of us, here?" Petrok asked, asserting his dominance with every ostentatious breath like a dying rooster with its chest puffed out. He looked just as ridiculous. "Why, right here, it was I who suggested the march on Winter Garden. On Croft Hold! Don't you dare mock me, your elder, the living breathing symbol of all who have come before you! A representative of the Ancestors, themselves!"

Gawen had heard of Petrok's conquests when he was a younger man. How he indeed instigated the attack on Winter Garden, as he often reminded the much younger Guardsmen. How he led the charge against the Gold Capes when Brochet and Morfit clashed. He was ruthless, the rumors claimed, however, to look at him now, it was hard to imagine him able to harm anything larger than a beetle. Gawen held his hands up, trying to subdue the ancient man. "Elder Petrok I meant no disrespect." Rumor had it that Petrok had been a part of Lair experiments in his younger years and was much older than he even seemed. Many attributed his erratic behavior to these experiments, as well.

"I know. I know," Petrok said, mood shifting instantly. "I know you didn't. Now, boy," he warmed like an unfurling snake, "tell me. What are your topics of concern?"

Gawen hesitated, scratching at his hair at the base of his scalp again. It was clear Petrok had not prepared anything and was attempting to rely on Gawen's naiveite. Petrok hobbled across the room and crumpled into a wooden chair on the far side. "Speak!" he shouted, pointing a wrinkled, shaking finger.

"Elder Petrok, I..."

"I command you, as Elder, tell me what you plan to discuss!"

Gawen sighed, annoyed, understanding he had little choice, knowing the stupid old man couldn't conceptualize what he meant if he tried. Alas, he spoke anyway. Petrok gave him little choice.

"A new sleep shift."

The old man laughed to reveal yellow teeth. "The men have kept the same watch for centuries."

"Stagger the shifts so all men see the light of moon," Gawen countered. "And each other. Moral will boost."

"Goaded dog!" Petrok exclaimed, throwing his wrinkled hands up. "We have always done it one way. It cannot change."

"Why not?"

"The men will not allow it."

"Actually," Gawen countered, having recently polled his companions in the North Gate dormitories, "I've spoken to many and they like the idea." He paused, then added, just for insult, "Most prefer it."

Petrok grumbled, visibly displeased, plan to plagiarize near-foiled. "Do you have anything else, lad?"

"Why don't you tell me what you have prepared, Elder?"

"Nonsense," Petrok muttered, smoothing his sickly grey beard as he leaned away.

Gawen frowned. "I insist," he said, this time firmer, taking a step towards the old man. "Or let us wait for Budic."

Elder Petrok glared hate at the presumptuous, know-nothing youngster. "Naturally," he replied through yellow, clenched teeth. "Naturally."

Then, their Commander entered through the towering arched doorway.

Budic impressed dominance easily. Late in middle-years, he wasn't imposing in height or features, with a medium frame and pleasant round face, complexion rich brown and eyes burgundy red like a royal swallow's feathers. His voice was soft, almost unimpressive, but his glare was intense, his words impactful, and his reputation brutal, preceding him as he entered the engulfing hall with a straight back and poise. Commander Budic kept his hair shoulder length in tiny brown braids, as was typical of most traditionalists in Westerviolet. Unlike the other Guardsmen, he bore a palm-size ouroboros emblem to secure his weighty emerald Guardsman cape, in brilliant glinting silver, indicative of his rank.

"What'd I miss?" Budic said lightly as he strode into the high-ceiling room, hobbling steps irregular instead of rhythmic as he limped across the floor. Budic reached the sturdy round table in the middle where both Gawen and Petrok stood and placed his hands on it. He leaned forward and eyed his two closest advisors. "I heard what sounded like a lively debate as I came down the hall."

"We were discussing our Topics of Concern," Elder Petrok said, leaping to his feet as quickly as an old man could, to pace shakily around the strategy table.

"Go on."

"I propose a new sleep plan," he shouted like an actor in a caravan.

"You do, do you?"

"You... you... you like the idea? I... I was telling my young mentee all about it."

"Oh no," Gawen answered with a slow-growing grin, "I couldn't possibly take credit for your ideas, Elder." He stepped backwards, leaving Petrok teetering alone. "That would be very disrespectful of me. Please, go on. Tell us all the details, yourself."

"You are to explain what I told you," Petrok commanded Gawen, frown drooping deep into his jowls. "It is an order."

Gawen didn't relent, hiding a smile by biting his bottom lip. "No, Elder, I insist. The credit should be yours."

Elder Petrok coughed loudly once, then again, before devolving into a fit of coughing. "Excuse me," Elder Petrok said then coughed more, "I must," he coughed, grabbing his throat, pointing with phlegm-dripping fingers to the door. Then the old man hobbled with a crooked back out of the gaping arched doorway.

"Between you and me," Budic confided, "I cannot bear that man."

"Truth?" Gawen asked, in amusement, turning his head.

"Curses yes," Budic replied. "Old Clemmo was a glutton and a pig, but he could control Petrok."

"Actually, Commander, the sleep shift change is my idea."

"Is that so?" Budic pushed himself to stand upright. "How do I know that is truth? How do I know you don't steal Elder Petrok's thoughts and brand them as your own?"

"With all respect," Gawen said, tilting his head, "you know."

Budic conceded with a pleasant smile, crossing his arms in front of his chest. "It is obvious, and a shame the Law of the Elder exists at all."

"Why does it exist?"

"It's been in our dogma since the beginning," Budic said. "The Guardsman Elder is a key in devising strategy because he can provide helpful counsel from the past."

Gawen approached the table. "But if your elder's counsel is no help, what is Strategy really for?" He leaned forward and looked down at the inlayed map of the Kingdom's sixteen realms, plus Echo's Omen. "Why hold it at all?"

"I've been dealt less than enviable advisors in all my time as commander, but still found them useful," Budic said as he limped slowly around the table. "I've done this a long, long time, Guardsman Gawen. I've learned it's critical to listen to the viewpoints of all, no matter how diluted they may be. Petrok is helpful in providing…" He paused in search of a tactful word. "Alternative viewpoints." He sighed. "I'm hoping your appointment breathes life into our stale routine."

Gawen narrowed his already naturally squinted eyes. "Is that why you meet with the Lord alone?"

"No, son." Budic shook his head. "That has always been the way. Since the great Lord Robert himself, the Guardsman Commander consults the Lord once per fortnight on affairs of the realm. Someday you'll have my seat and it'll be you to lead the men and you can decide how you structure Strategy. By that day, there will be another to replace Petrok. There will always be men like him and you'll never know what to do with them." He crossed his arms. "We are here now. Tell me of your ideas."

Without warning, a small teen years girl with braids down to her waist sprinted wildly into the room in tears, tattered beige smock smothered in brilliantly red blood. Gawen rushed to her as she tumbled into his arms.

"Are you hurt? What's wrong? What happened?" he asked intensely, holding her, stroking her head. Gawen was somehow extremely empathetic and kind despite his training. That was a part of himself he had kept mostly hidden from the moment when he was chosen as a small child to be a Guardsman and taken to the barracks.

Budic stood on the defence, hand on his dagger hilt. Eyes alert and ready, honed from years of battle. War.

The girl was trying to make out words, but her wails made her speech indecipherable. "He… He… He…." she sobbed pitifully, chest heaving, throat cutting with shards of tears. "I…. I… I f…f…found him…"

"Calm yourself!" Gawen commanded. "Who hurt you?" He spoke more softly. "Breathe, with me," he said, adrenaline pounding in his veins. "Ready? Out, and in. Out. And in. There, well done."

The girl breathed with Gawen until she was calm enough to speak. In and out she exhaled, still trembling like a leaf in a storm. But before she could say anything, Budic did. "I recognize you." He spoke slowly, as if uncovering the information piece by piece in his mind. "Aren't you the one running around with my nephew?"

Although not permitted, occasionally, Budic looked the other way when it came to inconsequential love affairs amongst his men and the maidens. What was the harm? Marriage was out of the question. Guardsmen never married. And, if a spawn were to arise, both it and the maiden would be dealt with accordingly, and the realm would keep running, just as it always had.

"He's... he's..." The wilted girl sniffled, struggling to breathe.

Budic pointed at her violently. "Spit it out!"

"HE'S DEAD!"

"How?!" Gawen shouted.

"No," Budic whispered.

"It's true! This blood is not mine." She looked down at her smock in shock, then wailed in sorrow all over again. Gawen held the girl close, rocking her gently.

Budic paced in a fury. "Where did this happen? Who did this?!" The girl only squealed and wailed louder than before. "What possesses you?!" Budic shouted sternly. "My brother tasked me with protecting that boy. Tell me what happened! Where is Aslf?!"

Through heavy tears the girl cried, "He was not there at morning call!"

"He's simply missing?" Budic's voice tinged with hope. "Why do you say he is dead?"

"I went to look for him. First, to his quarters, but he hadn't been back at all since before he left for post last eve. That was when I got worried. I ran around looking for him until..." The girl's voice cracked and she howled like a trapped ruby fox.

Budic and Gawen exchanged worried glances.

"Who did this, flower?" Gawen asked softly.

"He did!" she exclaimed with horror-filled, bloodshot eyes.

"It couldn't be," Budic said instantly.

"It's the most horrible t...t... thing I have ever seen. He didn't even leave a message. Nor token. He didn't tell anyone. If he had told me, I would have stopped him!"

"What did he do?"

"He slit his own throat!"

"That's preposterous," Budic said. "No," he shook his head. "The boy was the most eager, the most grounded I know. There is no way he did as you say."

"I saw it with my own eyes!"

"Did you touch the body? Move it in any way?" Gawen asked. There could be vital clues to why Aslf committed the act on his person, he thought.

"I did!" she cried. "I held him," she said softly, squinting her eyes, clinging to Gawen's muscled, armoured figure for dear life.

"Curses," Budic said under his breath.

"I'll take her back to her quarters."

Budic spun aggressively and pointed at his Second. "Hold it right there, no you won't. Call Cador to do it. I need you; that's an order."

Gawen nodded. "Yes Commander." He squeezed the girl's shoulders once and leaned close to her to whisper comforts in her ear. How his heart broke for her. He felt her pain.

He stood, leaving Miri shaking and shivering, sobbing on the floor, walked quickly to the doorway and shouted outside of it. "Cador!"

Deep grumbles came through the door frame.

"Girl, come here," Gawen said. She took hurried steps across the chamber, pulling her shoulders into a protective slouch as she grabbed his hand timidly. Gently, he led Miri out and handed her off to Cador.

He returned into the chamber with Budic standing in front of an unlit, cold fireplace. The war-worn commander stared at the empty space as if it were roaring with flames. Hands on his hips, Budic was still like stone.

"Commander, I am so sorry," Gawen said as he re-entered the chamber. He'd never seen the stoic man so shaken.

Budic turned to face him, brow furrowed and eyes glassy. A

shadow of the mighty man he was. His voice lowered. "Drop everything. Son, you will run point on this investigation. Do you hear me?"

"But, Commander, with respect, the girl said it was by his own hand."

"You believe it?" Budic half snorted. "If you spent a mere moment with him, you'd know Aslf would never."

Gawen nodded. He knew of the lad, although he was a Low Guardsman. Overly confident given his meek disposition. Always attempting to be seen as great, like his uncle. The men teased him ruthlessly for it. "Aye, he's eager, that Aslf. Or, was," he added. "If what she says is true."

"I swore I'd keep that boy safe. I need to know what happened."

"Yes, Commander," Gawen said solemnly. "I'll get to the root of it."

"Go," Budic grunted. "And speak to no one."

"Commander?"

"For all we know there is a snake amongst us. Best to be cautious."

"Aye," Gawen said, nodding once before swiftly leaving the Strategy Room.

Once Budic was alone in the lofty chamber he lowered his head and loudly sighed. Hot tears streamed down his cheeks, but he resolved himself not to openly cry. It wouldn't be proper.

NARROW ROAD

"Have you ever seen a deadblood?"

Ryd exhaled through flared nostrils. "What now?" he asked. He couldn't take much more of this.

"A deadblood," Digory said. "You know. The monsters in the Deadlands that eat men for sup?"

The Deadlands hugged the Vanguard Kingdom, from the Cursed Hills in the east to the Bone Mountains in the west. Everything beyond on either side was dead or dying. Irradiated from the war that drove the Vanguards from earth in the first place, hundreds of years before the Landing, during the time of the old gods. Thousands of years before the present day. Currently, it was infested with deadbloods.

Ryd shook his head and looked down to study small, rounded pebbles embedded in the path. They were just like what he played with when he was a boy. Westerviolet children, low and high native alike, were not allowed toys.

"I've agreed to ride with you," Ryd said, noting the unintentional patterns of the pebbles, like water swirling a brook. "I've agreed to go to Anstout with you. Isn't that enough? Can't I enjoy this view without your questions? Without your thoughts?" He exhaled and glanced up. "Look around," he said, gesturing at the wide valley below them.

They'd been travelling for two days. This section of road trekked up a hillside to avoid traversing a dense, swampy valley full of stinging insects and biting snakes. From the hilltop ridge they had a spectacular view of a blue sky filled with foamy clouds. The valley below was vibrantly alive with countless layers of brilliant green foliage reaching up towards the warm sun with lively candour. Drab birds with shrill chirps flitted about thorny fairymoss. Pleasant, welcome winds spun about fine, tall grass in a whooshing cadence. Swampy riverweed bobbed.

"Yes, yes. Beautiful," Digory said absently. "Beauty is everywhere. It's boring. I don't care for it. Ugly is interesting." Ryd scoffed. Digory ignored him. "You have travelled along the Cursed Hills. I hear they are full of them. Deadbloods. Surely you've seen them."

Ryd groaned. "Leave me be."

"Listen to me. You must tell me. Have you seen a deadblood? We stand to walk into a castle of them. I would like to know what that means."

Ryd relented. "Graves are only half."

"I thought you didn't know anything about Vanguards?"

"Some things everyone knows."

Ryd knew of rumors, mostly. Petra told him once that just looking into the eyes of a man with dead blood would turn one to stone. He'd overheard passing Baneswood traders recounting their run-ins with members of the Brotherhood, how the Gravesblood could walk across the Dead Line unscathed. How they were immune to Dread. And, of course, he'd heard his father's tales, about how, despite only having half dead blood, Graves was not man anymore. They were the same as deadbloods. They had no love left within them. The Ancestors shunned them for their unholy nature. Their souls were gone.

Having recently encountered the monsters himself, that concept shook Ryd to the core.

Digory shrugged. "They've got generations of dead blood. Much more than half."

Ryd's heart sank into his stomach.

"Disappointed, are you?"

"No, it's nothing."

"What is it?"

"That's just, a lot," Ryd said quietly, "I can't imagine what half would be like and…" He trailed off.

Digory smiled, turning his head to study his companion's

heavy blond brow. "I knew that you knew." He paused. "Now you must tell me."

They passed the crest of the hilltop and descended into the next valley blanketed with tiny blue thimbleweed flowers. Beyond that valley was another, thick with wide-faced sunblooms. In all areas of the Kingdom suitable for farming, meadows that were not utilized for agriculture had been long ago planted with either flower, particularly around Littlebell. Sunblooms healed the soil while thimbleweed was the key ingredient in nearly all human healing tinctures, salves and potions. In the present day, both flowers were everywhere.

The sound of the horses' hooves clopping against small pebbles echoed in the lull of this hot, breezy afternoon.

Ryd wiped sweat from his brow and with a look of defeat, sighed again. "It wasn't long ago I faced them."

"Tell me."

"Last month's merchant mission."

"You lie! I would have heard if you…"

"It's true," Ryd interrupted. "Clemmo represented Lord Tomas and I tended the livestock. We had three others with us."

Digory nodded. Second Clemmo died during that trek. "I heard," he said, recalling the gossip he'd gathered from the other North Gate men. "I know you were the only to return."

"The journey to Croft was no problem at all," Ryd said as he jostled atop Mable's saddle, horseshoes clapping loudly beneath him. "Surprised us, really. Each day was as uneventful as the last, even as we passed through Baneswood and entered the Morfit's realm. Clemmo was nervous it wouldn't hold," he added, in reference to agreements made by the Vanguards during the fallout of the Uprising decades earlier.

"But it did?"

Ryd nodded curtly. "It did. Truth, we avoided Baneswood proper and kept to the outskirt villages. We didn't want to spur conflict wearing the Brochet emblem."

"Fair," Digory said knowingly. "I'd wager there are still hurt sensibilities."

During the Uprising, Baneswood fought for the New and Westerviolet the Old. The Old prevailed. Many lives were lost on both sides. It was a brutal, bloody war for New independence but the Old squashed it like a boot on a snake. Although the Old's victory did nothing to quell the resentment and often downright hate felt within New realms for Old ones. In the years following, these feelings only grew. There were often conflicts along the borders for this reason.

"I don't blame them." Ryd had heard stories about Westerviolet's victory, recounted in great theatrics and ceremony throughout the entire realm each Vanguard Day, in the dead of winter. "I'd be bitter too if I lost so many men."

Digory scoffed. "They only lost traitors."

"How can you say that?" Ryd widened his eyes. "They fought for you!"

"Not me."

"I mean to say they fought for the rights of your kind. All our kinds. All but the *Vanguards*." Ryd spoke the word Vanguard as if it was the highest insult, just as his father had, although doing so spurred his own anxiety. He silently said a prayer to the Ancestors, apologizing for his blasphemy.

Ryd, if nothing else, was a man in conflict.

Digory shook his head. "They fought for their own pockets, the same as everyone else. It's far more convenient to blame the Uprising on furthering the good of the people, than the truth."

"What truth?"

"The New Vanguard bloodlines were weary of the Old bloodlines having all the power and coin, mainly through control of trade," he explained. "Had the New prevailed, they would have unlocked parts of the Kingdom forbidden to trade in. Take Lyonshall. Lyonshall mines trade only with the Old realms. Imagine if Demos or Morfit had direct access to them? And so on. You see, it's far more than for the good of the cursed earthblood."

Ryd winced at the slur but didn't respond. Silence fell upon them like a thin sheet. A gust of wind billowed the train of

Digory's guard's cloak in flapping waves until Ryd broke the lull. "Why do we travel through Baneswood to Croft instead of through the Omen?" His brow pinched.

"There you go having Vanguard knowledge," Digory said, to which Ryd shot a glare. "Yes, that is true. However, at the moment, we're at odds with Basil, and I hear Lachlan as well, he and Tomas had a disagreement, I heard, so we avoid Lyonshall's border too for now. Word is, the old man has a temper. And is losing his mind in his late years."

"You heard," Ryd said. He turned in his seat to face Digory. "Why do you say 'we' like you're one of them?"

Digory scratched at his short, dark beard. "Westerviolet is home."

"You know they don't see you that way. You know they don't see you at all," Ryd said. "My father..."

"Deadbloods," Digory sharply interrupted. "On with it."

"Right." Ryd didn't want to poke his new companion too hard. Digory deeply intimidated him and Ryd was not sure what would happen if he was provoked. "It was after we left Croft Hold. I thought things went well with Morfit. Elder Goodman Morfit is, well... *good*." Digory snickered. "He is," Ryd defended. "The man I met was reasonable and fair. They agreed to continue the accord."

"They?"

"Him and Clemmo, speaking for the Lord," Ryd clarified. "Not target or plot against the other's blood, despite politics."

"Ah," Digory nodded. "I heard."

"You heard?"

"Word got out in the barracks." He turned his head to look at Ryd. "A lot unhappy about it. They say it's like fucking the enemy." Ryd only shrugged. "After you left Croft Hold," Digory urged.

The sound of their horses' hooves cut through the warm air as Ryd rubbed beads of sweat from his brow, then smoothed his curls. "I promised the old man I wouldn't say..." he sighed, "but what's it matter now? I might as well tell you."

"Old man," Digory turned. "Clemmo? Before the raider

attack?" Ryd shook his head. "Tell me. Was it deadbloods, instead? Is that how he died? They kept his body hidden, so it was surely gruesome. I must know what we're getting ourselves into."

"Don't lie, you're curious as well."

Digory turned to reveal a roguish smile. "Aye."

Ryd sighed. His memories were heavy and painful, haunting his dreams each time he closed his eyes. "We left Croft Hold's castle along a different road than we came. Instead of taking the Gilded Bridge, we were directed to the southern route that went down straight through the realm instead of back along the border edge of Baneswood. It was supposed to be much faster and safer."

"How well did that go?"

"Not very well."

"How were you attacked by deadbloods in the middle of the realm?" Digory turned his head. "I didn't think they could survive for long so far outside the Deads."

"The path we took didn't lead us through the center of the realm," Ryd said with a weary sigh. "It took us to the base of the Hills, through the edge of the abandoned Horne Territory now infested with the cursed things."

"Brilliant!" Digory laughed. "Why? Did Clemmo misread the map? Smudge it with his fat fingers?"

Ryd's ample lips curved into a displeased frown. "It isn't right to speak that way of the dead."

"Everyone hated him. And he was fat. It's true whether or not he's dead."

Ryd shrugged. "We realized we'd gone the wrong way once the blue Hills rose up before us. But, by that time, night fell. We chose to camp and decide what to do at daybreak. I went off to gather the kindling, yet, as I walked through the woods, something was odd."

"Odd?"

"Yes," he nodded. "It was silent."

"You were in the woods. No men around. Surely it was."

"No, not quiet," Ryd retorted. He remembered how he felt

that eve, like it was yesterday. Every sense was on alert. "I mean silent. No birds chirping, or animals rustling leaves, or crickets humming as the sun set. The entire forest hushed like it was holding its breath, all at once. I looked down and saw small vermin and reptiles slithering past my feet in flee."

"Deadbloods?"

He nodded furiously. "I dropped the kindling and ran back to the others."

"Did they believe you?"

"By the time I got there, it was too late."

"What do you mean?"

Ryd flexed his jaw, swallowing hard as he conjured the memories he had of his travel companions being ripped into pieces while still alive, images that would forever be branded on his brain. "The deadbloods reached them before I did," he said with a guilty lump in his throat. "I ran out of the woods into the clearing to find the men on the ground, Agan and Opin with large gashes across their stomachs, intestines spilling out on the meadow floor. Opin was bleeding and twitching, nearly dead, but Agan was frantically trying to scoop his flopping innards back into his body."

"Sounds pathetic."

Ryd frowned. "They were good men," he said. Eyes distant. "It was bad."

"Right, right," Digory said quickly. "Tell me of them. The deadbloods!"

"I only saw the one who had Clemmo," Ryd said as he swatted at a shiny green beetle flying by his head. "He cut open Clemmo's stomach with his claws as I ran into the clearing. Then he gripped him by the neck. The old man's eyes almost bulged out of his head. I think he was too shocked to say anything at all."

"I would have liked to have seen that, the pompous old bag," Digory spat.

"The dead..." Ryd warned.

"The dead are dead. I'll talk of them as I please," Digory replied. "How did he hold fat Clemmo's neck in one hand?"

"They are large," Ryd said distantly, remembering the fearsome pale giants.

"Their hands?"

"Everything," he said in darkly fascinated awe. "Their hands and feet. Their claws. Their shoulders. Their jaws. They are taller than a Vanguard, even taller than Graves. Their skin is light grey. Like they really are dead."

"What else did it look like? Do they really have fangs like we tell the little ones?"

"No," Ryd said. "Well," he added without confidence, "not really."

"Not really?" Digory was captivated. He'd been entranced by deadblood stories since boyhood. They were common in tales told to children, urging them to obey orders, or else they'll be snatched up in the night.

"I think they file their teeth into points. They look sharp. But, not like an animal."

"Do they walk like a man?" Digory asked eagerly. "Or crawl like a beast?"

"Like a man, but faster and stronger, with white hair and grey-white eyes to match their skin."

"Do they wear clothes?"

"No."

"Interesting." Digory brooded, wiping sweat off his forehead with the tail of his cloak. "Did it say anything?"

"I heard a commotion while in the thick of the woods, but I only saw the one that killed Clemmo. He didn't talk to me. He didn't say anything at all," Ryd said, setting his brow low, lying with difficulty. He didn't mention the deadblood's eloquent warning, how he spoke with command, in the common tongue, indistinguishable from a Vanguard Lord.

The deadblood looked Ryd dead in the eye and Ryd felt as if he'd been plunged into a snow stream. "Young man," the deadblood said, expression empathetic and pained despite blood dripping from his hand and the dead men at his feet, "you must not let them have her. It cannot happen again."

"Have who?" Ryd asked. But the deadblood turned and in an

instant was gone into the treeline. It was disconcerting, to say the least.

"But it saw you?" Digory asked earnestly.

"Yes, he did. As I ran into the clearing," Ryd said. "He looked like he was just about to leave."

"Why didn't it kill you?

Ryd hesitated. "I…I don't know. He saw me and ran off."

Ryd thought it best to lie given the gravity of knowledge imparted on him. He didn't even want to know it himself. To think that the deadbloods were a civilized people, that they could speak, that they somehow cared for others, that there was a woman they thought required protection, that they were not a group of deranged savages, was unthinkable. Since he hadn't told Lord Tomas and the others what transpired, he saw no reason to tell Digory. He didn't trust the Guardsman. Not at all. He didn't want to know the information himself. He pushed it out of his mind.

"You said there were three men with you as well as Clemmo. What happened to the third?"

Ryd shut his eyes. He exhaled, guilt bubbling in his chest. "Rowem was scouting for water and returned not long after I did, but alas, he was the first to react."

"Alas?"

"Yes," Ryd said sadly.

"What happened?"

He looked down to study the path. "It should have been me."

"What happened?" Digory wondered what his fearful companion could have possibly had done.

"Rowem ran to tend to the wounded men," Ryd said, shame scalding him with each word. "He grabbed Agan's head to calm him and help him as he lay dying. Like a coward, I just stood and watched. Like I was frozen." He didn't mention that he actually did feel frozen by the glare the Deadblood had given him.

Digory shrugged. "What's wrong with that?"

"It saved me," Ryd said hollowly. "I just left both there to die. I'm a coward."

"How?" Digory turned to study Ryd's forlorn expression. "I mean, how did it save you?"

"I saw the dark grey poison first," Ryd remembered out loud, gaze distant, totally trapped in the past. "It started at Rowem's hands where he held Agan. It was the same place that he must have been touched by the deadblood."

"Dread Death?"

"Yes." Digory nodded grimly as Ryd went on. "It hit him faster than I could imagine. The stories about it are true. Worse. So much worse."

Dread Death was an incurable disease that sprung from contact with deadbloods. Some, it took quickly. Others, slowly. All went painfully. It was the very same disease that took out nearly all Vanguards two hundred years prior, referred to commonly as the Plague.

"You stayed clear and avoided the Dread?"

Ryd nodded, glancing to Digory, then back straight ahead. "All I could do was stand and speak to them from afar as they died."

"Did Clemmo say anything?"

"He was barely conscious and bleeding fast when the deadblood left him," Ryd said distantly, "but yes he did. That's why I kept it a secret. He asked me to."

"Why?"

"I thought it was obvious."

"Tell me."

Ryd swallowed hard. "The Morfits betrayed us," he said bluntly. "One of them told Clemmo to take a different route through the old Horne territory, hoping we never made it back to Westerviolet. Then the whole plan for the Accord would fall through."

"Who?"

"He didn't say." Ryd rubbed the back of his neck. "Clemmo told me something is brewing. This is the start of it. He made me swear to hide what happened."

"Why?"

"He feared if Tomas discovered the insult, he would invade

Croft Hold," Ryd said gravely. "Thousands of lives would be lost. More. A new war would begin. He said the Kingdom is teetering at the edge of it already. One assault and it'll all fall to ruin."

"Surely anyone who saw the bodies knew the truth?"

Ryd shook his head. "I was careful to protect myself and I tightly wrapped each body in their own sleep bag. I slung them atop the horses and led them all back home. It took a fortnight longer than it should have. I cannot tell you how badly they stank by the end. The others took my word for it that their deaths were caused by raiders. Didn't want to look at the sun-rotted flesh. The smell was enough. The bodies were burned not long after I returned."

Digory couldn't imagine why anyone would ever go through so much trouble, simply for honor. He would have left the bodies behind, only taken their daggers, if it had been up to him. "You told Tomas the truth," he asked, hoping the answer was no. "Surely he knows?"

"No."

Digory raised his eyebrows. He'd misjudged the young stablemaster. "What about Budic? Does he know what happened to his Second?"

"I don't think he does," Ryd said wearily. "I didn't tell him. I didn't tell anyone."

Digory smoothed his beard. "Interesting."

"Do with the information what you wish," Ryd said with disgust. "I'm done keeping Vanguard secrets. I only want to find my brother."

"Which Morfit betrayed us?"

"I told you," Ryd muttered, turning his head to look at him, shielding the sun from his eyes. "Clemmo didn't say."

"Who do you think?"

"I don't know."

Digory was unrelenting. "You went on the trip that just returned as well, didn't you?

"I got back not long before you stumbled into my stable."

"Where did that one take you?"

"The Cursed border."

Digory nodded. "Why would you agree to go after what happened with the deadbloods?"

Ryd shrugged. "I didn't want to draw attention by refusing." And he didn't want to betray his father's legacy. His father never said no. His father was fearless; a trait young Col inherited that Ryd was painfully lacking yet mimicked adequately enough. Although Digory saw right through the façade.

"Did you see any that time?"

Ryd shook his head curtly. "No."

Then, an arrow flew inches from Digory's shoulder with a terrifying *whoosh*. It landed deep in a white birch trunk at the cusp of a forest to his far left with a twang.

"Down, get down!" he yelled, instinctually rolling off his horse. "Raiders! It's an ambush!" Digory shouted as he plunged behind a fallen tree off the path's edge. Arrows fiercely pummelled from the ridge on the right.

"I can't leave the horses!" Ryd yelled back, crude arrows landing loudly to his left. "Shit!" he shouted as one barely missed his thigh. Following Digory, Ryd jumped clumsily off Mable and scurried over the dirt and pebbles of Narrow Road until he joined his position behind the large log. Arrows dotted the log, cutting through the wind and striking with heavy pops as the shafts implanted in the old, dead wood of the fallen tree.

"Ready yourself." Digory loaded his svelte, tactical crossbow, pulled from his back, already expertly assembled. "What are you waiting for?" he again yelled at his unmoving companion.

"My sword is on Mable," Ryd shouted woefully.

"Who the curse is Mable?"

"My horse!" Ryd screamed over the sounds of arrows flying at them, pointing at the brown mare galloping away down the road. She'd been hit in the flank by an arrow and was followed closely by Digory's mount Chester in fast pursuit. The pair watched as Ryd's weapon bounced from its position secured to one saddle. The rations hung from the other. The mounts faded into tiny specks on the green, hilly horizon, then disappeared into nothing at all. Soon, the horses were gone.

"You left your blade!" Digory bellowed, then muttered to himself, "Curses. He *is* useless."

"You told me to get off!" Ryd yelled back. "Let me use yours! Your dagger!"

Digory paused, despite the twangy assault of crude arrows and loudly rustling breeze he felt eerily at home and calm. He assessed his panic-stricken companion's gaze for an unnecessarily long moment, then said slowly and deliberately, "No."

"You can't be serious," Ryd cried back, shaking from terror, clinging to the log.

Digory's fiery eyes burned with intense focus, studying the adjacent ridge's matching white-birch treeline. "Do you see where they are?"

"See them? See who?" Ryd spun, hands white-knuckle gripping a shard of old wood protruding from the dead log. "Give me your weapon! Please, anything!"

"The raiders, you dolt. Where are they!?"

Ryd didn't respond due to overwhelmed terror.

Digory sighed. "If I give you this dagger you will surely die," he said as he gestured to it, "as you have no idea how to use a real weapon. You'll likely lose mine as you did your own. You're surely untrained." At the look on Ryd's face he added, "You know it is truth," in a chillingly deep tone. Ryd looked away. He nodded once, swallowing his pride in a gulp. Digory continued evenly. "The first arrow came over my shoulder. That means one of them is over that way." He pointed to his right into a particularly dense thicket of trees on the ridge. "Can you see anyone?"

"I'm not sticking my head up. Not for you."

"This isn't for me. Don't be a child. This is for us. And since you are a dolt and have no weapon of your own, the least you can do is help me use mine."

"Is there another way?"

A high-arched arrow landed perpendicular in the ground directly behind their backs with a threatening twang. Had the wind been a bit different, it would have gone right through either one of them.

"What the curses I'll do it myself," Digory said, words tumbling out in breathy frustration. He shot his head up quickly over the log once then dropped back down just in time to avoid a flurry of arrows. "I was right," he said as he looked sideways to Ryd. Digory took a deep breath as he readied his crossbow, popped back up above the fallen tree, then released. His arrow flew towards the tree line, followed by a loud moan and a thud. Digory lowered and sat with his back against the log again. He looked to Ryd. "Curse you, you know that?"

"Hey."

"No, I'm serious," Digory said surely. "I have to do everything. How have you travelled these roads before and never met raiders? How do you not know how to fight? How do you not grab your weapon as first instinct?" He paused, thinking. "How do you not have a better weapon?"

"I've never..." Ryd paused, sighing. "I've never met raiders," he admitted. "I've never fought. I lied when I said I'd travelled far. I've only been the one time to Croft Hold and then on last moon's mission to the border. Before that, I've transported grain across Vice Provinces, or consulted with the other realm's stable masters, but never outside of Westerviolet," Ryd admitted softly, lowering his head. "And I've never used a weapon."

"Why would they take you to Croft if you're useless!?"

"My father died," he replied. "There was no one else."

"You know nothing of trading then. Or fighting." Digory's mood fouled further. "Marvelous. I brought along a horse fucker. And now I don't even have his fucking horses."

Ryd glared.

Digory changed the subject, speaking mainly to himself as he glanced at the surroundings. "We must have just crossed into Littlebell's realm."

"How do you know?"

"Besides the trees," Digory said condescendingly, gesturing to the white-birch line in the near distance, "raiders would never attack the Brochet emblem on Brochet land. But Littlebell... Littlebell is ripe, here where the land isn't protected. It's supposed to be neutral, but raiders in don't seem to care about things like that."

"Why isn't it protected?"

"Minney doesn't have forces. None at all. Don't believe in it." A barrage of angry arrows thudded against the log as Digory turned to Ryd. "How do you not know that?"

"I knew that," Ryd lied. "I thought this was near Morfit land," he added defensively.

"With what you just told me of their treachery, you wonder why the Morfits don't keep our border?"

Ryd's eyes widened in understanding.

Digory raised up again to gauge the position of their assailants as a new bombardment of arrows cut precisely through the air, narrowly missing him. He lowered his head just in time. "There are three more of them. Maybe four." Digory looked down at his feet; six arrows left. "This is going to be tight. Too bad we don't have more weapons."

"You said to get off the horse!"

"Shut up I can't think," Digory growled. "Useless. Cursed useless."

He reloaded the crossbow as another arrow whizzed at them from behind a large boulder halfway down the ridge, closer to the path. Digory popped his head up, and, this time, fired on instinct without assessment. A blood-curdling scream erupted when the arrow hit its target.

"You're a good shot."

"I know."

"How long did it take to get that good?"

I was born this good, Digory thought. "Not. Now," he said.

"We have ya surrounded!" an orotund declaration bellowed from behind the treeline. "Lay down yar weapons..."

"Weapon," Digory muttered under his breath.

Ryd frowned.

"...and we may let ya live. I will now step out of me position. If ya honorable men, ya won't shoot. We'll speak terms!

Agreed?" the disembodied voice shouted.

Digory shouted back an enthusiastic, "Aye!" as he reloaded behind the fallen log.

"You're disgusting," Ryd said under his breath.

Digory flashed a cavalier smile.

"I will now come forward. I repeat, ya not to shoot!" the deep voice shouted after which a short man with downturned eyes and a shiny bald head not fitting the voice at all stepped out of the tree shadows and into the light. He was dressed in dark rags with crudely fashioned sandals, equipped with an oversized wooden bow and a quiver of arrows. He was a raider.

Digory stood while Ryd stayed crouched behind the fell tree. "Who are you?" Digory yelled up the hill at the short, middle-years man.

"Kon, of Hill's Shadow!" the man hollered down at Digory with practiced command. "Ya be of Westerviolet," he assessed, noting Digory's attire.

The Hill's Shadow raiders were a jovial band of thieves who believed they were doing the right thing. Most were family men with wives and children who got tired of a life of poverty and banded together in the wake of destruction after the Uprising ended, fifty years prior. They hated Vanguards, particularly from Old realms. They were also a subset of the Faith of the Horned that had been long-ago exiled for they refused to pay homage to Glassy Stream or participate in the annual sacrifices. They primarily occupied Flower Valley, deep within abandoned Horne territory, however, commonly pilfered merchant caravans on the outskirts of Littlebell, Westerviolet and Baneswood. Some infiltrated Westerviolet, when hungry enough.

"Aye, *were*," Digory clarified with bravado. "We've escaped!"

Ryd whispered up at Digory. "Why do you lie?"

"Go with it," Digory hushed back without looking down through smiling teeth.

"I cannot make out ya words!" Kon's shout echoed from afar.

"Come closer!" Digory shouted back, still grinning, "And

bring your friends. I won't shoot," he said, feeling his elite weapon deep in his palm. "We are brothers!"

The raider nodded and gestured to his left. A tall man with an oblong face and a thin man with a balding ponytail emerged from the woods, both with similar features to Kon, exchanging confused glances with each other.

"What did ya say about escaping?"

"Why, did you not hear?"

"What do ya speak?" Kon asked loudly, walking forward more.

The men whispered to each other as they approached while Digory didn't move from behind the tree, still holding his small crossbow loosely in his hand, down to his side, hidden in shadow. When the group was markedly closer, he spoke again. "We've revolted against the tyrant Budic! Tried to take the Guardsmen and failed," Digory lied loudly. "Now we flee."

"Why do ya travel the Narrow?" the thin man asked, taking careful steps through the tall grass. "What business do ya have in Littlebell?"

"Who says we go to Littlebell?"

"That's the way ya head," the tall man retorted. "Where else would ya go?"

Digory smiled wide. "My Lords, why, we are here for you! How fortuitous that we found you. Or, rather, you found us."

The approaching raiders exchanged confused glances.

"Us? Why would ya look for us?"

Ryd whispered upwards sharply at Digory, "Yes, why would we look for them?"

"Quiet!" Digory chided down at him through his clenched, false-smiling, bearded jaw. "We sought you out to join your ranks, of course!" Digory cried out to the apprehensive raiders. "We have heard of Flower Valley's sanctuary."

The three raiders converged in front of Digory and Ryd on the opposite side of the pebbled road's edge. The short raider, Kon, held his bow and arrows. The tall raider had a hand on the hilt of a curved, finely fashioned sword, now dinged and rusted, likely Morfit made, scavenged from an old war. The thin one's bow was pulled tight in warning.

"Unheard of," Kon balked. "Never in history has a Guardsman aligned with Hill's Shadow. We be enemies."

"Yes, and all the more reason for us to join you, and now we are both enemies of the Guardsmen. Obviously," Digory said with a grin. "Good to greet you, brothers!"

The thin man asked with a squeak, suspiciously, from behind his bow. "How do we know we can trust ya?"

"Put that down, Hirsh," Kon chided, "as a sign of good faith. Ya heard the man. They mean us no harm." He gestured with his hand and placed it on his comrade's slight, rag covered shoulder to pull him close in a huddle. The tall raider joined suit. All three now had their backs to Digory and Ryd. Digory smiled.

"Don't," Ryd whispered, flinching in anticipation, but it was too late. Digory had already raised his crossbow and fired at the huddle.

In the instant the first arrow took off, Digory was reloading. Before taking another breath, he let off a second shot.

The first shot fell on the tall man. He collapsed forward with an agonizing wail and landed on his companions, chest pulsing spurts of blood. The shock in addition to his size and weight staggered the two smaller men, yet, before they could react, the second arrow burst through Kon's eye and poked out of the back of his skull, knocking off a portion of bone to expose pulsing brain underneath. Kon's body dropped dead to his knees, then face first into the dirt with a sad crunch. Viscous blood pooled in a red lake beneath him. The tall, large man wailed at white clouds above him as he died in what appeared to Ryd to be excruciating pain next to Kon's warm corpse. The thin, balding raider, Hirsh, reacted just in time. He rolled away from Digory's barrage. A well-placed arrow narrowly missed his neck.

"Curses," Digory said under his breath. "Almost had him." He reloaded. Hirsh readied his own crude bow and fired on Digory, just as Digory dropped behind the arrow-speckled tree.

"What'd you do that for?!" Ryd shouted.

"What?" Digory half turned, visibly proud. "What'd I do what for? Save your life for? I really have no cursed clue."

"No. No no no," Ryd said as another arrow landed with a thud in the tree. "You told them you wouldn't shoot but you shot anyway. It's not permitted, Digory," Ryd whined, thinking of the law, "they were speaking terms. That means you murdered them! You'll hang for that!"

The barrage ceased briefly. In its place, footsteps echoed more and more softly through the rustling grass.

"Hear that? He's moving away," Digory said. "That means he's trying to flank us."

Meanwhile, Ryd was distraught. "You swore you wouldn't. How could you just murder them like that? They were speaking terms! Why did you shoot?"

"Let's first not die. I like not dying. Then ask me any cursed question you want." Digory's tone dripped venom. Ryd frowned. "The raider shooting at us from over there will soon be shooting at us from up there, and that will be very bad," Digory added as if speaking to a child, pointing from beyond the adjacent tree line, to over their shoulder up a higher ridge. "If I can't get him before he gets the high ground, we've got to make a run for it."

"You're going to shoot him too?" Ryd asked. "Cursed First, you are!"

"You sound like a cursed Minney child. He's shooting at us. Obviously, I am going to shoot him."

"I can't believe I agreed to come with you."

"Not now," Digory said. "Follow me."

"Right," Ryd rolled his eyes, "or else you'll shoot me."

"I do have one more." Another arrow lobbed high in the air and landed straight into the ground between them. Glancing at it, Digory said, "We'd best move. Ready?"

"No," Ryd replied, almond eyes wide with fear.

"Go!" Digory shouted, leaping instantly over the tree barricade.

Ryd yelled, "Now?!" but was too late, as Digory was already

ten paces ahead of him. "Wait!" Ryd pleaded, running behind him.

"Don't run straight," Digory shouted over his shoulder as he darted back and forth through the high-grass meadow. "Run like a snake," he yelled, running in a looping pattern. He paused when Ryd didn't listen. "You dolt, serpentine!"

"What!?" Ryd shouted, unable to hear, still sprinting in a straight line.

"Like a snake!" Digory answered. "I mean run like a..."

Then, an arrow landed deep in Digory's left shoulder with a sickening pop. Shards of pain shot through every vein in his body, like white-hot fire. "Argh! Curses!" he yelled as he collapsed onto his side.

Ryd, still sprinting straight, reached Digory cursing on the ground, cradling his shoulder.

Ryd shouted down at him. "You've been hit."

"I can't tell," Digory growled back through a clenched jaw. He touched the arrow protruding from his shoulder. It had pierced through an impossibly tiny gap in his chainmail. He began to yank it out but yelped pitifully as another arrow zipped through the air and landed by his foot with a twang.

"You're hurt. Grab my hand."

"Are you mad?" Digory asked with a low growl, like the wounded beast he was.

"Grab my hand. Let's go."

"You don't hear me," Digory said angrily, another arrow narrowly whizzing by. "Fortune is with us that the wind has picked up and he's not a good shot. But fortune will change," he said, shifting his weight, groaning. "Take this," he added, wincing again in agony as he handed his crossbow to Ryd. His good arm was useless to him now. He had no choice but to trust the man with his weapon, and life. It was a necessary risk. "He should be right over there," Digory said, gesturing to a clump of peeling white birch trees. Ryd slowly took the weapon and turned it over unfamiliarly. "For curse's sake, Ryd!" Digory bellowed. "For curse's sake shoot him back!"

Ryd, panic-stricken, heart thumping out of his chest, quickly fired. The arrow flew in a lazy arc through the sky. It didn't even make it half the distance to their attacker before dropping flat into a sea of seeded grass bobbing in the breeze.

"What the curses Ryd!?"

"I'm sorry!" Ryd cried. His cheeks burnt hot. "I've never done this before, I'm sorry!"

"Curse it. This is the last one." Digory, dizzy with pain, loosing focus, tossed Ryd the last arrow. It toppled lazily, point over tail to the ground. "I wanted to save this for you but curse it." Ryd frowned as he clumsily scooped the arrow from the dirt and reloaded the delicate weapon with Digory's guidance. "No, the other way you dolt," he hissed, directing Ryd trying to insert the arrow the wrong orientation. He couldn't believe how useless this man was. Barely able to call himself a man. "Careful! Quickly! Oh curses, another one! Watch out!" Digory shouted, shoulder pulsing, vision fading as another arrow from the birch ridge whizzed by.

Ryd ducked just in time.

"How many does that guy cursing have on him? I'm a bit impressed," Digory said, face paling, woozy from blood loss and shock, clutching the arrow still jutting from the left of his chest. The wound site sizzled. His vision pulsed. *Nighthorn poison*, he thought. *Perfect.*

"Will you be quiet?"

"He'll have reached that ridge by now. Look, over there. See him. He's aiming once more. Now!"

Ryd breathed out slowly, said a silent prayer to the Ancestors and aligned the weapon with his target. He clenched his eyes tight and fired blindly at Hirsh, the slim and balding Hill's Shadow raider.

"Fuck!" Digory shouted. "Cursed fuck!"

"What? What happened?" Ryd shouted back, breaking his eyes open slowly.

"You got him! I don't cursing believe it. You got him!" Digory cheered as he pumped his good fist in the air, then winced in pain, hard. "I didn't think you had it in you."

Ryd dropped to his knees in the dirt and high grass, taking a deep breath in, then exhaling slowly. "I got him?" he asked, half-shocked, shaking wildly. "Are you sure?"

"Right in his chest you did! I saw him fall. How's it feel?"

Ryd turned. "How do *you* feel? You're the one shot."

"I feel good. I'll get another scar. I love scars. Proof I'm alive, that's what I say."

Ryd rolled his eyes. "You're pale."

Digory winced, barely able to see, dizzy from pain. "I'm fine."

Ryd stared at him, subconsciously clutching his own shoulder in empathetic agony. "Really?"

Digory side eyed him. "Really what?" Glinting beetles buzzed in front of his ashen face.

"You didn't say thank you."

"Why would I?" Digory shifted his weight, hands sticky with his own blood. He gestured at his wound. "This is because of you."

"I saved your life," Ryd argued. "What if I ran? That raider would have killed you."

"Maybe, or I would have survived just fine, then hunted you down for betraying me."

"That's not how it…"

"You need me more than I need you. It was a good shot, but fortune saw you. I could have done better."

"You really are the worst."

"I know," Digory said. He flashed a proud smile. Then, with his shoulder pouring blood, his vision faded. He groaned in pain as everything turned black.

WESTERVIOLET LORD'S STUDY

Lord Tomas Brochet sat behind the legendary elderdesk as he rifled through the latest documents delivered from Animus Rock, as he did at the cusp of each new moon. Edicts, advertisements, and invitations scattered across the massive face.

Public demonstrations in Animus Rock now permitted.

Jewel blossom pollen PRESENTLY available from Graceview. Place orders promptly to ensure timely delivery. Note: Thorneblood not liable for ill effects, including chromatic tears, sensory bleeding, or in rare cases, death.

Lady Verity Bellamine's birthday is forthcoming. All bloodlines are cordially invited.

Tomas glanced through the parchments and sighed. Nothing worth his time. After smoothing his thick hair with one hand and removing square spectacles with the other Tomas rubbed his eye with a finger.

"Where shall we begin?" he asked, without looking up.

Budic stood across the room holding his helmet in front of his body with both hands.

"Sit," Tomas commanded, tapping the edges of the papers on the desk, then placing them down. He set his oblong rock on top then folded his spectacles and placed them also on top of the parchments aside the infamous stone. "What's going on in my realm?" he asked in a groaning croak, like a slowly opening door.

Budic crossed the room with a clanking limp then rested adjacent the Lord. He sat with a clinking rustle of chainmail. "We received word today of another attack on the Narrows,"

Budic said, eying the stack of papers.

Tomas glanced up from underneath his bushy eyebrow. "Raiders again?"

"Aye. Raiders."

"Bastards," Tomas spat under his breath. "How many did we lose?" Budic was silent. Tomas looked up. "How many?"

"None, my Lord."

"None?"

"There was an attack, but it was the raiders that fell," Budic said carefully. "A Fellowship caravan arrived an hour ago with the bodies as proof. Expecting coin, of course, for the trouble."

"Naturally," Tomas said with a flit of his wrist. "How many?"

"Six of them."

"Any word of our hero's identity? The weapon?"

"None," Budic said. "And arrows are my guess."

"Guess? Wouldn't arrows remain as proof? You're certain not spears? Or swords?"

"Nay," Budic replied. "Whoever it was took them when they left. There are holes where arrows should be, nothing more. They must have been a good shot, too. One was right through an eye. Dead through."

"Any threat to us?"

"Not that I can see, my Lord."

Tomas nodded, satisfied for now. He placed great trust in Budic and if he didn't worry, then Tomas didn't. When Tomas was young, he was sharp, but with age came dullness. Although, when the moment called for it, he still had his signature charismatic personality. Tomas rubbed the bridge of straight nose, squinting in thought briefly. "If someone wants to kill my enemies for me, fine. The larger question remains. Why so many attacks by the Hill of late? Commander, how that can be? Clemmo discussed the Minney border two moons ago. Where are the Morfits?"

"My men have not seen them at all," Budic said studying the dark iron helmet he held in both hands in his lap. He popped his head up. "Not once."

"Not once since the Morfit accord six moons ago?"

"Not once."

Tomas grumbled, "Old Goodman is a fool to test me."

Tomas Brochet and Goodman Morfit had never quite seen eye to eye, the opposite really, coming to a head nearly every Council session in their younger years. Tomas was as Oldblood as Vanguards came, while Goodman was New. But in spite of their stark differences, politically, socially, even morally, they were cordial.

Goodman was known for his softness, in fact. Tomas certainly didn't see him as a threat.

"Why would he betray Brochet?"

"The New rotted his brain." Tomas remembered the cheerful dolt's gullible temperament well. Elder Goodman Morfit was well liked amongst newbloods and natives, however, hated by oldblood Vanguards for his progressive ways. "Must be. That and the whisperings of his earthblood whore of a wife," he grumbled. "It's the Uprising all over again."

"I don't think Goodman Morfit betrayed you, my Lord," Budic said, then fell into an expectant pause.

"What, then? What is it?"

Budic steadied himself internally. "The word is the men follow Lord Rupert now."

"The son?!" Tomas exclaimed, chuckling to himself, shoulders bouncing in amusement, remembering a tale he'd heard of the boy, when after Sybil bested him in a horse race, he cried. "Sybil's old friend? The copy of his father? The soft one? Sent to Animus Rock years ago to keep him out of Croft's affairs," he added with a dismissive wave of his hand.

"He was," Budic said, "but he's returned. And he's trained as a sweep fighter now, the men say."

"Goodman would never allow it."

Budic's naturally thin eyebrows pinched. "I tell you, he…"

"Let's talk to the earthblood again," Tomas interrupted, growing more cavalier with age. "The one who brought back Clemmo's corpse."

"Burkhart's son? Why?" Budic leaned forward. "My men

already questioned him."

"Something isn't right," Tomas replied slowly with squinted hazel eyes. "After we're finished here, fetch him and bring him to me. I'll do it myself. See what he knows about the traitorous Morfits."

"Yes, my Lord."

"What else, Budic?" Tomas's tone was unimpressed, as if each breath threatened a sigh or yawn.

"Basil sends word."

"That old dolt," Tomas huffed. "I forget about him, rotting away in his First hole." He insulted Echo's Omen, although deep down, deeper than he'd ever admit, he was impressed by the massive structure and the obedience of those under Basil Graves' command, mad he was. Nearly jealous.

"They think it's paradise."

"One dog's shit is another dog's meal," Tomas spat. "What does the bastard want now?"

"He sends his regards."

"He's gone soft. They all have," Tomas grumbled.

"Not only that, my Lord."

"Good. Sentiment doesn't suit him. Nor I. What then? What's he want?"

Budic paused, mulling over his words carefully. He knew no matter how he put it, though, Tomas would receive the sentiment poorly. "Basil begs you to reconsider," he finally said. "To remember the agreement."

Tomas's pleasant countenance clouded. He did his best not to think about the pact his grandfather Lucien made so long ago. To him, it was inconsequential and paled in comparison to the older, deeper debt that Graves owed to Brochet. But Gravesblood, particularly Basil Graves, didn't see it that way. "I told him from the instant she was born he couldn't have her!" he rumbled like thunder. "She's my only granddaughter. The youngest of my blood. I don't care about the cursed agreement," he said angrily. "Curse Graves!"

"Basil reminds you of the alliance. He writes that your bloodlines need each other and..."

"Horseshit," Tomas interrupted. "Curse his alliance!" He gave the pinkie, holding his left hand in a fist, with pinkie stuck straight out, gesturing in a sweeping, upward motion violently. A truly vulgar Westerviolet insult. "I won't permit his dirty deadblood son to fuck a Brochet. Out of the question!"

Amidst Tomas's tantrum, Budic was a center of logic and calm. He had weathered the Lord's storms many times. "He invites you to visit the Omen. He says it's been too long. He questions your dedication."

"He's lucky I don't hire Warn to clean out his precious Omen."

Budic ignored Tomas's gripes and went on. "He writes that Lachlan is fading, my Lord. Worse, the thread that holds Regnard to the Old is about to snap, again, if it has not already. He fears the worst. He says that true Old bloodlines must strengthen their alliances even more now." Budic paused then added cautiously, "He has a point."

Tomas frowned, standing from his seat behind the elderdesk, sauntering with an impressively lively gait to the massive window overlooking the stable and gardens. "Why?" he asked, white cloak edged in emerald billowing behind him, blinding in the light, like snow. "Ogo Regnard is no match for his father," he said surely, thinking of the pimply teen biting his nails that he remembered, as he looked out at the stable yard below. "He's only known Council meetings and political squabbling. He acts tough, although beneath it, he's all nerves. But Lachlan is a soldier. Lachlan controls the Red Plumes. And Lachlan is Old through and through. He's been through a war," Tomas said, voice rumbling. "The old man and I may not see eye to eye all the time," not even remembering himself why they were currently feuding, "but he would never betray us like his forefathers did. He's proven where his allegiances lie."

"Fair," Budic nodded, "but Lachlan grows old. Ogo holds elderclaim. The realm is his eventually, anyway."

Tomas squinted his eyes in thought.

Then, Budic stood from his seat and took a few steps until

he reached Tomas's side. "I have studied the Tree, my Lord. Ogo's daughter is wed to Rupert Morfit."

He didn't have to say another word.

Tomas frowned. He knew the Morfit boy's ambitions from his childhood friendship with Sybil. Despite his softness, he wanted power. It's why Goodman sent him away from Croft Hold to begin with. "So, it is another war they want," he said grimly.

Budic nodded once. "Seems so, my Lord."

"This is why old Goodman betrays me. He's lost control. The losers of the Uprising are back for a second lashing." Tomas remembered the Uprising well. It started when he was a younger man, closer to his daughter's age than his now, and newly married. At the time, he was full of ambition. He remembered how power-driven young men can be, and war particularly creates opportunities for the power hungry.

"But where does Basil fit?" Tomas turned from Budic and paced back to the elder desk as Ogo's sister popped into his mind. "Old Lachlan heard this from Xoana, his daughter. It must be. Her sons with Hadrian. The Bloody Norlands. She must despise what her brother has done to their name in alliance with those earthblood lovers. She must. She's her father's daughter. She's oldblood to the core," Tomas said surely. "Hadrian must have a stake," he added. "Xoana is insane. She'd never allow her husband a moment's rest if her blood realm fell back to the New."

"Are Regnard women really like they say?" Budic asked, breaking Tomas's cadence. "I've not had the pleasure to meet one."

Tomas shook his head, thin villainous lips curling into an amused smirk. "Not like they say. Worse. They're brash, and loud, and jealous like a defix. And, ugly as sin. Uglier than Busks, except instead of those long, dull Busk faces, they have snub, pig, Regnard noses. Consider yourself fortunate not to meet one. Awful," he spat. "If it weren't for their ancient blood, I'd say to the First with them, but in our Kingdom, one can't be too particular about allies."

"Would Hadrian Norland really use Warmen against Lyonshall if Ogo took control?"

"He'd march the whole cursed army on Lyonshall to ruin Regnard if he could."

"That would start a war," Budic said wearily. He'd been through one and could do it again, but he'd rather not.

Tomas stopped at his desk, resting up against it in a half-leaned seat. "Norlandblood craves an excuse for battle, no matter the cost. Past that, this is Hadrian. It's personal for him. He's ambitious and barely kept in check by old Cornelius. I know an attack on his wife's blood realm would be enough to justify action. He would tear open the wounds barely healed from the Uprising without rebuke."

"He'd dare attack Lyonshall without backup?" Budic looked surprised. "It's impenetrable." At that, Tomas scoffed. "Besides that," Budic added, "newblood surrounded!"

"Only if Demos and Dale want another war it is," Tomas replied.

"Surely they would march to defend their ally?"

"It's not yet been fifty years since we nearly wiped them from the Kingdom," Tomas said, shaky baritone grating. "If they are smart, they will stay out of it."

"My Lord," Budic offered, "the younger generations don't remember war."

"It is the way of the Kingdom," Tomas scoffed. "Our parents told us stories from their parents of Blood Wars, and yet they made the same mistakes during the Uprising."

"Aye," Budic nodded, remembering the endless bloodshed all too vividly. "The Uprising was a continuation of the Blood Wars, one hundred years later.

"Seems they do not learn," Tomas replied with a tired sigh. "They rise up and are slaughtered, again and again."

"Young men wish to start the wars that old men wish to avoid."

Tomas crossed his arms. His eyes glazed with memory. "I recall Hadrian as a boy, born during the Uprising. Escaped Animus and was raised at Graceview. His sister wasn't so fortunate. Oldblood girl with green eyes. Frail thing. Hadrian adored her."

"What happened to her?"

"He told me that he watched her fall from a window," Tomas said. "He counted to ten before she hit the ground, she fell from so high. He said the man who threw her wore gilded armor."

"Morfit."

"Morfit," Tomas agreed. "Hadrian grew up with a bad taste in his mouth for them. He never forgave Brynmor for it."

"Why'd he blame Brynmor?"

"He thought his uncle was at fault. He was Norland elder at the time and supposed to keep them safe. Hadrian told me that was why Ismelda died. Brynmor didn't protect her."

Budic walked from his place near the window, back to a seat. "Sounds like a troubled kid."

"That wasn't the end of the trouble for Hadrian," Tomas replied. "Years after losing his sister, he lost his beloved cousin."

"Aye?" Budic shifted in his seat with a clink of chainmail. "Morfit again?"

"Brynmor's daughter Serverine. Beautiful. Mix of Thorne and Norland, so, refined and blonde and chillingly pale. With eyes so intense, they could cut glass."

"What happened to her?"

"Conned by Morfit," Tomas replied. "Fled to Croft Hold. I hear she has a mongrel daughter," he added, making a face as if something stank. That was the highest betrayals in the eyes of the Oldbloods. Mixing pure Old blood with New.

"Why didn't Brynmor march the Norland army to bring Severine home?"

"The men follow Cornelius," Tomas said simply. "And Cornelius is cautious."

"But, Brynmor is the elder?"

"He was," Tomas said. "After Brynmor lost Serverine, Hadrian led a mutiny. I'm surprised we haven't discussed it. It wasn't that long ago. Regardless, Cornelius took charge. This put Hadrian in line for elderclaim instead of Brynmor's own son."

"I see," Budic said. "Then, what of Serverine?"

"In a twist of fate, Cornelius refused to retrieve her."

"The bastard."

"One would question his motivations," Tomas said with a smirk. "Overthrowing Brynmor for not going after Serverine, to then not go after Serverine himself. Hadrian was enraged, I've heard, but Cornelius quickly appointed him Lord of Warmen."

"And all was forgiven?"

"I know not. Seems so. It's none of my concern. Let's not waste breath on the squabbles of other bloodlines," Tomas said. "Cornelius is old. Hadrian will soon be elder and in control the Warmen. He is also a Brochet ally. That is what's important."

"Aye," Budic nodded. "It seems Norland is a needed ally of Brochet now more than ever."

"Yes, what is your point?" Tomas eyed his Commander curiously. "Speak plainly."

"Once Norland, or Graves, or any of them discover our reigniting of the Brochet alliance with Morfit, our position in the Kingdom is threatened."

"If it's discovered," Tomas countered. "The purpose of a secret alliance is that it is secret."

"Aye," Budic said carefully, "but in light of the Morfit's assumed betrayal, I fear they intend to betray us to the other Old bloodlines as well."

"Goodman would be a fool to cross me."

"My Lord, it isn't Goodman. As I said..."

Tomas waved his hand dismissively.

"Put yourself in his position," Budic postulated. "It's best for Ogo Regnard if the Old is fighting amongst ourselves."

A wave of realization swept over Tomas. "While we're busy bickering like maidens, he plans to take Lyonshall."

"Exactly," Budic said, nodding, "leaving Westerviolet as the only Old realm east of the Missi, apart from the Omen. It wouldn't take long for Ogo to march South. He would take the Omen on the way. Attempt to, although I'd like to see that battle," he added. Red Plumes against Omen brothers. Both were notoriously brutal. He wasn't sure who would win. "With Old Regnard dead, Graves's outpost crippled, and Brochet conquered, think. The New would actually have a chance at defeating the Old."

"That's their plot?" Tomas thought out loud. "Basil writes that Lachlan loses grip as the Morfits betray us. It all lines up."

"You made the right decision when Goodman commanded his bloodline," Budic reassured. "If the Morfit alliance held we would have been one step closer to…"

"Curses, it wasn't," Tomas interrupted sharply. "Couldn't have been the right decision. I've led us into a hornet's nest."

"We can mend this."

"How?"

Budic frowned and looked down at the hammered helmet in his hands. Then, his head popped up, jostling the thin, brown, snake-like braids around his ears. "What about Sybil?"

"Use her to hold the Kingdom together? To clean this mess?"

"Prove to the other Old bloodlines that Brochet hasn't faltered," Budic added. "She's young. She's fair. She'll have a child and it'll secure position. Even if they hear rumor of the hidden alliance, they'll disregard it as false."

Although he had already considered it privately, Tomas angered, cheeks beating red. "If you think I'm handing the jewel of Westerviolet to those dead-blooded heathens fucking each other in the Cursed Hills you have lost your mind! Never a Brochet wed to those dead men." For his harsh ways, he loved his daughter and would never give her to Gravesblood.

"My Lord, I didn't mean Basil or his brood. What of Hector Graves? Or a Norland?"

Tomas's voice dropped an octave. "Not Hector."

"But he is…"

"I said. Not. Hector." Tomas boomed. "Never."

There was something about Hector that Tomas couldn't quite put his finger on, but it made his blood run cold. And that was saying something. If there was a man who embodied the rumors about the Graves bloodline–cold, unfeeling, deadblood-like, dangerous–it was him.

Budic nervously swallowed hard. "Then a Norland. One of Xoana's boys?" he asked. "A bit young, but they will do."

"The Bloody Norlands?" Tomas nearly laughed, lightening considerably. Hadrian's four sons were given the nickname after rumors spread about the Kingdom from their own realm. What they did to the earthblood there. Hunted them, tortured them and killed them in interesting ways for sport. To avoid a scandal, and to secure Norland's alliance to Graves, Hadrian gave them to the Omen. "Those boys are hardly a step above Basil. I'm not sending my daughter to Echo's Omen to join in the debauchery of their Brotherhood and that's final."

"With respect, My Lord, was her mother not from the Green Wing?"

"You forget your place. I am not sending her there. Do not press me."

"Herman's boy?" Budic leaned forward, placing his forearms on his knees.

Herman Graves, Hector's brother, was the only one of his bloodline who held moderate views. Although now married to the sister of the King, he had one son from a previous union.

"His son is young, too young, and hardly a Graves. A mongrel," Tomas spit. "Besides, the boy was chosen by the Guild moons ago. He's off at Wraithswail. Herman shares the features and name but none of the blood beliefs with his kin anyway. Same goes for the boy. They've been warped by the looseness of the Capital after so many years with the Bellamine dandies. It's a shame how the Bellamines fell. But what can be expected after tainting their storied legacy with earthblood? No, no. Sybil will not go to the weak bastard of the Graves bloodline. If our goal is to win Old allies, that is not the correct Graves to bed, I assure you."

"You're right," Budic nodded. "But it wouldn't hurt to be near the King."

"Like I said, it wouldn't work."

"I've heard you tell her she is overdue for marriage. Why, now that it's time, do you refuse to discuss it? You won't entertain my suggestions."

"I would if they were worthy ones."

"My Lord…"

"You do forget your place. No more of this."

"My Lord, there will be war and if you do nothing. No matter who wins, we will lose," Budic cautioned. "Brochet will lose."

Tomas stood up, sighing loud from the back of his throat. He ran both hands through his thick, salt and pepper hair. "What will you have me do?" he asked with rare vulnerability. "You know Sybil."

"Aye," Budic said, nodding, thin braids jumping. "I know she'll do as she's told if it's you telling her. We need allies," he added, standing from his seat, placing his helmet to rest, walking until he was up against the desk across from Tomas. "You know it's time." Budic put his hands carefully on the desk. He leaned forward, meeting eyes with his Lord.

Tomas massaged the bridge of his nose. "This is why I keep you around, Budic."

"You'll do it?"

"She already believes I'm going to. I might as well," Tomas exhaled. "I hate to lose her."

"It is for the best," Budic reassured. He stood upright and crossed his arms. "What of Alain?"

"His branch was disgraced. He lost elderclaim," Tomas said, thinking of Brynmor's grandson. "Why would we ally with the least powerful Norland?"

"I know him. He's a good lad. Handsome. Dutiful. Strong."

"I don't care about him being a good lad if he's got the wrong blood," Tomas said harshly. "Table it for now."

"But you will consider it?"

"Enough, Commander," Tomas said firmly, returning to his seat behind the elder desk. The conversation was over.

"Aye, my Lord," Budic nodded, quickly regaining his seat adjacent the Lord.

"What else?"

Budic rubbed his thumbs over the smooth hammered metal helmet in his lap again. "Graceview is asking for an update."

"Already?" Tomas raised bushy eyebrows high. Every year Graceview lent Westerviolet coin to facilitate their lemons and barley industries, and upon harvest, all was repaid. Once a wealthy realm, Westerviolet's coin had been lost during the Uprising and had yet to regain it. Although this knowledge was not common. In the eyes of the Kingdom, they were as rich as Thorne themselves. "They know harvest does not begin for a moon. They'll have their coin when the leaves fall. It's that way each year." He paused. "What has happened? What's Thorne up to?"

"I don't know. They ask that you pay now."

"Who does?" Tomas questioned sharply.

"The letter is from Montague Thorne."

"I should have known it was Monty," Tomas laughed, thick hair dancing as he bucked. Montague Thorne, known as Monty, was the son of a friend of Tomas's. He'd mentored Monty in his younger years, when he would visit Animus Rock for the quarterly Council sessions. "He is always up to something," he added, then he cocked his head abruptly, pausing, thought striking him light a bolt of lightning. "Budic, wait a moment."

"What, my Lord?"

"You don't think Thorne is in bed with Regnard, do you?"

"Are Thorne and Regnard allies?"

"Thorne follows coin," Tomas said, papered skin pulling into deep wrinkles as he frowned. "They support battles, but don't fight in them. And, doing so they reap the rewards. It's why we owe them so much cursed coin in the first place. I'm still paying back what Father borrowed from them half a century ago."

"Is Thorne in support of the New or Old?"

"Hard to say," Tomas replied. "I'm suspect whether Ivor shares Monty's viewpoints."

"Why wouldn't he, if they're blood?"

"Remember, Hadrian Norland is Ivor Thorne's cousin, and closest friend."

"Oh," Budic said quickly, recalling the relationship now. "That complicates things."

Tomas nodded. "It does."

"Didn't you say there's a Regnard at Graceview?" Budic asked.

"Olegaria. Ogo's youngest sister. She's married to Wallace. You know, the famous one from the Uprising? Old man now. Hastien's son. Monty's cousin. Untouchable."

Budic nodded. "Could she have a part in this?"

"Olegaria? No, of course not," Tomas said dismissively. Budic raised an eyebrow. "I don't see how," Tomas added in response.

"Have you met her?"

"Well, no, but ..." Tomas trailed off.

"What if she's in line with her brother?"

"They share blood, but I doubt she'd recognize the man in person."

"Why?"

"They've never met," Tomas replied simply. Budic waited for explanation. "She doesn't leave Graceview," Tomas added casually.

"Olegaria Regnard is a prisoner?"

"Not exactly."

"What then?"

"More like," Tomas said, "the spoils of war."

"Explain."

"Wallace Thorne funded the Old to victory during the Uprising," Tomas told him. "It amazes me despite their heavy hand in the outcome, Thorne is absolved of wrongdoing just because they themselves never drew a sword."

Budic frowned. "My men recognize them for what they are."

"As they should," Tomas agreed. "The rest of the Kingdom is hopeless thinking Thorne is looking out for the good of all, instead of the good of Thorne. They're clever. In the right place at the right time. And it's nearly impossible to say no to them. Something about their nature. A remnant in their blood from a more powerful time."

"Why does Thorne hold Olegaria prisoner?"

"You know how The Uprising ended?"

"Naturally," Budic replied. "It is now legend," he clarified with half a smile. "Lachlan's betrayal."

Lachlan Regnard was the breaking point in the Uprising. A much younger man at the time, Lachlan rebelled against his newblood father and reclaimed Lyonshall for the Old. It was the turning point. This sealed the fate of the war.

Tomas nodded, confirming, remembering his own role in it as well—it was all his idea in fact, instigated by his grandfather Lucien—but he left that bit out. "Do you have any idea how Lachlan made it all the way to Ravenshroud from Lyonshall?"

"None," Budic replied. "That's clear across the Kingdom. During war, how'd he do it?"

"Wallace Thorne."

"I thought Thorne was the coin. Didn't get involved."

"Oh, they get involved, just not with spear or sword."

"Why help Lachlan betray his father?" Budic asked in shock. "What did Wallace Thorne have to gain?"

"Regnard swung the balance to the New during the Uprising, since they'd fought for the Old during the Blood Wars. Xabob Regnard's choice to switch sides after his father gave his sister to Graves nearly ended us all."

Budic's eyes widened. "That's why Lachlan's grandfather went New?"

"Yes," Tomas said with contempt. "No one wants their kin fucked by the dead. We have that in common. Unlike Xabob, I didn't go and marry a cursed Morfit in rebellion."

"Lachlan's got Morfit blood!?" Budic balked with paramount, palpable surprise. "I thought Regnard was oldblood?"

"That's what the old bastard would have you think, but nay," Tomas corrected with jesting contempt, "they were until Xabob. Xoel was worse."

"Xoel?"

"Xabob's son, Lachlan's father. He married Earthblood."

Budic was stunned. "Elder Lachlan of the proud Regnard bloodline has a *native* mother?"

"Oh yes," Tomas replied with a cheery inflection, fully amused. "He's always despised himself because of it and so was sympathetic to the Old since he was a boy. He blamed his father and grandfather for his tainted blood. He even wears darkened spectacles as to hide his earthblood eyes. We teased him ruthlessly for it at Academy. The scandal is fantastic."

"I see," Budic said slowly. "Wallace Thorne helped him because…?"

"The coin, why else?" Tomas asked rhetorically, adjusting thick peppered hair. "The sooner the Old prevailed, the more Wallace had to gain. The Old was losing and that was bad for business. Thorne doesn't lose. And he didn't just help him."

Budic leaned in anticipation. "No?"

"No," Tomas said definitively, enjoying Budic's audience. "Whispers say Wallace convinced him. Some rumour there was a deal struck."

"What kind of deal?"

"Not many know the full truth, but I have ways," Tomas said cryptically. With a mischievous twinkle in his eye, he continued. "Wallace offered Lachlan his birth right, Lyonshall's legendary Red Throne. He'd even give Lachlan a Thorne wife, his only chance of a respectable oldblood Vanguard taking him and his mixed blood. But, alas, Wallace had one condition."

"What was that?"

"He demanded a standing favor, to be redeemed at any time, no questions asked."

"That doesn't appear ill-advised."

"You know the saying," Tomas said with a smile. "Never gamble with Thorne."

"What happened?"

"Lachlan took the deal and moved to Ravenshroud. There, he was married to Wallace's sister Lilwen. Ogo, their firstborn, was birthed at Ravenshroud. After, the family moved to Graceview. There Olegaria was born, less than a year before the Uprising ended. When Lachlan went to finally reclaim Lyonshall, Wallace demanded that his sister stay at

Graceview."

"Why?"

"I know not," Tomas dismissed with a flit of his fingers. "But Lachlan refused, so Wallace called in his favor. He told Lachlan he could take his new Thorne wife Lilwen, but the infant Olegaria must remain."

"Lachlan left his daughter at Graceview?"

"He certainly did," Tomas confirmed. "Come to hear, years later she grew up to be quite beautiful. Imagine that, a beautiful Regnard! Must have gotten only Thorne blood. Poor Xoana can't stand it, the homely bird. She got the Regnard face, unlike her sister."

"What became of the girl?"

"Olegaria? Wallace married her." Budic made a face in disgust. Tomas nodded with bravado at Budic's reaction. "His own niece," Tomas added, shaking his head in agreement and loathing. "So many years younger. Despicable. As if they were Beaumonts. It's worse still what happened when Lilwen got word of what her brother had done to her daughter, his own blood niece."

"What happened?"

"She ate an entire jar of mad honey. The whole thing. A gift from passed down from Allen, himself. Needless to say, the honey was more potent than when first gathered."

"No," Budic said in a low whisper, deeply aghast. He had memories of that drug he would never forget. Could never forget. It had been decades, he'd only tried it once when he was young, and still he ached for it. It often called to him in his dreams. "It surely killed her."

"It did," Tomas nodded, voice resounding through the cavernous chamber. "After several hours." He paused briefly. "It's rumoured she scratched away all flesh from her face and neck first."

"That would make me turn on my father. If I were Ogo."

"Perhaps."

"You said there are Thorne children?"

"Three daughters. Near Rose's age."

"Interesting."

"Olegaria's girls play a role?" Tomas asked rhetorically. "Nonsense."

"Considering all possibilities, my Lord."

He flitted his fingers. "Yes, of course," Tomas mumbled. "Of course."

WESTERVIOLET GARDENS

Gawen neared the scene of young Aslf's demise. A tidy group of maidens and handmen huddled around the body beneath the fourth ancient oak, speaking in hushed whispers.

"Step aside everyone, step aside please!" Gawen said with command, yet the crowd didn't budge. "Did any of you see anything?" Gawen questioned to and fro and he passed through. "Know what happened?" Everyone shook their braided heads and glanced to their bare feet. A few said quiet "no" with narrow eyes cast down.

It was as he expected. Westerviolet natives were typically tight-lipped with Guardsmen.

"Show some respect!" Gawen said more harshly, frustrated by the buzzing unhelpful busy bodies. "Step aside. Go back to your duties." A dissatisfied mumble passed through the onlookers, clutching their pendants, uttering prayers. All had varying complexions of walnut-tone skin and squinted red eyes that glanced back and forth to one another, questioning if they should obey Gawen's command, like timid squeaking mice. "Must I alert the Commander of your wasted time? Or perhaps your Lord himself would like to hear?"

At Tomas's mention, all dispersed instantly, scurrying to the reaches of castle and grounds. In the crowd's wake, the air hung and warm and stale about the low-lying gardens. Gnats buzzed in Gawen's ear as he scanned the perimeter. Quickly, the sounds of people were replaced with the hum of the birds, high-pitched chirps in sing-song bursts. Gawen rubbed his forehead to focus and sighed as he approached the body. He was finally alone with the corpse.

"What happened to you?" Gawen whispered at dead Aslf as

he surveyed the scene.

The body was propped up against the fourth weathered oak's charred bark. The matted leaves and grass around its base were slick with congealed red blood, heavy with agitation from when the body was discovered, and from curious onlookers after. Handprints and fingerprints covered the young guard's face, arms, and cape from so many handling the body.

Gawen walked a bit closer. He squatted with a creak of chainmail to investigate.

Harsh daylight flickered across the gory scene through lush oak leaves. Aslf's young pimpled neck was slit clean across in a gaping wound that his whole head hinged on. If it weren't for the bark propping his head up, it would likely fall backwards and snap away entirely. The river of blood he lost from the gash appeared to be what killed him.

"You must have been determined. To go this deep. The whole way," Gawen said under his breath, inspecting the throat closely.

Aslf's head was nearly falling off.

His right hand clenched his glass dagger. Gawen attempted to pry the Guardsman's weapon away, but the boy's fingers were stiff. Gawen noted that Aslf clearly died holding his own dagger as he dropped the clammy stiff hand back to the ground with a thud.

"Why didn't you leave a note?" Gawen whispered to the body, checking Aslf's pockets to find a piece of bread and post keys.

"And why didn't you give back your keys first?" Gawen jiggled the keys then sniffed the perfectly fine loaf of barley bread. "And why waste good bread?"

A Guardsman approached in attire matching Gawen's, with traditional hair and an oversized head. "Second, the girl is in her quarters," the man said, naisly from his long-ago broken nose, squashed into a bump and flat from his profile.

"Thanks, Cador. Did she say anything else?"

"Nay," the large man replied, shrugging. "She cried so I left her with Petra."

Gawen nodded. "I want to speak with her, but it sounds like it'll have to be once she calms down."

"That's smart, Sec. Girl's a mess." Cador shifted his weight. "Why do you think he did it?"

Gawen did not glance away from the slain body. "Did you know him well?"

"Not well," Cador said, eyes also glued to the corpse. "Fortune held and I'm not dawn post."

No one liked dawn post. Sunrise, for natives, tended to be painful. It hurt their eyes.

Gawen nodded.

"I trained him for a moon when he was a recruit, though."

"What was he like?"

"Something to prove."

"I got that too. Must be because he's Budic's."

"The men cursed him. Thought he didn't deserve it. Thought Budic handed him a dagger for free."

"Is that what you think?" Gawen appreciated Cador's counsel, even if he didn't always agree with it.

Cador shrugged, glancing away. "I didn't know him well. He did his job. All I care for. I didn't have to like him."

"Do you think someone cared enough? Enough to kill him?"

Cador raised an eyebrow, looking back to Gawen. They met eyes. "Hard to say."

"Did you know of anyone who wanted him dead?"

Cador shook his head. "You know what I know, Sec. Kid was a pest. Not a threat. No one liked him but who'd kill him?"

"You'd be surprised."

"I tell you he did it to himself, the cursed coward," Cador growled, pointing at the body. "Look, he still holds his dagger. He was a waste of a blade. Why do you kill your time? Throw him in a pyre and scatter him in the Hills. Come spend time with the living."

"Budic's orders."

Cador nodded. "Aye. Good luck fucking yourself," he said warmly. "This one's not doing it for you."

"We'll see," Gawen said distantly, still staring intently at the body.

"Are you done here at least? Let's give him to Hudde. You'll be out of the heat and so will he." Cador gestured towards Westerviolet's Apothecary. "You don't want him stinking up the garden."

"Fair." Gawen was unable to take his eyes off the fleshy pink inside of Aslf's flayed throat. He'd never seen anything quite like it. He was disgusted and intrigued, all at once. "Arrange to deliver him."

"Yes, Second."

"While you go, I'll debrief Budic," Gawen said. "He'll want an update. Then I'll meet with Hudde."

"Do you think he's done with the Lord?"

"He should be soon."

Cador nodded. "See you in a bit, Sec."

NARROW ROAD

"How much further?" Ryd asked Digory. No response. "Hey, wake up. Don't fall asleep." Ryd tried poking his unlikely companion again, behind him on the horse. "Hey."

It had been days since they'd seen lemon orchards or barley fields, nearly ready for harvest. Now, forest sprawled out in front of them and on either side of Narrow Road, shifting from scraggly pines to modest, thin-trunk birches as they left Westerviolet and entered Littlebell's realm. High-grown weeds encircled many of the trees as if they were trying to squeeze life out of them and creeped out to the road's edge. The lanky, white trunks with papery bark dominated the treeline, with neat meadows blanketed with blue thimbleweed in between. While the scraggly pines in Westerviolet's realm felt cold and intimidating, these birches seemed to welcome the travellers with open arms.

The young men rode along the Narrow, cutting through the overgrown forest atop one underfed black horse. In the far distance were patchworked fields of lush, mature crops. Corn mostly. It was Littlebell's biggest crop and export.

Ryd was too distracted to appreciate the changing landscape. He was too worried. Digory, shirtless and tightly muscled, wound pumping trickles of blood beneath dark-crusted emerald rags, was slumped up against Ryd's back.

After the attack, Ryd scouted on Digory's woozy, insistent command. He searched the surrounding woods and found a steed left by the raiders. They continued along the Narrow once Digory ensured Ryd collected all arrows and any loot from the fallen. Before they departed, Ryd snapped the arrow protruding from Digory's shoulder in two, ditched the bloodied, tattered chainmail as well as all other evidence he was a Guardsman, apart from his dagger, as it was relatively well hidden where it sat. He wrapped the wound in a makeshift sling using strips of the emerald Guardsman's cloak.

Now, as they rode, Ryd controlled the steed while Digory sat behind him. Ryd went carefully, wincing in concern at each horseshoe-fall, for Digory's condition worsened by the moment. He had lost a lot of blood and faded in and out of consciousness in the deep afternoon heat. The sun threatened retreat, bobbing behind the wake of trees.

"What is it?" Digory came to. "What?" He grumbled. "I'm up."

Ryd glanced over his shoulder. "No, you aren't. Stay awake or you'll fall off." The black horse walked slowly, knees wobbling with the weight of the two men, hooves clacking heavily against small stones in the path. Digory grunted. "Hey," Ryd poked with his elbow. "I'm serious."

"Hmm ow, stop that." Digory moaned. "I told you I'm up."

"Then tell me how much further it is."

"Hmm," Digory mumbled incoherently. He felt his vision narrowing. His thoughts, muddled.

Ryd poked him again. "Wake up!"

"Curses!" Digory growled loudly. "Don't do that."

"I have to make sure you stay awake," Ryd said, but Digory only mumbled under his breath. Ryd half turned. "What did you say?"

"Nothing," Digory spat. He was bordering delirious.

"How much longer?"

"Do I look like a map?"

A lone crow cawed at them from a tree's branch as they passed. The blunt leaves were lush and green apart from one low limb; the tips of that foliage had faded early to autumn's brilliant gold. The Kingdom was on the cusp of fall, when everything around them was beginning to die. Ryd looked forward to it. Not only was it beautiful, but autumn held his favorite Westerviolet festivals. The Day of Fists was coming up. And Coupling Day. Ryd always wondered if he'd be coupled. Lately he awaited the festival with excited anticipation and year after year left disappointed and wanting. Although up until his father died, he wasn't sure it would be required. But still, Ryd often imagined what it would be like to touch a woman.

Then, the crow squawked again and shook him from his reverie.

"You said you knew."

"I don't."

"It's getting dark." Ryd bit at his lip, feeling a nervous knot in his stomach as he assessed the unfamiliar surroundings. "We should camp here, then."

Digory moaned again as he was jostled, then collapsed into his side, cradling his wound. "Keep going," he grunted.

"Not if you don't know how much further." But Digory only moaned pitifully. "I won't be riding all night just to ride all day tomorrow. The horse need rest. We do too."

Digory spoke more softly and slowly. "Not much further," he said with panting, pain-filled breaths. Ryd pulled the horse to a stop. "Don't," Digory whined.

Ryd shouted backwards at him. "What is wrong with you?!"

"What the curses?" Digory protested. His words slurred.

"Do you know where we are or don't you?"

Digory grunted and mumbled. His sweaty brow slumped up against Ryd's blond locks. Ryd poked Digory harder with his elbow, to no avail. "Stay awake!"

But Digory mumbled and collapsed, dead weight against Ryd's back completely.

Ryd loudly sighed. At this rate, they were never going to find Col.

"Oh great," Ryd said, turning to steady him, but the body slipped and Digory fell to the road with a heart-dropping thud. "Curses," Ryd muttered. He exhaled slowly as he pulled the horse to a stop again, then dismounted and darted to Digory's side.

The fallen man was still breathing, but barely. Ryd sighed with relief. Despite himself, he was growing attached to his companion. At least, he felt the need to keep him alive. He dragged the body to rest under a tree with much difficulty, then tethered the wretched horse to a nearby, sickly evergreen heavily overtaken by ivy. After, Ryd sunk to the ground aide his companion. He wearily closed his eyes. Digory lay unconscious, matted with brown blood, shallowly panting, his head half-propped up against the sapling beside him.

The next morning, a blinding sunrise of sharp oranges and white sunlight woke Digory. He peeled open his heavy eyes as shrill birds chirped above him in a flamboyant cacophony. Each tweet was a fresh dagger in his head's ache. The sun stabbed him too. He winced. A light breeze rustled creeping weeds on a nearby ridge. Digory saw that crusted blood caked his tan hands. He noted the makeshift sling around his arm clumsily fashioned with hasty knots and torn edges, emerald stained dark brown.

Despite the deep throbbing in his temple and the sharp pain in his shoulder, Digory was alive. Pleased by this, he smiled and lifted his head, neck stiff, and assessed his surroundings.

To his left was a black stallion. It was dirty, underfed and unkempt, fitted with an unfamiliar worn saddle and hitched to an overgrown split pine. The raiders' steed, he surmised. Narrow Road lay in front of him through a meadow of blue thimbleweed. On his right, the white-trunk birch forest, tall papery trees in neat rows, and the younger man Ryd curled on his side. Digory examined the Stablemaster's solemn expression even in sleep, then coughed loudly. Ryd stirred slowly, as if out of a dream. He stretched, then straightened quickly, and turned to Digory while rubbing his eyes with both hands.

"You look surprised," Digory said flatly.

"You wake."

"As do you."

"I wasn't sure you would."

"Were you worried about me?" Digory asked with half a smile.

Ryd looked forward quickly. "Unbelievable," he said rubbing sleep from his eye with his thumb as he shifted to sit.

"How'd you rest?"

Ryd glared at him sideways. "I don't get you."

"And here I consider myself a legible parchment." Digory turned to face Ryd, wincing pitifully in pain the whole time. "What don't you get? I'm being polite. I don't care how you slept."

"You still have not thanked me."

"I never asked you to save me. I owe you nothing."

"But just because..."

"You saved yourself," Digory interrupted. "You are selfish. I shouldn't have to thank you for that."

"I did no such thing!" Ryd shouted. "You really are something." He stood in a fury. Digory raised a coy eyebrow. "Don't look at me like that," Ryd said. "Stop it," he commanded loudly as the raucous fowl above increased in volume, each bird in fierce competition with the next, fully irritating Ryd further. Digory shook his head, still silent. "What is it!?" Ryd bellowed at him again, so loudly it disturbed the flock of birds perched on the sickly evergreen's branches. They dispersed in a cloud of displeased squawks.

"You saved me because you think you're the type to save a man," Digory said, rubbing sleep from his own eye. "It has nothing to do with me. You'd never betray yourself. If you could have, you would have left me to die. Deny that you thought about it. You can't. You wish you would do as you really desire. But you won't." He examined his wound with a wincing poke. "You're trapped by yourself, by the man you think you are," he said through the pain. "You saved me because you're weak."

Digory believed that everyone, no matter how pious, was self-serving in the end.

"I deny it," Ryd replied proudly. He smoothed his tunic. "I saved you because I need to get to Littlebell. To find my brother."

"You know just as well as I do how to get there now. Especially now that I am wounded, I'm no protection. And you care not for my mission. Really, you would have been much better off if you left me. You would have been free. But like I said. You're weak."

"Because I don't leave you to die, I'm weak? What is wrong with you?"

"I see the world as it is. Not as I'm told to see it."

"Did your father never teach you…"

"Who says I have one?" Digory retorted. "Who says I didn't rise up from the Lord's Lair unborn?"

"You are evil, that's what you are," Ryd spat. "There's no heart in you."

"If that's what you have, I wouldn't care for it. Seems messy."

"Enough, enough." Ryd sighed, defeated. "You're exhausting." Digory smiled. His strong jaw flashed beneath his dark beard. "Don't look at me like that," Ryd said.

"Like what?" Digory asked. "You can't even see me."

Ryd didn't have to look at him to know the expression he made. "Don't look so pleased with yourself."

"This isn't pleased," Digory clarified. "I'm in pain."

Ryd rolled his eyes.

"It really does hurt, you know." He shifted, adjusting the make-shift bandages, peeking at the green puss-oozing wound. "I just make it look good."

Ryd ignored him. "Why did you break your word?"

"What now?" Digory's pleasant grin fell to a bothered scowl. "Dare I try to lighten the mood," he said poking at the arrow's shard in his shoulder again.

Ryd looked deeply troubled by what Digory had done. "Those men back there. You told them you would not shoot. You even called them brothers," he said swatting tiny insects waking at dawn. "Then you killed them. You shot one straight through the eye."

"You're still tethered to that?" Digory half turned. "It was a good shot."

"There was blood everywhere."

Digory chuckled and faced forward again. *I've caused far better bloodshed than that*, he thought, remembering the time he attacked a whole merchant caravan full of Baneswood natives for Sybil, framing Hill's Shadow, just to get her a lower price on a ruby fur shawl. Now that was a fight.

Ryd felt like a pot near over-boil. "My father taught me to be an honorable man. Honor is what separates man from beast," he said surely, words resounding, yet tone unconvinced. "It's why our people are pure and it's the *Vanguard* blood that's tainted." He paused, smoothing dirt from his trousers. "I need to know why," he said. "Why would you turn on your own kind? Why would you lie to them? They may have let us go!"

"Aye, they may have let us go," Digory placated, "or they may have shot us through our eyes." He gazed in more clarity at his injury, arrow-shaft still protruding from the gruesome, blackening wound in his left shoulder. Nighthorn poison was no small matter. It worried him, but he didn't show it.

"Don't do that," Ryd said, watching Digory poke the infection.

Digory ignored him. "You know I'm right." He winced as he pulled at the crusted emerald rags a third time. A new gush of brilliantly black blood spilled from the wound. He gasped and bit his lip hard, drawing drops of blood there too.

"So what?" Ryd eyed the blood and shook his head. "Because you lie, you think they will too? The Kingdom can't function that way."

Digory laughed through winces in pain. "The Kingdom does function that way, you childish dolt. I know they will lie because they do lie. Unless you'd like to be shot you must learn to shoot first." Ryd made a face. Digory looked up, muscled and scarred chest soaked with his own putrid blood. "Did your father not teach you that? You would rather ask the raiders nicely not to shoot us?"

"Well... yes."

"My point," Digory sighed, pressing around the wound site, seeing if it was possible to remove the arrow and shaft from his chest.

"What point? I don't hear a point. Only nonsense."

"They asked nicely. Look what happened to them."

"But!" Ryd took an incensed step forward. He pointed. "You…"

Digory interrupted. "Your way only works if everyone does it that way. If one man realizes that it's faster to shoot instead of asking…" Digory trailed off. "You see?" He gestured for emphasis with his right arm as his left lay dead in his lap. "It's nice to think everyone is nice but they aren't, so best prepare for the worst. They may not shoot us, but best we shoot them first to be done with it."

The sun rose higher in the sky blanketed with gauzy clouds that cast a blinding, austere glow across the land. The wind whipped with the promises of a new day. Ryd began to pace in front of Digory. He'd never met anyone so callous, so cruel, but he shouldn't have been surprised. Digory was one of the Lord's Guardsmen, after all. The most feared men in the whole realm. Some thought, the whole Kingdom. Even more than the Red Plumes. The Brotherhood. Gravesblood. What had he expected?

"What kind of Kingdom is that? Where everyone shoots first?" Ryd turned from Digory, relieving himself atop a cluster of stones scatted in the nearby dirt. He spoke half looking over his shoulder. "We'll all soon be dead."

"You surely will be."

"No," Ryd finished, pulling up his threadbare trousers. He turned. "I refuse to believe it."

"You can believe anything you like. Until someone shoots you," Digory said. Ryd frowned. He looked like he was going to speak but he didn't. "Cheer up," Digory offered. "Now you're with me. Your odds of survival have vastly improved."

"You'd be more convincing if you hadn't just been shot."

"Good one." Digory chuckled. "That was funny."

Ryd hated Digory and yet still somehow liked him. Digory was that way. As charismatic as they came. You couldn't help but want to be near him. Appreciative of his approval, Ryd half smiled.

"You'll continue the journey?" Digory asked eagerly.

"You're still going to deliver the letter? Do you even still have it?"

"Sure do. Right here." Digory tapped his trouser pocket. "And, aye. No other option."

"And you claimed I was in love with her."

"What now?"

"Nothing, nothing."

"Once we're done at Anstout you're free to go," Digory added.

"You make it sound like I don't have a choice until then," Ryd said. Digory looked away, and didn't respond, although the man was right. He knew too much. Digory had to keep an eye on him. His plan was to be rid of him before they returned to Westerviolet. If he wasn't taken by the perils of travel before that point. It would be easier than trying to explain why he took the Stablemaster with him on business Tomas had not approved to begin with. Ryd walked back to Digory and squatted down on his haunches. He leaned in and asked with open eyes, "My brother can come with us? Once I find him. Hopefully not long after we make it to Littlebell."

"Who?"

"My brother, Collen," Ryd said in a displeased exhale. "The reason I agreed to travel with you."

"Oh, yes," Digory nodded once. *The boy I killed in Pinewood*, he remembered. "Of course," he lied. He locked steady eyes with Ryd. The young man had no idea his brother was dead. None at all. That was clear. "Sure," he said.

"Then yes," Ryd nodded, satisfied, pushing himself to stand. "I'll go to Anstout." He swallowed hard. "You have my word. You're sure we'll be granted safe passage? You've heard the tales?"

Digory's tone was nonchalant. "Who hasn't?" Ryd shot him a nervous glance. "Yes, we've been guaranteed passage," Digory clarified. "The Brochet emblem…"

Ryd interrupted, "Look at you. You're covered in blood and

no longer bare the emblem. Remember, I discarded your ruined armour, on your command, mind you. Won't it raise suspicion?"

"Trust me, will you?"

Ryd wanted to retort, then only sighed, scratching coarse curls at the base of his neck. He finally asked quietly, "Graves are really more than half deadblood?"

"Aye."

"I can't fathom…"

"Sybil speaks of them as equals," Digory said with clear contempt. "If I didn't know better, I'd think she's a bit impressed." Ryd grimaced. "Aye," Digory acknowledged Ryd's face. "Yet I hear they're far from their aims."

"Aims?"

"Still no Graves able to walk there."

"Where?"

Digory snorted, coughing red spittle and phlegm to the left. The gore landed in a small patch of clover. "The Deadlands," he said.

"Not one?" Ryd asked, surprised. "But I thought…"

"Not one. Sybil says Graves can survive longer out there though, and are likely immune to the Dread," Digory interrupted to explain. "I'll admit both are useful, but at what cost? If deadbloods are anything like you say…" He trailed off into a brooding glare. Not much shook him, however Sybil's plan to conspire with Graves behind her father's back, regardless of her aims, made him nervous. He did not trust Graves, and although Sybil was powerful, he was convinced that she would not be safe.

"I wonder how they do it," Ryd thought out loud. "You think they actually fuck them? Are there deadblood women?"

Digory paused and turned his head. "You know, I've never thought about it." Although, he had. Everyone who heard the legends, from the emergence of Haulfrun Graves himself, had an opinion on how Graves was able to combine their bloodline with dead blood. Graves never spoke on the matter. It was a Kingdom-wide mystery.

"There must be."

The young men lulled in contemplation.

"You said the deadblood you met filed its teeth," Digory said. "That would be one hell of a barekiss."

"I wonder if Graves really eats us," Ryd whispered, missing Digory's joke entirely, gaze glassed and distant.

Digory laughed. "That's what you've heard?"

Violet heat rushed to Ryd's cheeks. "Don't they eat us?"

"They don't eat us, you dolt," Digory said, smiling. *Not like those Horne heathens were said to*, he thought, glad the entire bloodline was long-ago extinct. "Gravesblood experiments. Like the rest of the Old realms. And they breed their own blood over and over and over, generation after generation, with deadbloods."

There was a time, before Old and New, that all the realms experimented on their natives. Long before the Plague, when there were hundreds of thousands of Vanguards of every bloodline. This went on for many years, centuries even, following the Landing. It's why in the present day, natives of each realm tended to have extremely characteristic traits making it easily identifiable where they hailed from. For example, Westerviolet natives all had particularly skittish dispositions. Traditionally, only the meekest, most subservient, apart from stock reserved for Guardsmen, were permitted to breed.

The same was generally true in other realms. Baneswood natives had exceptionally good hearing and eyesight, which helped immensely with hunting and trapping. They were also particularly large and unusually strong, because the Vanguards pitted them against each other in fights for sport. Lyonshall natives were hulking and dull, well suited for mine work. Morfit natives were sturdily built and dutifully minded, as were Animus Rock natives, as they were primarily farmers. Hellswater natives were either stunningly clever or stoutly built for river work. Ironbark natives tended to be good with their hands, known for production of everything from weapons to clothing. Littlebell natives were creatives and artisans of all kinds. Busk natives were in large part descendants of escaped convicts. Ravenshroud natives were either exceptionally large, bred to be Warmen, or exceptionally small and subservient, like the natives of Westerviolet. Anstout natives were rarely seen, therefore little was known of them. The same was true of Graceview natives, as they were said to be xenophobic and stayed within their own realm. Anstout natives were docile and agreeable, believing anything that they were told, typically following each other around like sheep.

Echo's Omen natives tended to be a mix of the natives from the surrounding realms, as it was the newest realm, carved out of the already existing Kingdom for Graves and Brochet during the Blood Wars.

Then there were the natives of the abandoned realms: Duskfang, Hunter Post, Whisperfield and Winter Garden. Duskfang natives were feared and avoided for their alleged knowledge of Calvanese charms, Hunter Post natives were mostly thought to be religious zealots and kept to themselves in the eastern reaches of Baneswood Forest, Whisperfield natives were very small and distrusting and finally, Winter Garden natives generally were jovial, self-sufficient, and produced beautiful jewellery that was prized throughout the Kingdom.

"What about Anstout, or Echo's Omen natives?" Ryd crouched to a full seat. He crossed his legs and leaned towards Digory, fully engrossed, like a child.

"The lucky ones become Brothers," Digory said, thinking of what he knew of Echo's Omen, "then their bloodlines are protected and permitted to carry on." He took a breath. "It's the lowly earthblood curses who don't pass Assessment and fall victim to the Brotherhood and their other pursuits that you should be sorry for."

Ryd's pale eyebrows pinched. "How do you know all of that?"

"I told you, I eavesdrop," Digory lied flatly. "Trust me they don't eat us. What they do at the Omen is much, much worse. This is what you get for choosing to be in the dark." Digory shook his head. "You wish they simply eat us."

Meanwhile, the cast-off birds squawked loudly, chattering in the nearby woods.

"What else, then?" Ryd asked, mindlessly picking at a blade of grass, tearing it apart in his fingers, squinting because of the sun's blinding dawn rays. Pollen-filled wind drifted through the blue meadow towards them. "How do they have dead blood in their veins without the dead madness that comes with it?"

Digory kicked his feet in a series of sorrowful groans and yowls until he was able to sit up, with Ryd seething annoyance in the background. "I didn't say Gravesblood weren't mad," he finally said once upright. They just have more control. Or maybe, just better clothing than true deadbloods, I know not." Ryd rolled his eyes. "Because you said they wore none."

"I get it, but it wasn't funny."

"We'll find out about Graves soon enough," Digory added with finality. "For now, Littlebell."

"Are you fit to ride? You've lost much blood. Not had drink nor sup."

"I'm fine," Digory unconvincingly winced. "Tether me to yourself or the beast, if it makes you feel better. That way, if I die you don't need stop until you dump my corpse into the Missi."

"Lovely," Ryd retorted. "Are you sure you're ready? It may be a while until we rest again."

"My guess is we're less than half a day's journey."

Ryd stood quickly. "You tell me that now?"

"No use dwelling on the past."

"It's not the..."

"Hoist me up. Let's go."

Ryd shook his head in futility, eating his words again. He sighed and obeyed the command, as he was bred to do.

———————⊖χϵ———————

Turned out, Digory was right.

In half a day's time the pair spotted the haphazard arabesque that was Littlebell's city in the distance. The well-known Bell Tower was first to reach above the horizon, high-soaring over red and brown thatched-roof homes all crammed together amidst thin, winding streets that zigged and zagged. The Bell Tower was in the center atop a massive rectangular brute of a structure made of yellow stone. All other buildings seemed to swirl around it like silt around a drain. From the direction they approached, Digory and Ryd had a view down at the riverside metropolis. It sat at the lowest point in an expansive, neatly tilled valley squeezed up against the murky-brown Missi.

"Look! There it is," Ryd shouted, brimming with excitement. He'd imagined the utopia his father told him stories of his whole life. "Littlebell!"

"Oh, you're right," Digory peered over Ryd's shoulder. "Finally."

"We made good time."

"If only you'd ridden slower, we'd have gone backwards."

"I had to be sure you didn't fall off!" Digory smirked silently. "I can't wait to get you to the Apothecary to be rid of you."

"That's not very nice."

"Neither are you."

A squat middle-years man with coal-black skin, leather sandals, and a fawn-colored braid trudged with his head down ahead of them. His robes were foreign; decorated with dreadfully ostentatious, clashing patterns and they were markedly feminine, with loose draping and a tassled, braided belt. He was a typical Littlebell native wearing typical Littlebell attire. Ryd had never seen such fashion. Did all Littlebell men dress that way? The man pulled a sturdy handcart piled with row after row of neat-stacked corn. A small, nearly identical child wrapped in an orange and pink cloth with inquisitive, almond-shaped eyes perched amongst the ears. He stared shamelessly at Digory, unblinking and wildly curious.

"Keep moving," Digory said, eying the child from overhead as they passed on the horse. "From the looks of it, not much further."

"We can rest if you'd like."

"I'm fine," Digory growled.

"You're slurring."

"You are."

"Are you mad?" Ryd half turned, pitiful steed neighing under the weight. "You sound like you're in pain," Ryd pulled the horse to a halt off the side of the path, allowing the trickle of travellers to pass by. Digory only incoherently mumbled. "You must tell me if you're fading. I won't have you falling off again." Digory muttered nonsense. "Oh no. If you're about to pass out…"

Alas, Digory collapsed. His chin dug sharply into Ryd's back.

"No!" Ryd jostled Digory with his elbow. "Not now. We are so close." Ryd groaned, eyeing another ostentatiously dressed man with short-cropped hair and many rings on his hands passing slowly with a cart full of dead fowl. He looked like the other yet held himself differently.

What Ryd didn't know was that there were two classes of society within Littlebell. The North natives and the South natives. From the outside, they seemed similar but if you were from Littlebell, they were as different as night and day.

"Why couldn't you wait?" Ryd moaned. "You chose the worst time, like you knew." Regardless, Digory stayed unresponsive and slumped. Then, still tethered to Ryd and the horse, he began to convulse and vomit bile.

"Oh, woah!" Ryd shouted. He hurried to untie the knots holding their binds together then lowered Digory to the ground the best that he could as soon as he'd freed himself from the cord, steadying Digory's head from behind with shaking fingers, brow beading in the mounting heat of the rising morn.

Digory's body flopped about before going limp in the long grass aside Narrow Road's pebbles. Shiny green beetles buzzed in the air. A few more travellers passed by, dressed not unlike the others, pulling carts filled with various wares, and didn't pay the pair any heed. Littlebell natives were kind to their own but wary of strangers. It was safer.

Ryd leaned to investigate Digory. He was morbidly still. His face was sweaty and pallid while bile dripped from his beard. Ryd slowly lifted the cloths covering his wound, already crusting over with an opaque ooze. It smelt of death. The wound-site's edges were black and curling into themselves. Ryd brought his wrist up to his mouth. He gagged at the putrid stink.

"Nighthorn," he whispered as he stood. He turned his head away to fill his lungs with fresh air.

Kingdom wide, everyone knew to beware of the tiny purple berries that grew on dark green vines. Occasionally, children fell victim to them. Nighthorn grew nearly everywhere and in the later moons of the year the fruit appeared juicy and delicious, not unlike the commonly enjoyed duskberry that grew on bushes near streams and was often used to produce a popular condiment called duskberry chutrel, a deep violet spiced preserve used East of the Missi in lowborn households, often spread onto hard bread or roasted meats. Although the Nighthorn berries were poisonous, the large yellow flowers that bloomed in Spring were where the deadliest effects came from. Hill's Shadow notoriously soaked their arrows in poultices made from them.

Ryd looked around. He noted a clearing, around a bend of tall birch trees, young trunks abundantly springing from the valley floor like grass. A good place to make camp. A good place to let Digory die. With much more strength than he even knew he had, Ryd squatted and hoisted the much larger Digory over his shoulders. Grunting loudly, he slogged step after step through thick tufts of wild grass and pointed thistles swarming with bumbling bees, until finally, he dropped Digory with a thud.

Then Ryd collapsed in exhaustion at the edge of the treeline.

After collecting the sad black stallion and tethering him to a tree, Ryd lay on his back. He looked up at wisps of grey clouds backlit by late morning sunlight and it reminded him of the plants blanketing Westerviolet's most southern Vice Province.

Cotton. Another one of Westerviolet's key exports. He liked traveling there when it was time to find new colts to break. The memory of home steadied him. He exhaled a deep breath.

When Ryd sat up and looked around to assess his surroundings, he nearly jumped in surprise. At the far side of the meadow hidden behind a massive-trunked willow was a small, green-stone cottage with a thatched roof and neatly manicured garden. Ryd rubbed his eyes in disbelief then nearly turned to Digory to comment on the discovery, forgetting his precarious state. From the looks of it, the man was dead. Digory's only chance was if the inhabitant of this cottage could help him, for Ryd had done all he could. He hoped to the Ancestors that who ever lived there would know what to do.

Ryd mustered all his strength and lifted the dense Digory once more. Ryd carried Digory across the entire meadow, legs burning, joints aching, slow step by slow step, until he finally reached the cottage. He dropped Digory in the brown dirt near a patch of moon flowers with a thud. After, Ryd knelt quickly to check the man's breathing. It remained. Barely.

Despite the risk, Ryd knew he had no choice but to knock on the cottage door, for Digory's life depended on it.

So that's what he did.

WESTERVIOLET EAST TOWER

ybil, finally asleep, woke with a start to the chiming of a bell. She bolted upright, irritated and confused, looking for the source of the din. It sounded as if it was coming from nearly, within the castle. Perhaps from a different tower. Sybil slapped her own cheeks, believing she was dreaming. Often, she had unbelievably vivid dreams.

But no, the slap hurt. The warm air dragged lazily across her face, billowing thick green curtains hung over her bedroom window. The crickets sang outside and the river fangs and frogs splashed in the moat. She ran her hands over her embroidered bed linens and indeed, they were just as she remembered. Finely crafted, beginning to pull from her incessant rubbing, in the night, when she couldn't sleep.

Sybil frowned, laying back down, shutting her eyes, attempting to reclaim the dream that she'd been thrust from violently. Rosen's arms around her in the buttery morning light. But it was gone, as he was. She opened her eyes wide, rolling onto her back, sighing, reliving his absence all over again. It was a cursed First that she could not free herself from.

She stood and went to the window, overlooking the castle grounds, moat, wall, and grey city beyond. She took a deep breath of the oppressively warm air and imagined it all under her command. *Soon*, she thought, knowing her father, despite the Ancestor's aims, could not live forever. Soon, she would be elderclaim. Soon, the Emerald Throne would be hers.

Knowing that sleep would continue to elude her, Sybil left her chamber, dashing through the cold green-stone halls glinting in the candlelight, down wide staircases, around bends and turns, until she exited the North Tower completely and made it to the Throne Room. She pushed open the high reaching doors with difficulty, creaks echoing loudly in the depths of night. It was an engulfing space nearly rivalling the main hall, lined on either side with reaching pillars, with huge torches in between them, unlit and cold. Different versions of the Brochet's emblem hung all over the walls, from centuries of battles and wars, speaking to the enduring power and sanctity of their bloodline. There was dust on the floor. The Brochets had not used it since the Plague, when nearly all of the bloodline died. It was closed to honor the Ancestors lost. But that didn't stop Sybil from visiting, often.

Her footprints were the only marks on the floor. On nights that she didn't feel like leaving the castle, she'd go there. She'd study the old emblems. She'd run her hands over the walls. She'd sit in the enormous throne carved from one glinting emerald gemstone, imagining it was an earlier time. Imagining all the other Brochets, and Vanguards Kingdom-wide, bowed to her. Like the castle, the Emerald Throne had a pulse. A heartbeat. It *felt* like something to Sybil, and after sitting in it, similarly to how she felt after laying in the white bindweed, she was renewed.

The bell sounded again. Sybil, again, was snapped from her reverie with irritation. It plastered her face.

"What the curses *is* that?" she said out loud. She looked around the empty, engulfing hall. Apart from the old emblems, she was alone. She sighed, standing, descending the massive throne's steps, gliding back through the hall. She glanced back wistfully before shutting the towering doors with a groan.

She craned her ears, walking through the shallow-filled corridor outside the Throne Room, old Brochet Ancestor portraits watching her with amusement, malice or judgement— possibly all three. Her white sleep gown dragged over the cold stone floor behind her.

The bell chimed again. She spun her head, hair falling over her shoulders. Was she imagining it? Was it real? She wasn't sure, but it was coming from the east. She went that way.

Sybil passed by the Main Hall and the corridors that led to the kitchens and assorted maiden and handmen chambers, the stairs leading to the root cellars with adjoining passageways to the Lair and dungeons. She passed more portraits and several statues, some of which she recognized but many she didn't. Brochet, caring so greatly for beauty, was quick to immortalize their visages, more so than any other bloodline. The gorgeous faces of the Brochet Ancestors were everywhere.

This was a large part of why the natives of Westerviolet considered the castle to be haunted. It was difficult to feel at ease with so many eyes watching constantly, with cruel gleams in gazes. It was natural to imagine their spirits remaining in the walls of the huge, daunting green-stone castle, floating from chamber to chamber. Although, the reality was, it was only Sybil. Occasionally, a native caught a glimpse of her in her flowing sleep garments running through the open stone breezeways, further fuelling legends of spirits. But there were no spirits. It was only Sybil haunting.

The bell chimed again. The sound was near, yet removed, as if it was coming from high above. It was the sound of a large, loud and resounding bell. *It must be in one of the towers*, Sybil thought. It couldn't be the North Tower, because that's where she just came from. It would be unlikely to be the South, as it was for it housed the Grand Library or the West, for it was filled with mostly chambers once occupied by various Brochets, now reserved for Vanguard or the occasional high native guest, but it couldn't possibly be the East Tower either. The East Tower had been closed for centuries. Again, the bell chimed. It was still coming from the east.

As Sybil walked with bare feet on cool stone, she thought. Sybil was always thinking. She thought about her daughter, worrying for her that Academy would not be kind to her. Worrying that the other Vanguard children would not understand her pensive ways and that she would be a target for her beautiful, doll-like face. She worried about sending her to mix with New Vanguard children, as Rose had already proven to be easily corruptible. She worried that she would not be able to stop her father from giving Rose to the Omen.

That thought brought Sybil's thoughts to others, centred on

herself. She thought about her plans for marriage. How she didn't want to wed a Norland or a Thorne, handsome as they could be. She certainly did not want a Regnard, or even a Dale, brutish they were. The plans she had put into place by giving Digory the letter, she thought, were larger than just marriage anyway. They were a strategic move, pushing her closer to her goal. And keeping Rose safe in the process. She knew her plan was not without risk, but she also knew it was the only way.

Sybil reached the East Tower. The bell chimed again. It was certainly coming from within the Tower, Sybil thought, furrowing her brow.

The large wooden door to the East Tower held with detailed iron fastenings and was shut as it always was. She'd once tried to enter and had been scolded so harshly by her father that she avoided that part of the castle all together, since she was very young. But even if she had been curious, it was locked. She knew from when she first pulled on it. It was shut so tight, it would take a Dale of legend to pull it open.

Sybil shook her head, turning away, feeling silly for chasing fancies, then the bell chimed. She turned back, tempted. She placed her hand on the ancient door. It was warm, almost buzzing with energy. She narrowed her eyes and pushed it. It opened easily.

No one knew who built the castles, or how old they were, or how they were built. The Vanguard Kingdom had sixteen of them, all enormous and reaching, all full of hidden passageways and secret doors. Sometimes, to Sybil, it felt as if Westerviolet's castle was rearranging itself for her as she walked through it. Like it had an opinion all its own. It felt like, to Sybil, that the castle was beckoning her to enter the forbidden East Tower.

In the dark of night, cast in shadow, Sybil happily obliged. She pushed through the door easily and it swung open to darkness. Unlike the natives, she couldn't see anything. She frowned, left momentarily to grab a candle from a sconce on the wall, and returned, heart pounding excitedly. The bell chimed again. This time, it was right above her.

She looked around the chamber. It was filled end to end with artifacts, old armor, chests full of defunct Westerviolet coins, gowns on decaying wooden mannequins, and mirrors. So many mirrors, of all sizes and kinds, strewn haphazardly about as if placed there in a great rush. There were also portraits too. Lots of portraits, mostly like the ones throughout the castle, but older. Most of them were falling apart. The subjects within them wore clothes unfamiliar to Sybil and had hair and adornments unfamiliar as well. They were particularly beautiful. They must have been particularly ancient Ancestors, Sybil thought to herself as she stepped through the clutter towards the spiral staircase at the back. It looped tantalizingly upwards around the perimeter of the round chamber, leading to the above floors.

Sybil reached the stairwell, bell growing in volume each time it chimed. As she ascended her thoughts drifted to her weighty Brochet history lessons, particularly regarding the castle. She remembered when the wall had been taken down, partly, during the Blood Wars and then rebuilt. She remembered lessons about when the Gate House had been extended, and when the Apothecary was built, long before she was born. She even remembered why, allegedly, the Ancestors had chosen Westerviolet to settle in. It was the tiny violets and their associated powerful properties. But nothing about a bell in the East Wing's tower.

The second story of the tower was more of the same—a large chamber instead of many, like in the other wings—full of ancient, interesting clutter. Sybil paused briefly eyeing a glittering diadem on a stand, behind several rusted swords and a toppled chest of drawers. Then the bell chimed again. She continued upwards.

Finally, after several stories of more of the same, including one hall with rows of old handwritten books, she reached a final landing. The top of the East Tower. It was round as the other halls, with gaping, open windows that stretched into the reaches of the pointed spire. The wind blew fiercely up there, whipping Sybil's hair. The walls were stone as the rest, and bare, apart from wild marks all over. Massive scratches, as if a great beast had once been contained there.

And in the center of the chamber, there was a large, defunct bell.

AROUND WESTERVIOLET

Gawen was deep in thought. In all his years at Westerviolet, there had never been such an attack. Never a Guardsman struck down within the safety of the moat, not until now. Nervous rumors and gossip flew throughout the barracks. The Guardsmen, a highly superstitious group of men, postulated about what young Aslf's demise could mean for them, particularly in the wake of the Fourth Oak splitting. For Westerviolet. For the Kingdom. Some thought it warned of a deadblood attack. Others believed that the young Guardsman was driven mad by lack of Oblivion Tonic. Many believed Aslf was struck down by the Ancestors, themselves. All agreed it was a bad omen.

Gawen felt heavy weight on his shoulders, pressuring him to solve the case quickly.

He paced away from the moat gardens, thumb rubbing over his glass dagger hilt, mind looping over the details of the case, not really where he was. He took long strides through the hot afternoon with the sun on his back. Today there was low wind and high humidity. The morning clouds had already burnt away leaving no barrier between flesh and searing late summer heat. Gawen's skin prickled underneath his weighty chainmail and heavy cape. His head boiled in his helmet. His face was shiny with sweat beneath it's sharp, triangular nose guard.

The monstrosity of Westerviolet Castle was the largest structure in the city as well as in the realm and could be seen for creeds all around. It was constructed of grey-green stones three times the height of a man, stacked into four, four-sided towers named for each direction of the compass, with the legendary Air Hall as the fifth and highest point in the center.

The North Tower functioned as the grand entry to the castle

with an arched, impossibly reaching wooden door carved from one block of wood, allegedly from the mythical Jasper forest. It was the most enviable of posts for the Guardsmen. The Ancestor Walk, a series of black marble statues of strong-jawed men with brooding frowns yet playful expressions in their eyes, glaring with secrets they could never reveal, lined the path up to that gate. All looked much like Tomas. At the bases were etched nameplates on mirrored silver, starkly contrasting the black marble. There were tokens of homage left at the feet of the pedestals. Food, candles, even clothing. Several clusters of worshipers huddled at the bases, clutching stone amulets, muttering prayers.

Past that was a grassy, short-trimmed lawn dotted with plush white sheep spanning the commons until the North bazaar. At the far North end of the lawn nearest to the stalls and Apothecary was a step not more than half the height of a man cut down sharply into the lawn then flattened back out leading to the road, lined high with flattened stones. The step kept the sheep on the lawn; they would never leap off it for fear of the height, ever so small.

Around the extended perimeter of the castle and all outbuildings, gardens, and grounds was an opaque black moat, viscous and black, full of slender yet astoundingly long snakes with diamond-shaped heads and yellow eyes, fading light brown towards the tail. River fangs. Specially bred creatures that only existed in Westerviolet, said to have been created by the first Vanguards. Unlike most snakes, these Brochet-bred serpents were active during both day and night. Their venom was also much more deadly. The river fangs teemed in pulsing knots and clumps amidst the murky, black-mirrored water, causing it to perpetually churn, particularly in the late summer months when they were breeding. The poison serpent moat could only be crossed by a thick drawbridge at the North Gate. Even the quickest dip into its mirrored waters would be a sure death.

The entire Commons perimeter was lined by a stone curtain wall with a path atop it and various gates, all routinely patrolled by the Guardsmen. Around the castle lay the city of Westerviolet. A depressing, grey village full of low-born natives, policed by a few high-born ones. Beyond that, in all four directions were the Four Vice-Provinces of the Westerviolet Realm.

Gawen walked the Commons. He cut through the plush lawn instead of taking the customary path, as it was faster. He smiled at the fluffy livestock dotting the green grass. He'd always liked the sheep. Lost in thought and nearly to his destination, he stepped deep into sheep excrement.

"Cursed First," Gawen said under his breath as he examined shit up to his boot laces. He sighed as he wiped the mess on the short-chewed grass the best he was able before continuing his trek across the grounds to the south-facing gardens. Gawen passed by the maiden's dormitory, briefly pausing to assess the formed grey building with horizontal slits for windows, wondering how Miri was doing, before moving on.

Gawen took the southern entrance into the castle and went up the back staircase, intended for natives. It was thin, barely wide enough for two men to stand side-by-side and spiralled upwards violently. Gawen looped around and back on himself for several dizzying stories, each curved wall reaching up in cool greenish-grey stone, until he popped out down the hall from Lord Tomas's study.

The hallway was dimly lit by low-burning candles every few steps placed on heavy sconces set far into the walls between deep-set doors. Each doorframe was lined with grey stones and a forest-green keystone above a dark-stained door with iron bands. Upon the hall's emerald-toned stones hung gigantic oil-paintings, portraits of Brochets past, many recognizable from their mighty statues on the Ancestor Walk. Others, with stories all but lost to time.

Gawen had only been to this hall once before and the grandeur still intimidated him and his humble sensibilities. Each long-dead Brochet ancestor had the same devious smirk, or frown, depending on how you looked at it.

Feeling the stares of many hazel eyes from the past looking

at him, Gawen cast his gaze down. Chainmail clanking, he hurried the rest of the length of the hall. It ended in a large arched door with a broad, weighty iron knocker in the very center, in the shape of the Brochet emblem. He held the icy ouburous and knocked twice. It reverberated loudly.

Tomas's old voice groaned. "Who's there?"

Gawen cracked open the door enough for those within to see him. Tomas gestured once after an uninterested glance, then pushed his square spectacles back to the bridge of his nose.

Gawen hurried inside and saluted. Tomas nodded and Gawen dropped his hand. "Apologies for the interruption," he said, "I am Commander Budic's Second." Gawen raised his narrow red eyes confidently to meet Tomas's rounded, twinkling hazel. "There is pressing Guardsman business that he has requested timely updates on, my Lord." Gawen spoke with poise beyond his years, befitting his station.

"It is so urgent that you interrupt your Lord?"

At first, Tomas was nearly impressed with the young earthblood. The stones on him to barge in so. Although when Gawen said his name, Tomas remembered his blood and then understood why the young man carried himself as he did. He was no ordinary native. Not at all.

"Yes, my Lord."

"What then?"

"My Lord," Budic intruded, standing from his seat adjacent Tomas, old armchair creaking, hammered metal helmet clenched in his hands, knuckles white. Turning his body, he attempted to block Gawen from Tomas's view. "I can speak to my Second outside. This is an internal matter. I will brief you after the investigation has concluded."

Tomas's etched brow furrowed into sunken lines. "Investigation?"

"It is controlled," Budic said, voice calm, burgundy eyes wild like royal swallows in flight. "I have the top men on it. I've appointed my Second," he gestured to Gawen. "Here he is. Evidence that he's diligently working away."

"Budic, tell me," Tomas looked to his commander. "What is

going on?"

"My Lord…"

Tomas waved a long-fingered, wrinkled hand dismissively at Budic, glossy tunic billowing around sinewy arms beneath his white, emerald lined, side-toggled cloak and told Gawen directly to speak.

"My Lord, I…" Gawen began to protest, glancing at Budic.

"You heard me," Tomas darkened, overgrown eyebrows furrowing, lips curling down. "As your Lord I command you to reveal what you investigate." He paused, lifting his bushy brow wide and high. "In my realm," he added, rumbling slow. He adjusted his thick hair with a pat.

Gawen glanced at Budic. Budic hurriedly nodded twice. His snake-like braids danced.

"A body was found today," Gawen said, walking further into the study.

"What body?"

"Aslf, Commander Budic's nephew," Gawen said, removing his helmet, clasping it behind his back. Glancing to his beloved Commander briefly, then back to his Lord, Gawen said sombrely, "He is indeed dead."

"Who would do this?" Tomas said. His face reddened as he rose from his chair. Murders in Westerviolet–particularly within the moat–were unheard of. He sauntered to the wide, rectangular window then half-turned to Budic. "Commander?"

"My Lord," Budic took a limping step forward, "that is it."

"Speak plainly," Tomas commanded. "Tell me."

"It appears the boy did it to himself."

Budic stepped in. "We don't know that. Aslf was a fighter. He'd never end it that way."

Suicide was the lowliest of sins within the ranks of the Guardsman, and to have committed it ensured erasure from record. No dagger ceremony. No proper pyre. No ashes scattered in Stonewold. Although there had not been one in recent memory. The Guardsmen of Westerviolet were notoriously proud.

"I know the boy. Raised him. I smell something," Budic said, uncharastically distressed. "I've asked Gawen to investigate for me. If there's a traitor among us," he said as he paced through the enormous, starkly decorated chamber, then lowered his voice for emphasis, "we must know."

Tomas paused then himself began to pace the study. Budic retreated to a seat in a more modest chair off to the side of the chamber, near the gaping, soulless fireplace.

"If you say he's not the type, then find out who did this," Tomas said, pointed boots clicking. "I won't have murders at Westerviolet. Especially not within the Commons." His voice boomed. *Clack. Clack. Clack,* he paced. "Not within my men. My realm."

"Aye, my Lord," Budic said. He turned, spinning his braided hair. He barked at Gawen a bit too loudly. "Where is the body now?"

"In route to Hudde. Thought best to get it out of the heat. I can go there to begin the investigation. I will debrief you on what I find once you're complete with the Lord."

"So be it," Tomas boomed.

Budic straightened himself, rubbing the proud emblem insignia on his breast instinctively. "Aye," he said, with renewed composure. "So be it."

Then, Tomas demanded to hear what Gawen had discovered thus far. Budic leaned forward, listening earnestly.

"Not much," Gawen said honestly. "As the girl described to us, he had his own dagger in his hand and a wound on his throat that looked as if he'd done it to himself. In his pockets, no clues. Only post keys and a portion of bread."

"Girl?" Tomas turned.

"Aye, a maiden discovered him."

"I see." Tomas shut and pursed his thin lips. He rumbled low. "Question her."

"Yes, my Lord." Gawen never broke eye-contact. A difficult feat when speaking to Tomas. Impossible for most. "She was my next stop after Hudde and the body."

"I've heard what I need to," Tomas dismissed with a flit of his wrist. "Off you go." He turned to the Commander, "I expect a timely report, Budic."

"Aye, my Lord." Budic. said. He glanced quickly at Gawen. "Go, son."

Gawen nodded. He turned and jogged with clanking chainmail out of the storied study.

It took trudging back the way he came in the sticky heat for Gawen to reach the Westerviolet Apothecary at the far North of the Commons, on the cusp of the moat, near an outcropping of reed grass and oblong lily pads. The air filled with the sound of snakes splashing.

A large portion of the grey building overhung the onyx waters. Like all other buildings within the Westerviolet curtain wall, particularly in this section of courtyard, the Apothecary had a darkened, triangular, roof, looped silver-tinted gutters and intricate, ornate detailing, particularly around wide, languid front entry porches. The roads here were hard-packed, lined with ancient square-cut stones matching the curtain wall and the castle herself, along each side. In between these neatly maintained, greenish grey-tone roads, it was overgrown violet grass. There were few natives, and all kept their eyes down. If this courtyard was a person, it would seem at the brink of death–barely alive.

Gawen rarely visited the Apothecary. He was rarely injured or ill. Fortune seemed to follow him, and he never required Hudde's assistance. All the better, because he didn't like the man.

He entered beneath a hammered copper awning, green and tarnished from age. Gawen grasped the pyramid handle and pushed through the keyhole-shaped door slick with hard-dried resin. He stepped tentatively into the dimly lit, smoky room.

Pre-plague books littered the walls and some corners of the room and floor, each obviously ancient with tattered covers and yellowing parchment. After the Second Tower was burned, before the Plague, most of the books that remained and were not too damaged were spread about the Kingdom, to each realm's Apothecary for safe keeping.

There were shelves on every wall. Where there weren't books displayed there were strange gadgets and odd sculptures and jars with specimens in syrupy, yellowed liquid from days long-past, aside dusted over windows. While meticulous and brilliant, Hudde was not tidy.

At the front of the room were beds with men sleeping, obviously infirm. Injured or ill women within the curtain wall were sometimes tended to by Petra or the other maidens, but usually, they were put down. On wide tables at the other end of the room were vials and bottles full of liquids and substances of all different colors wafting pungent scents. Healing tonics, mostly.

When Gawen stepped fully inside, his head felt light. A warm haze washed over his thoughts like a thick hide blanket. He removed his helmet and ran his hand over his sweaty hair. He patted his cheeks twice with his hands and took a deep breath in and out.

"I see you aren't taking your Tonic," a monotonous voice floated through the thick air.

Gawen turned. "I've never liked it. It makes me feel," he paused and yawned. After, he finally said, "fuzzy."

"You have no tolerance at all."

"If I didn't know better, Hudde, I'd say you were making fun of me."

"I don't make you anything," Hudde retorted in monotone. "You make yourself what you are."

"Right, sure," Gawen rolled his eyes. He was tired of the Guildman's riddles already.

"You should take your Tonic," Hudde chastised. "The Guild has proven it's beneficial."

Oblivion Tonic was strongly encouraged to be taken by all natives within Westerviolet. It was reported to give the people strong constitutions, a better ability to withstand the heat, and, most notably, dreamless sleeps. It was also associated with piety and looked on favourably by the Ancestors. Nearly all

Westerviolet natives took it happily.

Gawen studied the man through the Apothecary's smoky haze. Hudde blended with the shadows. He had long, stringy, oily greying hair and squinty red eyes. He was very short with an average build and impeccable posture, as if he was always trying to be taller than he was. His chest puffed out beneath his sleeveless, taupe brown tunic as he stared up at the strapping young Second with innate pride.

"Now I remember why I don't come here," Gawen said mostly to himself. "Are all Guildsmen as strange as you, Hudde?"

"Guildsmen vary as much as men vary themselves."

"Why did they pick you to be one of them?"

No one outside of the Guild understood why they chose who they did. In the past, in pre-Plague times, the Guild was primarily Vanguard, and all had powers, or so the legends said. In the present day, the Guild assessed all children, Vanguard and native, typically only choosing one or two for their ranks every generation. Most realms had only a handful of Guildsmen, some far less. Traditionally, one ran the Apothecary within the realm, tending to every type of ailment and occasionally providing counsel to that realm's elder, while the others resided at Hidden Den in Wraithswail.

Hudde ignored the question, unblinking. "Are you here to examine the body? It is this way." He gestured behind himself to an arched doorframe hidden with an emerald cloth.

"Right," Gawen said, yawning again, rubbing the back of his sweaty neck. "How can I wear this off?"

Hudde shook his head curtly, once. "There's nothing to be done," he said. He focused his already narrow eyes at Gawen.

"Right, surely not," Gawen mumbled.

Hudde, obviously disapproving, turned to take shuffling, bare-footed steps across blackened wooden floorboards. "Do you follow?" His flat voice tinged frustration.

"Aye, behind you," Gawen replied dutifully, yawning again. Every movement was laboured; his limbs felt like rocks. As if slogging through mud, Gawen followed the much shorter man behind the emerald cloth into the hidden back room all the while rubbing his eyes, squinting, and yawning.

The body lie on a long table in the center of the rectangular, thin room, illuminated by an old chandelier. All clothing had been stripped away and Aslf's corpse was cleaned of blood. His shell was limp and dead grey like the courtyard outside. Aslf's poor head lay far backwards at an inhuman angle from the huge slice in his neck. His throat was opened and visible, facing towards the doorway. It was the first thing that Gawen saw when he entered. He covered his mouth with his hand on instinct, in disgust, nearly gagging, bile biting the back of his throat. He forced it down, swallowing, never once averting his eyes as he entered the chamber slick with death.

"The incision is," Hudde poked at the slice with an implement, "considerable."

"Aye, I thought the same," Gawen glanced down at the flayed boy, senses screaming in horror, yet outwardly calm. "Why so deep?" As Gawen turned his head to Hudde, typically focused gaze faltering. His eyelids lay heavy. "Half of that would have done the trick."

"It would have taken the boy substantial strength to continue this depth of an incision from here," Hudde pointed with the implement, "to here."

"He was puny," Gawen remarked, eying Aslf's underdeveloped muscles. "Was he strong enough for it?"

"It doesn't appear so, and yet it is done," Hudde answered. "The hand still clenched in rigor mortis as if holding the dagger. I pried it from his fingers myself."

Gawen nodded. He swallowed hard as he looked down at Aslf's cold, colorless stare. Glossy as if encased in glass.

When life left a native, so did the red of their eyes.

"There is something else," Hudde said.

"What more?" Gawen asked eagerly, yawning again unintentionally as he leaned closer to the corpse. "Show me."

Hudde noticed his yawn with a double take glance and glared briefly. "Over here," Hudde said, pointing to Aslf's head.

"I don't see anything." Gawen stifled yet another yawn.

Hudde silently shifted the boy's dull braids to reveal pooling bruising. "That wasn't there before," Gawen said.

"At times, visible contusions only appear after death."

"This was underneath his helmet?"

"Yes," Hudde answered surely. "His head struck extremely hard while wearing it. A fall, perhaps?" The men postulated in silence in the dim-lit room, staring down at the clammy body.

"Could it have been caused by a blow to the head?"

Hudde looked up. "Perhaps," he said carefully.

Gawen's naturally narrow eyes opened as wide as they could. "I must go," he said quickly. "Thank you Hudde. Please, continue. Let me know if you find anything else."

Hudde nodded his head. "Best of fortune, Second," he said unconvincingly to Gawen's back as he rushed out.

Gawen tried to say thank you but had to stifle a yawn. He exited the hazy bungalow in a hurry then hungrily breathed in the fresh air once he was free from the Apothecary. The Tonic's heavy cloak slowly lifted.

WESTERVIOLET HALL

S o much had happened in less than a moon.

Rose had gone from prisoner to true Vanguard, nearly over night, in her own mind. She tasted freedom only to have it ripped away by her mother. Her true dream was to be sent to Animus Rock for Academy schooling with the other Vanguard children. She yearned desperately to finally see what the rest of the Kingdom was like. She'd always imagined making friends with the others, just as Mother did back when she was at Academy. Sybil would often tell Rose stories of her times there, the lessons she learned, the boys who fancied her, and the rivalries between the young women, and between the men. Rose yearned to be as her mother was—the center of society. Known for her wit, beauty and charm. And even so, Rose's heart was troubled. It ached, missing Collen horribly. True, Col betrayed her, but she understood why. She always understood why everyone did everything, and she couldn't bring herself to stay cross with him. The only ones she was cross with over Col's death was her mother, and her mother's Guardsman. She hated that man more than anyone.

Rose sat at the broadside of a thick mahogany table with intricately carved details in homage to the ouroboros on the legs, and deep-etched along the sides. Diamond-shaped serpent heads biting their own tails decorated it primarily. From the lofty rafters hung an iron chandelier that dripped heavy with layer after layer of various shades of wax. Currently, pale yellow stumps burned low. Warm wax accumulated in drippy pockets on the chilled iron above.

Rose stared down at her roasted boar and barley in broth, a Westerviolet staple, wishing it was time for sweets. She stirred the contents with a heavy hammered spoon clanking against the sides of the delicate bowl–*clink, clink, clink.*

"Rose," Sybil commanded, forcibly clearing her throat. "Rose," she warned again.

Rose kept stirring–*clank, clink.* Candlelight glistened off her silken smock, ruffled around her neck and at her shoulders.

"Rose, enough," Sybil said. At the command, Rose dropped her spoon. She let it slide down into the bowl while looking up smugly at her mother, dark waves framing her play-innocent, conniving glare. "You're not hungry?" Sybil asked rhetorically, sharp eyebrows raising. "You haven't eaten a thing."

Tomas sucked on his teeth and patted his hair, then pinched bushy eyebrows in displeasure before speaking in a grunt. "I was not much older than you during the Uprising," he said. "Do you think I wasted food?" He gestured with his spoon. "Didn't finish a meal? No," he boomed. "I won't tolerate this behavior." He dipped the heavy spoon into his own glass bowl, then, hand shaking slightly, slurped a sip of soup. "Your mother coddles you," he observed, swallowing. "I will not stand for it."

"But grandfather..." Rose interjected with a small voice.

"No," Tomas's voice deepened. "You are a child with child's problems." He set the spoon on the mighty table with a clank. "You think you know pain?" His voice echoed in the high-ceiling hall. "Speak back once more, and I will teach you pain."

"Father!" Sybil gasped from the far end of the dining table.

Tomas sat opposite her, but despite not wearing spectacles rubbed the bridge of his nose as if adjusting them. "I'll not have it from you either," he said. "I am her grandfather. Your father," his voice gained confidence and bite with each word. "*Never* speak back to me."

Sybil adjusted her brilliant white gown while inwardly pouting. Over it, she wore a gauzy shawl, crocheted from fine thread, delicately draped about her ivory skin and distinct, boney shoulders. She pulled it tighter and intertwined her fingertip with a loose yarn. As she glared, she twirled the yarn subtly between her pointer finger and thumb in her lap.

Rose looked down sheepishly at the spoon floating in her

broth and poked at it, until it fell deeper beneath a drowned cut of chewy meat. The candles on the chandelier flickered like stars amidst the cavernous blackness of the high-reaching sup hall ceiling above her.

"Eat, girl," Tomas commanded Rose, still glaring resentfully at her bowl. He gestured again with his spoon. "Eat!" he bellowed. The shout rang through the high-ceiling hall. Rose jumped. She hurriedly fished the spoon out of the clear bowl and wiped it on her lapcloth. She took a small bite.

"Now, I have a matter to discuss," Tomas said slowly after taking a leisurely bite himself, gnawing, lips open, chomping on the chewy meat with back teeth, then washing it down with a drink of Animus wine. Sybil and Rose glared at him.

"Well, what is it?" Sybil finally said.

Tomas casually looked up from his meal. "I am so glad you asked." His eyes sparkled. "I've made my decision." He paused, head swooping from the left to glance at Rose, then back straight to meet eyes with Sybil. "I am sending both of you to Animus Rock."

Rose dropped her spoon with a small splash as it fell back into the soup. "Really!" she looked up in excitement. She gripped the intricately carved table edge with both hands.

"Father," Sybil started, leaning forward, "I thought that..."

"My decision is final," Tomas interrupted. "Be happy, girl," he added. "You get what you want." Sybil furrowed her dark brow and glanced down. She poked at her food.

"What's Animus Rock like, Grandfather?"

"A great city! Or it was for many years. But now," he paused, with a sneer. "Under betrayal of the Bellamines..."

Since the Landing, the Bellamines had been the rulers of the Animus Rock realm, as well as the entire Vanguard Kingdom. Currently, Bellamine was the tether that held the Old and New together. But it was loosening.

"Father," Sybil flashed a brief smile, "you say it as if they have done a wrong."

"I know you are sympathetic to them, Sybil, but they are soft and cannot be trusted. Anyone to throw a proud bloodline like theirs away. And now, Bellamines are nearly earthblood themselves! Such a pity."

Tomas referred to the Bellamine bloodline's practice of marrying natives and having children with New blood. It had been in place since the Blood Council, marking the end of the Blood Wars more than a century prior.

"What happened to them, Grandfather?"

Tomas softened considerably. "They made a choice."

"How?" Rose pressed. "What did they choose?"

"Do you know about the Blood Wars?"

"Father..." Sybil warned, "she's just a girl."

"Hush," Tomas shushed Sybil. "If she's going to Academy she'll learn soon anyway." He shifted, turning his entire body instead of craning his neck to meet eyes with his granddaughter. "So, tell me," he said, ancient voice creaking. "Have you learnt of the Blood Wars?"

Rose shook her head no, eyes peeled open as she met Tomas's gaze closely. As he began to speak, she slowly furrowed her brow into a pinch, narrowed her eyes analytically and subconsciously pursed small lips into a pouting frown; the expression matched her mother's identically.

"Degory Bellamine was crowned King in 3850," Tomas started. "About two hundred years ago," he added, kindly for the girl's benefit. Rose nodded eagerly. "Degory trained his whole life to be King. He was smart, and fearless, and fair. The whole Kingdom loved him, even the earthblood for some forsaken reason. But it's said they did."

Then, Rose naively asked, "Was he a good King?"

"He was kind to the earthblood and friends with the elders of the Old bloodlines. He tied together the Kingdom."

"So, he made things better?" Rose asked hopefully, thinking that Kings must the best of all Vanguards, or else they wouldn't be allowed to be King at all. "Then he was good?"

"Hard to say."

"Why?"

"King Degory Bellamine contracted Dread Death. He died in 3860 at thirty years old, never having married. And he left no heirs."

"Then who became King?" Rose frowned.

"Exactly the problem. Clever girl," Tomas half smiled, eyes glinting. "Degory had no heirs, thus, his younger brother was crowned king."

"His brother?"

Tomas nodded, "Yes, Danil. The child was only fourteen years. Nearly your age. Imagine! He was said to be spoiled, immature, and insane from years of the interbred blood in his genes. The Boy King, they called him."

"Interbred?" Rose repeated the strange term. She turned her head to her mother.

"It means the Bellamines only married and had children with other Vanguards," Sybil explained. "There are only so many of us, particularly after the Plague. And when blood doesn't have a lot of room to mix, sometimes, madness will occur."

"That's right," Tomas affirmed. He knew this madness all too well. It lived in his late wife's blood. Sybil's mother. Rose's grandmother.

"Then why inter...breed at all?" Rose asked innocently, turning her head from her grandfather to her mother. "Why do it if some children turn out mad because of it?"

"You sound like the New," Tomas scoffed.

"Because, my sweet, we are special," Sybil said to Rose, ignoring Tomas.

But Rose still didn't understand, and her expression said as much. Kindly, Sybil tried to explain.

"Remember the Vanguard mission?"

Rose nodded. "They wanted magic?"

"Power," Sybil clarified, looking to Tomas.

Tomas nodded in agreement. "Whatever you call it, power, magic, abilities... yes," he grumbled, then hacking coughed once. The phlegmy sound echoed about the high-ceiling hall.

"What happened next?" Rose pressed.

"The next four years of young King Danil's rule led to the Blood Wars."

"Oh no," Rose whispered.

Sybil watched the girl's reaction while poking at her soup without eating. She rolled her eyes. Oh, how her father loved an audience.

"It was a long time coming," Tomas went on. "Degory had managed a shaky peace, but it was built on himself alone. And any kingdom built on one man will surely fall."

"How did it happen?"

"How did what happen?" Tomas barked, as he chewed another dry cut of meat. "Be clear child."

"The fall she means, father," Sybil interjected to Rose's aid.

Tomas nodded. "Danil's horrendous treatment of the earthblood is what did it," he said, still chewing. "The New bloodlines rebelled against him." He swallowed.

"Why'd he do it?" Rose asked with a small voice. "Treat them bad, I mean." She couldn't understand why a King wouldn't want to protect his own people. What else was a King for?

"Humfra Graves was Danil's great friend, you see," Tomas explained. "He was committed to the Old ways. Why, Humfra Graves himself founded the Echo's Omen's Brotherhood, with Brochet aid, naturally." He added, smiling. "Humfra Graves, along with others, convinced the Boy King of the appeal of the true Old way. That the Vanguard Mission is all that matters, and native concerns are secondary. That they are here for us, no better than sheep. Humfra Graves," and Lord Robert Brochet the Great, Tomas thought proudly, "convinced Danil Bellamine to fully embrace the Old tradition and reignited the necessary scientific procedures to see the Vanguard Mission realized once more."

Tomas went on to explain that, with Humfra's influence, Danil lost his regard for diplomacy. He began openly experimenting on earthblood with shameless bravado the like hadn't been seen for centuries. Sanctioned it Kingdom-wide as well. While the Old bloodlines were delighted with their brash new king, the New bloodlines were appalled. They did not stand for it.

"So, they fought back?" Rose asked.

"They did," Tomas said, nodding, peppered hair bouncing.

"For many years. Forty, actually." He paused. "It nearly ruined us."

"What stopped it?"

"Why, your ancestor," Tomas said. "Lord Robert Brochet the Great."

"Really?" Rose beamed.

"Father..." Sybil began.

Tomas interrupted, "I say it was."

"But Father, with respect," Sybil started cautiously, speaking low, "The Great Robert Brochet was dear allies with Humfra Graves. Why would he have pushed Ueli Bellamine to betray his father and pursue peace against the goals of his bloodline? You say it as fact, but there is little proof."

Sybil spoke of how the Blood Wars ended. How Danil's son Ueli secretly brought the elders of each bloodline together and came to an accord at an event later called "the Blood Council", then murdered his father and ended the Blood Wars.

"There wouldn't be proof," he retorted before sucking on his teeth again, long like his fingers, crammed together. "Robert was smart. The Bellamines take all the credit for peace when Brochet is owed due. At a time, it is true, Robert was close to Humfra. But he distanced himself. And, Robert was a practical man. A generation knew nothing but war. It served no one. He found how to stop to it. He counselled Ueli Bellamine."

"Maybe," Sybil conceded.

"You doubt me girl, but there are writings," Tomas said firmly, bead of sweat pooling on his brow, glinting in candlelight across the long table. "You know I have Robert's journals kept throughout his life. He speaks of this. You should trust your father. I know." Tomas gestured his spoon warningly.

"Yes, father," Sybil said softly, lowering her head, flexing her angled jaw. She poked at her food, silently seething.

"Now," Tomas continued to pontificate, "that doesn't mean I must like his choice to push the boy the way that Robert did. Truth, he ruined a great bloodline. The Bellamines were once unflappable. But he protected Brochet. For that I can respect him."

"What happened?" Rose asked. If she'd heard this tale before, she didn't remember it.

"Ueli Bellamine, the son of King Danil, with the help of Robert Brochet," Tomas added with a pointed look to Sybil, "called the elders from each bloodline together."

Rose looked to her mother. Sybil nodded. "That did happen. There are many recordings of it. It was later called the Blood Council."

Tomas cleared his throat. He then continued his speech, eyes alight like always when he was the center of attention.

"They met at Creed Point, in Ravenshoud's realm," he explained. "Ueli begged each elder to support his claim to the throne over his father, King Danil. He had terms. As king, Ueli would allow the Old bloodlines to operate as they pleased within each of their own realms, however, experimentation by force was outlawed. It must be voluntary only. And of course, interaction with deadbloods was to be forbidden. He couldn't have an epidemic of Dread Death, not again, not as they were trying to rebuild after war." Tomas took a breath, then a sip of wine. "To prove to the New bloodlines that he would not turn on them and their people as his father had, Ueli declared that from then on, every Bellamine King would marry earthblood. Humfra adamantly fought against it, as did Gauthier Norland, until Humfra's son Harrye Graves convinced them to compromise. He was friends with Ueli, and Ueli was sure it was the only way."

"Was he right?" Rose asked.

"Ill-advised, if you ask me."

"Why?"

"He lost the trust of the Old bloodlines. They continued to pretend at Council, but it bred disdain. It drove Humfra into the shadows at Echo's Omen where his son Harrye sired the first half-dead Vanguard. The child was named Haulfrun, and he certainly changed the face of the Kingdom. His descendants are Basil and his clan who run the Brotherhood, in fact. They roped in Norland and Regnard into their insanity as well.

However, a story for a different day."

"Father," Sybil's head shot up. "Brochet is also allied with Grav..."

"Quiet, daughter," he said sharply.

"Did the New bloodlines agree with King Ueli?" Rose asked Tomas, with the pitch of a child.

"They did," he grunted. "The New bloodlines bought in immediately. The Old reluctantly agreed to the compromise too, after much debate. The event has since been called the Blood Council, as your mother said. All bloodlines agreed to follow Ueli as their king. The next day, the Warmen under Gauthier Norland's command marched on Animus Rock and seized King Danil. They imprisoned him. In 3904, the Boy King Danil was beheaded on the front steps of Animus Rock for all to see. Ueli was sixteen years old. He was crowned King that night on steps stained by his father's blood." He paused. "It's such a pity he ruined his strong heritage as he did." Tomas sighed.

"By marrying..." Rose trailed off.

"*Earthblood?*" Tomas finished her sentence, slur shooting from his tongue like a dart. "Yes, child." His words were long and drawn out. Slow. "True they scour the land for the most beautiful and refined of the beasts, like King Nycholas did during the Uprising with one of the heathens from the North, as the cursed Nomad queen is now. But. I don't care for beauty if with it comes softness. And the Bellamines are so soft. Caring so for their clothing and jewellery. It's horrible how the New women jangle as they approach you. All the piercings. And that rank oil. I don't understand newblood fashion. It's ostentatious. Thank the ancestors you do not do that nonsense, daughter," Tomas said taking another bite of food. "You adorn yourself like a proper Vanguard Lady should."

"You have to admit," Sybil countered, always the defix's advocate, "they are very beautiful. Verity Bellamine is..."

"Verity Bellamine is a mongrel," Tomas spat. A spray of soup flew across the table's face.

"Father!" Sybil gasped, covering her smile quickly with her

hand, swallowing a snicker. "She's the King's sister. You can't speak of her that way!"

"If I didn't know better, daughter, I'd say you were sympathetic to the New."

"You said it yourself Bellamine was once great friends of Brochet. Are we not still allies to the crown?"

"That does not mean I need like or respect them," he said coolly. "We will interact with them as we must. For all I know you'll spend one day in the presence of Verity and come home to Westerviolet with ears full of cursed baubles shimmering and clanking like charms on a pet. I won't have you fall to that nonsense. My granddaughter either. Promise me, you will not embarrass me so?"

"I promise Father," Sybil said mock sincerely, flashing a brilliantly white smile. "Do not fret. I am a Brochet," she said. "I need not adorn myself in sparkly things to make men look at me." That much was true. When Sybil was around, men couldn't look away. It wouldn't matter if she was wearing a feed bag.

"That's my daughter," Tomas laughed. "Good, good. And speaking of men."

"Father, no…"

"My terms for sending you to the Rock. I've thought about it, and, I'll allow you to offer suggestions."

"Suggestions?" Sybil asked, already knowing what he meant.

"You have until the shortest day."

"And…" she trailed off. "I'm not following."

"I expect you to tell me who should be your next mate, as has been discussed," Tomas said with a bite. "Why it be best for Brochet. You have mourned long enough. I'll allow you a chance to decide your fate but choose wisely daughter. I will no longer consider your wishes in my decision if you disrespect this chance. Do you understand? That means I may give you, or the girl, to Basil and his Brotherhood if it pleases me."

Rose's heart dropped into her stomach. She'd never been told directly about the pact with Graves, but she gleaned from eavesdropping and passing conversations between Tomas and

Sybil that Graves wanted to bring her to the Omen and believed they were owed her. All she knew of Graves and the Omen was that they were very bad. Tantamount to Westerviolet's lair, or possibly worse. The idea of being handed over to them terrified her.

"Father! You would never," Sybil gasped, lowering her tone, glancing to the horrified look on Rose's face.

"Don't test me," he warned. "You'll leave with the girl for the Rock in a fortnight. I've arranged for you to stay at Monty's Villa. He's at Graceview now but will be there in a moon's time. He's invited you to reside there in his absence. Ustin is an old friend of mine. I mentored Monty for many years when he was quite young at Animus. Brilliant boy. He's a trusted ally of Brochet, I assure you, despite his political leanings."

"Is he married to an earthblood as well?"

"Bachelor," Tomas replied taking another bite. Sybil raised an eyebrow. "What, daughter?" Tomas asked as he chewed.

"I'm surprised you haven't tried to marry me to him, if you like him so much."

"Montague?" he asked rhetorically through a chewing bite. "Never. His father may be a respected friend, but he chose a different path," he said, swallowing. "One that I will not choose for you. I won't have a grandchild with mongrel blood. I'd toss it in the moat. I love Ustin and his boy Monty, but Ustin fucked an earthblood and Monty has half of that tainted blood. You are right if not for that he would be my choice for you. But things are the way that they are," he added. "Our Villa is undergoing repairs, and he has generously offered to house you and the girl for your stay."

Sybil nodded. "So be it."

"I trust you'll find it's more than adequate. Thorne has refined tastes. Rose will attend Academy, and you will sit on Council in my stead. It convenes shortly. It will hopefully give you some..." Tomas trailed off for an instant, searching for a word. "Perspective."

Sybil glared as Tomas took another bite of food. He looked smug and chewed loudly.

OUTSIDE LITTLEBELL

Ryd banged with his fist on the green-stone cottage's door two times, grinding his jaw as nerves knotted in his stomach. While he waited, he listened to Digory's shallow breaths.

He had never been so overwhelmed in all his life. First his brother went missing and now his only companion lay near death. Ryd's heart thumped in his temple, loudly, like banging ceremonial drums on Vanguard Day.

The sun was high in the sky and its' light, unusually dim for midday, only barely escaped through cracks in churning grey clouds. Digory lay on his back next to a flowerbed. He was unconscious with his right arm flopped over his head from when Ryd dropped him there. Countless tiny gnats, shiny-green beetles, and dark flies hummed in the meadow behind them next to the sweeping willow. A small butterfly flitted past Ryd's face. A tree tapper drilled nearby. Ryd waited patiently.

There was no response.

Was it possible the cottage was abandoned? Ryd glanced about, assessing the diligently weeded and watered beds next to the recently swept steps and porch. This property was maintained. Someone lived here. He knocked again twice, shifting his weight and swallowing hard.

A black curtain moved in the window to the right of the door. Too fast for Ryd to catch a glimpse of the person inside, but enough for him to notice someone was there. Then, the flash of an orange tail. "Hello?!" he shouted, taking several steps back. He pointed at the window. "I saw you!"

There was long pause, birds chirping behind him somewhere in the willow tree, then a high-pitched, timid voice.

"Who's there!?"

Ryd took a step back. "We need assistance! We're travellers. My companion is wounded. Please, let us in!"

The voice shouted back. It was shrill and pleasantly feminine. "How do I know you speak truth!?"

"I do!" Ryd cried as he looked down at Digory. "Please, please! I don't think he has much time left. It's nighthorn poison!"

There was a pause. It was silent apart from wind in the willow branches and the same whistling birds. Finally, a meek reply.

"I'm not supposed to let anyone in."

"Please! We were attacked!" Ryd shouted. He didn't know what else to say. He rubbed the back of his neck with his hand. The drums in his head got louder. "I'll step far back if you wish. Look out of your window again and you'll see a man unconscious by your flowers." Ryd put his palms out to show he was not armed and stepped many paces backwards. He saw the curtain shift in the window to the right of the front door just as quickly as before, followed by another pause. Wind rustled the willow branches still, and the red and black tapper was at it again, now drilling loudly in a birch nearby.

Then, the cottage's door creaked open. Ryd froze in shock as a gorgeous young woman emerged from the doorframe.

She had coal-black skin and a flawless complexion, heavy eyebrows and a delicate nose. Her honied hair was curled into tight, silky ringlets that fell to her shoulders in an uninterrupted mane around her head. She wore a vibrantly patterned, tailored, sleeveless gown, fitted at its scoop-neck across her ample bustline, down through to a tapered waist, then flounced out past her wide hips with floral embroidery at the base of the skirts. It looked as if blue thimbleweed, just like in the meadows outside, grew up the edges.

The young woman's eyes were blue to compliment the stitching.

"What happened?" Her sweet voice cut easily through the thick summer air, but Ryd just stared at her. "Well? What happened?!" She pointed at the pitifully injured Digory.

"Oh, yes. Right. Right," Ryd stuttered, flustered, blood flowing quickly to his chest and face. He'd never seen such beauty in all his life. Women in Westerviolet were typically boney, scrawny things with sunken eyes and sad expressions. Only the maidens had any hint of beauty, as they were the youngest and fairest in the realm. But this woman and her full body left Ryd breathless. "We were attacked," he said, clearing his throat. "He was hit in his shoulder," he added obviously, pointing to Digory while never breaking eye contact with the woman. His gaze was tethered to her loveliness. He knew he couldn't look away even if he wanted to.

"You couldn't make it further?" She pursed her lips revealing one dimple in her left cheek.

"I dragged him off of the road to die," Ryd admitted. "But he may have a chance now that I found you. Do you have aid inside?"

She lowered her voice. "How did you know? How did you find me?" She uncrossed her fleshy, un-muscled arms, coincidently pressing her breasts together in a plump line. She leaned towards him in confidence. "Do they know about me?"

"What? Know what?" Ryd straightened his back, forcibly looking up from her breasts in the foreign attire. He was genuinely confused. And, fully entranced.

The woman hesitated. "But…" She glanced from Ryd to Digory.

Ryd looked from the young woman to Digory's pallid face. "There isn't time," he finally said. "Help me bring him inside. I will not harm you," he added sincerely.

Although (and perhaps because) she was bewildered, the young woman didn't refuse. Together, they carefully hoisted Digory's unconscious body from its rest near the flower bed. With great effort the pair placed him on the only table within the cottage; a solid wooden piece a bit lower than usual tables, the ideal height for the young woman herself only, much shorter than most.

A meow followed by a hiss startled Ryd. He turned to see an orange cat with beady red eyes glaring at him from beneath the table.

"Don't mind Ruby," Vera said with half a smile. "She's not as foul as she seems." The feline seemed a bit put off by this statement and sauntered away to hide behind a rather heavily draped curtain on the far side of the cottage, away from Ryd.

It was strange to see a common pest kept as a house pet, but he was far from Westerviolet. Ryd realized he didn't know anything these people's customs. He coughed and nodded. "I think the arrow was tipped in Nighthorn poison," Ryd said. "Look at the wound." He lifted Digory's makeshift bandages to reveal the jagged, concave gash. Black rot crept out from the site in terribly noxious tendrils.

The young woman stood on the opposite side of the table. She furrowed her honey brow. "That's not good," she said quietly.

"I didn't think so either," Ryd replied, matching her grim tone. They met eyes briefly.

"Help me cut away this cloth."

Together they ripped away the remaining cloak tatters covering the wound to expose the length of arrow protruding from Digory's shoulder. The young woman bit her lip, cheek dimpling again.

"What is it?" Ryd asked, assuming by her confident movements that she had Apothecary experience. Fortunate indeed.

"Hmm," she said, poking at rigid, blackened skin before looking up at Ryd. Her blue eyes met his red ones. "You shouldn't be here. It's too much. You should go," she said, then turned away. Her embroidery-hemmed skirts swished loudly behind her.

"Wait!" Ryd reached out. "Where are you going? We mean you no harm."

"I believe you," she said, turning. "But he wears the serpent." She gestured to Digory, limp body in the center of the cottage with arms and legs flopped off the table.

"The serpent?" Ryd knew all Digory's guardsman attire had been long-ago ditched. Did she recognize his cloak's tatters?

His trousers? His boots? How did she know?

The young woman pointed at Digory's dagger hilt protruding from the sheath in his trousers. There was in fact a tiny Brochet ouroboros embedded in the green glass. "For all I know, it was my family who attacked you," she said.

"Your family?"

"Too much," she replied, frowning, turning again, shuffling to a wooden cabinet, withdrawing pieces of plain cloth. "You shouldn't be here," she added over her shoulder, ripping the cloth into make-shift bandage strips.

"Then why did you let me in?"

"I didn't know how bad it was," the young woman said in a whisper, looking down as she shuffled back over to the table to stand adjacent Ryd once more. "It would take too much," she added under her breath, as if he was trying to convince herself, not Ryd.

Ryd was very confused. "Too much what?"

"I can't, please. If my Mimi discovered you were here..." she trailed off. "She can't know. I've made a mistake letting you in. You must leave," the woman said fearfully. She looked to him with her chilly blue, child-like eyes. She backed away from him slowly.

"No, you misunderstand," Ryd raised his hands to reassure her, but the movement spooked her and she jumped back further, dropping the bandages she'd just cut.

"No, stop. Don't come closer! Stay where you are!" she shouted as ribbons of cloth drifted to the floor.

"Please! I'm sorry," Ryd backed up with hands raised. Digory lay unconscious between them, shirtless on the rectangular table in the center of the modest cottage, chest rising and falling shallowly. "I'm sorry," Ryd exclaimed, gesturing to Digory, "but he won't make it to Littlebell!"

"Tell me who you are," the young woman said shrilly. "If you aren't here for me, then why?"

Now, Ryd was supremely confused. "Why would I be here for you?"

"You don't know who I am?"

"No," Ryd said with exasperation. "Who are you?"

The young woman's wide-set gaze searched his quizzically. "I thought everyone knew…"

Ryd interrupted, "I don't. Are you going to tell me, then?"

"I…" the young woman stuttered, "I can't tell you."

"I don't care who you are," Ryd said, sighing, nearly gritting his teeth. He was exhausted and Collen's face burned in the back of his mind. He had to deal with Digory so he could continue to search for his brother. "If you're not going to help him, I will find someone who will."

"You don't care who I am?" The woman said hotly as Ryd fumed at her. "You're right," she added, glaring. "Your friend won't make it to Littlebell."

"He's not my friend."

"Why are you trying to save him?"

"It's a long story," he replied wearily. "I need him to find my brother," Ryd added. "He's missing."

"How many years is your brother?"

"Twelve."

The woman's indignation and terror gave way to concern. "What happened to him?" she asked gently, crouching down to pick up the fallen bandages.

"Word is he ran off to Littlebell." He cleared his throat, grinding his jaw once. "Are you going to let us stay or aren't you?"

"Who attacked him?" she pointed at Digory, but Ryd only sighed loudly in response. "Who attacked him!?" she repeated in a shout, standing quickly, clutching the bandages tight in her palm.

"Raiders! I told you!" Ryd shouted back. "He's helping me find my brother!"

The young woman dropped deep into silence and thought, pacing around the cottage with quick shuffling steps, skirts swishing behind her. Then, she peered out from behind a thick curtain blocking all the outside light. The cottage was very dim inside, lit by flickering oil lamps alone. "You are from his realm?"

"Yes, yes," Ryd said quickly, glancing down at Digory's bare chest snaked with blackened poison stemming from the arrow's wound, before looking back to the strange beauty.

"Ah ha!" the young woman pointed. "Brochet!"

"I maintain the stable!" Ryd shouted back at her. He paused, taken aback by his own outburst. "I want nothing to do with the cursed *Vanguards!* Now please, at least let him die here. I don't think I can move him again," he added more softly.

She nodded, then closed her eyes dramatically. She sighed as she opened them wide. She nodded once. "Okay."

Ryd's head shot up. "Okay what?"

"Okay, I'll help him."

"How can you help him?" he asked as he poked at Digory's injury with his finger, feeling the hardened edges of the wound. "What more can anyone do for him? There is no antidote for Nighthorn."

The young woman's expression pinched. She took a length of twine from a hidden pocket sewn into her skirts and fastened her unruly mane of curls into an organized knot on the top of her head. A few escaped the style and dropped down to frame her face by her cheeks.

"What?" Ryd asked. "What is it?

"I'm not supposed to."

"Supposed to what? What is your name?"

"I told you I can't tell you."

"I have to call you something." Ryd was unrelenting. "What do I call you?"

"Fine," the young woman sighed, rolling her eyes, worn down by persistency and Ryd's broodingly handsome glare. It had been so long since she'd seen anyone. Much less a man. Particularly such a beautiful man. And she was so lonely. Besides, she could sense he meant her no harm. "It's Vera."

"Vera" Ryd said once, instantly awash with pleasure at the tuneful sound. He liked how it felt on his tongue. Like sugar. He had tasted it once. Although, somehow this was better. "Okay, Vera. What do you mean you're not supposed to?"

Vera walked to a washbasin. She rinsed her hands in sitting

water, glancing up at her reflection briefly in a polished glass on the adjacent wall, eyes darting back and forth, then she shook her hands dry. She returned to Digory's side across the table from Ryd. "I need you," she said, breaking the dim cottage's shaky calm.

Ryd's heart leapt. "What did you say?"

"Don't be foolish," she smirked at him. "Your hands," she added, taking his calloused hands into her delicate ones. "I need your hands. It's easier if I have help."

"Help for what?"

"Here," Vera said as she placed Ryd's hands on Digory's chest around the wound's protruding arrow.

"What are you doing?"

She looked up and her ice blue gaze palpably washed over Ryd. He was thrust into a river of overwhelming calm and reassurance. It took his breath away all over again. "Trust me," she said intimately. At that, he was lost.

Ryd, wide-eyed and nodding, held Digory's chest firmly as Vera grabbed the young man from the opposite side to roll him. She grasped what was left of the arrow. While bracing Digory's body with the other hand, she slowly shoved the arrow through and out Digory's back. It pierced his skin, rupturing with a gush of infected blood.

Ryd gagged and nearly vomited as Vera set her jaw. Digory's body convulsed briefly, bucking forward and back with the shock of pain, eyes rolling back in his head, ghostly whites against dusky-tan skin.

"He'll bleed out!" Ryd shouted, internally surprised at his own concern. Vera ignored him. She lowered Digory to his back once more. His punctured flesh met the dark, sticky blood coating the table and dripping onto the floor. Vera placed Ryd's hands atop the wound, then hovered her own above his. Digory's flailing calmed. Soon, he again lay so still he appeared dead.

Vera asked Ryd with deep seriousness in her tone, "You're certain?"

Ryd's head shot up. "Certain?"

"Certain you want to help him?"

"Yes! Whatever needs done," Ryd said urgently. "Hurry! He's bleeding everywhere. He's dying!" The putrid bloody runoff covered the table and coated Ryd's feet burgundy, dripping with faint pattering drops to the floor. The flickering oil lamps cast deep shadows across the rank, viscous liquid.

Vera gave a slight nod and placed her own hands directly above Ryd's and the pulsing wound. As she locked his eyes, he absorbed her features. She was so unlike the women in Westerviolet. Unlike anyone he had ever seen! He almost didn't notice her eyes start to turn, at first. Ryd felt a wave of intensive nausea wash over himself as bile-green smoke pooled in her irises. As his own left arm began pulsing, Ryd resisted the urge to flee and vomit.

"Good, stay here. Just a while longer."

"What's happening to you?" Ryd asked, terrified as searing pain bubbled from within his own shoulder. "What's happening to me?!"

"Trust me," she said calmly with her face contorted. "I'll be fine." Her eyes filled to the brim with the black liquid, whites and all, until her entire gaze was dark and misty.

Ryd's uncontrollable sickness was so distracting he did not see the black edges of Digory's wound fade to pink. The spider web of infected tissue pulled back on itself in reverse. More shocking still, it was as if Digory's body were a sponge that reabsorbed the blood he'd lost. What had fallen to the floor inexplicably crept up the table legs and travelled back through the narrowing wound on Digory's shoulder. Even the blood coating Ryd's boots followed suit, magically sucking back into Digory's body like bleeding out backwards. All that remained was the black tinge of nighthorn poison all over the cottage floor.

Flabbergasted, Ryd pulled away from the trance held by Vera. She gasped loudly and coughed and wretched as Ryd ran to the washbasin. He vomited violently. Yellow-green bile from his stomach mixed with the lukewarm basin water. He briefly looked up into the polished glass to catch a dark smoke leaving his own eyes. His normal red was half-clouded, however, as he vomited more, his eyes cleared and returned to his natural hue. Once the nausea subsided, he was reminded of the stabbing pain in his shoulder. He pulled at his tunic to reveal an identical wound to Digory's, not quite as healed as Digory's appeared to be.

"What are you?" Ryd whispered under his breath, lowering his tunic, feeling the magical wound on his shoulder, glaring at the putrid clouds leaving his eyes. What have you done!?" He turned and yelled at her. Vera was doubled over in pain, coughing into a waste pail on the far side of the one-room cottage. Ryd immediately softened and rushed to her side.

"Are you alright?"

"I'm fine," she said quietly, coughing again. "It'll wear off soon."

"What happened?" Ryd asked in half horror, half awe. He touched his shoulder gently.

"That will heal," Vera said. "I'm afraid you will have a scar." Ryd half smiled. "What is it?" Vera asked as she stood, adjusting her gown and then her hair, wiping spittle from the corner of her lip.

"Nothing," he said quickly, glancing to Digory. The man's color was returning as his chest rose and fell with a hopeful robustness. His pink wound appeared virtually healed, puckering around a hearty scab, not fatal at all. He wouldn't admit it to himself, but Ryd was relieved. He didn't want Digory to die. Ryd walked to Digory's side. He rested his hands on the table aside him. "How did you do that?"

Vera sat down in a simple wooden chair, clearly exhausted. "I just can."

"Is it something about your sky eyes?"

She smiled wearily and untied her hair. "I like that," she said, curls bursting free from the twine, bouncing quickly back into a honey-blonde mane. "Sky eyes."

"Why did they turn a different color?"

"I don't know," she said honestly. And she truly didn't. There was nothing in the Teachings nor in the records passed down through generations of Minneys that explained it. Not even every blue-eye could do what she did. Only a few legendary ones. Her grandmother Laila Minney, for example, had blue eyes, and while she had a certain touch for healing and an innate empathy, she could not magically heal others as Vera so naturally did. "I can feel other people and if I want to, I can take away what's wrong."

"Feel other people?" Vera didn't clarify; only nodded. This made no sense to him, but he didn't want to pester her with more questions, although he was full of them. Ryd rubbed the back of his neck with his hand and looked at Digory quizzically. Then he lowered his hand and looked at Vera. "Why did you need me?"

"I'm stronger if I have help," Vera said. "With how bad he was, I had to use you." She pointed at Ryd's shoulder. "You wouldn't be left with that at all if you hadn't pulled away so soon."

"He'll be okay?"

"Yes, but he won't wake for nearly a day," she said. "We can move him to the cot to rest after I bandage his wounds." Vera took a deep breath and returned to her feet, clutching the make-shift dressings. She shuffled to Digory's side and expertly bandaged the wound.

"Where'd you learn to do that?"

"Mimi," Vera said as she moved to the base of the table. Ryd took the hint, grabbing Digory behind his shoulders while Vera held his feet. They shuffled him over a few paces to a cot against a wall with a window behind it, covered in a thick curtain.

Disturbed by their movements, Ruby darted out from behind it, meowing at Ryd disapprovingly.

Ryd, overwhelmed, rubbed his temple with a glance to the pest. "This is a lot. I need air," he said and rushed outside with a slam of the cottage's wooden door behind him. Churning dark clouds loomed. Ryd doubled over next to the flowerbed, taking deep breaths.

Hands on his knees, eyes clenched shut, Ryd heard the front

door creak open. Vera followed him into the humid meadow. She placed her hand on his back to comfort him, but Ryd withdrew, then turned to see the stung look on her face.

"I'm sorry," he said, "but…what are you?"

Growing wind bucked torpid willow branches in a looping, whooshing dance beside them. Squawks were less chirp-like and more urgent now, chattering, warning of the impending storm. The air felt charged.

"Can I trust you?"

"Yes," Ryd said. "You can." His eyes pled hers. "Tell me. What happened in there? Who are you?"

"I'm a Minney," Vera said dramatically. She paused, eyes searching his, waiting for a response.

Ryd didn't react.

"Vanguard," she said.

"You're Vanguard!?" Ryd nearly jumped. "I…I assumed…" He had never seen eyes such as hers before and thought all in Littlebell must look that way.

"I am not one of you," Vera interrupted. "Although, our people are New."

"New?" Ryd asked before he could help himself, inwardly angry he'd said something so foolish. Digory had mentioned the term. He had at best a conceptual understanding of what it meant from their days of travel.

"You really must be of Westerviolet. You know nothing of my world." Vera laughed. She was used to being the center of attention and gossip. As a child, everywhere she went, someone wanted to look at her. 'Let me see your eyes, girl!' they would shout at her with glee. It frightened her when she was small and grew bothersome as she aged. She'd never met someone who didn't know more about her than she knew about them. "How refreshing," she said to Ryd.

Thunder rumbled on the horizon as sunlight fought to break through rolling black clouds.

"Tell me of it, then."

"Why?"

"I'm interested," Ryd said. "Here," he gestured to a log

shaded by a large birch tree at the cusp of the papery woods.

"You want to hear what I have to say?"

"Yes." Ryd said. "Tell me." He took several paces, then lowered to a seat on the log. He patted next to himself.

Vera smiled. She glided over, pulling her intricately embroidered skirts up to reveal slipper-like booties, then took a seat at his side.

"You don't tease?" She leaned towards him. "You really don't know about us?"

"Well, I know some," Ryd defended as he adjusted his seat, conscious for the first time of his own threadbare trousers compared to her fine gown. He should have known she was Vanguard from her attire alone, he thought sheepishly. He'd only ever seen Lord Tomas or Lady Sybil wear such finery. "I know Brochet. I've learned bits of knowledge here and there. I have ridden on trading missions," he added, to sound impressive. "I know some things."

"Like what?" Vera asked with an eager gleam in her eye.

"Graves rumors mostly," he said nonchalantly, referencing the only thing he actually did have any grasp of. Vera nodded knowingly. "I've passed through Baneswood and been once to Croft Hold. But I know nothing of their stories."

"Why not?"

"I have my own."

"And yet, you're curious of mine," Vera smiled. "But I am Vanguard. How do you reconcile this?"

"You're different." He couldn't quite explain why. Maybe it was that she looked far more like he did than any other Vanguard he'd seen. Their skin was the same. "Tell me about being a, what did you say? Minney." He picked at dead peeling white bark, curling away from their seat of a log.

"Our castle is Littlebell. As is our realm."

"I knew that," Ryd said quickly, a bead of sweat catching in the corner of his eye. He rubbed at it with his pinkie.

Vera nodded. "I was born there and lived there as a child. My Mimi moved me here to keep me safe once I was of age."

Ryd stopped rubbing his eye. "Mimi?"

"My grandmother."

"What's special about her?"

"She is elder was the only Minney alive for half a century with the charm."

"Until you?" Ryd finished. Vera nodded, honey curls bouncing around her face. "Is that what your powers are called?"

"No," Vera said quickly. "It's just being born with blue eyes." She paused, then smiled wide. Ryd felt like the whole world brightened. "Sky eyes," she corrected. Ryd beamed and matched her grin as she went on. "I don't think any of the other charmed Minneys could do what I can. Mimi can't. Not like I can."

"It's just the sky eyes?"

She smiled again. "We believe the charm means better blood, but I don't know. I don't feel any better. Any different," she said, smile falling. "My family thinks otherwise." She looked down. "They believe I'm meant to fulfil some old prophesy. That's why, once I began the bleed, they moved me here to keep me safe."

"Safe from who?"

"The Old."

Ryd crumpled the papery bark between his fingers. "Who?"

"The last charmed Minney before my Mimi," she explained, "Great Grandaunt Lilli. She was killed by the Old bloodlines. They captured her. Mimi won't let that happen to me."

"What happened to her?"

Vera leaned back on her hands, kicking her feet straight out. She sighed wearily. She'd heard the story more times than she could count. The tale was one of her first memories, used to warn her of the dangers of the Old bloodlines, and why she was never to leave Littlebell proper. "The Norlands experimented on her, raped, and murdered her." Her tone was bitter and hollowly cold.

"Other Vanguards?" Ryd asked, aghast, shifting on the log. "Why would they do that?"

"They're Old. They believe in the Old way."

It hurt Ryd to hear and his almond eyes narrowed to study dozens of yellow and blue butterflies whirling in the meadow ahead of them. It was a beautiful scene to witness, although his thoughts were with the poor Minney girl's suffering. "That's awful," he said under his breath. Vera glared at him sideways. Ryd felt her looking at him. He spun his head. "What?"

Her face threatened tears. "How can you say that when your friend wears the emblem of Brochet? When you are of an Old realm?"

Ryd recoiled, leaning back from Vera, picking another piece of bark. "He's not my friend," he said coolly, looking away. Vera adjusted her position to sit upright, with legs crossed, but didn't respond.

They fell into silence watching dark clouds roll over the buzzing, shadowy meadow.

"I miss my brothers and being near Father, but I know living here is best," Vera said unconvincingly, breaking the lull.

Ryd turned his head to her. "How many brothers do you have?"

"Two."

"Tell me about them."

She half smiled, glad to have a voice after isolation for so long. She didn't realize how lonely she was until given a companion. "Prihim is my favorite. He's the smartest man I know. Then there's Leon." Her smile fell. "He hasn't visited me once."

"How long has it been?"

"Six years."

"Wow," Ryd said softly. "Don't you get lonely?"

Vera shifted her body away. She crossed her arms. "Mimi visits me," she said defensively. "And I have Ruby."

"Not your father?"

"Father can't."

"Why?" Ryd frowned, feeling sorry for her, instantly angry at the man he'd never met. "Why wouldn't he visit his daughter?"

"He would, but he can't," Vera said. Ryd gave Vera a questioning look. "He hasn't moved since he fell eight years ago," she answered his gaze. "He lays in a bed all the time," she added, looking down. "Mimi cares for him."

"Oh." Ryd was silent for a moment. "Oh, I'm so sorry."

"Me too," Vera said.

"You can't heal him?" Ryd clumsily tried to right the conversation, "With your eyes, I mean."

"I already tried," Vera glanced away. "Before I did, he was dead."

Ryd opened his mouth and tried to speak but no words came out. Instead, he listened as wind whipped in discordant gusts, heralding a late summer storm. The willow's branches ahead bucked and the white-birch woods behind swayed. Disembodied fowl of every type chirped, squawked, and cheeped all around them as the pair was quiet for several long, painful moments. Then, finally, Ryd spoke, desperately trying to keep the conversation alive as wind whipped his face. "What of your mother?"

Vera's shoulders slumped. "Mother died giving birth to me."

"I'm sorry," Ryd said softly, crumpling the bark in his wide palm to dust. He hung his head, running his other hand through his sweaty hair. He wished he hadn't said a thing at all. He had no idea how to talk to a woman, much less a beautiful one. Much, much less a beautiful Vanguard one.

"It's okay," Vera offered, smoothing dirt with her foot. "I am too."

Ryd, inspired by a glance at the dainty cottage alone in the meadow, changed the subject. He picked at another piece of papery bark. "Wouldn't you be safer in the castle with guards to protect you?"

"We don't have guards," Vera said. She sat upright and wind fluttered in her golden curls.

"You don't? That's madness!"

"You and Prihim would get along," Vera said with a chuckle.

"Why?"

"He thinks it's mad we don't have guards too."

"Well," Ryd studied her eyes, icy pools against coal skin, "why don't you?"

"We Minneys are peaceful," she replied. "We don't believe in taking up arms."

"Even to protect yourself?"

She nodded once. "Even to protect ourselves."

Ryd was perplexed. "How are any of you alive at all?"

Vera giggled, batting her eyes at him, turning her head. She was invigorated by his company. "The Morfits are our allies," she said, smiling. "They protect us. I think Prihim wants us to adopt their ways because he's grown so close to them. He's on Council and at Animus most of the time. He likes their way of justice better than ours of peace."

"He has a point."

"Prihim doesn't see the full picture. Neither do you."

"Tell me then."

"What is just isn't always what is right. Nothing can be won through violence."

"That's nonsense," Ryd said, breaking into a disbelieving grin. "Violence is how everything is won."

Vera raised a slightly arched eyebrow. "Are you certain?"

"Yes..." Ryd's confidence faltered. "Violence is how the Vanguards conquered. Without it, you would be nothing."

"Perhaps," Vera said, biting her lip, revealing the dimple deep in her cheek. "But" she continued, "consider how much has been lost because of that choice. Think of it. Thousands of lives over centuries, gone. Millions of stories forgotten, for what?"

"For what?" Ryd picked bits of bark from his palm. "Power, control. The same things men always fight for," he added, remembering Digory's pontificating. He looked to her inquisitively. "How is that not the way?"

She kept looking down, shuffling dirt around with her feet, dust billowing about the embroidered hems of her skirts. "It isn't."

"How can it not be?" Ryd said. "You told me just now that the Old is after you. Shouldn't you protect yourself?"

She stopped kicking and gave him a chilling look. "If every man threw first, we'd all be full of spears."

"But... but... protecting yourself is different from..."

"The Morfits protect us, despite our peaceful beliefs."

"I don't see any Morfits here."

"Mimi thought it best not to draw attention to the cottage," Vera replied. "It's safe, as long as I don't let anyone in." She didn't mention the necessary charms placed upon the cottage by the Guild, intended to make it invisible to any passers-by, apart from Minney blood. She had forgotten about them herself, awash in the excitement of Ryd's arrival and company.

As Ryd studied Vera, she glanced down with hot cheeks and hid a smile with her hand. Ryd's eyes grazed her profile. A delicate sloped nose and slanted jaw. "Tell me more about your bloodline." He didn't care what she spoke of, just that he heard more of her voice.

"I thought you had your own stories," Vera teased.

"You're different," Ryd said warmly. "I told you. I like yours."

Vera, deeply touched, smiled with glistening eyes. She'd been alone for so long that Ryd's attention was like a rainstorm in a drought. Thunder rolled in close and loud with grumbling booms but the pair was entranced with each other and oblivious to the down-turning weather. The cacophony of birds hidden in the trees serenaded nosily as the black clouds blocked out what little was left of the sun, leaving the whole realm dark.

Vera tucked part of her curly mane behind one ear as wind picked up. "What else would you like to know?"

"What does 'New' mean?" Ryd asked innocently. At Vera's shocked expression, he explained, "I have heard the term many times but..."

Vera giggled. "You really don't know anything."

"Hey," Ryd said with a smile.

"It means that our bloodline doesn't follow the old way of the Vanguard."

"The Vanguard?" Ryd asked. "You mean like your bloodline?"

"No, I mean the *Vanguard* Vanguard," she clarified. Ryd

stared at her blankly, unresponsive. Vera stared back at him in shock, "You don't know?"

"Tell me," Ryd replied, scooting closer to her on the log.

"You really don't know?"

"Enough!" he said, smiling wide.

And indeed, Ryd knew little to nothing of the ancient history of the Vanguards. The truth was intentionally kept from the natives of Westerviolet and any celebrations of Vanguard holidays, like Landing Day, for natives' purposes, were exceptionally vague.

With a grin, Vera began the tale. "I'll tell you the story Mimi told me of the old gods when I was a girl."

Ryd leaned to mirror her, listening with anticipation.

"The Vanguard was a vessel that could fly to the stars."

"To the stars," Ryd interjected, incredulous. "You mean, up there?" He gestured at churning black clouds above. "I don't believe you."

"It's true!" Vera pointed to the sky. "Mimi told me that before the Destruction, people could fly and talk across miles and had weapons that made horrible banging noises and shot fire."

"Destruction?"

"Just wait, let me tell the story!" Vera smiled, touching his forearm playfully.

Ryd smiled back, glancing down at the friendly gesture, then back up at Vera's striking face. "Go on."

"Thousands and thousands of years ago, more moons ago than you could count, there was a very powerful, very bad god who wanted to change people," she said.

"Why did he want to change people?"

Her eyebrows raised and she spoke with her hands theatrically. "To unlock power."

"Why?"

Vera thought for a moment. "To make people better," she said finally.

"Like you?"

Vera paused and chewed her lip, kicking dirt. "I think so,"

she said, although she didn't feel any better than anyone else. Ryd nodded, eyes wonder-filled. "He began his work on the land but was condemned by every Kingdom for creeds all around," Vera told him. "Once it was discovered what the god was doing, he was banned in every realm in the land. His only option was to continue his experiments elsewhere. He was named Alabaster Beaumont. If you don't know much of our history that name won't mean anything to you, but to Vanguards, it means a great deal."

"Why?"

"He was the first Beaumont of their whole bloodline." She looked up at him. "The Beaumonts are gone now."

"Oh," Ryd said, barely hearing her, lost in her ice-blue gaze.

"You don't even know what a Beaumont is, do you?"

Ryd shook his head sheepishly. Vera smiled warmly at him.

"What happened to Alexander?"

"Alabaster," she corrected. "He put together a team of gods who shared his views. Together they founded the Vanguard. Each of them had a different aim, but all had similar purpose of evolving humankind. Except for David Minney."

"David Minney." He narrowed his eyes. "The first of your bloodline?"

Vera nodded. "The legends claim he was the only god on the Vanguard who was not there by choice."

"Why was he there?" Ryd asked. Before Vera could answer, the realization washed over his face. "No!" Ryd nearly gasped. "They weren't..."

"Yes, they were," Vera nodded grimly. "David Minney was on the Vanguard as a slave. Legend says he was very powerful. Mimi says I must be like him. It's said he had the charm and passed it on to his descendants."

"That's awful," Ryd said under his breath.

"It is," Vera agreed solemnly. "Almost as awful as what happened on the land while the Vanguard was in the stars."

"Destruction?"

She nodded, bright face-framing ringlets glinting even with the overcast sun. "From the Vanguard in the stars they saw the whole world burn. The land below was ruined. The gods had no choice but to stay in the sky."

Thunder clapped loudly above, ear-ringing like the sound of a femur snapping, followed by a brilliant flash behind the black clouds.

Ryd was entranced by Vera and only briefly glanced briefly to the darkness. "They were trapped up there?"

"Yes," Vera said. "For hundreds and hundreds and hundreds of years until the Vanguard broke around the decedents of the original gods. Our Ancestors. *The* Ancestors. Then, they had no choice but to come back down to the land."

Instantly, the dots connected in Ryd's mind. So that was what the Landing was celebrating, he realized. He felt silly he hadn't thought more about the sacred Westerviolet holiday before.

"If David Minney was a slave, why are you not?"

"After the Vanguards landed, it was decided that the descendants of David Minney would be freed," she explained the old tale, wind whipping though the low-grown meadow, now scarce of all insects. Dark, grim lighting from thundering clouds cast the white-birch trees in shadow, lush leaves fluttering violently in the gale, muggy, hot summer air cutting with crisp gusts. Like they sat in the belly of a belching beast. "This decision was what many say first split us."

"Why?" Ryd asked in wonderment.

Such stories were kept far from the citizens of Westerviolet. Ryd had simply been taught to worship the Brochet Ancestors because they were above him.

"Some of the bloodlines disagreed, saying to release the Minneys was a betrayal of the original Vanguard gods. Others claimed that this is a new world and to survive we must peacefully adapt, not stubbornly fight. Those bloodlines Minney, freeing us and establishing us as our own bloodline at Littlebell. For many centuries though, natives were enslaved across the Kingdom. The only place natives have ever been truly free is in Littlebell. It is a sanctuary."

"I see. Old and New." Ryd ran his hands over his hair. "How can you tell them apart now?"

288

"By who we wed. The biggest difference today between Old and New is marriage." Vera spoke with her hands like most of Littlebell did. "The Old is traditional. They only wed other Vanguard blood. So much so, they've created the curse."

"What's that? The curse."

"Vanguards can't always mate with other Vanguards," Vera said delicately. "It doesn't always... work."

Vanguards had intermarried for so long that their blood, while potent, was prone to several issues. Madness and infertility, primarily.

Ryd gazed out at the dark-cast meadow. "Why would they only mate with other Vanguards?"

"It varies by bloodline, but all believe in one way or another that Vanguard blood is purer and more likely to lead to the power they seek." Rumor had it, in the forgotten past, even Minney's who mated with other Vanguards instead of natives were more powerful. Vera had heard such rumors from her brother Leon, who told her he heard it from a traveling Guildsman, although he wouldn't specify which one. Leon's beliefs tended to skirt the line between Old and New. After deciding not to mention any of that to Ryd, Vera added, "The New doesn't care about purity of blood. We don't cling to dead tradition."

"What's that mean?"

"New bloodlines marry our children to natives." Ryd smirked. His serious brow rose as he smiled. Vera eyed him, unamused. "It is truth," she said, adjusting her hair behind her ears.

Shocked, Ryd turned his head slowly. "You mean," he paused, choosing words carefully. "They are free here, truly?" Ryd had never heard something so ridiculous in all his life. While there were natives with power in Westerviolet, the Vice Lords and their appointed high natives primarily, they certainly were not free.

"Yes, absolutely." Vera's sky eyes twinkled, gorgeously contrast against her skin. "They're free here in Littlebell. They live alongside us. Why wouldn't they?"

"What do you mean they're free in Littlebell?" Ryd leaned towards her. "Explain what you mean by 'free'. They aren't indebted to your bloodline?"

Vera laughed and mirrored his movement gracefully, facing him on the log. "Not at all. They're free to come and go as they please."

Ryd couldn't process it. The concept was unthinkable. "How?"

"Natives who live on our fertile land farm it. They can keep as much as they like of the crops and whatever they choose to bring to Littlebell is for us. It's a bit like an offering. Or a customary, voluntary tax. They are rewarded by access to the pleasures of the city. Including, the ability to sell their crops at the Occident, to earn coin. With coin, they can purchase any goods they please. The land produces plenty. This way brings peace."

"They can do as they please, yet they choose to share their crops with your bloodline?"

"Yes, absolutely. In exchange, we maintain the city, Apothecary, trade routes, ports, and so on."

"How does your bloodline have any coin at all?"

"Taxes on the wares sold within our city."

"Amazing," Ryd said in awe. The concept was unthinkably foreign to him. In Westerviolet, Brochet commanded the people how much they were expected to produce. If they didn't meet the quota, deadly measures were taken.

"It is the way things should be. It's why I don't trust your friend inside."

"Why?"

"Because he wears an Old emblem," she said. "Because you're both from an Old realm. Littlebell's people tell tales of the horrors in Westerviolet just down the Narrows. Mothers warn their children to never travel that way by mistake, for they'll disappear to Lord Brochet's Lair!"

Ryd laughed. "That's absurd," he said, rubbing the back of his neck, chill running down his spine at the thought of the Lair. "It's not that bad," he added unconvincingly, although he knew in the pit of his heart that it was. Or worse. He'd been fortunate to have been the son of the Stablemaster and was therefore removed from most of the realm's horrors, although he lived close enough to the castle. It was hard to ignore the screaming.

"What's it like, then?"

Ryd's brick-red eyes were lost in her beauty as he gathered his thoughts. She watched him with a partial grin, amused. He finally said, "We're assessed as children for usefulness, then assigned a position. If you're proven to have valuable blood you're permitted to mate. Sons follow fathers. My father was stablemaster which is why I now am too."

His answer troubled Vera greatly. "You're assigned to where you work?"

"Yes," Ryd nodded. "All is assigned."

"All?"

"Why wouldn't it be?"

"You can't choose what you do?"

"Can anyone?" Vera looked sad. "What is it?" Ryd asked her.

"They assign everything? Surely not what you eat."

Ryd nodded again. "Yes, what we eat. For us low natives anyway, there are rations. I've heard the high natives live more like Vanguards, but there are not many of them. They stay in their Vice Provinces, mostly, and only come to Westerviolet proper for holidays. Although their children are educated in the castle."

She paused, studying the dirt at her feet. "What of your mating, then?"

"Assigned," Ryd said automatically. "When we reach of age, and only if worthy. And a suitable coupling is has been identified, of course."

Vera frowned. "You *are* allowed to marry?" she asked hopefully.

Ryd shook his head no. "I'm not."

"I thought you said you could mate?"

"Not marriage."

"Your father was not married to your mother?"

Ryd laughed at the ridiculous concept. Only Vanguards married. Vice Lords were permitted harems and occasionally Guardsmen had a maiden or two they were sweet on. But marriage? For a native in Westerviolet? Never.

"I never knew my mother," he said.

"But your brother? Certainly..."

"I don't know if Collen and I share the same mother." Ryd didn't notice the painful pinch of Vera's brow as he spoke, since the thought of his brother thrust him into a brief sea of guilt and longing. "Father needed help in the stable, so he was permitted to breed. Once he'd produced two able-bodied sons, that was the end of it." Vera was visibly upset. Near tears. She sniffed. His head turned. "What is it?" Ryd snapped from his own 292 thoughts. Concerned, he placed his hand on hers.

"I knew it was bad, but I didn't realize..." Vera trailed off. The story that Lord Tomas Brochet told the Council and thus trickled down into knowledge of Westerviolet for all about the Kingdom was far different. Most thought Westerviolet was much like Croft Hold, or Animus Rock, just impartial to strangers and inaccessible. She'd never imagined that a realm so close to hers operated so inhumanely and felt foolish and small and scared, all at the same time. Tears spilled in two competing drops down both of her cheeks. On the right, the drop fell into her deep dimple. She turned to look at him.

"Don't worry," Ryd said.

The sky, yellow green with black clouds, lit up with a crack then opened in a downpour of warm rain. The pair was quickly drenched. Vera and Ryd, screaming in surprised delight at the shower, leapt from their seats while still holding hands.

"Come!" Ryd shouted, pulling her quickly through the field. The pair darted into the green cottage.

By the time they were indoors they were both drenched. Ryd's modest tunic and Vera's vibrant, embroidered gown were soaked and dripping water all over the floor. Both Ryd and Vera looked down at themselves then up at each other and laughed. Ryd still held Vera's hand. As they faced each other, Ryd glanced briefly over Vera's shoulder at Digory. He hadn't moved at all since they left him on the cot. His chest rose and fell steadily. His eyes were tightly closed.

Ryd gestured with his head to where Digory lay. "How much longer for him?"

Above them, heavy rainwater pelted the cottage's thatched roof in a cadenced drum. A slow leak started in the far corner near the wash basin, dripping in rhythmic succession against the bare floor.

Vera studied Ryd's handsome, serious expression. She examined rainwater resting on his light eyebrows and square chin. She put her hand on his smooth chin. He jumped slightly but didn't pull away. Lightning illuminated the heavy curtains about the dim, oil-lamp lit cottage followed by a deafening clap of thunder.

Vera stroked rain from his cheek.

"What are you doing?" Ryd asked.

She closed her eyes. He leaned towards her.

Digory awoke to brain-splitting thunder, body throbbing like he'd been tossed from a cliff. Laboriously, he opened one eye. With a flash of lightning, Digory caught a glimpse of Ryd and a strange young woman in a passionate embrace before he slipped back into his fitful dream, hearing the dead stable boy's screams repeat over and over in his mind.

AROUND WESTERVIOLET

Gawen knocked once on the splintered door of the women's dormitory. The stark building normally cast long shadows across the path but today the sun was obstructed by black clouds rolling in from the West.

Gawen looked up as he waited, smiling in relief at the temperature drop the weather would bring. These late summer moons in Westerviolet were hellishly hot. As a child, Gawen was tasked with fanning the Lord in his night chamber and he still remembered how good the false indoor breeze felt, despite being far from that station now. He adjusted his armour and rubbed at his sweaty neck with the edge of his thick emerald cloak, thinking over the details of the case. He knocked again. There was no response. Beetles whirred amidst the knotted violet grass, low-grown up to the edge of the path. A bird called nearby in lonesome, whooping chirps. Gawen shifted his weight and knocked again twice.

A trembling voice clucked over Gawen's shoulder. "What are you doing, cock in the hen dwelling?"

He turned to see a shrivelled lady in a sullied apron. Her fine, white hair was pulled into dozens of snake-braids, long to the middle of her back.

"Petra," Gawen said with a smile, eyes crinkling at the creases. The sup maid was the closest most of the Westerviolet commons low natives ever had to a mother. Including himself. Gawen had a soft spot for her. "How are you?"

"Alas," she said, waddling over to him, beige trousers swishing, "I've been better." She shook a wrinkled finger. "Never get old, child. Never get old."

"Aye, I'll remember that one. How's the kitchen?"

"Damned as the First," Petra spat. "How is post?"

"The same," Gawen laughed.

"What brings you here, boy?"

"Guardsmen business."

"You won't give an old woman something to gossip about?"

Gawen shook his head and smiled at the notorious tell-tale. "Nay."

Petra's face crumpled as she frowned, narrow red eyes searching Gawen's for clues. "Is this about Budic's ward?"

"How do you know about that?"

Petra smugly glowed. "The walls at Westerviolet have lips, child," she said. "If you know where to listen, you hear all."

Nearby, a group of maidens scurried towards the dormitories arm in arm, beige tunics bucking behind them in the mounting wind.

Gawen snuck a glance at the legendary beauties, delicate like feathers floating in the breeze, then focused back on Petra. "Do you know what happened?"

"The whispers say it was his hand."

Gawen lowered his voice. "What do you think?"

"I think that *you think* it wasn't his hand," Petra shook her finger at Gawen. "You think…"

"I think that there are too many questions."

"You haven't said why you're here."

"Did you ever see Aslf with anyone in particular?"

"Aye," Petra nodded. "Miri. She was soft for the boy. She found his body." She paused, pursing her lips as she chewed the skin of her cheek. She crinkled her thin forehead skin into a dozen lines. "Do you wish to speak to her?" Gawen nodded. Petra remained unmoving, blocking the splintered door with her shrunken frame like a parchment drawbridge clamped shut. "You aren't going to harm her?"

Gawen leaned in close. He placed his hand on Petra's frail shoulder. He looked reassuringly into her eyes. "No," he said. "You have my word. I only need to question her, then she is free to go." His presence was so commanding yet soothing; the old woman accepted it without a second thought. He was a man easily trusted.

"Wait here," Petra barked. "I won't have you bursting in and rustling feathers! A Guardsman in the women's dormitory," she spoke to herself. "What next? A native in the Air Hall?!"

Gawen smiled at the old woman, clucking under her breath, white braids jumping with the shakes of her head. Like this, Petra disappeared inside.

Gawen waited as he watched dark clouds roll in. He always watched the clouds and noticed the weather, enjoying the patterns and light cast across the sky. He felt happy when it was sunny and rain made him feel as if he may cry. He had been that way, tied to the weather, since he was a boy. The air today was moist, heavy, and static-charged. Lightning storms would be coming soon. Beads of sweat fell down his brow and cheeks. He wiped his face with his hand then dried it on his pant leg. Finally, the dormitory door finally opened with a loud creak and Gawen saw the girl who found Aslf's body emerge with slumped shoulders.

Miri stood in the splintered doorframe, teary-eyed, ready for questioning. Her young face looked up at him in misery and fear. Her eyes were dark red, lined naturally by long, black eyelashes. She was slight, with sharp collar bones and visible ribs under the skin on her chest. Her face was puffy and swollen and she hunched and shook, like she barely had the energy to stand at all.

"I am so sorry," Gawen began, "but I need to ask you a few questions. Is that alright?" Miri nodded sombrely without meeting Gawen's eyes. "How long did you know Aslf?"

At the mention of his name, the girl burst into tears and collapsed into Gawen's arms, just as she had earlier. The Commander's Second gently held her. "It's alright. It's alright. Shhh," he cooed. "Miri, I need you to be strong, do you hear me? I need your help."

The girl asked, nearly inaudibly, into his chainmail, "How can I help?"

Gawen looked at her, gripping her firmly with a square hand on each shoulder. Miri rubbed the tears out of her eyes with her finger. She sniffled once.

"You can answer my questions," Gawen told her. "Can you do that for me, Miri?" Trembling, the girl nodded. "How long did you know him?"

"All our lives," she said with a crack. "I love him! He wouldn't do this. What did I do wrong?" She crossed her arms tightly.

Gawen held onto Miri, eyes burning with ambitious intensity, wanting to shake the girl and scream at her, yet his tone was soft. "He wasn't troubled?"

Miri shot her head up. "Not at all!"

"I wasn't saying he was. Tell me then, why not?"

"He, he.. He said we would be together."

"You couldn't be," Gawen said. Miri was a maid. While she was fortunate to have been kept alive at all, for most female babes in Westerviolet were discarded or utilized in the Lair, she had not yet begun the bleed, and her usefulness was still being determined. If she was not deemed worthy of maiden status, she would be sterilized and put to work in the orchards or fields, or or and gifted to one of the high natives, or another Old realm as a plaything. Or simply exterminated. "The law wouldn't..."

Miri interrupted. "He would rank up through the Guardsmen and change the law! Convince the Lord! He swore he would!"

"I see," Gawen said softly, nodding, scratching at the base of his matted hair. It was a common ambition of the youngest, most foolish of men. He'd heard similar plans before. None ever came to fruition.

"He wouldn't have done this! Especially without telling me why," she cried. "Oh, what did I do!?"

"You didn't do anything, flower. Tell me, is there anyone who wanted to hurt Aslf?"

"You think someone hurt him? Who!?"

By now, Miri's tantrum had drawn a slight crowd. Dozens of questioning faces appeared in the dormitory windows above them.

"Miri," Gawen said calmly, "I'm asking you, who would have wanted to?"

Miri furrowed her brow. "I don't know. I don't think anyone. I don't know! Who would have done such a thing! And, I saw him lying there. It was so horrible! Dagger in his hand. All that blood!"

"It's alright, it's alright," Gawen hugged the girl gently again, feeling the rattle of her breath and the unsteady rise and fall of her chest. His heart broke for her, but he knew the only way he could help her now is to find justice for Aslf. "Can you remember anything strange from when you found him? Anything at all, before the body was moved?"

"I don't know."

"Think hard, Miri. If someone hurt him, you will help me find them." Gawen waited while the girl thought, examining her closely. He finally asked, "Anything at all?"

She pulled away and looked at him. "I saw him with the blade in his hand."

"Yes. He held the dagger…"

"No," Miri interrupted, visibly frustrated. She stepped backwards from Gawen and pointed at his right hand. "He didn't use that one."

"But he clearly held the…"

"NO!"

"No?"

"He couldn't!"

"He couldn't? Flower, speak plainly. I saw it with my own eyes. He had it in his hand."

"Aslf promised me long ago not to tell anyone, for if the Guardsmen knew, he'd be removed from your ranks. He'd never have a chance of being Commander someday, like his uncle. Like he'd always dreamed."

"Girl," Gawen said forcefully. "What is it?!"

"He could barely use his right hand!"

"What did you say?" Gawen remembered Aslf's dead body clearly clutched the blade with his right.

"Something that happened when he was a boy. Something in the Lair," she claimed. "And besides, he favors his left anyway. He barely uses his right at all! He hides it."

Gawen leaned in closer to Miri. "Are you sure?! Tell me, you must be certain of this. If you are…"

"I am sure! I've teased him for it since we were children." She paused, eyes losing focus. "Why would he hold it in that hand?"

"Thank you, Miri, you have done very well," Gawen said. He hugged her quickly.

"What did I say?" She opened her red eyes wide. "What did I do?"

"I must go. Thank you! Go back inside and rest. When the investigation is over, I will tell you. Thank you, Miri!"

"What did I say!?" Miri yelled after him.

With pressing news for Budic, Gawen sprinted towards the Strategy Room.

Gawen passed unceremoniously through the stone-arched doorway into the silent Strategy Room. Budic was in a chair in front of the cold, gaping fireplace. Above it rested a tapestry of a picturesque landscape filled with slate mountains, cotton clouds, and winter-capped trees with a hawk soaring through the sky. Budic held a goblet filled with Animus wine. He leaned far back in the plush chair, studying the tapestry.

"Commander," Gawen said as he approached. He hovered by the older man's side.

"These are much better when they're colder," Budic said, remembering the time he had been given the pleasure of tasting iced wine, then took a sip. "But they still do the job warm."

"Aye Commander."

"Do you want one?"

"No, thank you Commander."

"What do you have for me?" Budic asked.

"You were right."

"You mean?"

"Aye," Gawen nodded, voice heavy with emotion, "afraid so."

"I knew it," Budic growled under his breath. "The boy would never take his own life. But how? What proof do you have of this foul deed? Who has done this? I crave justice, but I need evidence."

Gawen carefully took further steps in. "I have it, Commander." He removed his helmet and held it to his side.

"You investigated the body with Hudde?"

"Aye."

"What did you find?"

"The incision is deep, Commander. Very."

"Across his neck, with blade in hand?"

"Aye," Gawen said again. "The flesh of his neck was sliced clean through. Nearly to his spine."

"Was that all?"

"No, something else." Gawen paused. "The boy had bruising on his head. As if he'd fallen hard. Or been struck."

Budic frowned and swished liquid back and forth in his glass, studying it carefully as he spoke. He wasn't usually fond of drink, but given the circumstances, it helped calm his mind. He understood why so many of his men relied on it in their off hours. Those that didn't abuse Oblivion, anyway. "Surely the damage occurred after the wound. Could he have fallen?"

Gawen shook his head 'no'. Instead of blurting out his findings, he decided to lead Budic to them, in the same way he'd realized the truth himself. "Hudde told me it happened when Aslf was alive," he said pointedly. Budic's gaze darted up, pleading with Gawen's as he went on. "Hudde said it looked as if someone struck him with a heavy blow while he wore his helmet."

"You didn't mention this before when you debriefed me in the Lord's Study," Budic accused. "What reason do you have for keeping this information from Tomas?"

"None, Commander."

"Then why not bring it up then?"

"The bruising didn't appear until later," Gawen explained. "It wasn't there when I first examined the body beneath the oaks."

Budic's hope fell. He leaned back in his seat and exhaled

deeply. "This is your evidence for murder? I appreciate the..."

"No," Gawen interrupted. "Respectfully, Commander. I have more."

"What then? Speak it."

"I spoke to the girl who found the body."

"Aye?"

"She said the same as you. The boy would never do such a thing."

"I told you that."

"Yes, but then she remembered something," Gawen said with sparking eyes, like rubies in the light. "Something about Aslf."

"What more could the girl remember to help in this?"

"Which hand does the boy favor for his dagger?"

Budic stuttered. "I... I don't know," he sighed, then took a long, pensive drink. He looked up at the ceiling, "I'm so sorry Mallo," he said, shutting his eyes. "I thought I knew the boy and I don't even know which cursed hand he used."

Gawen stepped a bit closer. "Commander, the girl said Aslf favored his left."

Budic took another long drink and finished the burgundy liquid. "That is not revolutionary, Gawen. Some men favor the left. Not most, but..."

"Listen, Commander," Gawen forcefully interrupted. "You are not hearing me. Aslf was found with the dagger in his right hand."

Budic looked up and to the side at Gawen. "Aye?"

"Aye," Gawen said, but Budic seemed to already understand, face reddening in anger. "That means the boy couldn't have cut himself. Not like that, with the hand we found the blade in. And surely not that deep the whole way through."

"So, it must be..."

"Murder," Gawen finished sombrely.

Standing in a fury, Budic threw his empty glass so hard against the stone wall that it shattered into glittering shards. Then he sighed loudly as he hung his head, guilt and sorrow pounding in his mind. He scratched at his sweat-beaded braids.

"Bring me who did this," he said to Gawen, gruffly, without looking up.

"Yes, Commander."

"Why are you still here? Go!" he growled in uncharacteristic wrath, before crying out in a visceral scream of anger, vengeance, and pain. Gawen hurried away.

WESTERVIOLET EAST TOWER

S ybil became fixated on the East Tower, trying to learn it's secrets. Instead of going out to the white bindweed meadow, she began frequenting the forbidden wing when she couldn't sleep, in anticipation of travel to Animus Rock. She wouldn't admit it to herself, but she was nervous. She told Rose all about how everyone looked to her as the center of beauty and charm, but that was a decade ago. She knew nothing of Animus Rock anymore. She told herself that everyone would bow when she arrived, but deep in her heart she worried she'd been forgotten.

She would put the old diadem on her head, feeling a mist of certainty settle upon her, and step through the old clutter, distracting herself from her perpetual worry. Her angst over her plan for her own, and her daughter's, future. Her apprehension over going to Animus and her revulsion over the idea of choosing a mate in the way her father intended.

There was to be a ball at Animus Rock at the start of the season, in preparation for the upcoming Council session, and Sybil, despite loving an occasion to dress even more lavishly than usual and appreciating all eyes on her as they inevitably would be, did not want to go. She knew that she would feel like meat thrown to hungry dogs. So many oldblood men of breeding age would kill for a wife like her, and she despised the desperation. Further, she did not want to subject her daughter to such customs at such a young age. Although, she told herself as she rifled through old handwritten book titles, Rose was not much younger than she when she was first betrothed, then married to Rosen. But for some reason, Rose felt younger to her. Purer. More innocent and naïve. Sybil, herself, was never innocent. She was born manipulative.

She learned little about the secrets of the East Tower while she was there, although she did discover many interesting items. A chest that never seemed to be full, no matter how much she put in, nor empty, no matter how much she took out. A mirror that reflected Sybil as she wished she looked, not in reality. Even a handwritten book detailing all of the hidden passageways within Westerviolet's castle. That, she studied carefully.

It seemed like the East Tower was where all of the old charmed Ancestor artifacts had been stored in the wake of the Plague. Many, especially New bloodlines, believed that the Plague was caused by the old gods themselves, to punish the Vanguards for their general debauchery, selfish tendencies and brutal ways. Sybil realized while studying the items that her forefathers must have believed the same. They seemed to have written off the old powers totally, locking them away to be forgotten as a penance for what they'd done to deserve the Plague.

Then, there was the bell. It was covered in such a heavy layer of dust and grime that Sybil didn't realize it was silver at first. Only once she touched it and dragged her finger did the glinting metal shine through, brilliantly, giving her an idea of how impressive it must have been when it was still hung, catching the morning's first light. After she set eyes on the bell, it never chimed for her again, as if it had served its purpose. But still, sometimes, Sybil would sit, listening to the distant river fangs splashing in the moat, wishing she could hear the haunting ringing one more time.

LITTLEBELL

"You would think they'd have a wall, or a mote, or something," Digory said, nose high in the air, flaring his nostrils at the wafting stink. "Westerviolet has both, and the best forces in the Kingdom." He rode shirtless behind Ryd on the frail stallion, muscles etched beneath his tight-pulled skin.

The pair was nearing the city, trekking slowly down a sloped ridge. The rainstorm from earlier passed by and the sky was mostly clear. The sun now hung low painting faint western clouds orange and the horizon dusky blue. It felt different here, in Littlebell. Warmer. Brighter. More alive.

The closer Digory and Ryd got to the city proper, the more company they had on the Narrow. Loud, clanking carts and caravans full of bleating, mooing livestock made the last leg of their journey the most colorful yet. They rode more slowly now in a line to enter the city behind a high-piled convoy of red-tinted pelts, thick bushy tails the size of a forearm with either a black or white stripe on the tail. While the ruby fox furs were beautiful, orange tint to match the setting sun, the scent wafting up from them was putrid.

"Hmph," Ryd grunted. "Be still or you'll ruin your dressings."

Digory ignored him. He lowered his bandaged arm. "You aren't curious why they don't?"

"Don't what?"

"Have a wall or mote."

"I don't care," Ryd said, blocking his nose from the stench with his wrist.

"You don't care?" Digory mocked. "You wept when your beasts ran off on you, and yet you care not if these poor Minneys and colorful earthblood curses are ransacked by the next greedy band of raiders to get a big idea?"

Ryd was deeply lost in thoughts of Vera, muddled with his yearning to find Col. And he was angry at Digory. The man had not given him one word of thanks for saving his life. Again. "Hmph," he grunted.

"The Minneys are weak," Digory said into Ryd's ear.

"Why?" Ryd turned, frail stallion groaning with the shift. "Because they don't fight?"

"Because they don't even try. Pathetic to be that way. It leads only to disaster."

"How does not fighting lead to disaster?"

"Weak things find power in being weak," Digory replied. "It's like standing on softsand. When others rush in to save you, they'll be sucked down too."

"What's softsand?"

Digory began to explain, then, smiling, shook his head and basked in his superior knowledge of the Kingdom. "I mean that the only power in weakness is that there are many strong, stupid enough to protect you."

"Why is that stupid? It is noble to protect the downtrodden."

Digory laughed loudly. "They say things like that for dolts like you, stupid enough to believe it."

"Stop it," Ryd said, growing angrier, studying the fetid cart ahead. Despite feeling relieved that Digory didn't die, he tired of the Guardsman long ago. It was only the promise of finding Collen and fear of travel alone that kept him going alongside him. That's what he told himself.

They moved sluggishly in the line of merchants and costermongers waiting to enter the city. This last leg of Narrow Road cut through an assemblage of papery birch trees along with bursts of ferns that sprinkled the valley leading up to it. Miniature white butterflies danced between blades of grass. Birds sang in raspy chirps. It was beautiful. And fully lost on both young men as they waited impatiently.

"We've been through this. The strong are the ones who protect themselves and don't fall victim to the traps of the weak." Digory paused for emphasis. "Like the Minneys."

"The weak don't set traps," Ryd protested, watching the orange furs jostle and bounce ahead. "They really need help."

Digory patted Ryd on his shoulder. Ryd winced quietly in unexpected pain when touched. "You show how little you know of the Kingdom, friend. The strong fall when poisoned by the weak. I know you don't care for politics, but you should hear some of what Sybil tells me. This world is cursed. We have two choices. To side with the strong and survive, or side with the weak and fall. I don't know about you, but I'm not going to fall."

"It takes strength to be peaceful," Ryd countered, thinking of Vera. "And I'm not your friend."

"That sounds like something a weak man would say."

"Maybe there is a good reason," Ryd said cryptically. He thought back to Vera's explanation of her bloodline's ways.

"They are stupid," Digory dismissed flatly. "That's the reason why. It is stupid to leave a trade city unprotected."

Ryd drilled a hole in the stinky cart ahead with his gaze. "They are protected," he said under his breath.

"What did you whisper?" Digory nearly shouted in his ear. "I didn't catch that."

"Nothing."

"Did I hear you know something about the Vanguards?"

"Stop it, Digory," Ryd half turned. "I'm not in the mood."

"Tell me, companion, how are they protected? I do not see a moat, or a wall to keep anything out. And all know is that Minneys do not fight."

"I don't know anything about them," Ryd sighed. "You're the one who knows everything."

As they descended the valley's modest decline, Littlebell sprawled out in front of them in a winding maze of interconnected apartments, hovels, and town homes painted sunset colors. Rooves were thatched out of blue-tone river grass. In a coiling, curling pattern, the structures surrounded the pinnacle of the city; Littlebell's mighty rectangular yellow-stone castle topped with the lofty bell tower overlooking the muddled Missi River. Unlike the rigidness of Westerviolet, in

Littlebell, everything, even the architecture, flowed.

"At least you admit I know everything," Digory said. "You've learned something." He smiled and ran his hand through his beard, beginning to grow scraggly. "Look. The city entrance nears. For not having a wall, it takes a long time to get inside. I can't wait to get out from behind these shitting horses and stinking men."

Ryd studied the commotion ahead. The line slowed and bunched with men and women dressed in ostentatious, clashing patterns, brighter than he'd ever seen, griping and complaining amongst themselves behind high-stacked carts or livestock. The women were stunning with dark skin contrasted against blonde hair ranging from ice to honey, plaited in intricate, raised braids that ran down their backs. How shocking to see so many women, out and about freely! It embarrassed him, but it was hard for him to look away. Particularly because most were of ample size, including their bosoms. But that was not what drew his attention most. He squinted at the oddity of their hands. Most had red or blue nails. The men, in comparison, while dressed as brazenly in calico tunics with large belts, sported modest trimmed hairstyles or neat braids, and predominantly faces clean-shaven. Some of the men wore glinting gilded rings with inlayed gems. Ryd had no idea of the intricacies of Littlebell's social structure, but it seemed to him as if there were two different classes of people entirely. The men with rings seemed to only interact with the red nailed women. He noted this, intending to ask Vera why, if he ever saw her again.

Unbeknownst to him, Ryd was right. These differences spoke to the opposing political factions within Littlebell, indicated typically by staining of the women's hands or the way the men kept their hair and beard. Those natives who supported more progressive mindsets lived primarily in the north and wore red, and those who were traditionally minded lived in the south of the city and wore blue. The main road into the city split it in two. The factions often clashed and relied on final ruling from Littlebell's elder to determine the way for the city, and realm.

It had been that way in Littlebell for as long as anyone could remember.

The sun by now had nearly set, beaming over the skyline in a blinding ray. Ryd strained to see, shielding his eyes further with his wrist, hand clenched into a fist. Sunsets weren't as bad as sunrises, but they still hurt. He ignored Digory and didn't say anything.

"Did I damage your Minney-loving feelings?"

"Will you ever shut up?"

"Maybe once I'm dead."

"Can't wait."

Digory patted Ryd on the shoulder, sending an electric jolt of pain down his arm. "That's the spirit."

"Ouch!"

Digory balked with annoyance, not concern. "What happened to you?"

"Nothing," Ryd said, cradling his left side.

Digory squeezed Ryd's shoulder hard again. He yelped pitifully.

"Nothing, eh?"

Ryd pulled his shoulder away. "Stop that!"

"Nothing sure seems to hurt," Digory said. "You should come with me to the Apothecary. Can't have you dying on me. Won't know what to do with this curse."

He kicked the frail stallion who whinnied sadly.

"Don't do that." Ryd patted the animal gently to calm him. "He's tired," he said firmly to Digory. "It's nothing," he added, righting his posture slowly. "I must search for Collen."

"To your own be true," Digory shrugged. "I'll leave you where you fall. Can't say I didn't warn you."

"Some thanks I get."

"What now?"

Ryd opened his eyes wide in frustration, keeping them forward, locked on the burnt orange pelts ahead. "Nothing."

"Ah," Digory said lightly, chuckling to himself. "This again? I should thank you? When I didn't ask a thing from you?"

Ryd shifted his weight. He frowned. "I said, it's nothing."

"Did you not learn from last time?"

Ryd grunted, truly wishing he'd left Digory to die.

"Everything you do in this world is because you decide to do it," Digory said simply. "Only a dolt thinks the world owes him for the path he chooses himself."

"I shouldn't have saved you?"

"I wouldn't have if I were you," Digory retorted. "But it is your cursed life. Do with it what you will."

Ryd stewed as Digory paused, scratching his beard, squinting his eyes. He finally asked, "Why *did* you keep me alive?"

"I don't know," Ryd said in a sigh.

"Then, how?" he asked, sarcasm gone. "How did you keep me alive? Last I remember, you didn't think I'd make it. I haven't looked at the wound, but I feel…" Digory trailed off, wide-set eyes squinted in thought. He felt strange. Like his whole body was buzzing. Although he had danced with death many times throughout his life, he'd never come so close to it.

"It sure looks like they have protection," Ryd changed the subject, pointing to four guards stationed at the main entry point to the city in heavy golden armour, shimmery gold cloaks with cowl necks, tassels at the end, and jewelled fastenings. To Ryd, they looked like a Vanguard child's playthings, they were so overdone. Pants were tucked into black calf-high boots with golden seaming and buckles. Curved, tassled weapons fasted at each hip. Shields emblazoned with the emblem of a stoic woman blinded with a scale in hand, strapped to left wrists. The men had a variety of skin tones and serious red eyes beneath golden metal helmets with thin rectangular slits and sharpened pointed spikes on top. All four men bore reedy moustaches, squat trimmed close to their top lips.

When the line reached the guards, it split four ways. Each interviewed a traveller.

"Morfit," Digory said.

"They don't count as protection?"

"They prove my point."

"How?"

"The Minneys are so weak that they drag another bloodline

down to fight in their stead."

"But the Morfits are powerful," Ryd said, glancing to dark flashes of the women's colorful fingertips as many chattered in low-throated laughs, speaking in looping motions with their hands.

As he'd noted before, some fingers were stained indigo blue and others cherry red. Upon closer inspection, most of the fingertips were stained both nail and flesh, nearly to the first knuckle while few others, however, appeared precisely maintained, only staining on nail and exacting tip of finger. Only the wealthy natives could afford the expensive process of staining that kept the fingers clean. Most used cheaper methods, which resulted in staining of the entire finger.

Stranger still, many of the women, particularly the most youthful-looking and beautiful of the crowd, wore tangerine balm, made from crushed the tangerine iris found only along the riverbank in Hollowglade on their bottom lips, said to enhance attractiveness. In Littlebell, this indicated a woman was unmarried and actively looking for a mate. Ryd couldn't help but be distracted. It was nothing like he'd ever seen. Only Vanguards in Westerviolet wore face paints. Never natives, as it was forbidden.

"Clemmo told me of Morfit's pull in the Kingdom," he went on while noting the strange customs silently. "I witnessed Croft Hold! You should see the bridge," he said, thinking of the gilded entrance to Croft Hold's castle. "It's so beautiful. It's more beautiful than they say."

"For all of their might, and wealth, they are flawed."

Ryd was at the end of his rope. Physically as he hadn't slept or eaten properly in days, mentally as he'd been dealing with Digory for far longer than he could withstand. He exhaled loudly with little patience, "Why?"

"It's the same reason the New has never overtaken the Old," Digory explained hotly. "You're only as strong as your weakest. The weak will bring the strong down in the end. It's as it's always been and always will be. It's a fool's errand to do as the Morfits do."

Ryd's commanding tone faltered, but he pressed still, watching one of the guards frisk a beggar, tattered rags curling loosely from the man's fugacious frame. "It's honorable that the Morfits protect the Minneys."

"Aye, that's another word for stupid."

The line inched forward towards the entry, indicated by a break in looming sides of red and orange plastered buildings with blue-thatched rooves. A cacophony of competing accents, murmurs, and shouts mingled as the queued crowd festered, hands and elbows dancing as many spoke with the characteristically Littlebellian unusually wide and flamboyant gestures, bucking their loose sleeves. A nasally baritone cut Digory and Ryd's conversation in two.

"State your business in Littlebell," the nearest Morfit guard said, eyes zeroed in on Ryd. He gestured for them to approach.

Ryd's heart jumped. "I'm in search of my brother," he said quickly. He pulled the reigns, urging the steed to stand in front of the guard. "He's come this way, I hear."

"Runaway?" the Morfit guard barked upward, narrowing eyes at them. Beads of sweat dripped from his helmeted brow, dampening his square eyebrows. He seemed tired and a bit annoyed.

Ryd nodded, raising his hand to block the setting sun's light. "Aye."

"We get a lot of those," the guard nodded, eyes creasing in pity. "Where do you hail from?"

Before Ryd could respond, Digory interjected, "Baneswood!" from over Ryd's shoulder. He'd ensured his green glass dagger was out of sight and knew his crossbow and arrows were deeply packed away in a satchel behind him. There was nothing to indicate he was a Guardsman or that they hailed from Westerviolet.

"Is that so?" the guard said slowly, assessing the pair and their horse with a raised brow.

Digory muttered into Ryd's ear, "Trust me." Ryd nearly laughed at the presumption but obeyed. "It is so, good man," Digory responded ostentatiously. Ryd tried his best not to roll his eyes. He set his jaw impatiently.

The guard, in his single spiked golden helmet, seemed suspicious. "Why no provisions?" He squinted at the mangy steed. "Your horse hasn't been cared for properly. And your tunic is missing." The guard pointed at Digory's bandaged chest.

Digory couldn't resist. "You're observant," he said.

The guard immediately frowned.

"We were attacked by raiders," Ryd answered quickly, in unspoken apology for Digory, motivated by the fear that proximity to a guard sparked within him. "Our horses ran off. He was wounded. This is what was left." He patted the dusty old horse's trembling neck.

The guard eyed them up and down once more. "Pity," he said. "Best drop him off at the stable first. He nodded at the animal, insinuating that it would make a proper offering to Littlebell in exchange for entrance. "He doesn't look like he'll make it much further."

Ryd nodded gratefully, rubbing the back of his neck with his hand, feeling dust mixed with salted sweat.

The guard took one step, golden armor clinking. He glared Digory. "What is *your* business in Littlebell?"

Digory gestured to Ryd with his head. "He told you."

"He told me why he's here," the guard rebuked with a distrusting squint. "Why are you?"

"To assist him," Digory said obviously. He then leaned forward, lowering his voice a bit, an excited twinkle in his eye. "I will admit," he went on, "I have heard tales of reverie here. I do aim to experience it before we depart."

"Not so in Baneswood?" the guard asked casually, visibly relaxing, glancing at clanking pans hanging from the side of a hand cart passing by. It was quite common for men and women from about the Kingdom to travel to Littlebell to experience her pleasures, not available in other realms. "Pity," he said again. "I've always heard Dale is a fair bloodline. Rivalling my own." He scratched at the base of his nose, above his lip, where he grew a thin line of hair to match the other guards. It looked like a dark caterpillar crawling over his lip. "Heard Baneswood is nice."

"As nice as can be."

The guard frowned and looked at Ryd. "Baneswood?"

Ryd nodded fervently. Digory patted Ryd on the wounded shoulder again and popped his head out from behind to eye the guard intensely, "Aye, Baneswood." Ryd winced as Digory's grip irritated his new wound.

The guard had a final test. "Which part?"

Ryd's heart dropped, but Digory replied instantly. "Glassy Stream," as if familiar.

The guard nodded in recognition. "I've heard of it. Out of the ways a bit, eh?"

"Aye, that's the place," Digory replied, nodding. He'd never been to Baneswood, much less lived there. "Beautiful, with the waterfall and all," he easily lied, recounting the only Baneswood village he'd heard of in detail, squeezing Ryd's painful shoulder hard. Ryd nodded theatrically to confirm the tale, swallowing hard, pain shooting down his arm.

"Beautiful," he said.

The Morfit guard sighed and scratched at pooling sweat on his eyebrows, boiling beneath his single spiked helmet. Then he glanced behind Ryd and Digory at the growing line of travellers to the city. He turned, pointing to the right of the Bell Tower. This pair, while unusual, seemed to be no threat. They were certainly not the strangest travellers he'd seen. Littlebell attracted all kinds, from every realm in the Kingdom.

"Head straight then take a left at the square, before the Promenade. You will reach Artisan Alley," he said. "That'll take you to the stables."

"Artisan Alley?"

"Aye," the guard replied to Ryd with a curt nod. "Turn after you see the Potter. Look for a black sign with a white vase."

"Many thanks. Any idea where to look for my brother?"

"Young?"

"Yes."

"I'd try the Market. That way," the guard pointed West. "It's where the Free Boys roam."

"Free boys?"

"Visit the Red Tavern," he said simply. "If your brother is here, they may have him. Ask if they've seen him. I hear they're friendly to others from New realms. Just mention Baneswood."

"Thank you," Ryd said gratefully.

"Which way to the Apothecary?" Digory asked over Ryd's shoulder.

"Turn at the Potter's sign," the guard said wearily, eyeing the line behind them, obviously ready for them to move on. "It's at the end of the square."

"Good man," Digory said. "Let's go, friend." He patted Ryd harder than before on his wounded shoulder.

"Stop that," Ryd growled backwards at him as they slowly trotted away. Horseshoes clopped against old-worn cobblestones as they headed into the town buzzing with life. "It hurts."

"You want him to think we're friends, don't you?"

"No," Ryd shot back. "I don't. Because we aren't friends. Why did you lie?" He half turned. "We should have told him the truth. I thought Littlebell doesn't discriminate against..."

"They say they don't," Digory interrupted, lowering his voice to a hush, "and keep your voice down."

"But..."

"But," Digory continued, interrupting Ryd a second time, "you yourself told me of the Morfit's recent betrayal of Brochet. If any aren't welcome here, it's us."

Ryd shrugged.

Digory sighed and rubbed his hand over his dark hair with his palm, sending a mist of fine sweat into the evening air. "They would have given us a tail for the rest of our time here," he said, as if trying to prove his point, "and I prefer privacy."

"Tail?"

"They would have followed us," Digory replied dryly. "We have no business in New realms. No honorable business, anyway."

"Sure we do." Ryd said, half listening.

He was distracted and his eyes widened as the city engulfed them. Red and orange bricks reached up towards the dimming sky. The city's aura was warm, like an intimate hug. It reminded him of sitting around a fire on a cool evening, everyone exchanging tales, laughing. Even upon entry, the city felt happy, welcoming, and alive. It was unlike anything he'd ever experienced. He couldn't help but smile.

"Have you even known one of us to leave Westerviolet without command?"

"Never," Ryd replied quickly. "It's against the…"

"Precisely," Digory said loudly over their horse's foot falls and the crowd's ruckus, "and I hear compared to the other Old realms, ours is a dream. When New realms find an Old earthblood, it is usually bad news." From atop the feeble steed the pair had a view over the sea of bobbing heads, mainly blonde. "You heard him say that the Red Tavern was friendly to those from *New* realms, didn't you?"

Ryd winced at the term 'earthblood' as he studied crowd ahead. He pulled the reigns to avoid trampling slow walkers. "Why?" he asked.

"Because they were either sent to do a misdeed, or they are escaping." Digory squeezed Ryd on the shoulder. Ryd furrowed his brow at the hot dagger sent down his arm but steeled himself as to not give Digory the satisfaction of getting a rise out of him that easily. "If they're doing a misdeed, it's clear why they should be kept out," Digory went on, "and if they're looking for sanctuary it puts everyone in the realm they escaped to in danger. Only the Morfits openly harbour escapees at Croft Hold because Old doesn't dare attack them unprovoked. The gold capes are too powerful. Apart from Warn, they are the most powerful New bloodline. Or at the strongest army anyway. But certainly, they want to keep us far away from Littlebell. They can't have this defenceless city falling apart from the inside out."

"What would happen if we were discovered?"

Digory scratched his beard and chuckled. "We'd be sent back

to Westerviolet," he said with amusement. "Likely escorted to the Lord as traitors. My guess is, we'd be sent to the pyre." He paused, then smirked. "Well, you would be. Then scattered in Pinewood." Ryd winced. Digory leaned forward, sweaty chest rubbing up against the back of Ryd's arm. "Didn't realize the stakes, did you friend?"

"I realize the stakes," Ryd defended, making a face. "And don't call me that," he added quietly. "I'm not your friend."

"Too late to back out if you're feeling squeamish."

"I only care about finding Col. Whatever it takes, it's worth it."

Digory went to speak, then bit his lip. He heard the boy's final wails echoing in his memory. He leaned forward again. "If you don't find him?"

"I will," Ryd replied, setting his jaw with a frown of determination. Digory sighed and scratched his nose. "I've never seen so many in one place before," Ryd said, eying the pulsing crowd in awe. Bodies spanned the wide cobblestone road into the city, from side to side.

"Like vermin."

"No, no," Ryd shook his head. "That's not what I meant."

Digory laughed. "Westerviolet has the laws she does to avoid the filth that bubbles up when left unchecked."

"You're disgusting," Ryd frowned. "Can't I enjoy something without you shitting all over it?"

Their horse trotted slowly through hordes of pungent, sweating bodies in patterned, decorated tunics, cloaked in multi-colored capes, talking, yelling, and laughing. It was hot in Littlebell and you could smell it. The swirling stench of human perspiration and excrement wafted up from the dirty alleyways that snaked about the narrow, three-story homes and winding cobblestone streets. The pair rode along the main road of the city leading directly to the Bell Tower. The huge yellow-stone structure rose above them in the immediate foreground and blocked out the setting sun. The shade here was considerably chillier than on the Narrows. The twilight hour cast the massive, rectangular fortress castle in a dusky, dream-like haze.

Littlebell's crowd pulsed significantly at a dramatic fork in the cobblestone road. On the right, a colossal, trapezoidal building painted a brighter, bloodier red than the others took up the entire block. Although the roof was angled to match the others, it was lined in a layer of tight-grown ivy, leaves waxy and emerald green. Balconies wrapped the building's perimeter, outward facing the roads.

"I am right. Look over there," Digory said, pointing at the bloody structure.

Ryd's mouth fell open in shock.

Devastatingly striking bare-breasted women, nipples perked, smoky black flowing skirts wrapped around their navels, tied with a braided knot, tassled with rounded beads or shells, beckoned to passers-by and blew kisses into the crowd from the balconies of the bloody building. The women looked like sirens atop smouldering flames. Their searing, almond-shaped eyes were thick lined in smudges of black soot. Their silken, golden, corkscrewed hair was uncovered and un-braided in offensive vulnerability, like Vera's had been, left to cascade down over their writhing backs and wriggling shoulders. The ornaments on their skirts' tassels tinkled like windchimes. As did the baubles in their ears and around their wrists. All had fingers red-tipped to match the paint of the building. There were men too, markedly feminine, in similar adornments, acting in similar ways.

"Have you ever seen such a thing?"

"What *are* they?"

"Those, my friend," Digory said theatrically, "are bare women. And men."

Ryd's mouth still hung agape. He'd never seen a woman's bare form before. His face burned hot. "What's their purpose?" he finally asked in a whisper. He couldn't look away.

Digory laughed, shaking his head at Ryd's naivety. "Purpose? They are the surge of the First is what they are. Defix with breasts. Men throw away their souls and coins for cunt."

"You can... pay them? To..."

"Yes!" Digory nearly cheered at Ryd realization, reliving the first time he felt the same way. He glanced briefly at the beauties as they slowly passed by the red building in the flow of the pulsing crowd. If time permitted, and he had the coin, he wouldn't mind sampling their wares himself. It had been quite a while since he'd laid with a woman. Not that he had to pay, for Digory could seduce any woman he wanted, barring Sybil. But he thought it would be fun. "Wonderful, isn't it? I've only heard of them, but they look just as I pictured. This is what I mean when I say that there are rules in Westerviolet to keep filth in check." He gestured dramatically for emphasis at the bloody building, then glanced to scan the colorful crowd. "That is the filth."

"How do you know they are filth?" Ryd countered. "How do you know what they do is wrong?" He didn't peel his eyes from the gorgeous, fleshy women beckoning to him from the balconies. *How could anything so lovely be wrong?*

"Because they aren't real," Digory replied. "Like all evil, they are a beautiful illusion."

Ryd squinted. He tried to peer through the darkened windows at the base of the establishment. He saw gyrating shadows of hungry bodies entangled in warm embraces. "If that isn't real, what is?"

"Pain."

Ryd sighed loudly, pressing air against the back of his throat. "Shut up," he groaned. He threw his head back and shut his eyes.

"You know I'm right."

Ryd glared down the incoming path. "Digory, you make this shit up as you go along."

"It doesn't make it any less true," he replied, laughing.

Ryd pointed to a round structure looming on the left. "What about that? What's that, then? Is that filth?"

"It's a Temple."

Ryd assessed the odd structure. "A Temple?" The word rolled unfamiliarly over his tongue.

"Aye," Digory said. "Hurt your shoulder and lost your

hearing too?"

Ryd ignored the insult. "What's a Temple?"

The indigo building had round windows spaced palm's distance apart, about waist high, and gushed white smoke from a round opening in the top of the roof. Alleyways looped around each side against the high-reaching orange and red painted homes. The front entrance was a disk facing the road, like a half-moon. Landscaped all around the perimeter were two-petaled ivygreen flowers, common across Hunter Post, scenting the surrounding air in tart, resinous notes. They were sacred to those who followed the Horned Woman. The scent was said to bring one closer to Her.

"Well." Ryd nodded to the rounded edifice. "What is that?"

"You sure you want to know?"

"Why wouldn't I?"

"It's banned in Westerviolet."

Ryd shifted his weight excitedly, curiosity besting him fully. He took a deep breath of humid Littlebell air. He truly wanted to learn more about the Kingdom for the first time in his life. He almost didn't recognize himself, but he was too fascinated to care. "Now you must tell me."

"The Faith of the Horned."

"I've never heard of it."

"You wouldn't have heard of it," Digory retorted. "Old realms have no need for the nonsense. I told you, Westerviolet went so far as to ban it. That's why you haven't heard of it."

"Why?" Ryd asked, studying the half-moon door. It was strange, covered in symbols he didn't understand. "Why ban it?"

The door fell open and laid softly on the cobblestones. From the smoky darkness within poured a gaggle of small figures in hooded blue cloaks, faces undistinguishable from shadow, hair swept back neatly in taut braided buns. They kept together in a tight formation with their blue fingers straight at their sides, then hurried down a small alley way around the building before disappearing behind it. The half-moon door closed upwards, slowly.

Ryd changed his question, "Who are *they*?"

"I'll give you one guess."

"The Faith?"

"Aye. Priestesses of it."

"What are they?"

"A flavour of madness, nothing more."

"They seem nice."

"They're no different than men who pay the bares instead of feed their families." Digory paused, grinding his jaw once. "An addiction. A way to escape life's inevitable pain."

"The Faith makes people feel better? What's wrong with that?" Digory shrugged but didn't respond. "You know," Ryd went on, "there are some good things in this Kingdom. Maybe they are good."

"Nothing is good, friend."

"I'm not your friend."

"This must be the square," Digory said. And just like that, because Digory was done with the conversation, it was done. That's how he was. The Kingdom caved in around him.

The road they trod opened into a large piazza cobblestoned to match the entry path, lined with awning-covered shops, a hostel, and a tavern. In the center stood a towering statue carved from pristine white stone. The imposing sculpture wore a smile and faced them with his hands spread outward welcomingly, atop an intricately detailed pedestal with an engraved copper name plate, long ago gone green.

"He must have been someone," Ryd said, internally jarred by the ease with which Digory shifted personas and tones.

Digory glanced at the inscription beneath the statue as they passed it by.

Ryd looked up at the impressive figure with reverence and awe. It made him feel drastically different than the Westerviolet Ancestor walk. Instead of meek and afraid, this statue made him feel powerful. "Who is it?"

"David Minney."

The name sounded familiar. "Who?"

"I forget that you don't..." Digory paused, trailing off. He sighed. "He was the first Minney."

Ryd nodded, remembering the story Vera told.

Digory pointed to the tavern on his right. "Up for a drink?" Murmurous ale ballads wafted out to the square despite the heavy building's walls.

"No."

"Come on. Why not?"

"I'm going to the stable, then to search for my brother." Ryd looked to a wide street on the left, flags hung as banners from each roof across the way. It breathed life, filled with singing and laughter. "We've been over this."

"Right, but there is always time for a drink."

"I said, no. You shouldn't be drinking anyway. Go to the Apothecary." Digory just shrugged. "I have to ride through there." Ryd pointed to the flag covered street. "It must be Artisan alley."

Digory rolled his eyes. "Great."

"It looks like fun."

"It looks like trouble," Digory spat.

"Why?"

"It's the type of place you keep your hand tight on your purse," Digory said. "If you had one."

Ryd flexed his jaw. "Right."

They cut across the square, through swirling scents from thighs of poultry still on the bone, roasting over an embedded grill atop a nearby cart. Behind the cart, a cage of clucking chickens with brown feathers and a table laid with pressed fowl-meat pies. Although chickens were popular Kingdom-wide, they were particularly favoured in Littlebell, both for their feathers and their meat.

The next costermonger sold corn dumplings, and after that, a man with a cart full of sweets. Maple cane and chewing sweetgum mostly. A group of small children in pink and orange robes chased each other, giggling and screeching. The wild group cut cross their path and caused Ryd to have to pull the horse with a protesting neigh to avoid stepping on them. An orange cat pounced down to the cobblestones from the tavern's boisterous balcony and hissed in their direction, before hotly pattering away. It reminded Ryd of Ruby, and his thoughts drifted to Vera again.

Nearby, a priestess of the Faith stood on a pedestal in shimmering azure robes to match the deepening twilight sky. She shouted to a small group congregated around her. She was out of earshot, but the pained, stinging conviction of each word was still conveyed. Cheers followed her cries in a shrill staccato through the other natural sounds the street crowd. It was bizarre for Ryd to witness a woman who looked like him commanding such attention.

There were few horses, so Digory and Ryd were mostly above it all. The sea of dark faces and hair in thick blonde braids and vibrant garbs filled every path. It was nearly dark. One by one, using nimble folding ladders, yellow-robed attendants scurried up poles, lighting oil lamps along the way.

Digory started, gazing wistfully at the Tavern as they left it in their wake. "Are you sure I can't tempt you with…"

"I said, no," Ryd growled. "Let's get on with it." He shook the reigns. He was anxious to find Col.

As the sun set for the evening and the sky burnt dark like soot, the city felt like it came even more alive. The pair made their way through the pulsing crowd, past street performers of all kinds. Men who did not speak and only mimed reactions, painfully naked, with faces painted tangerine. Men who sang beautiful resonating ballads. Unlike the orange-painted men who were clean shaven, these singers had chest-length facial hair, competing with each other in shouting song across the way. There were several painters, sketchers, and drawers, and one sculptor they could see moulding the form of an ass from river clay. Homeless bodies of both men and women dotted the doorframes with eyes dilated and bloodshot, begging for coins. All around them the energy was churning. Within the shops that lined the path, there was a cacophony of pleasant bartering and ruckus laughter.

It was chaos. Functional chaos.

"There," Ryd said finally. "The Potter with the vase sign." He pointed to a white sign with black vase emblem, matching the guard's description.

"Aye," Digory nodded. He dismounted with a grunt, kicking up dust with his boots as they landed on the cobblestones. He unfastened his sack from the saddle and tossed it over his shoulder, then checked that his dagger was in place before patting their temporary horse on the flank, hard. The poor beast blinked his red eyes and neighed sadly, as if he was too tired to complain. His expression matched Ryd's perfectly.

Ryd looked down at Digory. "Meet back here at sunrise?" He gestured to the sign. "Right there."

"Aye," Digory said, surveying the surrounding scene instead of looking at Ryd.

Ryd nodded, satisfied enough. He was ready to be rid of Digory. He shook the reigns and urged the horse forward towards the stables.

Digory took a breath as he looked around with sharply raised eyebrows to gain his bearings. Scratching at his beard, he turned and walked towards the square, where the Apothecary should be.

WESTERVIOLET GARDENS

Everything was going to change for her, and yet, it felt like it already had. Rose's mind was awash with thoughts. She often spent long hours in the moat gardens. She liked listening to the frogs and thinking. She'd sit with Ellie and pet her, of course, but other than that, she liked to just think. Alone, with no one to interrupt her, aside Ellie. She'd think about nothing and everything. She'd imagine herself traveling to distant lands that she'd only heard of in ballads and myths. Like Winter Garden, with its frost flowers. Or Duskfang and its caves. She'd imagine having her own daughter someday to raise as she pleased. She would let her daughter play in the white bindweed around the Lunar Tower, surely. And she'd imagine what all those people were like. Who they were. The ones whose faces she couldn't get out of her mind every time she went to sleep.

Rose felt warm air dance across her skin as it filtered through the solitary garden. Today, she imagined what the other Vanguard children would be like when she finally made it to Animus Rock. She did her best not to think about Col.

She sat in a quiet area with tidy lines of manicured bushes, rows of polite low-growing primpetals, as well as strong-scented lemon trees. A pebbled path through the flower-speckled greenery led down the center and about the bushes and plants. Over-ripe fallen fruit collected humming bees. Butterflies swirled with each gust of wind.

The garden hugged the castle wall on one side. It crept into the blackened moat on the other.

The area felt other-worldly. When Rose needed it most, this was her sanctuary. She sat on a stone bench overlooking the black moat, watching an impossibly long river fang slither in pursuit of a frog. Ellie lay dutifully by her side, swishing her ploom-like tail.

Then, Sybil sat gracefully down beside her with a swish of coal-black skirts.

"How did you know I was here?"

"I know everything," Sybil said. "I am your mother." Sybil took Rose's hand in hers. "Face me, child. Look at me." Rose dutifully obeyed, turning to look at her mother, hiding her displeasure at being interrupted. Sybil took her other hand. "You must know that everything I do is for you. You may not understand, but you will see. Everything I do is for your own good. It is to protect you."

Rose furrowed her small brow. She glanced at Ellie's cautious gaze, watching the exchange. She could feel the dog's anxiety over what her mother may do, may say. How she may make her feel. Ellie was wary of Sybil, as Rose was. But unlike Ellie, Rose loved her mother.

"Do you understand?" Sybil pressed, black gaze burning. "Do you trust me?"

Rose, heart screaming, nodded silently. "Yes, Mother."

ABOUT THE AUTHOR

E.M. Willett was born to be a writer. It's her calling, apart from motherhood. She also enjoys baking, gardening and reading. She lives on a small farm surrounded by an old oak forest with her husband, young children and dogs where she writes late into the night.